Red

BY

KC KEAN

*Red
Featherstone Academy #4
Copyright © 2020 KC Kean
www.authorkckean.com*

Published by Featherstone Publishing Ltd

*This book is licensed for your personal enjoyment only.
This book may not be re-sold or given away to other people. If you would like to share this book with another person, please purchase an additional copy for each recipient. If you're reading this book and did not purchase it, or it wasn't purchased for your use only, then please return to your favourite book retailer and purchase your own copy. Thank you for respecting the hard work of this author.
All rights reserved.
This is a work of fiction. Names, characters, places, brands, media, and incidents are either the product of the authors imagination or are used fictitiously. The author acknowledges the trademark status and trademark owners of various products referred to in this work of fiction, which have been used without permission. The publication/use of these trademarks is not authorised, associated with, or sponsored by the trademark owners.*

*Cover Design: Bellaluna Designs
Proofreader: Sassi's Editing Servies
Formatting & Interior Design: Sloane Murphy*

*Red/KC Kean – 1st ed.
ISBN-13 - 9798575928157*

My days, I have officially dedicated a book to everyone in my house, except myself because obviously that's weird. But I'm quite sure I'll do it at some stage LOL. There are so many people in my life I could start with, outside of my covid bubble, special people who impact my life in a positive way. So, I decided to go with my crazy-ass friend, Valerie.

Valerie Swope.

You beautiful friend. I don't even know how you deal with me, but somebody has to right?

So, this one's for you, for giving me the strength and support to keep typing, and create this crazy fucking world.

I feel like I should go old skool and create a poem spelling your name out to describe your fabulousness!

Vibing
Amazing
Laughter
Ecstatic
Random thoughts
Incredible
Eating Canva

So, I hope you either feel fantastic or embarrassed, I'm not fussy haha!
Much love

There is something empowering in the art of finding strength from within to defend yourself and pushing to break down the barriers that surround you.
- *Jessica Watson, Featherstone Academy*

KC KEAN

PROLOGUE

MOTHER'S RULES FOR JESSICA

1) Be seen and ~~not heard.~~
2) Always dress accordingly – **fashion is life!**
3) ~~Avoid~~ carbs and sugary products – **make us smile.**
4) Be approachable ~~to men at all times~~ - **friendly, and polite. Unless they are a bitch!**
5) Children are ~~an expectation~~ – **a beautiful gift.**
6) You are a trophy – **and a motherfucking queen!**
7) Excessive body fat is ~~not acceptable~~ – **against the law.**
8) Always ~~look to~~ **fuck** your husband~~s~~ ~~for guidance.~~

<u>MY RULES</u>

9) Be fabulous.
10) Be memorable.
11) Don't be afraid to take what you want.
12) Be you!

RED

KC KEAN

ONE
Jess

This damn book has me by my ovaries, sucking me deep into the story, and I don't want to miss a second of it. I read the words on my Kindle, but it's like I'm right there in the book. The scene playing out right in front of my eyes as Eden gets her ultimate payback. Rolling on to my stomach, I try to get comfortable with my Kindle in hand, not wanting to lose my place, yet too nervous about moving on to the next page. Especially since I'm at ninety-eight percent of the book, and this story is nowhere near done. I can feel the cliffhanger already.

My parents are downstairs, setting up some fancy

dinner that I have no interest in, so I'm escaping the only way I know how. By imagining a world where women are badass bitches, holding down more than one man, and having the best sex of their lives.

Sighing, I swipe a loose piece of hair behind my ear as I feel the emotion coming through the words as if I was an Allstar myself. All the hurt and the pain they're feeling as they watch Eden before them, completely blindsiding them all as she hits them where it hurts. I feel smug as shit for her. Which they fucking deserve after all the shit they put her through. My bedroom door swings open and slams against the wall, making me jump out of my skin in shock.

"Jessica, I have been calling your name for the past fifteen minutes," my mother huffs, hands on her hips. "Our guests will be here in less than twenty minutes, and you are in no way ready to greet them like this." She waves her hand in my direction, unhappy with the fact I'm wearing my cute pink hearts silk shorts and shirt pajama set.

"I already told you, mom, I'm not going to your stupid dinner. I don't care who it's with or how it affects your image in the Featherstone community," I murmur in response, not lifting my gaze from my Kindle.

She doesn't continue to nag, and it's my mistake for

noticing it too late when my Kindle is ripped from my hands and thrown on the floor carelessly behind her with a thud.

"Jessica, what have I told you about your priorities? No man is going to care for you reading when he has other needs for you." She sighs, repeating the same things she always does. "To convince a man to marry you, you have to be what they envision. Pretty, quiet, caring, and barefoot in the kitchen." I mouth the words behind her back as she turns to stand in front of my floor length mirror, straightening her wrap around floral print dress. Her blonde highlights shine under the light as her scrutinizing blue eyes critique herself. Not a wrinkle is visible with all the botox she's injected into her now flawless skin.

It's always the same speech she gives, but she's living in the past. I don't want to stay at home popping out babies like a breeding factory, only to discover my husband is having an affair with his secretary. That's not me. It never will be, but until I can safely stand on my own two feet, I have to abide by my mother's rules or feel her wrath.

"Now, I won't repeat myself, Jessica. You have twenty minutes to make yourself presentable," she bends down to scoop up my kindle as she heads for the door. "And you can have this god awful device back tomorrow." She slams the door shut as she leaves, and my blood boils with all the anger I feel inside. Opinions and protests are always lost on my mother, but it's the pain in my soul from holding my tongue that causes the most damage.

Lucienda Paul married my father, Neil Watson, at eighteen years old. My mother was born into a bloodline at Featherstone, whereas my father was an outsider. I learned earlier this year, from one of my mother's many lectures, that she married my father to force him into the Featherstone fold. His scientific achievements had caught the attention of the criminal underworld, and my mother was given the assignment to make it happen.

My father will never discuss his feelings about Featherstone. I think it's because he likes to turn a blind eye. Making the weapons and chemicals they need but without seeing them be used and the subsequent consequences that follow. Allowing him to live in a bubble. My mother refuses to work. Instead, she is a socialite amongst the Featherstone community, always wanting to better our bloodline and gain a higher reputation. I've heard it enough times, how she could be so much better without my father and me, but she lowered herself for the 'greater good'. I don't know how they are even still together. It seems as though once my mother sinks her nails in, she just can't let go.

Sighing, I look around my bedroom. We live in a highly respected gated community, with a fancy in-ground pool out back and shiny cars parked in the driveway. I can only assume the brand is luxury because anything vehicle related goes straight over my head.

There are three large rooms on the ground floor of my family home. The living room is for looking, not touching. The dining room is filled with high-end designer pieces, from the dining table to the art pieces on the wall to impress our guests, but the kitchen is as basic as possible. I think the fridge could be older than me, but guests don't see it, so it doesn't matter, apparently.

Upstairs, money is only seen in my mother's walk-in closet. If my mother could have avoided bearing a child, she would have. Apparently, it's a high expectation to continue the bloodlines, which is the only reason I exist. So, spoiling me is entirely out of the question.

My room consists of a standard twin bed pushed up under the window, a dark wooden desk in the opposite corner of the room, a vanity beside my bed, and a small walk-in wardrobe. The walls are a dull magnolia color, with a few pink accents throughout. It plays havoc on my OCD that none of the pink items are the same.

I inhale a deep breath as I try to focus on the future. Two more days and I'll be out of here, forced into the world of Featherstone Academy, which, if the high school is anything to go by, will be terrible. I hate what they stand for. I have nothing to offer the criminal underworld. I'd prefer to keep it that way, but I've watched people be murdered in cold blood for trying to leave. I refuse to be another Featherstone statistic.

Taking a seat at the vanity, I do a natural look with my make-up. I love a sexy smokey eye, but my mother would throw a fit about it. So, I apply a light sheen of lip gloss and bypass my eye make-up altogether. Opening the door to look through my dresses, I find my mother has already taken the liberty of pulling out a black and pink floral print ruffle neck dress made of chiffon with long sleeves. Very prim and proper, not what I want to be wearing at all, except if I show up in anything other than what she chose, it will only anger her more.

Slipping the dress on, I slide into a pair of white sandals. The sound of the doorbell chiming tells me the guests have arrived. I have no time to tame my hair, so I quickly redo my ponytail, making sure no loose ends fall around my face.

With one final glance in the mirror, I run my hands down the front of my skirt, trying to shake my anxiety of having to sit through another dinner with families from Featherstone. They are always so brazen and happy to talk about what activities they have been up to, no matter the level of crime they've committed. It's like an adult version of show-and-tell.

Making my way downstairs, I hear chatter coming from the dining room. My heart sinks as I step into the room, instantly knowing this is my mother trying to marry me off again. Unfortunately for her, it's never going to happen with this guy. He's a fucking asshat.

"Jessica, darling," my mother coos all sickly sweet, and I have to force myself to smile politely. "Please welcome Mr. and Mrs. Wicker and their son, Reece." I step forward, automatically shaking their hands. Both dressed as if this is a business meeting, with their hair perfectly in place, I want to gag at their sense of prestige. As I come to stand in front of Reece, he sadly starts to fucking talk.

"Jessica, long time no see. I've missed seeing you

at the rest of the parties this summer, especially after Longridge." His hands clasp mine tightly as he attempts to give me a smoldering look, and I have to force myself not to roll my eyes at his shit.

"Oh, you two know each other already? That's even better," my mother says, smiling widely at us both. Snatching my hand out of his grip, I put some much-needed distance between us all.

"I'm going to help daddy bring everything in." I smile wide and turn quickly, cringing at myself. I hate saying daddy, but mother enforces it in front of others. All I can think about is a book I read once, and daddy kink was the main trope. To each their own, no judgment here, but now I have to say it in front of people. It doesn't really give me all the feels when I have to address my actual father in that way.

"Hey, pumpkin," my dad calls out as I step into the kitchen. A towel thrown over his shoulder, thick-rimmed glasses perched on the end of his nose, and peppered red hair wild around his face. He's wearing one of the minimal shirts he owns, with a pair of black pants. Looking nothing like my father, who collects old band tees and has the same jeans from when he was in his twenties.

I love my dad, especially compared to my mother. But he just seems to turn a blind eye to everything she says and does. No matter how hard I try to fight for myself, my own rights, he stands back and does nothing to help me. Dad knows how I feel about Featherstone, exactly how he must feel, I imagine, but he won't discuss his position at Featherstone or how it came to be. The words never pass my fathers lips. It's only ever the stories my mother cares to offer.

"Hey, dad. What do you need help with?" I ask, stepping up beside him. I love it when he gets to cook. It's always a proper, full-course meal and tastes delicious. It's hot as hell outside since we're at the end of August in Indiana. My father chooses to make pork tenderloin with a vegetable medley and an option for either mashed or baked potatoes.

"You can help carry these dishes in with me, please." He looks in my direction, and he must see my current mood written all over my face. Wiping his hands on the towel resting on his shoulder, he sighs. "Pumpkin, I know, okay? But there is nothing we can do. Just think, in a few days, she'll be out of your hair, and you'll be in a completely different state. Who will I have fun at the lab with then?

Think of your poor old dad."

He tries to hit me with his puppy dog eyes, but they don't work on me anymore, not like they used to before Featherstone's rules became my life. "Then I'll be trapped in a criminal world I don't actually want to be a part of, dad. Stuck with idiots like Reece Wicker," I complain, pointing a hand in the direction I just came from. Before he can respond, my mother interrupts.

"Will you two get a move on? Our guests are waiting," she grinds out under her breath, glaring at us before turning on her heels and heading back to the dining room. My father squeezes my shoulder as I turn to face him, my eyes widening in frustration.

"Pumpkin, if I ever find a way out of her grasp, for you, for either of us, I'll take it. That option just doesn't seem to be in the cards right now." Lifting the dishes in front of him, he follows after her, leaving me stunned as I gape after him.

He has never murmured such words, and the hope they give me is unexplainable. As small of a chance it might be, I could live a different life, and the fact that my father is on the same page fills me with so much emotion. Shaking my head, I focus on the here and now, but I can definitely get through this dinner much easier after that.

Grabbing more dishes, I head for the dining room, crossing paths with my father, who softly smiles as he passes. Everyone is in deep conversation as I enter the room, but I feel Reece's eyes on me instantly.

"Sit, Jessica," my mother says, pointing at the seat across from Reece. "Reece has just been telling me how you were friends at Featherstone High and went to a few parties together over the summer. Longridge has always been the best annual lake party of the year. I'm glad you know each other so well."

I smile tightly in response. We aren't friends, not even a little bit. We just happened to both be at the same party back at the beginning of summer. I got a little wild and carefree. Under the night sky and the campfire light, along with the mixture of alcohol, he looked hot. So hot, I made the mistake of hooking up with him.

He looked cute when his dark blonde hair was under his baseball cap. Combined with his six-foot height and thick arms, I was making stupid mistakes. It was probably because he had a familiar face, and I was happy to take his cheesy slick moves. I had gone with my closest friend since junior high, Valerie, and she hadn't let me live it down since. It's a good thing I love her because her choices are no better than mine most of the time; she is just as much of an irresponsible peckerhead as I am. We are totally bad influences on each other, even though we are a lot more distant than we used to be since she has no idea about Featherstone.

But this creep refused to give my panties back. Even in my drunken state, I cringed as he lifted them to his face, inhaling deeply before stuffing them in his pocket. I watch as he rubs at his nose across from me, as if remembering the same fact, and he winks at me.

"I wouldn't say we know each other very well," I answer, smiling politely around the table as I avoid his direct stare.

"Don't worry about that. You have plenty of time in the future to get to know each other more," Mrs. Wicker says, and I have to bite my tongue before I shout out 'over my dead body!' The table falls into silence as my father takes a seat opposite my mother, and everyone starts to dish their food out. I can feel my mother's eyes burning into the side of my head, warning me to take only a small amount so I don't embarrass her by looking like a pig.

"It's so nice to have another bloodline in the area," Mr.

Wicker says, looking at my father, but it's my mother who answers.

"Isn't it? Nobody else understands our lifestyle, so it's good to have a close-knit community nearby."

"What is it you think you will do in twelve months when you finish the academy, Jess?" Mrs. Wicker asks, and I groan internally.

"I haven't decided yet," I respond politely, but as always, it doesn't please my mother.

"She will either follow in Neil's footsteps in Science or proceed with the Paul bloodline and work in the L.F.G. department. I am personally hoping she may reignite the Paul family bloodline. I completed my assignment with Neil, so I no longer needed to pursue my career when he had his." This woman is so fucking crazy, and it confuses me why everyone at this table doesn't agree. Before anyone can respond, she continues. "Although, I don't think she has what it takes to truly be a Paul, which is why she needs to marry into a successful family." Lifting her wine glass to her lips, she looks like she belongs in a Disney movie as a villain. She loves nothing more than to break me down, but publicly being passive-aggressive with me is the final straw.

My father clears his throat, but I'm already rising to my feet. "Thank you so much for coming," I say, glancing at the Wickers. "But if you'll excuse me." I can't even throw out a reason for leaving; my heart is pounding in my ears as I fight back angry tears.

"You'll do no such thing, Jessica. Sit. Down. Now." I hear her warning, but I just can't take it anymore as words spill from my mouth with no filter.

"No thanks, mother." My hands brace the back of my chair as anger courses through my veins at her belittling me. "I'm not going to sit here and play the role of being in a happy family. And for you to think I'm going to marry Reece fucking Wicker? Especially when I already let him dick me? Well, guess what? He was a shitty lay, and there is no way in hell I would choose to go anywhere near him again," I growl before storming out.

I hear the clattering of plates and the anger in my mother's voice, but I don't stop, not wanting to face the consequences of my actions just yet. I race up the stairs, the sound of heavy footsteps following after me. I'm ready to slam my bedroom door shut, when it's stopped just before it clicks. My mother wouldn't be able to move this quick in her stiletto heels, but fear coats my body as my brain thinks it's Reece, only to see my father's face through the gap.

"Do you already have your suitcase packed for the academy?" He rushes out, and I nod in response, too afraid to open my mouth again. "Good, let's get you out of here."

I know that means going to Featherstone Academy early. Right now, I'd take that over my mother, and Reece. If I have to fucking be there, I need to shape up, stand tall, and learn to take what I want, just like everyone else around me. Instead of letting words cut me so deep.

Arriving at the Academy, after a flight and a chauffeur picking me up from the airport, I barely notice my surroundings as we drive onto campus. Nerves have my hands fidgeting, but I'm still processing what happened back home. My phone was ringing like crazy as my dad took me to the airport, so I haven't taken it off airplane mode since getting off the plane.

I had to wait four hours at the airport, but I'm lucky there was even a flight leaving today. At least I got some uninterrupted reading time away from all the stress going on around me. Dad paid for the ticket and gave me the cash he had on him to see me through. It's almost like he knew my mother would wise up and cut my credit card off.

The driver had handed me a box when I climbed into the car. It was filled with my schedule, dorm key, everything I would need to settle into Featherstone Academy. Which seemed much bigger than the high school if this drive was anything to go by.

Pulling to a stop, I finally focus on what's happening outside of the vehicle. Stepping out, I'm surrounded by six buildings, just like back at my old school. Aces, Diamonds, Hearts, Spades, Clubs, and Jokers, only this time, the buildings are bigger. I hate that we are categorized and separated accordingly. It stops people from getting to know one another for who they truly are, instead of what they may have to offer you based on their bloodline.

No other students are around, and I've learned the driver is a non-talker, so it's pointless to ask him anything at all regarding the academy. Wordlessly he helps bring my four suitcases up to my room on the first floor of the Diamond block. As soon as I have the door open, he's gone, leaving me to take care of myself.

Dragging my cases inside, I shut the door behind me and flop straight down on the bed. I don't see what the room looks like because the moment I know I'm alone, the dam breaks, and tears flow uncontrollably down my face. I allow myself this moment to get all this shit off my chest because once I have no tears left to cry, that's it. I'm going to find my inner strength and own the hell out of the next twelve months, by all means necessary.

KC KEAN

TWO

Jess

My skin prickles with goosebumps at the feel of his callous fingers moving painfully slow up the inside of my leg. Inching closer and closer to my core, a separate pair of hands cup my breasts from behind—a hard chest to my back, fingers stroking against my seam, as lips take mine. Trying to force my eyes open, I want to see who will bring me to ecstasy, but all I can see is the fireworks exploding against the back of my eyelids.

Everything is overwhelming as I roll my hips up off the mattress, against the thick length between my legs. Hitting my climax, my eyes spring open, locking with Maverick

Miller's deep brown eyes.

The surprise sends another shockwave through my body as I crash to the floor.

Shit.

Holy.Fucking.Shit.

Sitting up, I lean my back against the side of the bed as I try to calm my rapid breathing. Damn wet dream, with inspiration courtesy of last night's steamy read. These damn reverse harem books are ruining me, in the best way possible. The extra addition of Maverick Miller, my Combat tutor, comes from laying my eyes on him for the first time yesterday.

Fumbling around on the bedside table, I grab my phone to check the time. Two minutes before my alarm is due to go off, perfect timing. I'm relaxed too, after my extra special morning orgasm. Unraveling myself from the blankets, I throw them in a heap on the bed, taking a seat on the edge— the vision of Maverick, repeating in my mind.

Damn him and his haunted brown eyes. The way his brown hair looks like he's just stepped out of the bedroom has me wanting to run my fingers through it. His body frame and golden tan only enhance the visual.

Shaking my head, I need to get a grip on myself. He's

my damn tutor, a sexy one, but he would never look twice at me, not when I'm a student. Especially after everyone else threw out some hot as shit moves yesterday, including my new friend Luna Steele, who drop kicked Wren Dicktrichson to the floor.

I was shit, totally awful. I could feel the burn of *his* eyes at my back as he watched me make a complete mockery of myself. My movements were awkward and jerky. With Roman literally standing still, there was no real fight between us.

The alarm sounds on my phone, and I quickly shut it off. Dragging my fingers through my hair, they get tangled in a knot, and I can't help but sigh at the inconvenience of the bird's nest on the back of my head. I shouldn't have stayed up so late last night, but yesterday was my first official day of classes at Featherstone Academy, and I was missing excitement.

I had to stay up late to venture into my new book purchase, which was released yesterday. I'd waited weeks for the latest book in the Sin's of Neverland series, and before I knew it, the time was almost two a.m. but totally worth it. I'm just lucky my dad managed to swipe my Kindle before we took off. Otherwise, I don't think I would have survived. Wiping the sleep from my eyes, I stand and stretch, loving the feel of the tension leaving my body.

Glancing around, I take in my small dorm room. My twin bed sits neatly in the corner, a vanity facing it, the perfect spot for natural lighting when I do my hair and make-up. On the other side of the room are a small walk-in closet, my desk, and the door leading into my tiny en-suite. It may be small, but I didn't have to share it with anyone, so I was allowed to decorate the space however I wanted to. Which meant it was all pretty in dusty pink and light grey. Twinkly fairy lights hung on the wall beside my bed, and my trio of favorite candles sat on my nightstand.

This is my home, my safe haven for the next twelve months, and I'm going to rock it - no more quiet and timid, Jessica Watson. I'm going to be me. I just need to find the confidence to actually see it through.

Stepping into the en-suite, I notice there is barely enough space for the toilet, shower, and sink, but it works. The charcoal tiles make it look sleek and modern, but even smaller than it truly is. I rush my shower, the smell of my favorite coconut body wash filling the air around me, as I wrap a towel around my body and stroll over to the window by my bed. I'm not high up in the Diamond block, but no one can really see in from outside.

I have a view of the courtyard in the center of all the school blocks from my room. Watching as the other students mingle with their friends and cliques while I wander aimlessly alone, just like in high school. Nobody wants to be friends with the girl whose dad makes gas explosives for The Games. My father is an Organic Chemist, which means nothing here. My bloodline doesn't bring wealth or fear with its name. Ultimately, making me a nobody, which is why my mother is always trying to push us further up the table.

The bloodlines of Featherstone Academy only tolerate me because I've been lucky enough to be placed in the Diamond block, under my father's new bloodline name. But other than that, they don't even breathe in my direction. Which is better than being bullied and beat into the ground, I guess.

Taking a seat at my vanity table, I apply my make-up quickly, with the level of precision you only get from hours of practice. In high school, I would sit and improve my skills every night, wanting to bring out the best of my features and experiment with bold looks. I never wore anything other than my natural tones, accentuating my naturally red hair and blue eyes.

Finishing my look with lightly curled hair, I drop my towel and slowly step into my latest purchase, a satin cobalt blue two-piece bra, and pantie set, with matching garter and tan stockings. My fingers tremble slightly as I stroke across the material. Taking a deep breath, I straighten my spine, my pink cheeks cooling as I force myself to stand and see the woman looking back at me.

The girl before me looks confident, sexy, and in control. I'm willing to boost my self-esteem in any way possible, and this is, by far, my favorite plan. Stepping away from the Stepford housewife vibes my mother throws at me, I love it. Sexy lingerie, just for me, and damn does it feel good. Every day, for the next twelve months, while I'm here at Featherstone Academy, I *will* own it. This is my time to find myself, which is why they were the first thing I packed.

I love how good I feel in my sexy ensemble. Now I need to find someone to rip the scraps of satin from my body and let me see how good it looks crumpled on the floor.

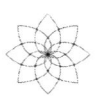

A bell sounds through the sound system in the science lab, and the tutor claps his hands. "Okay, that's it for today…"

"Obviously," someone scoffs from behind me, making the other students chuckle like hyenas. I'm sure Oscar O'Shay, the childish Ace, is leading the pack. Shaking my head at them, I place my tablet into my oversized purse.

Carl Perez, the Science tutor, clears his throat, "Thank you for that, Aiden Byrnes." Pushing his glasses up his nose, he frowns at the guy directly behind me. "Wherever you are seated now is your spot for the rest of the school year. Today was a general introduction to Science class here at Featherstone, but during our next class, coursework will be assigned."

He arranges his briefcase on his desk, effectively dismissing us. The room is large, with two rows of workstations filling the entire space with us each sitting in fours. It would look like an ordinary science lab to any random person, but the lesson plan is worlds apart. From learning the components to make bombs to understanding the breakdown of crystal meth. Even chemical compounds for therapeutic drugs. How is this even a thing?

Standing from my seat by the window, I glance at the other students as they begin to filter out of the room.

Following behind the other's seated on my row, I'm stopped abruptly by someone slamming their hand down on the stool beside me.

"Hot damn, shorty, your pouty lips are so fuckable. Why'd you need to leave like that last week? I've missed you. Especially since you ran out on our family dinner so quickly."

The tight grip around my wrist has me lifting my gaze in confusion. Seeing Reece next to me, his eyes leering at my lips, has my heart rate increasing instantly. I'm stunned at Reece's complete disregard for what I said at dinner, and I cringe at the fact he thinks his creepy glare makes him look hot.

Trying to pull my wrist from his grip, he uses his hold on me to pull me in against his body. I can't tell what's going on around us, my brain is overwhelmed by his close proximity, and the smell of his cheap aftershave. Raising my other hand to his chest, I try to push him back, but he doesn't move, and I can't seem to find any words to warn him off.

All I can hear is my own breathing in my ear as he leans in close, his nose brushing against mine, until he's suddenly gone. I can't stop my eyes from blinking rapidly as I glance around me. Reece is on the floor, glaring up at Oscar O'Shay. I think he might be the reason Reece is no longer touching me, and my shoulders sag in relief.

"Jessica Watson is a friend of the Aces. Keep the fuck away from her," he grunts, glaring around the room at everyone who has stopped to stare. His blue eyes glare at everyone as he stands confidently in front of me. "Your gang-green dick will fall off before it goes anywhere near her. Do you understand?"

Reece rushes to the door. "Fuck you, O'Shay, she's *mine*." He scowls in response before looking at me again. "I'll catch you back at Diamond, wifey," he mutters, standing straight, rearranging his blazer, and storming out of the classroom.

"Are you okay?" Oscar asks as heat rises in my cheeks, knowing there are still others lingering in the room, watching the scene unfold.

"I'm fine, Oscar," I grind out. "Just because you happen to have your greedy eyes on my new friend does not mean I need your help with anything, asshole." Shouldering past him, I hold my head high as everyone tracks my movement, praying they don't see the shake in my hands.

As I near the door, Aiden Byrnes, the mouthy asshole,

with his blonde hair swept to one side and cock-sure grin on his face, holds it open for me. His crystal grey eyes hold me captive, but all too quickly, I step into the hall, and the world moves on around me. Aiden Byrnes is an enigma, always loud and demanding attention. But no one ever seems to get close to him, except his twin sister, Trudy.

Shaking my head, I move for the elevator, I make sure Reece has gone, before checking the rest of today's schedule on my phone, as the doors shut behind me. Lunch followed by Combat. *Perfect.* My muscles will be killing me by the time it's dinner. Leaning my head back against the mirrored wall of the elevator, I sigh. Screw this shitty Academy but thank god for its hot men.

Luna is waiting outside of the academic building, standing at the bottom of the large stone steps, with her classic resting bitch face in place. It's funny how I've only known her for less than a week, but she knows me better than anyone else here. Her silky brown hair is always tied up, falling perfectly down her back with little effort. Her green eyes are sparkling with annoyance more than happiness. She is a natural badass.

"Red, Frappuccinos at the coffee house again?" Luna asks as I link my arm through hers.

"You read my mind," I murmur when my phone vibrates in my pocket, glancing at the screen, '*Dad*' flashes across it. Answering the phone with a sigh, my father's voice greets me.

"Hey Pumpkin, I just wanted to see how your first few days at the Academy have been going?"

His question leaves me speechless for a moment. I haven't really spoken to him since he threw me on the last-minute flight to Virginia. All I know is he's got his hands full with my mother while I'm dealing with Featherstone. I want to tell him that I hate it, but it currently beats being around my mother. With every fiber of my being, I don't want to be here. I have cried, screamed, and raged at him for forcing my hand, giving me no alternative but to live this life over the years, but there is no point repeating myself.

After dinner the other day, I know he knows, and in some way, this is him trying to protect me from my home life. So, here I am, carrying the burden of my bloodline, forced upon me, just like everybody else around me, except I don't have a real skillset as they do. They're just hoping my Science is as good as my father's because if the Pauls were that good, they wouldn't have been happy for my mother to *not* continue the Paul bloodline.

"Everything's fine, Dad." Simple and short. I can't offer him anything more without my emotions getting the best of me, even though I know deep down it isn't his fault.

"How was Science?" I can sense his smile by the pitch of his voice, but it only grates on me.

"It was fine, Dad." I sigh. "All I want to do in this world is make chemical weapons for the damn criminal underworld. It beats being a Paul at least," I whisper angrily into the phone, feeling Luna's eyes on me the entire time. I refuse to meet her gaze, focusing on the surrounding trees and flower beds instead.

"I see now isn't the best time to talk, Jessie. I'll give you a call this weekend."

The phone cuts off just like that. Every time our phone calls end in the same way. With my father not offering me any form of outlet for the pressure I feel being here, representing a non-existent bloodline.

Taking a deep breath, I put my phone away, finally looking at Luna. She stares at me with her green eyes filled with questions but thankfully ignores my little outburst.

"So, an extra shot of espresso in your frappuccino then?" She asks, and my shoulders sag in relief as I nod enthusiastically.

Damn, I've needed a friendship like this for far too long.

KC KEAN

THREE

Jess

"Again, Red," Luna calls out, and if I could catch my breath, I'd tell her to fuck off. But as it is, my hands are braced on my knees, my insides raw as I try to pull a full breath into my lungs.

"No, please, no," I manage to mutter, but she just grins down at me like the devil. I'm glad I chose to wear my loose-fitted grey shorts today instead of my bike shorts because they'd have stuck to me like glue. Sweat drips from every part of my body while my so-called best friend chuckles.

Grabbing a bottle of water from the edge of the mat,

Luna uncaps it and holds the container out for me to take. The ice-cold liquid is half gone in two gulps, and yet she still picks the boxing pads back up, ready to go again.

"Luna, you've had me on the treadmill, the bike, lifting weights and throwing punches for the past twenty minutes. I can't take any more. This is the limit for today."

Lowering the bright red pads to her side, I take that as a win, dropping down on my ass right where I am. The water bottle in my hand splashes over me, but I'm already wet because of sweat anyway. Resting my arms on my knees, I hold my head in my hands as my heart rate slowly calms down.

"Fine, Red, you can have the rest of the day to relax. But next time, we have to push for more if we want to increase your skills, agreed?"

"Agreed," I grumble, wondering if my life is about to flash before my eyes if I don't get my breathing under control.

"You know sitting down only makes you feel worse right?"

I don't lift my head to meet her gaze or even open my eyes, but I manage to use my strength to give her the finger, and her chuckle surrounds me.

"Don't be such a drama queen. Come on." Patting the side of my leg, she grabs my hand and pulls me to my feet. "I'll even leave you to spend the rest of your evening lost in one of your steamy books," Luna says with a smile that I manage to match.

"You, Luna Steele, are the devil," I grumble, grabbing a towel from the rope around the ring we stand in. "Every time you train me, it feels like a near-death experience. You better believe I'm going to shower, grab some food, and spend the rest of the day in the sunshine, laying on the grass with my book."

I jump out of the ring, brushing my damp hair out of my face as Luna joins my side, hip checking me as she passes.

"Are you sure you don't want to come up and have dinner with me and read in my lounge?" She asks. I wrap my arm around her shoulders as I catch up, stretching my arm out since she is a lot taller than my small five-foot three-inch self.

"Do I need to sing the best friend's song to you again? Because you are too damn sweet to me," I say with a grin, and she rolls her eyes at me.

"No, you fucking don't. I take it back, get out!" Her

shout has no bite, especially with the smile on her face.

"Best friend, my very very best friend…"

"Nope. No. Seriously, get out." Luna cuts me off, and I can't stop giggling as we walk out of the gym. The lobby is quiet, but it's late afternoon, so all the cliques are stationed in their usual spots outside.

"Remember what I said, Red," Luna whispers under her breath, and my back instantly straightens.

"Fake it till I make it." Repeating her words pushes me to own it. "I'll see you in the morning."

Stepping out into the courtyard, I feel eyes on me. Not because I'm anyone exciting, simply because I am a nobody, and I just walked out of Ace block like it is no big deal. The campus is new to all of us, but back at Featherstone High, I would have never been invited anywhere near the Aces. Now, my best friend is one of them.

We've been here for less than a week, and already so much shit has happened around me. This place is a viper's pit, and I feel as though I'm barely holding on to the side, merely missing their bite. Crude words have always been thrown my way, but I've thankfully never been physically hurt.

Walking past Wren Dietrichson and her sheep, I feel

their eyes burn my skin as I hold back my sneer. They're causing the same shit as they did when we were in high school, but this time, Luna is in their sights. I've always avoided them, but I won't back down from Luna's side because they're jealous of her.

"Run along, bitch, back under the rock you came from," Wren calls out, making her friends chuckle. My hands ball into fists at my side as I keep my mouth shut and continue moving.

I manage to make it back to Diamond without further interruption and quickly shower. Changing into a pale pink floral print dress, all floaty and hitting just above the knee. I braid my hair to the side, allowing it to dry, deciding to leave my face bare of make-up. Slipping into a pair of white lace ballet shoes, I throw a blanket into my oversized purse, along with my Kindle, and head for my favorite spot on campus.

Picturing the most perfect oak tree by the Main Hall, I pick up speed. It's quiet and peaceful here, with pretty flower beds surrounding it and my favorite pink roses blooming. This spot also keeps the sun for the longest on campus and is the best location for watching the world go by. Students and tutors are coming and going from the main hall, and the on-site shops and food outlets in the opposite direction. It's the perfect place for being alone, but I'm not really alone.

I enjoy the walk, making a quick stop to grab a sandwich and bottled water on the way. After choosing a spot just out of the shade of the large oak tree, I place my pastel blue blanket on the grass. I slip my shoes off and lie under the warm rays of the sun beating down on me.

Time passes me by as I enjoy the outdoors, my latest novel on my Kindle, consuming my mind. The love, passion, and ecstasy that fills the pages come to life around me as I get lost in their world.

"Hey, Rick, wait up!"

A deep voice calls out, pulling my attention from the story I'm in. Tearing my gaze from my kindle, I look to see where the shout came from. I notice Maverick, my Combat tutor, waiting on the steps up to the Main Hall, and a guy approaching him from the open doors.

Holy fuck. I can't take my eyes off him, the guy talking to Maverick. Short brown hair and bright blue eyes are what capture my attention. But it's the fit of his tight t-shirt and the broad set of his shoulders that make me get all flustered. Seeing them side by side, I could totally use this visual.

I can't hear their conversation, but they seem happy enough in each other's presence. With a clasp of hands and a pat on the back, they walk in opposite directions from the Main Hall. The guy with the hot, deep voice, and piercing blue eyes, follows the path closer to where I'm sitting. I can't stop myself from tracking his every movement.

As if feeling my gaze on him, his eyes find mine. My breath stutters in my chest, leaving me frozen in place. I'm sure my mouth is gaping wide open, but I can't seem to close it. Someone walks straight into him, or him into them, I'm not sure, but our intense moment is broken.

Shaking my head, my cheeks flush beetroot red with embarrassment. It feels like the hot sex scene I was just reading is written all over my face. His deep voice, his eyes, and Maverick's messy hair only enhance the words.

Damn it. Now I'm too horny to be in public. I guess I need some time with BOB, my Battery Operated Boyfriend, to help alleviate the need inside of me. I'm glad I've eaten because good energy levels make for excellent orgasms.

West

"Thank you, everyone, for joining me on such short notice," Barbette Dietrichson addresses the room. Everyone wears neutral faces, but I can't be the only one internally cringing at the grate of her voice.

She's gathered all the tutors in the conference room in the Main Hall, likely to tell us about some shit she's excited to torture the students with. I think it's her favorite pastime. Barbette was just as much of a bitch even when I attended Featherstone Academy as a student.

I only have to teach Weaponry twice a week to the boys in Diamond and Hearts, along with all the students from Ace. The rest of the time, I'm called away to either do Featherstone's dirty work, or I would travel to visit Luna and Rafe. Now, Luna is here, knowing all the secrets we've been keeping, and I'm at a loss of where I stand. I've spent so long following the words of a dead man, promising to protect Luna from harm, yet here she is right in the path of pain and destruction.

Maverick throws himself down beside me, a sigh bursting from his lips that doesn't go unmissed by the others seated around us.

"What?" He grunts at everyone looking his way, and they all quickly turn their gaze back to Barbette.

"Mr. Miller, how nice of you to join us," Barbette says with a sneer. "I won't keep you long. I just wanted to advise everyone the assignments will be going out tomorrow. A fabulous surprise for our enthusiastic students, I'm sure."

I can't stop my teeth from grinding together. So high and mighty the Headmaster sits, but not every student here wants to be a part of this world. That decision is taken out of our hands the moment we are born.

"Anything else?" Maverick asks, making Barbette sigh.

"No, Mr. Miller, nothing else. We are to surprise the students tomorrow, understood?"

Maverick is up and out of his seat the second she stops talking, storming out of the room like he usually does. As much as I can't stand Barbette Dietrichson, Maverick has no patience like the rest of us and he doesn't even hide it.

Offering a polite nod to the bitch standing before me with her hands on her hips, I follow after him.

"Rick, wait up. Rick!" I shout, and he finally slows once he's outside of the building. Glancing over his shoulder at me, I see the haunted look in his eyes.

"What, West?" He murmurs, glancing down at his feet.

"You aren't sleeping," I state, and he shakes his head.

"It doesn't matter, West."

"If you would just…"

"West, I appreciate your concern, but I'm fine."

I know when it's not worth an argument with him. I consider Maverick a friend, as much as he can be one anyway. He's always distant, only ever offering what he wants you to see, hiding his pain and internal struggle from everyone. But I know what he's lived through. I can't imagine the mental strain he feels.

Patting his arm, I step back, "Okay. Catch you tomorrow. You know where I am." He smiles appreciatively at the fact I don't continue to push him.

I want to check in with Roman to make sure Luna is okay. I know she doesn't really want to speak to me at the moment, because of all the secrets between us. But I need to make sure she's okay.

Taking the quickest path to Ace block, I feel eyes on me. Looking to my right, my steps falter when I see the most beautiful red hair braided over the shoulder of the woman lying under an oak tree. Her blue eyes flutter as she looks me up and down. The second our eyes lock, I'm captivated by her. Who the hell is that? She looks sweet and delicate like a freedom rose while lying on the grounds of Featherstone Academy. She seems completely out of place.

I stumble back as I collide with someone in front of me. "Sorry, man. Are you okay?" I ask, keeping my balance.

"Watch where you're fucking going," the little asshole grunts, continuing towards the Main Hall. I want to smack the shit out of this mouthy nobhead, but I have to remember I'm a tutor, even if there are only four years between me and the students. He quickly continues by me, and as much as I want to call him out, my eyes drift back to where the pretty girl was.

Looking back to the oak tree, the pretty redhead has gone, walking the path toward the dorm blocks in front of me. She's like a bright ray of sunshine in this dark world. I can't stop myself from watching her leave, drifting through my fingers before I could even get close.

KC KEAN

FOUR

Jess

Something is wrong. I can feel it in my bones. Luna didn't show up to class this morning, and she isn't here in Combat. Which isn't like her since this is likely her favorite class with all the fighting involved. Taking my phone into the Combat class, I don't see Maverick anywhere. So, I hang by the door and try to call Luna again.

The ringing soon reaches her voicemail service again, and I give up trying to leave another message. Sighing, I glance around the room, spotting Oscar, Roman, Parker, and Kai sitting on some of the benches. I wouldn't usually approach them on my own, without Luna here, but desperate times call for desperate measures. Roman screams 'fuck off' with his permanent scowl in place, while Kai taps away on his phone, not looking at his surroundings but likely knowing everyone's movement.

As I near, Parker lifts his gaze, swiping his curly hair out of his eyes, which crinkle in concern. His move draws Oscar's attention my way too.

"Jessica Watson, where's my hot baby girl at?"

"I, uh, I don't know," I murmur, playing with the phone in my hand. "Luna hasn't shown up anywhere today, and she isn't answering her phone." I show them the screen of my phone like they can fucking tell from that, and internally groan at myself.

"What do you mean?" Roman Rivera growls, instantly rising to his feet.

"I mean, I'm worried because I don't know where she is," I grumble back, not liking his asshole tone. "But forget it, I'll figure it out myself." Spinning on my heels, I head back for the door when someone catches my arm.

"Ignore that grumpy fucker, Jess. I'll come with you," Parker says, glancing down at me with worry in his eyes that matches mine.

"Where are we going?" Kai asks, and I look at him

in surprise.

"Combat isn't my strong suit. Any excuse to leave and check up on my friend is easily taken," I respond, heading straight for the exit, feeling them all on my tail.

Just as I step through, I walk straight into Maverick. Throwing my arms out to stop my fall, they meet his chest as he grabs my waist to catch me. Frozen in place for a moment, I see turmoil swirling in his eyes, full of pain. His pupils widen as he stares down at me, and I can't bring my mouth to close as I gape up at him.

Leather and sandalwood intoxicate my senses. Goosebumps prickle my skin, where his fingertips brush my hips. Holy hell, Maverick Miller this close has me speechless.

As if he intentionally wants to ruin my perfect moment, Roman interrupts. "Good catch, Maverick, but how about you let Jess go so we can get a move on?" Like I've caught fire, Maverick releases me from his grip, stretching his shoulders as he stands tall, frowning at us all.

"And where do you think you're going? I'm about to start the lesson," he grunts, making Oscar laugh.

"Right, about that. We have places to be. So, thanks."

The Aces take his lead and head down the hall, leaving

me panicked in my spot. Maverick sighs at the guys but does nothing, instead, he turns his icy gaze on me.

"Get back in the sports hall," he says, his voice void of any emotion. But I don't miss his eyes lingering on my waist where his hands held me moments ago.

"Actually, that's my friend they're going to check on, so…" I move to step around him, but his growl makes me pause.

"Did I fucking stutter? I said, get back in the sports hall."

Turning to face him, my hands clench by my side, wanting to crush the phone in my hand.

"Wow. My friend hasn't responded and could be in danger in this fucking hell on earth." I take a deep breath, stopping myself from letting my true rage show. "So, no, you didn't stutter, *Sir*, but I'm not staying when she needs me."

My heart pounds in my chest at disobeying a tutor, so I run before he can stop me, heading straight for the locker room to grab my things. I don't want to waste time changing, but as I pick my uniform up from beside my bag, I notice that the black material of my jacket and skirt is frayed. What the hell? Holding it out in front of me, my already beating heart goes into overdrive as I realize someone has slashed my uniform. Who the fuck has done this? And why?

Fuck. I don't have time for this. As racked with panic as I am over my uniform, I know it in my bones that Luna needs me. So, I stuff it all into my bag and head for the door, putting it to the back of my mind.

Stepping to the hallway, I notice Maverick has gone, but Reece is lurking by the doors to the Combat hall, and I can't seem to suck in a breath. Lost in his gaze, my anxiety increases at the darkness in his eyes, while my steps slow.

"Let's go, Jess," Parker calls from the other side of the main doors, standing by an SUV with the door open. "We'll all travel together in the SUV. It'll be quicker than traveling in separate cars." I don't argue as I climb in with them, the driver taking off as soon as the door shuts behind Parker.

"When was the last time you spoke to Luna?" Kai asks quietly from beside me, and I retrace my steps.

"Yesterday, as we left History. Then we went our separate ways, but Luna did go to Ace when I went back to my room."

Nobody responds as we all consider how strange the

situation is. She's her own person. It just seems out of character for her to go off the grid so suddenly. The SUV comes to a stop outside of Ace quickly, and Roman throws the door open. We all file out of the back and head straight inside.

The guys rush for the elevator, but I stop, spotting Thomas off to the right.

"Thomas, have you seen Luna anywhere? I'm worried about her."

"Oh, Miss Watson. She is up in her room, I think. I sent food up earlier."

I sigh in relief, "Thank you, Thomas!" I call out as I run for the elevator, squeezing in with the guys.

It feels like it takes forever for the elevator to reach the top floor, but the moment it does, Parker is out and banging on Luna's door. He yells at the top of his lungs while the others hurry behind him, panic in their eyes.

"I swear to fucking god. I'm about to bust this fucking door down if someone doesn't fucking open it. Right. Now."

It takes a moment before the door is finally open, as I stand behind them.

"What the fuck are you doing in her room?" Parker

snaps, and I frown, unable to see around them, see who he's speaking to.

"Roman, I swear to god, calm him down. He's not helping the situation, and I won't let him through like this, she doesn't need any extra shit right now."

That voice sounds familiar. As the guys push into the room, I stand frozen in place as the hot guy from the other day stands before me. His blue eyes look tired, but he's staring into mine with recognition. He looks as though he hasn't slept well, bags under his eyes, and frown lines mark his forehead. I want to run my thumb along them, release his tension.

"West, I'll calm him down when you tell us what's going on. We've been trying to get hold of her since Jess said she'd heard nothing. Now we finally get in here to find you, West, a tutor. You need to tell me what's fucking going on."

West? Who the fuck is West, and how does everyone know him but me? I really, really need to get to know him.

"West!" Luna calls out, her voice is weak and gravelly. I bypass him, heading straight for my friend, needing to see her with my own eyes to make sure she is okay. As soon as I see her lying before me in her bed, I release the breath I hadn't realized I'd been holding. As bruised as she looked, I was just glad to see her alive. You never know with this place.

I stand quietly in the corner as West recounts what happened to my best friend. Luna was beaten and attacked in her own block with the lights cut out. It sounds like more than one person was involved. I know Wren had something to do with it, I can feel it in my bones, but I feel helpless. What can I offer her to make this better and ease the pain Luna is in?

When she tries to get out of bed, I watch as Roman offers her a gentleness I've never seen from him before, and it catches me by surprise. Such a big guy with a delicate touch, and I can't help but want that for myself. The hopeless romantic in me wanting to be loved even in moments like this. Shaking my head, I focus on what is in front of me, and right now. I need to keep busy, and Luna deserves a Frappuccino.

"I'm going to go and get Luna her favorite drink. Does anybody else want anything?" I ask, but a chorus of 'no thanks' greet me.

"Let me get the door for you," West murmurs with a small smile, and my nerves kick in all over my body.

I follow behind him, watching his ass flex under his tight denim jeans, fucking drool-worthy. He stops as his hand wraps around the door handle, but he doesn't move to open the door. Looking up in confusion, I cringe with embarrassment when I find him already staring at me, a knowing grin on his face. I can feel my cheeks deepen in color, which only makes him smile wider. His eyes sparkling with mischief.

"I don't believe we've been properly introduced. I'm West." His deep voice washes over me as he holds his hand out.

"Jess," I breathe, my hand tingling as I place it in his, lost in a trance. "Uh, how do you know Luna and the guys?" I ask, our touch lingering for a moment longer before I remember to release his hand.

"I'm an old family friend of Luna's and the Weaponry tutor here." I watch as he tucks his hands into his pockets.

"How does such an awful place have such hot tutors?" I whisper under my breath before I can stop myself, biting my lip shut.

"What was that?" West asks, leaning closer slightly in confusion.

"Uh, nothing. Nothing at all." I wipe my hands on my

shorts and nod at the door handle, encouraging him to open it, which he thankfully does before my embarrassment kills me.

"Well, it's very nice to meet you, Jess." My name sounds like heaven on his lips.

As I step past him, I squeeze his arm, as if it's natural to touch him without question. "You too, West."

West

Holy shit. So, the pretty redhead has a name, and she is somehow a part of Luna's life. This world really can't get much smaller. Her presence is like a candle in the dark, a ray of sunshine through the dark clouds Featherstone hangs over us.

I have barely slept since someone attacked Luna right under our noses, but a moment in her soft and gentle presence has calmed my erratic mind, and relaxed my tense muscles. It feels strange, wanting to spend more time around Jess, but I couldn't come up with a reason quick enough. Usually, I find a girl after fight night, fuck, and run. The only girl I spend more time with than that is Luna, who is apparently drawn to this girl just as much as me.

I wrack my brains on whether there is anything official in the rule books about tutors and students together. I've seen it happen before, the students are all of age, but it *is* frowned upon. Yet, shooting and killing others is perfectly fine. It doesn't make sense at all. There is something about her presence that makes me not give a fuck either way.

Turning from the front door, I adjust myself discreetly, but Kai observes me from the bedroom door. He says nothing, just raising his eyebrow at me and steps back into the bedroom. Fuck, I'm getting hard for a student, yet I just can't seem to give a shit.

For now, I need to help play this giant game of chess Featherstone has set up and try to get us all out of it alive.

KC KEAN

FIVE

Jess

The past few weeks have been crazy. Between Luna's attack and classes, there has barely been a minute to relax. So, I'm excited for the Fall Ball tonight. Featherstone makes my blood boil, but they sure know how to throw a party, and I love any excuse for getting all glammed up. It also means I can hopefully relax and have some fun for a few hours.

I'm even more excited that I also get to work my make-up magic on Luna too, since she willingly agreed. Well, agreed to shut me up, but I'll take that as a win. I'm looking forward to making her look girly compared to her usual edgy vibes.

Her mother bought so many dresses, we didn't need to go shopping, and the make-up station she has means I don't need to take anything with me. Now, I just need to get my ass into gear. It's just that my body aches so bad.

Since Luna was jumped, Roman has agreed to continue my training at my reluctance. If I thought Luna worked me hard, I had no idea what was happening now. Roman's self-defense classes are way more aggressive. He's only doing it as a favor to Luna, and out of all the Aces that are currently vying for Luna's attention, he is my least favorite. Simply because when I beg to stop training, he makes me do ten more reps of whatever I'm doing. He's a real son of a bitch.

Roman can tell me he's doing it to help me, but really he just likes torture. My muscles burned to begin with, but I refuse to admit his constant cardio and weight training is getting easier. I'm slowly starting to predict his next move. But, I'll hold back, then BAM! I'm going to get this fucker back.

Finding myself under Luna's wing has also led to Roman, Parker, Kai, and Oscar offering me protection by association. Usually, the ruthless Aces take care of no one but themselves, yet they are currently obsessing over my bestie, and it's hilarious seeing this side to them. The way their eyes follow her every movement. They'll fight to give her everything.

Their constant closeness also means I haven't had any further encounters with Reece. My gut tells me it was him who cut up my uniform, and secretly, he's the reason I'm pushing myself with all the self-defense classes they're giving me. I don't want him to hold me like he did in Science the other week, I felt helpless.

Pulling myself away from the anxiety bombarding my mind, I jump out of the shower, I throw on a black mid-thigh skirt, and tuck in a white tank top into the waistband. Slipping my feet into a pair of sandals, I leave my hair up in a bun since I can style it when I get over there.

Locking my door behind me, I take the stairs down to the ground floor. There's no fancy lobby here like over at Ace block, no gym or fancy on-site chef service either. The ground floor is simply more dorm rooms. The process is the same, though. The higher up the building, the higher your bloodline within Featherstone.

Which is why I take the stairs. Being on the first floor comes with both pros and cons. I'm not at the bottom of the

Diamond pile, and I can take the stairs easily since it's only one flight. But all of Wren's little friends are on the top floor of the four-story Diamond block, and they make sure everyone knows it. They think they're the next best thing when no one from Ace is around, and it's embarrassing how much appearances matter.

The hallways are quiet, and the usually busy outdoor space surrounding all the blocks is deserted while everyone prepares for tonight. The automatic doors open for me, and Thomas, the doorman at Ace, smiles politely as I head straight for the elevator. Since my best friend is on the top floor, I don't fancy the four flights this time, not after my earlier workout.

Pounding on Luna's door, I can hear her grumbling from the other side. It's crazy how natural this is now, walking into Ace without a care in the world.

"I'm not fucking here!" she shouts, and I grin.

"Open the damn door, Luna."

The door swings open, and her frown is already in place, but I pay her no mind as I step past her, heading straight for the stunning dressing room she has adjoined to her bedroom. Racks and racks of clothes are lining the far wall, along with bags and accessories. While her vanity sits perfectly by the window, offering the best light.

"You do whatever makes you happy, and I'll shout for you when I'm ready," I call out over my shoulder, and she barely offers a grunt in response. She leaves me to do my thing, and I can't help but get lost in all the clothes. Fashion is life. I want to read books and look good doing it. My fingers skim over the fabrics, silk, lace, and velvet. The designer brands have me super jelly, Gucci, Chanel. The list goes on, and I'm beyond lucky that she is so openly willing to share this experience with me.

It takes a little while to go through all the high-end make-up products she has too, and I love every second of it. Deciding to do my make-up first, I go for a sexy smokey eye with painted red lips and pin the top half of my hair back in a cute half up/half down style. I feel sexy as hell, especially with the lingerie I'm wearing.

"Okay, Luna, I've narrowed down these dresses to the top three for you. Now choose so I can do your hair and make-up," I yell, having no idea where she is in her room.

Walking in, her eyes go straight to the three dresses hung near the floor-length mirror for her to try. All ankle-length, there's a green, deep blue, and dusty pink option.

"I'm not wearing green this bright," she grumbles, and

I just chuckle, loving to wind her up. "You can do my hair and make-up first, then I'll try the dresses," she finishes, and I clap excitedly.

"Fabulous, sit. Are you sure you don't want me to go a little crazy with this?"

"I'm sure. If you give me an over the top look, I won't go." She scowls, but I roll my eyes at her. Turning her away from the mirror, I pull out all the products I need and get to work. Styling her hair perfectly, I curl it and make a loose messy bun at the back of her head.

"Are you sure you are happy to share the dresses, make-up, and shoes with me? I don't mind going back to my dorm to get ready with my things," I murmur, feeling a tad guilty that she's so openly sharing with me.

"Don't be crazy, Red. You appreciate all of this more than I do. I'll be upset if you don't choose your whole outfit from here. It's ridiculous how much stuff there is. Veronica went over the top with it all," Luna responds with an eye roll of her own.

"Thank you, Luna. For being the best friend I've always needed. Not just for sharing all this with me," I murmur, my hands swirling around us. "But, for putting up with my non-stop talking, and letting your guard down around me."

"You're making me blush, Red. You encourage me to be this way, with all your positivity and the lightness inside of you. All your rainbows and unicorn glitter is rubbing off on me."

My heart warms, but neither of us say anything more as I cover her face with a mixture of bronzes and golds. I don't go as bold as my own, and when I turn her to the mirror, I know I made the right decision.

"If I do say so myself, Captain, you look stunning, now choose a dress. We've got about half an hour until the guys get here," I say with a smile, and head for her bedroom to give her some privacy while I can also get changed too.

Stepping into the beautiful dress Luna has let me borrow, I zip up the back and take a look in the floor-length mirror. The dress is rich red in color, with a deep V to the front and a high slit up the left side. I'm in love. The skirt has layers and layers of chiffon and lace floating at different lengths, from my hips to my ankles. Stroking my fingers over the material, I feel like a princess. I shake my head at the absurdity of it all.

Loving the fact that I wear the same size shoe as Luna, I slip a pair of black stilettos on, fastening the clasp around my ankle. Adding a pair of Luna's earrings and a delicate bracelet to my wrist and I'm ready.

Now to find myself a prince charming, or two, or maybe five. Tora, the leading woman in my favorite paranormal harem romance, has three and I want that many too. At a minimum, more of those dreams I had about Maverick Miller and all those other hands caressing me.

The room in the Great Hall is beautiful. It's like a fairytale, with floral arched walkways and red carpet paths. But sitting at one of the many large tables covered in gold satin tablecloths with huge pale pink floral centerpieces, I have never felt so awkward in my life. I can barely understand what is going on around me as my nerves continue to take over. Along with Luna and her guys, Wren and her date, Tyler, are also sitting with us. I'm ready to claw my eyes out.

Her vile mouth has done nothing but cause tension, and Luna is already on edge. I'm not entirely sure why, but I can tell she isn't fully focused on what is going on at the table. Her eyes keep drifting to the table where The Ring are sitting. She doesn't need this bitch adding to her concern. Wren loves to stir up trouble, and she's getting on my last nerve. My inner bitch wants to ask her whether her ass is jealous of her mouth with all that shit she's spewing, but I don't have the lady balls to say it. One day I will, just not today.

"Miss Dietrichson, your grandfather wishes to see you alone." A steward advises, approaching the table and leaving just as quickly. I enjoy watching the color drain from her face and the tremble in her hands as she stands. She's barely left the table when Roman tells Tyler to fuck off too, and I feel us all slightly relax at their absence.

My attention is drawn to the singer on the stage with a live band singing Taylor Swift's 'Lover.' A shadow falls over Luna's other side. I watch as West whispers in her ear, his eyes meeting mine, and the magic they hold gives me butterflies. I want to know what it feels like to have him whisper in my ear, his deep voice up close, giving *me* goosebumps.

Standing tall, he asks Luna to dance, and I can't help but feel a snippet of disappointment that it isn't me. I feel the guys' anger around the table, watching her head for the dance floor with West. Roman's hands are clenched tight on the table, while I can see the indecision in Oscar, wanting to go and tear them apart. I'm left gawking at how damn handsome West looks in a suit. Charcoal grey pants and blazer with a matching tie and black shirt, tailored to fit his body perfectly.

I'm even more surprised there doesn't seem to be any gossip from anyone about a tutor dancing with a student. I distract myself with a sip of water, needing to cool down and not look so obvious when Kai clears his throat.

"So, Jess, Luna mentioned your assignment for Featherstone." He leaves the sentence open, maintaining eye contact as he waits for me to respond. My palms sweat with the stress this damn assignment is giving me.

"Okay," I say, not really knowing what response he actually wants from me.

"Do you mind if I take a look at the devices before you hand them in?"

"You want to look at the gas explosives I'm expected to make?" I ask in confusion, and he nods. "Why?"

"Because we are linking all of our assignments together, and it feels as though there is a bigger game at play here," Parker says, giving me a little more insight than the others.

"Well, I'll probably make them the day before the deadline, so I'm sure I can have Luna let you know before

I pass them on. But they won't be in my possession for long. I want as little to do with Featherstone as possible."

Roman smiles as his hand slaps the table. "Good, that's what we wanted to hear."

Did Roman Rivera actually not be a moody asshole for a minute there? He must see the surprise in my eyes because he shakes his head at me, looking back to Luna on the dance floor. I can feel someone's eyes on the side of my face, and when I turn to see where the burning sensation is coming from, my eyes instantly collide with Maverick's.

His hair is no different than any other day, messy and tousled as if he's just got out of bed. Other men would spend forever trying to get their hair to look that good, but you can tell he makes no effort in any of that. He's dressed in a simple pair of black pants with a matching tie and shirt, which fits him like a glove. The thickness of his arms causing me to almost moan in delight, my vivid imagination wondering what they would look like coiled tight with him above me.

His eyes hold me captive until Luna retakes her seat beside me, pulling me from my smutty thoughts. West looks me over as he turns to leave us, a smile playing on his lips, leaving me flustered after my previous stare-off with Maverick.

Feeling eyes on me from the left, I peer out of the corner of my eye, and my body stills at the sight of Reece shaking his finger at me in disappointment, a sneer on his lips.

Another server approaches the table, and a flurry suddenly surrounds us, drawing my attention back to the table. I don't really understand what is going on, but one-minute Luna is on the phone, and the next, she's sending Parker and Roman outside. Rafe, her guardian, is approaching the table. Murmuring between themselves, I stand ready to leave too. Laughter catches my attention at the table on the other side of the dance floor. I don't know what's going on. But Aiden Byrnes has everyone at his table laughing at whatever joke he's telling, playing to a willing audience as always.

Oscar is suddenly at my side, arm around my shoulder, steering me towards the exit. It sounds like a riot is starting behind us, but Oscar doesn't give me a chance to see.

"Let's get you out of here in this dress, Jess. We don't want any of the boys here getting ideas they can flirt with you or anything," he grumbles, patting my head like a child, and I elbow him in the stomach, making him huff out a breath.

"You are a total shit, Oscar O'Shay," I mutter under my breath, which only makes him chuckle. He wraps his arm around my shoulder, guiding me towards the door, and I can feel eyes on me every step of the way. Glancing over my shoulder, I quickly whip my head back around when I see Reece burning holes in the side of my head. That's not the attention I want.

We meet Roman and Parker out by the limo we came in for the two-minute drive we have, but Luna's men wanted to ride all together. An SUV would have been more than sufficient, but apparently not for the Aces.

The further away from the ball we get, the more disappointment I feel. I've spent the evening surrounded by my best friend and her guys, which is fine, but nobody wants to approach me, get to know me, nothing. I want a crazy sex life and spontaneous moments, yet I'm on my way home to get my fix from a book again, instead of the real-life experience.

Something has to change, and it seems that's going to have to be me.

SIX

Jess

Straightening my blazer, I check my reflection in the mirror. The tight black skirt sits just above the knee, the slit up the back dangerously high. The white blouse reveals the top of my cleavage, while my blazer defines my waist. The bright red 'F.A.' emblem is standing out against the dark material, and the gold trim finishes off the look. Slipping into my heels, I grab my bag and my phone from the bedside table.

I notice messages and missed call notifications flashing across the screen as it turns on automatically. Frowning in confusion, my phone lights up as another call silently comes through. *Parker* flashes across the screen, and I swipe my thumb across it, answering his call immediately.

"Jess! Jess? Are you there?"

"Hey, Parker. I'm here, is everything okay?"

"Oh, thank god. Everything has gone to shit here, Jess. Luna is on her way back. She'll likely be there any minute, but I don't want her to be alone. Can you go over?"

"Yeah, of course," I say, rushing for the door and hurrying down the stairs. "I'm on my way, but why is she on her way back from DC already, Parker? She said she would get the job done, and leave this evening."

He sighs down the phone, and it only adds to my concern. "It's hard to explain, and there is no time. We aren't far behind her, but Luna wasn't herself when she left."

"Okay, let me know when you guys get here," I answer before throwing the phone in my bag as I step out of Diamond block.

There are a few students gathered outside, but everyone is still likely getting ready for the day. I smile at Thomas as I step inside Ace and head straight for the elevator. It feels like it takes an eternity to reach the top floor, but the second it does, I'm out and banging on Luna's door.

"Luna, I know you're in there. Open the door right now," I shout, not wanting to waste time.

"Now's not a good time, Red," she calls back, and I can hear the pain in her voice.

That's when the piece of paper stuck to her door catches my attention. Ripping it from the door, I read the notice in my hands.

FEATHERSTONE ACADEMY
THE PYRAMID
YOU ARE REQUIRED TO ATTEND THE
TRIAL GAMES TODAY AT 12 NOON
ATTENDANCE IS MANDATORY
YOU MAY BRING ONLY ONE WEAPON OF
YOUR CHOOSING BUT IT MAY NOT BE A GUN
YOUR SACRIFICE FOR OUR ORDER IS
HONORABLE

Oh, fuck no, she isn't going through this alone. Not when I know something was already wrong before she got here and saw this.

"Don't give me that shit, Luna. If one more person calls my phone, I'm likely to launch it. Now let me in so I can help."

"No."

"Now, Luna!" I yell, slapping the door as worry consumes me.

"I'm doing you a favor, Red. Be grateful I can see through all this fog in my brain to recognize your importance to me. I can't promise the same when you're in here," she answers, and I want to cry at her words, but I refuse to back down, not when I know she needs me.

"Luna Steele, open the fucking door now."

The door swings open, and I take in her disheveled appearance. Wrinkled clothes, wild messy hair, and her face is red with anger, but I force myself to smile at her sweetly and brush right past with the notice in my hands. I head straight for the kitchen, flicking the coffee machine on and pulling two mugs from the cupboard.

Luna follows me into the kitchen. Her usually bright green eyes are dark and dim.

"Your eyes aren't the same," I murmur, unable to keep my mouth shut. Luna doesn't respond, so I continue, glancing down at the notice beside me.

"What will be better for you, catching a few hours' sleep or powering on through?"

"I took a nap yesterday morning and have been awake ever since, so about twenty-two hours, but my brain isn't going to switch off right now," she answers honestly, and I nod in response.

"I won't ask if you're okay because I know you're not. You don't even look like you right now. It's weirding me out a little," I say with a smirk, but I still get nothing in response.

A knock on the door sounds, and I can tell she's about to blow. Frustration is evident in the clench of her fists and the tight set of her jaw.

"You want to be my best friend? Then you get rid of whoever is on the other side of that door. I'm done with all of this shit," she growls, locking herself in the bathroom.

Okay then. Best friend duties it is. Hopefully, it's the guys, then I can get some more answers to what's going on here. Swinging the door open, I glance over my shoulder, swinging my arm out wide to let them in.

"Come in, tell me what the hell has…"

I'm cut off as an arm wraps around my neck, and a piece of cloth is brought to my face. A sickly smell fills my lungs as it covers my mouth and nose. I try to wiggle out of their hold, but the shock is taking over my body. My brain is malfunctioning as I try to remember what Roman taught me. My eyes search frantically around as my attempts to scream are muffled. There are three more people dressed head to toe in black. I can feel my brain getting foggy and my eyes blur as I struggle to fight them off. My arms feel sluggish, and my legs begin to wobble. I stumble, a hand on my arm whirls me around, pinning my back to their front as I feel my body becoming limper.

Just before the darkness takes over, I can't help but frown internally. Someone sent four people, yet they only really needed one because I'm so damn weak. How fucking pathetic.

My head twitches, and my fingers tingle, as I try to register where I am. My body aches from head to toe and I feel like I'm standing yet floating all at the same time. Trying to lift my hands to swipe at my eyes proves difficult, but I have to, my eyelids feel glued together with gunk. My hands feel as though they are made from stone, and I just can't lift them.

Glancing down at my fingers, I wiggle them slowly, the motion sluggish as my brain tries to catch up. My chin rests against something around my neck that feels completely out of place. What on earth is going on? My bare feet are only just visible in the darkness surrounding me, and I can't shake this distorted feeling. I can hear chatter, squeaks, and bangs, but I don't see anything. Nothing covers my mouth, but I'm too freaked out to say a word. Even if I wanted to alert anyone, my tongue is like lead in my mouth.

I don't realize I'm leaning on something until I try to move, and what feels like a thin pole is at my back, forcing me to remain upright. What the fuck is going on? A groan beside me in the darkness catches my attention, but I can't see anything in the cocoon that blankets me, separating me from the noise and outside world.

Taking a step forward, I'm instantly thrown back by a rough pull at my neck. My hands instinctively rise, pushing through the ache, trying to process what is holding me in place. The touch of thick, coarse rope wrapped around my throat catches me by surprise, sending my shock levels through the roof.

I pull at the rope frantically, but it's no use. I can't seem to lift it over my head. Shit. I need to calm down, relax, and assess the situation like Luna taught me to. But that's easier said than done right now as fear courses through my body.

I take a deep breath, followed by a second and a third. Squeezing my eyes shut, I strain to hear what is going on as the noise level rises around me. It takes a moment, but the sound of Barbette Dietrichson's voice is recognizable through a sound system.

"The aim of the game is for both Luna and Tyler to make it past the three rings to fight it out at the top. The winner there must complete the final act before winning The Death Pyramid!" she shouts with glee.

Death Pyramid? Holy shit, is this Luna's Death Pyramid assignment? Where the fuck am I? I zone out as I try to process her words until her voice booms through the speakers louder.

"To add extra incentive for the main runners to win, I would like to remove the cover from the top of the pyramid," she pauses, and I'm suddenly thrown into the light.

I blink, my eyes taking a moment to adjust to the bright lights, but when I finally take stock of where I am, my heart stops. I'm too high, too high up in the fucking air. My fingers are wrapped tightly around the noose at my neck as I glance below. Fighting rings are set up in the shape of a pyramid, and I'm standing on a platform at the top.

A whimper catches my attention, just like earlier, and when I look to my left, I'm stunned to see a naked Becky Brown strung up just like I am. She's shaking, and I can't tell whether she's cold from being unclothed or afraid. I'm sure the anxiety and panic in her eyes match mine as we stare at each other for a moment. Glancing away, I quickly stare down at myself to make sure I'm not naked too. I can hear Barbette continuing to speak, but I don't really focus on what she's saying, until her words have fear like ice through my veins.

"As the battle commences below, the two girls at the top will slowly start to be hung. They must reach the top and cut the rope in time. Now, I think I've covered everything. Shall we begin?"

I'm going to be hung? What the fuck for? Tears prick my eyes as dread consumes my body. I'm going to fucking die here, at the hands of Featherstone and their stupid games.

I can't see Luna or a familiar, comforting face in the crowd as Dietrichson's voice fills the room, followed by the wail of a siren.

"What the hell is going on?" Becky shouts, venom in her eyes as she takes me in like it's all my fault we're here.

"I … I don't know," I murmur, as the noose around my neck seems to tighten with every breath. Glancing above my head, I notice a device slowly pulling the rope high. They're going to kill us, and there's nothing I can do about it.

Facing away from where Luna must be, I can't see what is happening, but I can hear the sounds coming from the fighting below. Every second feels like hours as the rope pulls tighter and tighter.

"You can't fucking do this to me!" Becky screams, tugging on the rope just like me.

I don't yell or shout, but my fingers ache from the friction of the rope as I try to get out of the hold, but it's no use. I'm suffocating. Standing up onto my tiptoes, I have nowhere to go while my lungs burn for more oxygen. I can see all the people in attendance out of the corner of my eye, as I get dizzier with the tightness of the rope.

The sound of flesh hitting flesh as people brawl near us gets closer, yet feels even further away. My head lolls forward as my body grows slack, unable to stand strong on my own any longer. I'm dying, and I never got to live the way I wanted to or become who I am meant to be.

As if knowing I'm close to taking my last breath, I feel

the tension in the rope give way and my body falls to the floor in a heap. Pulling oxygen into my lungs causes too much pain, but I need it like never before. Barely able to open my eyes, I know she saved me.

"Luna," I try to shout, but it's barely a whisper passing my lips as I lie on my back, trying to focus.

"Breathe, Red, just breathe. You'll be okay," she murmurs from above me, and I feel tears track down my face as my emotions get the better of me. "I'm so sorry, Red, so sorry that you were dragged into this. I'm going to make them pay, every last one of them."

Before I can reassure Luna that it's not her fault, an oxygen mask is placed over my face. Callous fingers trace my hairline soothingly, but tears blur my vision, and I haven't got the energy to see who it is.

"I've got her from here, Luna. They're waiting for you to address the room," someone murmurs before lifting me into their arms. I can't fight to stand on my own two feet, knowing I need help and support right now.

I feel my body turn to mush as my breathing becomes labored. "It's okay, Jessica. I have you now. Don't worry, just rest."

Forcing my eyes open for just a moment, I notice the

stubbled jaw and piercing green eyes of Maverick Miller, and I know if this is the last vision I ever have, it was the best one yet.

RED

KC KEAN

SEVEN

Maverick

Fuck. My heart pounds in my chest as the scene unfolds before me. A new trial for Featherstone's annual games event plays out before us, and the wreckage it causes clearly demonstrates the carnage, based on the bodies lying broken in Tyler's path. A vast difference to the path Luna Steele is leading, since I've helped carry two of the three bodies out of the ring to safety on her order. Any other time I would have told her to fuck off, but I see the determination in her eyes to cause as little damage as possible.

I just need her to get the fuck up to the top and release

Jessica Watson from the rope, but I can't see the ring where she is currently fighting with Tyler. They're out of view, and no one has risen to the final platform yet. After taking Aiden Byrnes to the medical center, I brought back a small oxygen mask and a portable oxygen tank. For the moment, I pray Luna cuts the rope and frees Jessica.

My eyes trail over Jessica again, standing tall at the top of the pyramid. I started the trial standing dead center between both paths up to the top, but the more I watched Tyler enjoy the pain he was inflicting, the more I moved to Luna's side. I notice her family bloodlines' in the boxes on the opposite side of the hall. It surprises me to see their eyes moving back and forth from Luna to Jessica, making sure they're both alive and okay.

I can see the fear in her eyes as the rope around her neck lifts her further off the floor. I want to storm the fucking game and cut her free myself. She doesn't deserve this, any of it. From the first moment she walked into my Combat class, I knew there was something different about her. She's innocent in a way Featherstone will surely ruin. But the fire that runs through her veins when she truly believes in something, is what holds my attention and drives me crazy all at once.

The memory of her standing toe to toe with me and not backing down when she was fearful for Luna, runs through my mind. Her defiant side surprised me after I caught her from falling. I still remember the soft feel of her skin under my fingertips. Wild red hair around her face, her blue eyes were wide as the pulse at her throat pounded rapidly.

She didn't falter at my growl or whimper like the shy girl I expected her to be. Instead, she fired my words back at me, giving me a taste of her bite, leaving me stunned in place as I watched her go.

Movement catches my eye as I see Luna, covered in blood, lift herself onto the platform. My feet are moving before my brain even catches up, climbing the pyramid as quickly as I can. I don't hear the cheers and whistles at Luna's victory from the crowd. My mind is solely focused on removing Jessica from this mess.

Stepping onto the platform, Luna is hovering over Jessica as she lays on her back, blood dripping from Luna's face. She's muttering to Jessica, but I can't hear her words. Instead, I focus on getting the mask over Jessica's face, giving her the oxygen she needs to breathe better. I pause as I look down at her, the angelic touch to her features forces me to stroke the frown that marks her forehead. Her mesmerizing eyes are bloodshot, and her neck is raw with rope burns. She whimpers slightly at the touch, her eyes closed as she takes deep breaths.

"I've got her from here, Luna. They're waiting for you to address the room," I murmur, slipping my hands under Jessica's body and holding her against my chest. I watch as Luna slowly fills with rage, grinding her jaw as her hands clench at her sides. I glance towards the box where Luna's family waits, to find them running around preparing for her to come down from the pyramid, so I know they've got it handled.

Sighing in relief, I turn all of my focus and attention to the woman in my arms. She shifts restlessly as I slowly carry her down, and I find myself muttering reassuring words, "It's okay, Jessica. I have you now. Don't worry, just rest."

The words feel strange on my tongue. I'm never one to offer kind and gentle words, but to put her mind at ease and to relax, I'd say just about anything right now.

Compared to the other people I've carried down, I take my time, making sure to keep my movements to a minimum so I don't disturb her. Bypassing everyone in the hall quickly, without a backward glance, I head straight for the medical center. The door is at the opposite end of the room to the main crowd of people, who are gathering around to hear from Luna. Pushing the door open with my back, I turn us into the hallway and rush us into the nearest empty room.

Gently laying her on the medical bed, I brush her soft red hair from her face. Her eyes remain closed as she seems to sleep.

"Mav, another one?" Dr. Ethan Phillips asks, exasperation clear in his voice as he stands at the door, running his hand through his disheveled hair.

"The most important one, Ethan," I answer, glancing over my shoulder at him, and his eyes widen in surprise at my words.

"Are you okay for two minutes while I finish with another patient? If you need to go..."

"I don't need to be anywhere, just hurry," I growl, wanting him to get his other shit done so he can get back here.

"Okay, two minutes," he rushes out, patting the doorframe. I nod in understanding, turning my gaze back to Jessica at the sound of her soft murmur beneath the oxygen mask.

Big blue eyes flutter open as her long dainty fingers rise to her face, pulling the mask off. Looking around the room, her gaze finally catches mine. Her pupils widen with relief when she sees me, making my lips tilt up slightly.

Leaning over her, I move to put the mask back in place. "Jessica, the mask is to help you with breathing. Put it back …"

"Always so grouchy, Maverick Miller," she whispers. The softness of her skin surprises me again as she lifts her hand to my face, my body freezing beneath her touch. "Why are your green eyes always storming with turmoil?" She asks softly, her gaze locked on mine as her thumb strokes across my cheek soothingly as if I was the one nearly hanging from the ceiling and needing comfort.

Her words startle me, and combined with her touch, she holds me captive, looking up at me with wonder in her eyes. Her blue eyes, full of hope and adventure, pull me in. My thumb strokes across her lips in response. I can't seem to process when or why I moved my hand to her face. Pulling it away feels out of the question.

Subconsciously, I move closer to her, two opposite ends of a magnet drawn together without choice, her natural glow drawing me in. The tip of her nose brushes against mine. "You need to smile, Maverick. It will do you a world of good."

Her breath blows against my lips as she speaks, but I can't find my tongue.

"Sorry about that, uh, sorry," Ethan stumbles, pulling my attention from Jessica. Quickly pushing off the bed, I put some much-needed distance between us, but I instantly miss the touch of her hand against my face.

"No, we're done here."

"Maverick," Jessica calls quietly, but I refuse to look at her.

"Ethan, Jessica was one of the girls hanging from the rope. Make sure to take extra care with her," I force out before storming for the door, slamming it behind me.

Moving through the medical center, I know I need to get out of here and far away from the woman who stirs emotions inside me. Feelings I've never felt before or even considered, and I don't want anything to do with them.

Straightening my leather jacket, I push through the doors into the hall where people stand gossiping about the spectacle they've just seen.

"Maverick! Maverick!" I stop in my tracks, turning to see Parker racing towards me, and before I can respond, he grips my shoulders. "Jess, where is she? We need to get her out of here to leave with Luna."

"What? Jess is going nowhere. She's with a doctor, where she needs to be," I grind out, feeling my back stiffen and my defenses rise.

"Luna needs to leave now, but she won't rest without Jess by her side. A plane is ready for them, with a doctor on board waiting. So, where is she, Maverick?"

Clenching my hands at my side, I take a deep breath. "Are you sure Jessica will get the care she needs?"

"Of course. Nobody else will be with them, except Rafe and Juliana."

My gut tells me to keep her at my side, protect her with my life, so she doesn't get pulled into this bullshit ever again. But my head knows we'll both be better with her as far away as possible.

"She's in the medical center with Dr. Phillips."

Not waiting around, I walk away, barging through the crowd. I need to get out of here, clear my thoughts, and get Jessica Watson out of my fucking head. My phone vibrates in my jeans pocket, and I know ignoring it will be no use.

UNKNOWN: Friday. Byrd Field. 10:00 AM.

Two Days.

Sighing, I pocket my phone, my brain going into autopilot, preparing for Friday. It's just what I need, and the perfect distraction from the red-headed flower I need to forget about.

KC KEAN

EIGHT

Jess

New York. New fucking York. I could scream with excitement, but I can see Juliana Gibbs shaking her head at me again. Although, the sparkle in her eyes tells me she's amused with my giddiness. It feels nice, enjoying a morning of shopping after everything that happened yesterday. I should probably be back at Juliana's apartment with Luna, resting, but apart from the bruises around my neck and a sore throat, I'm okay. I'm not ready to relive the whole ordeal, I'm going to focus on the fact that I'm alive, breathing, and in New York! Good times and good vibes only.

"Ladies, are you ready for me to take your order?" The server asks as he approaches our table. Juliana insisted we eat at The Modern, at the Museum of Modern Art. I feel a little out of my depth in a two Michelin-starred restaurant.

"We will take your selection of six to share between us, please," Juliana answers, thankfully taking over instead of leaving me to sink in the menu choices. By the looks of it, the chef will choose six items off the menu for us to sample. I can get down with that.

"Perfect. Would you like the wine pairing as well, ma'am?"

"No, thank you. We will take two waters instead, please." Nodding, the server leaves us, and Juliana's ice queen mask slips off her face when it is only the two of us.

"How do you do that?" I ask, unable to stop myself. "Sorry, I mean..." Clearing my throat, I can feel my cheeks redden at my big mouth, but Juliana smiles.

"You mean, how do I slip a mask on and off so easily?" She asks, and I nod, biting my lip to keep my mouth shut. "I picked it up quickly when I was at the academy, actually. When I had to hide my emotions from others. Now, it's natural." She shrugs, and it makes me smile to see her so casual.

We've been out for hours, shopping like my life depended on it. Thankfully, Juliana loves to shop too, along with Rafe's credit card, she's gone crazy. She insisted on buying a few items and fresh supplies for both Luna and me, and I'm grateful for the care she extends my way.

I've also enjoyed distracting myself from the giant Maverick Miller sized hole in my mind. I struggled to sleep last night, remembering the touch of his fingers stroking my face and lips, and his stormy eyes up close. I was so close to brushing my lips against his, then Ethan, aka my new friend, Dr. Phillips stepped in, and Maverick hightailed it out of there like his pants were on fire.

I sigh, annoyed with myself for thinking about him, even after he stormed out like that. My phone vibrates on the table as Juliana thanks the server for our drinks.

"The boys again?" Juliana asks with a grin on her face. I purse my lips as I check the screen, and it's no surprise to see Oscar's name flash across the screen.

"I mean, if you can guess which one, you get an extra point," I say, unlocking my phone and thumbing back through the group chat messages.

"Hmm, the frown lines between your eyes scream Oscar." I scrunch my nose in disapproval, and she chuckles, knowing she's right.

>Oscar: How is my baby girl today?

>Oscar: Hello?

>Parker: Give her a minute to at least respond, Oscar.

>Oscar: Okay, it's been three minutes. How is my baby girl?

>Kai: Oscar, stop.

>Roman: Can we kick him out of the chat? He's pissing me off.

>Roman: But if you could just tell us how she is, please, Jess?

>Oscar: Screw you, Rome.

>Oscar: JESSICA

Oscar: WATSON

Oscar: ANSWER

Oscar: MY

Oscar: MESSAGES!!!!!

Oh my god, how fucking ridiculous are these guys? I swear to god I am determined to get myself a harem, but if they act like this, I'll pull my hair out.

Me: She is resting. Refusing to see anyone for the moment, so we are giving her the space she needs and deserves after what she endured yesterday. Now, when that changes, I will message you.

I place my phone on the table and it starts vibrating again, this time a phone call. Even Juliana rolls her eyes as I pick it up without bothering to look at the screen this time.

"Oscar, how many times do I have to…"

"Jess?" The voice on the other end asks, and I recognize

the deep tone instantly.

"West?" I respond in surprise, straightening my hair like he can see me.

"Yeah. Sorry, I know you have a lot going on right now. It's just … after yesterday, I've been worried, and I just needed to hear from you for myself. So, I convinced Rafe to give me your number."

Holy. Fucking. Shit.

West Morgan is worried about me. ME. I can feel the flush creeping up my neck as I turn myself away from Juliana, feeling her gaze on the side of my head.

"No, no. I really appreciate you calling. I'm okay, just some bruising on my neck, a little ache in my muscles, and a sore throat. It's nothing really, especially compared to what Luna went through." Fuck me. Even with a sore throat, I still can't seem to shut my blabbering mouth.

"Don't compare your injuries, Jess. You both went through completely different experiences," he soothes down the phone, and I feel butterflies in my tummy. I have barely slept, but I refuse to discuss my personal ordeal with anyone, not wanting my weaknesses on full display.

"Thanks, West."

He clears his throat and pauses on the other end of the

line before his deep voice fills my ears again. "Do you know when you guys will be back?"

"Honestly? I haven't really spoken to Luna yet. She needs her space, but when she's ready to talk, we'll go from there," I answer, my fingers trailing the floral pattern on my dress.

"I understand. If you need me for anything at all, no matter the time, just text or call, okay? I'll answer."

"I will. Thank you, West," I murmur, feeling the call coming to an end, and wishing I had something to talk to him about to keep listening to his voice.

"Anytime, sunshine. Take care," he mumbles back.

"You too."

I don't know how I manage to press the red button, ending the call, but I find myself staring at the phone even when he's not there. I make sure to add him to my contacts, excitement zinging through my fingers as I do.

"Well, I must say you played that cool, Jess. It's just a good thing you weren't standing in front of him. Otherwise, they would have seen how red you were getting." I lift my gaze to Juliana, whose smile covers her whole face, making me shake my head.

"I don't know what you're talking about," I mutter as

the server brings over the food, all of which is entirely new to me. "Thank you," we both say in unison as they place the last plate and leave again.

The buzz of my phone catches my attention, but I refuse to pick it up when the food has been served. I have manners, but what flashes across the screen has my heart skipping a beat.

WEST: I'm glad you are okay! Anytime you need me, I'll be there, I mean it. See you when you get back to Featherstone.

West

Damn, I could feel her sunshine vibes through the phone. I don't know how, but without even seeing Jess, my soul feels lighter. I want more of her, even if it is a text or a conversation over the phone. I sent a quick text, unable to help myself, then forced myself to put my phone away.

Turning off the lights in the Weaponry hall, I close the space down for the night. Class finished a while ago, and everyone is long gone. The Aces were being annoying, so I gave them the weapons we were working on and proceeded to ignore them. The usual anger I always see in Roman's eyes was distorted with sadness.

Once upon a time, I would have asked what was going on, but our friendship became strained a long time ago. Now Luna is here at Featherstone, and Roman doesn't like the idea of having to share her with me again. Although, he doesn't seem mad about sharing her with the other Aces. I try not to take it personally, especially since I don't see Luna that way. She may be my moon, but to me, that makes her my sister. He'll get over it eventually, since my mind is consumed with a pretty redhead, who is like an angel amongst demons in fancy Featherstone Academy uniforms.

Hoping Maverick is still in the Combat hall, I lock the doors to Weaponry and step outside into the late afternoon air. I jog over in just my training gear, thankful when the door swings open. There is a gym at our apartment complex just off campus, but there is more chance of bumping into other tutors there. Nobody comes out this way, leaving the Weaponry and Combat buildings peaceful for Maverick and me, just how we like it.

"Rick?" I call out as I step into the main space, spotting

him in the far corner where the weight stands are. He doesn't answer, which is a good sign since he hasn't told me to fuck off either. I always take Rick at his word. If he wants to be alone, he means it, and I will always respect that.

"West," he murmurs as I come to stand in front of him. Lifting his eyebrow at me, he rises to his full height.

"Ricky, we can't keep matching like this," I say, indicating our matching black skin-tight t-shirt and loose black shorts. He frowns, turning away to grab another set of weights. "Okay, Mr. Miller is not in a fun mood today. Do you want to spar?" I ask, hopeful I can get my hands a little dirty. When he turns to me with the smallest grin on his face, I know I'm in luck.

"Fortunately for you, I have some shit to get out of my system," he grunts, pulling tape from the bottom shelf and throwing it in my direction.

Methodically going through the motions, I tape my hands, but my mind is still focused on my previous phone call.

"What has you grinning?" Rick grunts, and I sigh.

"Have you ever been in the presence of someone who instantly lifts the burdens we carry, making you feel lighter, just by being themselves?" I ask, not wanting to disclose details, but I can't get past how she makes me feel.

Frozen in place, he doesn't answer straight away. "Yes." Shaking his head, he moves to step on to the thick red mat in the center of the room.

I don't push him further, sensing his one word is the end of that conversation. I barely step onto the mat before his arms are swinging. Thankfully, I'm always prepared for his outburst of strength, swarming me from the start. I have no clue how much time passes as we lay blow after blow on each other, a familiar dance between two friends, always avoiding the face. We don't put all our weight behind our moves, but just enough to feel the impact.

Sweat drips down my back as I quickly wipe my brow, but Rick comes at me quickly, not missing his opportunity to side-kick me to the mat. Panting, I rest my eyes, exhaustion taking its toll. "Time," I call out, and I hear Rick drop to the mat too.

"Fuck me, Rick. Please tell me you got whatever was bothering you off your chest?" I groan, my ribs aching, and I know they'll be bruised by morning.

"Have you ever had someone get under your skin?" He asks, catching me by surprise.

"In what way? People who piss me off enough get under my skin."

"No, not in that way. A girl," he grinds out, ruffling his hair. "She fucking walks on clouds, leaving a rainbow in her path, but you know you'll darken her pure spirit the second she sees the real you?"

"About a girl?" I ask, needing clarification as I look in his direction. It is *never* about a girl with Maverick, not anymore. He's already shaking his head and rising to his feet. He stalks off, pulling his damp top over his head, and I don't push him any further.

I guess we both have women on our minds, except his thought process makes me pause. Would I do that to Jess? Dampen her light?

Fuck. Now I'm confused. Maybe I should put some space between us. Although, with the adrenaline pumping through my veins from fighting, mixed with the thought of Jess in her stunning red dress at the Fall Ball, I'm hard as steel.

I need a damn cold shower.

RED

NINE

Jess

I'm so fucking ready for this week to be over. We've been back at the academy for less than a week, and it's been shit. The only shining light is the Byrnes' party happening tonight, which Luna actually agreed to go to. I need some shots and dancing, in that order.

My jackass Combat tutor has done nothing but glare at me throughout every Combat class I've attended. There is definitely no discussion of what had almost happened after The Pyramid. Then, I sent West a text when we got back to campus, and I've received nothing back in response. ZILCH. So much for being there. Cue Luna eye roll. So, tonight I'm going to forget all about them, in the sexy new dress I bought in New York with Juliana. I am going to party hard tonight.

Dragging my case behind me, I step into the lobby at Ace. Before I make it to the elevator, an arm wraps around my shoulders, catching me off guard.

"Jessikins, how is Luna? I need insider details because she won't speak to me." I look up to Oscar as we step into the elevator, Kai and Parker following us in. It's as if a cloud is permanently over their heads at the moment while they mope around over Luna.

"She's doing better, but whatever you guys are doing isn't working. Maybe I could give you a little shove at the party tonight," I answer, and he spins me to face him, hands resting on my shoulders.

"The Byrnes' party? You and Luna are going to that?" His eyes search mine, and I nod in response, making his gaze darken as he frowns. "Roman is going to need to hear about this so we can form a plan together." The elevator dings, and the doors open. I barely get a hold of my suitcase before Oscar is steering me towards Roman's room instead of Luna's.

Parker smiles at me as he steps in front of us and

unlocks the door. Following them inside, I rub my arm uncomfortably as we all stand in front of Roman's questioning gaze while he sits on the sofa.

"Hey, what's going on?" He asks, arms braced on his thighs as he looks between the four of us.

"Tell him," Oscar says, glaring at me.

"I didn't have to tell you, you know? So, stop glaring at me, or I'll show you some of the new moves Luna has been teaching me," I glare back, refusing to feel intimidated by his shit.

"Does someone want to get to the point?" Roman interrupts, but I won't back down from Oscar's glare so easily, leaving Parker to finally answer him.

"Luna and Jess are going to a Byrnes' party tonight out behind the Library."

"But Luna doesn't party," Roman growls back, and I finally turn to look at him. It's actually good to see the fire in his eyes, compared to the lost soul I've seen all week. Roman not being his usual prick-ish self is highly noticeable.

"Well, that was only because she was trying to keep her guard up here. Rafe told me some crazy stories about her. She usually parties if she feels safe enough or if everything is too much and her mind needs a break. Which do you think it is right now?" I ask, hands on my hips as I glare around at them all.

"Does Luna even fucking know what goes down at a Byrnes' party?" Roman grunts and I shake my head.

"Okay. Obviously, she's going to clear her mind, but she drank with us after the Fall Ball because she felt safe. So, no matter what shit is going on right now, we'll be there. That way, she can relax her mind, and we'll be there to catch her if anything gets out of hand," Roman says, scrubbing the back of his neck, and I'm actually impressed.

"So we're gonna let her go?" Oscar questions with a frown, and Kai quickly shuts him up.

"Shut up, Oscar. Luna is her own person. We don't tell her what she can and can't do. If she's going, we go too. Simple as that." He nods, and Parker agrees.

"Okay, well, my work here is done. See you tonight. I plan to get us there after 10, you know, fashionably late and all that. With the treats I've got planned, you won't be able to miss her," I say with a wink, heading for the door. "Oh, but a hint for your plan, let Kai do the talking. He doesn't lead with his dick."

Shutting the door quietly behind me, I smile at the

direction tonight is going in. It'll be good to have them there, watching us instead of blocking us. That'd only piss me off and Luna more so. Stepping across the hall, I knock on Luna's door, brushing my hands over my leggings.

The door swings open, and she offers a soft smile, the most I've seen out of her all week. "Captain, get ready for some fun because we are going to have the best night," I sing, stepping into her space. I don't miss the roll of her eyes, but she doesn't disagree. "I have a treat for you too. Courtesy of my shopping trip with Juliana in New York," I add, waggling my eyebrows.

"Lead the way, Red," she finally says, and my excitement kicks up a notch.

Moving into my favorite room in her miniature condo, I look around her closet. One day I'm going to have one just like this, it doesn't have to all be designer, but it'll be filled to the brim of clothes I've earned all on my own.

Prepared for my bossy side, Luna willingly takes a seat at the vanity, and I get to work. Throwing her hair up into a sexy messy bun with loose tendrils falling around her face, I decide what make-up would work well with the outfit. I manage to cover the scar on her forehead that's forming, a battle wound from her brawl with Tyler in The Pyramid, framing her green eyes with pale creams and golds. Black-winged eyeliner with a touch of blush and bronzer, and she's all set.

"You are fire. Now, give me a few minutes, and I'll be dressed," I say, ushering Luna into her bedroom with the red two-piece outfit from New York.

Slipping into my cobalt blue bodycon dress, I feel amazing. I can't wear a bra with the open crisscrossed straps at the back, leaving me exposed. The low cut V to the front makes the dress extra sexy. Fastening my favorite pink heels around my ankle, I take a look at myself in the mirror.

My wavy red hair falls around my shoulders, and my classic smokey eye finishes the look off perfectly. Now, the party can begin. I'm going to be fabulous and fun. I'm going to be Red.

Pulling up to the party out by the library, Luna's eyes widen at the size of it. It's dark outside, but you can still see the Gazebos set up everywhere, with the dim lights that have been placed perfectly around the whole space. Some with open sides for the dance floor, bar, and seating area, while others are closed off, offering hot sex and high-quality drugs inside.

I step out of the SUV, bringing Luna along with me, and soak in the music that filters out around us. 'Don't Call Me Up' by Mabel plays through the speakers, and I'm ready for a shot or two before I start dancing. Linking my arm through Luna's, I pull her towards the purple gazebo serving drinks.

"What's going on over there, Red?" Luna asks, but before I can answer, Trudy stops in front of us. She looks hot in her sheer black dress and smokey eye ensemble. I love how she's always daring with her outfits.

"Luna, I'm glad you could make it," she says to Luna before turning to me. "Jess, right? We have Science and L.F.G. together."

"Yes, and we do. Luna was just asking what the deal was with the restricted areas. You want to explain it to her?" I ask, running my hands down my dress, wanting to hand over the reins of this conversation.

"Oh, you mean the good stuff? I'll give you a mini-tour," Trudy offers with a wink. She looks between Luna and me for a moment before stepping around us. "I can tell there's no room in the linking for me. So, would you like to follow my lead?" I don't argue with her statement because this girl is right.

Happy to follow in her footsteps, she gives Luna the tour of the black and red tents. I'd never actually been in the narcotics tent before, back at the high school, because the rules didn't apply there either. Still, I was surprised to see how classy it actually looked. When we stepped into the well-known 'sex tent,' my body temperature instantly rose as I recalled my recurring dream, which now includes West too. Even as we step out of the tent now, goosebumps still prickle up my neck. Watching the orgy taking place across the scatter cushions has me so turned on.

I can still see the three people towards the back of the group, lost in each other. A guy sits on a huge cushion, with a girl full on naked and riding him like her life depends on it, all while sucking off the guy standing beside her. God, to feel that full. I could only dream. The guy on the bottom turns his head our way, Reece Wicker, and his brown hair damp with sweat continues to lift the girl up and down his length. Winking, he nods his head to beckon me over, and as turned on as I am, it's like an ice cold bucket being dumped over my head. I made that mistake once before, and I refuse to let the memory ruin my night. But I will never be going near him again.

The light breeze does little to cool my overheated body as we walk through the crowd outside, leaving Trudy to oversee everything.

"Shots time!" I cry, squeezing Luna's arm, pulling her towards the drinks tent.

As we approach the bar, Luna's current 'non-boyfriends' watch her like hawks. I know they aren't going to leave us alone, so I may as well make use of them.

"Who's getting the shots in?" I ask as we come to stand by them, and they all perk up, but of course, Oscar is the quickest. Demanding the whole bottle of tequila and some shot glasses from the bartender, even though he's already serving someone.

Stepping forward to help with the shot glasses, so we can get this party officially started, when all of a sudden, hell breaks loose. Brett Rhodes has his hands on Luna, but only for the smallest moment before Parker steps in, reminding everyone of the Ace he is without Luna by his side. I stand frozen and helpless as Brett's friends move in but are instantly stopped by Roman, Kai, and Oscar, who moves from my side at the bar lightning fast.

Glancing around the space, I'm not the only one to

watch the scene unfold as everyone within range watches as the Aces takedown these guys with little effort at all. Blood covers Kai and Oscar as they beat the shit out of the guys trying to help Brett. In contrast, Roman and Parker are surprisingly less brutal in their attack. I watch as Parker drops Brett on the pile of broken and beaten boys before turning and giving Luna his attention. It makes me chuckle how she is turned on, yet she still refuses to give into them.

Picking up the tray of shot glasses, salt, and lemon wedges, I carry them over to the table. Luna is standing by, and I see the pleading in her eyes. I can see her walls dropping from here, but she's a stubborn ass and doesn't want to give in.

"One shot, then it's girl time on the dance floor, understood?" I call out, watching her shoulders sag in relief as the guys frown in annoyance, except for Oscar, who has a wicked glint in his eyes as he stares Luna down. I watch as the others follow his lead, preparing to take shots straight from her body, and I count them in with my own tequila at the ready. Needing the distraction from the sexual tension building around them.

"3 .. 2 .. 1 .."

Licking the salt from my hand, I down the shot, feeling

it burn my throat before I bite into the bitter lime. Hot damn. I shake my head, feeling the buzz from the alcohol run through my veins.

"You ready to dance?" Luna asks, making me giddy.

"Hell yeah I am." Grabbing Luna's hand, I drag her towards the center of the dance floor as upbeat dance songs play through the speakers. I instantly start singing along to 'Change My Heart' as my body sways to the music. My eyes close as I feel the music pump through my body, my hands rising above my head as my hips dip and sway on their own accord. I love the strobe lighting flashing behind my closed eyelids, enticing me to open them and watch everybody move around us.

When 'You should see me in a crown' booms through the speakers, I can't help but step back, pointing my finger in Luna's direction and letting the song do the rest. If a song was ever written for Luna, this is it. I don't care about anyone around us, letting myself be me, be free. Luna finally catches up and grabs my hand, dancing together like we aren't at the shittiest academy on earth. I love being able to have this moment of freedom, especially with Luna, all the crap that looms over her forgotten as we dance like all the other girls our age.

Trudy approaches us out of nowhere, begging to join us for a few minutes of peace from everything going on around her. I feel Luna's reluctance, but the desperation in Trudy's eyes is apparent, and I can't bring myself to say no. Grabbing her hand, we move to the beat as Luna lets go. There is no tension from her. She just mustn't trust her like she does me.

Lost in the music, Trudy and I dance around each other, I feel fucking amazing until she squeezes my hand tight, pointing over my shoulder. My body freezes for a moment as I stare at the side profile of Aiden Byrnes, who has his hands around Luna. He looks fucking delicious in skinny ripped black jeans and a tight black Henley, enhancing his light blonde hair and grey eyes. The twinkle in his eyes always reminds me of meeting the devil in person. Oh, so tempting and always up to no good.

A part of my brain wants to be pissed that his hands are on my friend, yet his hold on her seems nothing more than friendly. It's just that damn mischief in his eyes I can see, that tells me this isn't going to end well. Especially when I see Roman already making his way over, picking up speed as Aiden leans in to whisper in Luna's ear.

He's barely up close for two seconds before Roman

rips him off Luna and throws him across the dance floor. Trudy doesn't release my hand as she rushes towards him, pulling me along with her. Aiden props himself up on his elbows, grinning wide at Roman as Trudy drops to her knees beside him.

"Damn it, Aid. Why do you always have to cause trouble?" Trudy groans, gripping his chin to check him over, but he doesn't pull his gaze from Roman.

"Are you okay?" Luna asks from behind me, but I can't take my eyes off him.

"All good, buttercup." He offers a thumbs up, antagonizing Roman further, and I can't stop myself from shaking my head at him. I hear Roman and Luna arguing behind me, but I can't focus on anything else but Aiden's icy grey eyes looking deep into my own.

I feel his gaze look me over from head to toe, and I stand in a state of shock, letting him do so. Goosebumps rise on my arms under his scrutiny as I watch his tongue sneak out to lick his lips. Holy shit.

"Red, are you okay if Oscar gets you home?" Luna shouts, pulling my attention from the hot mess on the floor in front of me. I glance around at them all and nod in agreement, unable to find any words.

I watch as she storms off, leaving Kai to chase after her. "I've got this guys," he says, and I can't help but interrupt before he leaves.

"Don't pull a Roman, okay? I can't help you idiots out when you act like that." I glare, and he must agree because he doesn't argue back.

Turning back around, I'm surprised when there is no longer anyone on the floor next to me. Instead, Aiden is standing right beside me, his eyes staring intensely at my lips, making me nervous.

"Aiden, do not fuck with Jessica too," Trudy whispers, stepping up beside him, but he doesn't offer his usual snark in response.

"Since when does Jessica Watson have the backbone to stand up to someone? Never mind an Ace?" Aiden asks, a real curiosity in his eyes, but his question annoys me.

"Wow, screw you," I grind out, turning to join Oscar and Parker as they try to calm Roman down, but a hand on my arm stops me in my tracks. I know I've read hundreds of books that mention a spark that travels between two people when they have a connection and touch for the first time. Never in my life have I felt anything close to that until this very moment. I feel like every inch of Aiden's fingerprints are burning onto my skin, marking me for life.

He must feel it too, when he pulls away quickly, glancing down at his hand like I burned him. "I didn't mean to be rude. Your sass just caught me by surprise." He continues to stare at me, and I can't bring myself to move away. "Come have a drink with me," he murmurs, catching me off guard. "Please," he adds, and I know that word doesn't come naturally to him.

"I, uhh," I look over my shoulder to see Oscar glaring over at us, and I just know he's going to have something to say about it. He forgets I'm my own damn person, ever since he made his off-limits statement in Science a few weeks ago. Aiden must catch my thought process and murmurs to Trudy, who rolls her eyes and links her arm through mine.

"Hey Oscar, we're going for a drink. Let us know when you're leaving, and I'll personally deliver Jess back to you guys." Her words are confident, and as Parker and Roman also stare at me, I worry they'll know I'm a fraudster and tell me to get in an SUV and go home. To my surprise, Parker nods and draws the attention of the others away from me.

Without missing a beat, Aiden takes off for the booth

in the purple tent where the drinks flow freely, and food is readily available.

Well then, I guess I'm spending some time with Aiden fucking Byrnes. I don't know whether I should send for help now or later.

RED

KC KEAN

TEN

Aiden

My hand moves to her back instinctively. The feel of the material crisscrossing against her skin goes straight to my dick. Fuck me. Jessica Watson has always been a wet dream. A *very* unattainable redheaded, hour-glassed shaped bottle of sin, that just so happens to be in my presence, finally.

I can feel Trudy glaring at the back of my head, but I refuse to let her bad vibes ruin my moment. As if it's a twin thing, I can hear her thoughts like they are my own.

'Look at him, thinking he's got charm.'

'This poor girl doesn't know what's hit her.'

'He's nowhere near finished having the shit kicked out of him by the Aces.'

Shaking my head, I look down at the beauty beside me as she glances up. Even in her heels, I'm easily still five inches taller than her. The usual cheery spark in her eyes is mixed with desire, and it's a look that suits her well. She could say jump right now, and I wouldn't even ask how high. I'd just start jumping until she was pleased. Jess smiles up at me, looking every inch the tempting seductress without even trying.

Stepping in front of the booth at the end of the gazebo, I sweep my arm out wide, encouraging her to take a seat. No one ever sits in this booth, always wanting to be more central to the party, but this offers the perfect seclusion from everyone while still basking in the essence of a good time.

"Right, asshole, I have shit to do. Shit you should be doing too, but I'll leave you to do your things as always, Aiden," Trudy says, shoving my shoulder in a mix between playfulness and actual annoyance with me. Looking past me, her demeanor changes as she addresses Jess. "Have fun, girl, but if this little shit gets to be too much, just let me know, alright?"

"He'll have got what he wanted and be on his way in no

time. Don't worry, Trudy." She smiles brightly at Trudy as she takes a seat, and my twin leaves.

"I'll get what I want, huh? And what is that exactly?" I ask, bracing my arms on the table as I lean over, but she just shakes her head at me, offering nothing in response. "Okay, beautiful, what are we drinking?"

She thinks on it for a moment before clasping her hands together on the table and responding, "Shots." Short and sweet with no room for argument.

"Don't go anywhere," I murmur as I walk as fast as I can to the bar. I don't bother waiting for a bartender, I was the one here earlier helping set up the damn thing, so I step around the bar eyeing the shot options before me.

Looking over my shoulder, I check she is still where I left her, to see her sitting comfortably in the booth, glancing down at her phone. Deciding on the untouched bottle of Sambuca in front of me, I grab two shot glasses and head back in her direction.

Seeing me approach, she places her phone back in her bag, and I don't think I've ever seen anything so refreshing. Most girls here at Featherstone are glued to their phones, barely coming up for air, and when they do it's to take selfies.

"Shot for the beautiful girl sitting in my booth," I say,

placing the bottle and shot glasses down on the table in front of her. Her hands instantly wrap around the bottle, reading the label in confusion before glancing back up at me.

"I've never had this before."

"Sambuca?" I ask, and she nods in response as I take it from her hands and unscrew the lid. "I had it in Europe over the summer. It tastes like aniseed, a drinkable fireball, but if you don't like it I can always get something else too."

"No, this is good." She places the shot glasses in front of me as I take a seat beside her, filling them to the top.

"I think we should play a game."

"Well, I thought that would be obvious. You are the king of games after all," she responds, humor in her voice as she looks at me with mischief in her eyes. Fuck me, who knew she had all this sass underneath her angelic exterior?

"I'm not going to ask what you mean by that and pretend I have no idea what you're talking about." She chuckles at me with a shake of her head, not moving away, even though she knows my usual MO.

She knows my reputation, it's no secret. Once I've

hooked up with someone, you've had all the attention I'm going to give you. No commitments, no spoken promises, just pure unadulterated fucking. And by someone, I mean people of any gender. I actually tend to lean more towards guys because they don't expect more and hang it over my head like girls do. But Jess is worth breaking the pattern, even if only for a moment.

Everybody who is present at Featherstone High knows my sexual preferences, and girls either think they can change me or turn their noses up at me. Yet, Jess sits before me with the same smile on her face that she offers to everyone, not a single ounce of judgment. I'm always the center of the party, surrounded by people who want to hang with me. I just want to have a good time, not caring who it's with. But right now, I'm aware of every move Jess makes, my eyes following her hand as she brushes her hair off her shoulder.

"How about twenty questions? If we don't answer, we take a shot," I offer, wanting to know more about her while I have the chance. Always seeing Jess in class is very different from seeing her up close like this. She's hot as hell, and there is so much more in her eyes this close.

"Okay," she murmurs, rubbing her hands on her

thighs, a hint of nerves in her actions, and I love it. "You can ask first."

Clapping my hands, I stare her down, trying to decide what to ask first. "I'll start you off easy. What is your favorite color?" I ask, and her nose scrunches as she frowns.

"Purple, but I didn't take a seat to talk colors, Aiden. I want shots, and your questions aren't going to help with that." She shakes her head, leaving me gaping in surprise at her little outburst, and I can't stop the pulse of excitement leading straight to my dick.

I move closer to her, angling my body, our knees brushing as I brace my arm behind her on the booth. Her pupils widen in surprise at my close proximity, but she doesn't back down, which only adds to the tension surrounding us.

"Your mouth is going to be the death of me, Jessica Watson." Her name rolls off my tongue so sweetly as I stare at her lips. "Okay, how about we take a shot, and you show me the kind of questions you want afterward?" I ask, and she nods subconsciously, grabbing the shot glass closest to her. Picking up my own, I hold it between us, and she taps her glass against mine before lifting the liquor to her lips and downing it all at once.

My eyes are too busy tracking the swallow of her throat and her hooded lids, as I remember to take my own shot. Quick to catch up, I feel the burn trickle down my throat as the Sambuca leaves its mark.

"Oh my god," she whispers, her head tilted back on the booth, a breath away from where my hand rests. I'm surprised she isn't coughing and spluttering like some do. Instead, she's smiling, and I don't miss the swipe of her tongue across her bottom lip.

I can hear the music playing around us, and I can sense the presence of others here at the party, but my focus is solely on this girl in front of me. I can't stop my fingers from grasping her hair beside my hand, slowly rubbing it with my thumb. So soft and pretty, but my brain wants to see it messy and laid out across a pillow. Fuck.

Moving my gaze from the strands of hair, I find her looking at me through hooded eyes. Fuck me. I've seen Jess around Featherstone since I was fourteen years old, and she has always been unobtainable with her angelic aura. Now, here she sits, offering me a deeper look inside her soul. My head instinctively begins to move closer to her, wanting to bring our lips together, but she cuts me off.

"How many times have you fucked your own fist today?"

Whoa, I did not expect that question to leave her lips, but my smile widens at her brazen attitude I'm getting to sneak a look at.

"Do you want the answer, beautiful, or are we doing shots?" I ask in return, and she simply shrugs her shoulders, but I don't miss the daring glint in her eyes. "Twice," I answer honestly, and her bottom lip drops in slight surprise.

"So hot," she murmurs under her breath, and I know instantly that wasn't for me to hear. It doesn't help the pulsing of my cock against my tight jeans though, and I can't bring myself to rearrange the situation.

"My question."

"Is it going to be better than my favorite color this time?" She asks, a devilish grin on her face, and I don't hold myself back this time as I get closer to her.

"What's your favorite sex position?"

Biting her bottom lip, she considers my question, which has clearly caught her by surprise. The way her eyes frantically search mine, to make sure she heard me correctly, is fascinating. Obviously, trying to decide whether to answer or not, I give her a moment to see how daring she really is.

Releasing a sigh, she doesn't move an inch, keeping me nose to nose with her. "Honestly, I need to try more positions to decide."

My pulse picks up, but I can't let that be enough. "As in you haven't tried any or …"

"I'm not a virgin, Aiden. I've just had sex with boring guys who want to fuck missionary and not let me even ride them as an alternative," she says, lightly shaking her head, making my jaw drop at her openness. Holy shit. Damn, I want to rock Jess's world even more now. My dick is hard and fighting to be released so that we can show her a good time.

"And did they play with your body, Jess?" I ask, my desire taking over, but she just giggles.

"It's not your turn for a question," she responds with a wink, and I'm done. Cupping her chin, I tilt her head back, instinctively her hand lands on my chest, stroking up to my shoulder. I hold the position. I want to see how bold she really can be. Watching her gaze flicker between my eyes, the realization dawns on her that she has to make the final move.

I'm not sure whether she will back down or rise to the

occasion, but as I watch the sultry look take over her eyes and feel her fingers tighten around my neck, I know I'm not going to be disappointed.

Her lips touch mine, all soft and full, taking exactly what she wants from me. My lips feel on fire as she bypasses any gentle build-up and pushes me to kiss her back with the same level of fierceness. Keeping my fingers under her chin, my other hand instantly finds her waist trying to pull her in closer, I swipe my tongue against her lips, gaining instant access to her mouth.

Her fingernails scrape against the back of my head, and I moan against her lips. Who the fuck is this woman? Because the Jessica Watson I expected was not this damn seductive. We need to be alone before this gets out of hand here in the booth.

"Sorry to break up this party for two, but Oscar is searching for Jess, and I don't think he'd be impressed with what he found if he came over right now." Trudy's voice breaks through the lust, making me growl. Jess quickly pulls back, desire in her sparkling blue eyes.

Dropping her hands from my body, I refuse to do the same. "Oscar O'Shay can fuck off. I still have eighteen more questions," I grind out, holding on to anything I can to keep her here with me, but I can already feel her pulling away.

"Oscar seems to have it in his head that he's my keeper, and Trudy is right. He throws out threats all the time when it comes to guys who even walk past me," she says softly, maintaining eye contact with me.

"I know, I heard him the first week in Science, but you're your own person, Jess."

"You're right, I am, but I don't want to see you be pushed around again, tonight at least," she says with a grin. "At least I got a taste of the elusive Aiden Byrnes, right?" She murmurs, stroking her thumb across my bottom lip as I reluctantly drop my hands from her body.

Without a word, she stands from the booth, running her fingers through her hair as she smiles at Trudy and me. I'm left sitting in a state of shock as I watch her walk away, Oscar approaching her moments later with a frown on his face. Whatever he says must piss her off because she jabs her elbow into his stomach and storms off, making me grin.

"For once, Aiden, I'm glad you don't pursue girls past more than a little fun. Otherwise, you'd be in a shit load of trouble chasing her," Trudy says as she leaves me on my own.

Yeah, no pursuing girls past one time, even if it was only a kiss. Scrubbing a hand over my mouth, I know the truth. I'm fucked.

RED

ELEVEN

Jess

Sitting in the back of one of the Diamond SUV's on a Monday morning is never how I want to start my week. Waiting for it to fill so we can head over to Combat.

Stifling a yawn, my brain plays Friday night on repeat again. I can feel the heat on my neck as my skin flushes, remembering the feel of his lips against mine and the way his hands caressed my body. Aiden is known for being elusive, and his sexuality is always the first thing people whisper about, surprisingly not in a negative way. It seems to make people want him more. Especially if you are a girl, simply because he never sticks around for more than one night. Something about us being needy, which is why there are always more rumors of him with guys.

God, he makes me feel confident. I promised myself I would 'fake it till I make it' as Luna said, and with Aiden, I felt comfortable enough to say what was really going through my mind. It's a shame he never does repeats, even if it was only a kiss. At least I took a seat at that table with him with no further expectations in mind, which was completely out of my usual comfort zone anyway.

Although I wish we hadn't been interrupted, and I could have gotten up close with his dick. If the rumors are true, I wouldn't have been disappointed. Instead, I let Oscar walk me to my room, even though that fucker was quizzing me on my whereabouts. I took care of myself as always, with the help of BOB. Which reminds me, I need to order batteries.

So, life would go back to normal, Aiden wouldn't acknowledge me ever again, and I'll leave with the memory of his touch and the way he reacted to my touch. Damn, the way he moaned against my lips makes me shiver.

Movement from the open door gains my attention as Reece climbs into the SUV, trapping me against the other door as his friends climb in behind him, along with a few girls I'm not overly familiar with. It's hard work since he's a Diamond as well, but he won't leave me the fuck alone whenever he sees me. It always seems to be when Oscar isn't around too. Otherwise, I'd actually encourage him to protect my virtue.

I try to keep my focus out of the window, watching the campus fly by, as Reece strokes his hand over my knee. My body stills at the contact, my next breath trapped in my lungs as I forget how to breathe.

His breath fans over my ear as he leans in close. "Wifey, I feel like you've been avoiding me, and that.. Just. Won't. Do." The hairs on the back only neck stand on end when brings his lips to my jaw. "I saw you watching me in the sext tent at the weekend, I know you want me, again."

Taking a shaky breath, I find the strength to finally use my mouth. "Get your hand off my leg, Reece. Please."

His snicker sends a shiver down my spine as his hand tightens around my thigh, slowly travelling higher up my leg. "Don't worry, Jessie baby, my friends know about our family agreement, and the fact you're my wife-to-be." His friend sitting facing me chuckles along with him.

My eyes close on their own accord as I try to find the inner strength to stand up for myself. I want to bitch him out, he sure ask fuck wasn't worried about his wife-to-be in the orgy tent at the weekend. But I know anything I say will only encourage him.

The moment his hand meets the apex of my thigh, I turn to meet his gaze, my hand rising to hit out at him as the SUV comes to a stop, halting my movement.

I sigh in relief as his hand moves from my body, with the Combat building coming into view, my heart pounding with fear. "Later, wifey," he purrs before stepping out of the SUV with the others.

I take an extra moment to calm myself. My reaction time needs to be much quicker if I want any chance of being able to fight him off if needed. But deep down I hope he's just all show, and no action.

Walking towards the crowd of people, hovering around outside the building, I push Reece to the back of my mind. Now, I have the pleasure of Maverick's icy glare, still pretending there wasn't a moment between us after The Pyramid. At this point, I'm wondering if it was all just in my head.

Spotting Luna waiting with the Aces by the entrance. I wordlessly slip my arm through hers, and we head inside before the guys can protest.

"Hey, Red. Everything okay?" Luna asks, and I smile, brushing my hair from my face. I'm such a fucking softy for a nickname, and hers just makes me melt every time.

"I'm good. It looks like things are amazing with the guys again," I respond, glancing over my shoulder to see them glaring at the fact I stole her away so quickly. But nobody puts up an argument, they just follow behind us.

"Yeah." Her voice sounds almost dreamy, making me grin, but I won't mention it otherwise she'll force herself to lose the happiness she's basking in right now. After she argued with Roman on Friday night, Kai chased after her. I can only guess what happened from there because when I went around on Saturday, all the guys were there, and everything seemed back to normal again. It still makes me chuckle now when there was a spider in Luna's bathroom, and my badass bitch best friend freaked out.

Leaving the guys behind, we change quickly in the locker room. Maverick didn't let Luna spar once last week with her injuries from The Pyramid. However, she still changes into her workout clothes.

"Oh my god, Red," she shouts, surprising me as I'm about to pull my t-shirt over my head.

"What?" I panic but frown in confusion when she

strokes the top of my stomach.

"Red, have you seen the definition coming along here?" I look down at where she's touching, and my tiny muscles are showing. It makes me blush that she notices, and there are other girls in here likely looking over too, but I refuse to acknowledge them. "Man, Roman must have been putting you through your paces in the gym. I like it," she says, finally stepping back and meeting my gaze.

I can feel my embarrassment at her praise as my cheeks turn pink, which she notices and grins, fucking pinching them playfully. Whacking her hand away, I fake glare at her, which only makes her chuckle at my expense.

"You should definitely leave the tank top off, Red. Rock your shorts and sports bra look, and show off your trim frame." She nods enthusiastically, and I pause, considering her words.

Glancing down at myself, I'm wearing loose-fit black shorts and a pale pink sports bra. Which is casual enough in my own space, but in public? My mother would die … and it's that thought that makes me fold the loose grey t-shirt up and put it back in the bag. Before I change my mind, I fasten my hair up in a hair tie at the top of my head and let Luna pull me to the main sports hall.

Linking her arm through mine, Luna grins at me. "I'm proud of you, Red." I smile in response, not wanting to open my mouth and back out of my new show of confidence.

As soon as Oscar catches sight of us walking towards them, he goes from sending Luna some attempt of a sexy grin to full-on glaring at me. Before anything can leave his mouth, Luna has her finger raised and pointing in his direction. "If you so much as say shit to Red, I will cut you off from all the sex you could be having in the near future. Do you understand me?" She growls, and I stare at her in awe. Oscar does nothing but clamp his mouth shut and attempt to smile sweetly at her, which makes Parker, Kai, and Roman laugh at him.

"Nice of you to join us, ladies. Now how about we get on with the lesson?" Maverick shouts from behind us, and my back stiffens. He is such a jackass.

"I wonder what crawled up his ass this morning?" Luna whispers as we take a seat with the guys.

"His sense of fucking humor," I mutter back, and she chuckles.

"Sorry, ladies, is there something you wanted to share with the class?" Maverick grunts, but I refuse to respond, just smiling in response. Although, I can tell my annoyance is shining in my eyes. He's just being pissy and petty right now for no reason.

Thankfully, he doesn't push further, sending us to do two laps around the outside of the space. Luna pats me on the shoulder before taking off. She loves this shit, usually doing an extra lap. In comparison, I'll take my time, so I don't need to do any extra. I must admit I find it a lot easier since training with Luna and Roman. There is something therapeutic in the movement, but I actually take more joy from sparring, not that I'm going to tell any of these assholes that. They'll push me harder, and I'm happy with the pace I'm currently at.

There is something empowering in the art of finding strength from within to defend yourself and pushing to breakdown the barriers that surround you. I like it when my fist connects just right, the adrenaline pumping through my veins and the sweat dripping down my back.

When everyone has finished, Maverick starts calling names out to pair off on to separate mats. "Roman, take Luna to the far corner. Do not make me bench you for another week because you pushed too hard, though," he says, making her clap her hands in excitement. He continues to read names off until I hear my own. "Jessica and Reece." Shit. Please no. I do not need him having an actual excuse to put his hands on me right now.

Reece waves from a mat across the room, his eyes trailing over every inch of my body, as I try to keep my facial expression neutral. Heading for Maverick, who is looking down at the tablet in his hand, having dispersed everyone, I take a deep breath. My hands shake a little at having to approach him, but anything to avoid Reece right now.

"Hey, uh, Maverick. Is there any way I can be paired with someone else? Literally, anyone …"

"What's the matter, little girl? Is it too difficult for you to just take instruction and just get on with the lesson?" He grinds out, glaring down at me. Wow. Bouncing on my tiptoes nervously, I try again.

"No, I just …"

"Listen, I don't give a shit. Not about you, and not about some sparring partner you might have an issue with. Now, get the fuck on with it." Turning, he storms off, leaving me standing alone. My nostrils flaring with the rage I'm trying to contain. What a nobhead.

"Let's go, Jess!" Reece shouts from behind me, and I try my best to relax my posture as I head towards him.

Luna catches my eye as I walk over, raising her eyebrow in question about what's going on, but I just shake my head. The quicker I get this over with, the better. "You ready to get beneath me again, wifey?" He murmurs as I approach, and I hold back a gag.

"Let's just spar, shall we?" I refuse to take him on. I don't want to encourage his advances.

"Whatever you say, I'll take it easy on you."

Shaking my arms out, I don't respond, preparing myself for his first move. He starts easy, placing slow practiced hits on my arms as I block him. His brow crinkles, but I don't question his thought process, instead continuing through the motions. He tries to get me in a headlock, but I remember the move Roman taught me, dropping to the mat and rolling back up to my feet quickly.

"Who's been training you?" Reece questions, but I shake it off.

"That's irrelevant."

"You think I don't have a right to know what you're doing, and who you're doing it with?" He huffs. "Well, we'll see how much you've learned," he adds, and his tone sets me on edge.

Kicking out, his leg hits my thigh with much more

force than he'd previously been using, which instantly catches me by surprise. The sound of his skin slapping against mine echoes around me as I try to move, but his forearm hits into my stomach, taking the breath from my lungs. In the blink of an eye, he's lifting me in the air and dropping me to the floor on my back, covering my body with his.

I feel a little dazed and a hint of fear as he looms over me, squeezing my wrists together in one hand above my head as he gropes my breast with the other. His body is shielding his hand from the view of everyone else, and I feel frozen in place, trying to catch my breath and find the strength to get him off me.

"Your tits are so fucking perfect, wifey. When we're married, I'll get to play with them all the time," Reece leers from above me, sending ice through my veins.

"Over my dead body," I grind out, finally finding my tongue and bringing my knee up to hit him, but it does little to make him move.

"Your mother was very disappointed in your behavior at dinner, but I promised I'd whip you into shape in no time."

Fuck that. Fuck him and fuck her.

"Get off me!"

Just as I lean forward to sink my teeth into his shoulder, a shadow falls above us before Reece is literally removed from my body. It takes a moment for him to release my hands as he's being moved, and he manages to lift me to a sitting position. Trying to catch my breath, I process what the hell is going on.

Maverick stands above Reece, fire burning in his eyes as he leans over him. "Both of you, my office now!"

What the fuck? Is he joking? The anger in his eyes as his fist clenches at his sides, tells me he's definitely not. Rising to my feet, I rub my hands on my shorts.

"What's going on, Mav?" Roman shouts from across the hall, where Luna is also looking over in confusion, but I just turn and head for the door where Reece is already leaving. I don't wait to hear what Maverick has to say in response because I already know this is a load of bullshit.

I don't bother to hold the main door open for him as I head straight for his office across the hall, hoping it smacks that peckerhead in the face. Reece is already waiting, hands on his hips as he glares at me. The room isn't big. There is a big window on the opposite wall, filling the room with natural light, with a mahogany desk and filing cabinets, the only furniture in the room. A large leather chair sits on the other side of the desk, surprisingly empty of anything personal.

The door slams, making me jump as I whirl around to see Maverick breathing rapidly as he looks between us. He looks hot when he's brooding, but he shouldn't look this hot when I can see the fury in every fiber of his body. His hands are fisted at his sides, his veins bulging up his arm, right under his tight white t-shirt.

"You," he fumes, suddenly charging at Reece. I watch him try to move backward but hits straight into the wall beside the window, leaving him with nowhere to go. I'm shocked when Maverick doesn't stop his charge, punching him directly in the face and making me squeal. "You ever touch anyone inappropriately like that in my class again, and I'll kill you with my bare hands. Do you understand?"

"The fuck, man?" Reece shouts, cupping his cheek as he frowns at Maverick.

"Get the fuck out of my sight before I do it now."

Reece glances between us for a moment but must decide he's done with this as he swings the door open and makes a run for it. Maverick slams the door shut behind him as I still stand in shock at what is even happening right now.

"Are you okay?" He asks, but his eyes don't meet mine. They're zoned in on the slight outline of a handprint covering my left breast where Reece touched me. The material crinkled from the way he squeezed.

"I'm fine. Can I go now?" I try to fold my hands over my chest to cover the mark as he approaches. I find myself against the wall behind me as he crowds my space. Fuck, he smells so good, all leather and manly, it's intoxicating.

"Next time, wear a damn t-shirt over your bra. Maybe then there won't be any groping issues," Maverick spits out, and I gape up at him.

"Are you actually serious? No other girl out there has a t-shirt on," I answer, instinctively lifting my hands to his chest to keep him back. "You also don't get to tell me what to wear, and even if I had nothing on, it doesn't give Reece or anyone else the right to touch me." I'm furious. How dare he point blame at …

The stroke of his thumb against my pebbled nipple beneath my sports bra renders me speechless as I suppress a moan at such a delicate touch. Lifting his gaze from my chest to my eyes, I'm surprised to see them so green, like fresh grass. He suddenly shakes his head, as if remembering himself and dropping his hand.

"Maybe if you didn't open your legs for just about anyone, people wouldn't be so drawn ..."

SMACK.

Shaking in shock, my hand pulses with heat as the sting courses through my bones. "Oh my gosh. I should not have done that. I didn't mean to. I just ... I just ... I'm sorry. You don't know shit about me, and you have no right to say that," I rush out, tears pricking my eyes at the fact I hurt him.

His eyes finally meet mine as he clears his throat and steps back. "You can leave. I'm sorry, I shouldn't have said that to you, or touched..." he whispers, trailing off as he walks around to sit in his chair. I pause for a moment, trying to decide whether I should stay or go, but deep down, I know staying won't fix anything right now.

Slipping from the room, I quietly shut the door behind me, my shoulders sagging with sadness. Deciding to skip going back to the gym, I head for the locker room. I hear Maverick curse and the slam of a fist on wood, but I don't stop. I have no idea what the hell just happened or what came over me, but I need some space right now.

KC KEAN

TWELVE

Jess

Taking a seat in the lunch hall opposite Luna, I'm still reeling from everything that happened back in Maverick's office. When Luna and the other girls came back to the lockers, I'd freshly showered and dressed, acting like everything was fine.

I don't think I've ever been this wound up before, but I'm a comfort eater, mostly when I'm not at home with my mother. I'm waiting for a large plate of mac and cheese to be delivered to the table with a calorie-packed soda. I don't think I have time for ice cream, but I could really do with a huge tub of Ben & Jerry's cookie dough right now.

"Seriously, Red, what's going on?" Luna asks, clearly sensing my internal turmoil, and I sigh, lacing my fingers together as I contemplate whether this is safe to talk to her about. She has enough to deal with.

"Well, I need you to promise this is for me to take care of. I don't want you taking on my shit too, okay?" She looks ready to argue, but I raise my eyebrow, and she reluctantly nods.

"So, before I arrived at Featherstone Academy, I had a huge blow-up at home, that involved my mother and her guests. I may have said a thing or two that made her unhappy, and my father got me on the next plane to Richmond." The frown lines on her forehead deepen as I talk, and I realize I've never really spoken about my life before here.

"Okay... Do I need to go and smack a bitch?" She grunts, and I chuckle.

"I do not need you to go attack my mother." I grin, "Yet," I add, and she nods for me to continue.

"Well, the argument started because Mr. and Mrs. Wicker, and my mother, were basically preparing my wedding to their son." Glancing around, I make sure the Aces aren't on their way over yet before continuing. "Their son happened to be someone I had a drunken hook-up with earlier in the summer. One I regret, and I do not want to be chained to that limp-dick for the rest of my life. So, I may have said something along those lines, but their son still seems to think it's going to happen."

I bring my eyes to meet Luna's as her fingers tap the table between us. "And that guy would be the one from Combat just then?" She asks, and I nod in response.

"Yeah, Reece Wicker."

"Reece Wicker is a dead man walking," Luna grumbles, but I reach my hand out to hers on the table.

"Please, Luna. He's harmless. I swear, if I need you to intervene I will come to you. But I'm trying to stand tall for myself, and learning to not take anyone's shit. I feel like I'm always having to be defended, and it's not what I want."

She stares me down for what feels like forever, but she must see the sincerity in my eyes, before leaning back in her chair with a sigh.

"Fine. But if I think anything is getting out of hand, I will get involved." I nod eagerly at her response as I release my hold on her hand. "So, I have something to talk to you about," Luna says as the guys order her food with theirs.

"Oh yeah?" I murmur. When I meet her gaze, I'm surprised to see the tension around her eyes as she rubs her hands. Leaning forward slightly, I brace my arms on the table as my brain starts to go a mile a minute with worry over what's bothering her. Her persona has instantly changed from moments ago when she was offering to smack a bitch for me.

"Soo, I want you to move into Ace, in your own room," she rushes out, faking confidence in her words, and it takes me a moment to process what she's saying.

"What? No way, Luna. Are you crazy?" I recognize too late that I went to high pitched, and I can feel other students looking in our direction. How would that even happen?

"It's for your own safety, Red. Rafe promised nothing changes for you when you move into the Gibbs room. You'll continue with your bloodline as normal but stay in Ace with us, on the same floor as Kai and Oscar. It's a win-win." I can see she's trying to sell it to me, but the determination in her eyes tells me I'll be moved in as soon as possible, whether I like it or not.

"I'm going to ask again, are you crazy? I can't just start living in the Gibbs' room. It's not mine, and I refuse to owe anyone for this." I'm stumbling to find grounds for my argument here, but I don't want to move in there and have to live by someone else's rules, not after living with my mother. At least at Diamond, I have my free will, although deep down, I know Luna would never put me in a situation like that. If she truly knew my home life, she'd have me emancipated by the end of the day.

"Look, Red, I know I can't keep you holed up in my room with me, okay? But it's not safe with you being in a different block. Not after The Pyramid, Jess. I need you to compromise with me a little here. I've given up any attempt to push you away. So let me offer an alternative, where we both get what we want." Neither of us blinks, staring each other down, and the raw emotion in her words makes me give in like I was always going to.

"Okay, but I need more details than this," I murmur, pointing at her with my strongest glare, but I know it doesn't have the desired effect. The Aces take seats around us, but I refuse to give them any attention when we are having such an important talk.

"So, you told her then? We're gonna be neighbors, Jessikins. This means I can monitor any boys you're not telling me about who try to sneak in and out of your room,"

Oscar says, wagging his eyebrows at me, which only adds to my internal stress at this very moment. Squeezing my eyes shut, I try to take some deep breaths before I end up smacking someone else today.

Looking across the table to Luna, I sigh. "I really want to punch him in that special way you showed me."

"I'll help you out," Roman says before Luna can respond, and with a wink, he turns and slaps the back of Oscar's head.

"What the fuck, Rome? There was no need for that," Oscar growls, but I can't stop the giggle from escaping my lips as a little tension leaves my body. Roman holds his fist out to me, just like he does after we've been training, and I meet him in the middle, bumping fists and wiggling our fingers.

"Did you guys just fist bump? I'm confused." Luna asks, a deep frown in between her eyes forming as she looks between us, which only makes me laugh harder.

"Don't hate me cos you ain't me," Roman sasses, and this calm, fun side of him catches me by surprise. The server arrives with a plate filled with mac and cheese, which is mine, making my tummy grumble. Quickly taking it out of his hands, I don't even pay attention to what the others are eating. As we all sit eating in silence, I consider what I actually need to be asking Luna about this whole moving into Ace idea she's come up with.

"Fire them at me, Red," Luna says, and I take a big gulp of my fizzy drink before I decide where to start.

"Do I have to change any of my classes?"

"No, your schedule stays the same."

Good. I don't want to be changing every aspect of my life when I've just gotten slightly comfortable.

"Do I have to compete in the Games?" I ask, my heart pounding in my chest at what her answer may be.

"Definitely not, Red. If that had been a condition, you wouldn't be moving in. I promise." My pulse calms a little as I try to wrap my head around how this has even happened.

"How is Featherstone allowing this?"

"Juliana has been listed as your guardian, and before you ask, your father is aware." She nervously messes with the napkin in her hand, and my heart stops. I can feel everyone at the table staring at me, and I need to act normal. Holy shit, she basically *is* emancipating me from my hell without evening knowing.

"Oh, cool. I guess," I mutter, taking a drink of my soda,

ending the conversation there. Internally my brain can't function without understanding the whole picture. Still, the thought of Juliana as my guardian, as opposed to my own mother, makes me want to cry with joy. Could this be real? Like a way for me to finally wash my hands of my mother?

"Sooo, you're okay with that?" Luna presses on, and I know I need to give her an answer. I just don't want them to see the level this actually affects me.

"Well yeah. Juliana was really nice when we went shopping to get some clothes. I get she's freaking ruthless. I heard her on the phone at one point going batshit crazy at someone, but she was really nice to me. Plus, she loves you a lot, so I'm not going to complain."

Seemingly happy with my response, she glances down at her phone, leaving me to get lost in my own head. I want to leave so I can speak to my father, to Juliana, anybody that can offer me a little more information without raising the suspicions of these protective fuckers.

I can sense something going on with Luna, but she doesn't mention anything, even as she stands with Roman, yet I can feel the tension rolling off her. "We're going to head out. I need to get the keys off West so we can get you moved in tonight."

"Tonight?" I ask in surprise, and West has the keys? It's a shame he ghosted me. Otherwise, I would have got them off him myself. Although, it seems there is more to the meeting between them by the twitch of Roman's jaw.

"I'm not wasting any more time, Red. I've been trying to set this in motion since we were in New York. You have a free period now, right?"

"Yes."

"Perfect, get your shit together. I've got you four hot guys to help with the moving." I cringe at her words, and my response flows without a filter.

"They're all taken, and they're not all that hot."

"Hey, you better take that back. I'm Oscar fucking O'Shay. I'm hot as shit," Oscar interrupts, acting like a hurt pageant queen.

"Oh, Ozzie, I'd love to be able to see things from your point of view, but I can't get my head that far up my own ass," I say with a grin, making the table burst into laughter as he pouts like a child. Without another word, Luna and Roman leave, and I'm itching to do the same.

"Do you want me to head back to Diamond with you to help pack up your things?" Parker asks, and I instantly shake my head.

"Thanks, Parker, but I'll be alright." Grabbing the bag at my feet, I get ready to leave, my brain going a mile a minute, and I need to speak to my dad. Smiling at the remaining Aces sitting at the table, I head for the exit. Stepping outside into the fresh air, I take a moment to calm the pulsing in my ears when a hand grasping my wrist catches me by surprise, pulling me to the small alcove where people can sit outside.

When my eyes finally catch up with my brain, my back is pressed against the wall, the bricks rough against my back as Aiden stands tall above me. I stare up at him in surprise, and before I can ask what the hell is going on, his lips meet mine with his hands moving to cup my face.

Holy fuck. The heat of his lips against mine consumes me as I let Aiden take what he wants without question. All too soon, he's pulling away, leaving me gasping for more. Resting his forehead against mine, he holds a small piece of paper between us, making a show of slipping it into the front of my bra.

"Now you have my number. I expect you to use it by the end of the day," he murmurs, stepping back and straightening his jacket. I can't stop myself from biting my lip to stop the moan slipping out at how good he looks. His blond hair slightly ruffled at the side, and his grey eyes are blinding in the afternoon sun.

"What is this?" I finally ask before he leaves.

"Honestly? I don't know, but you better use it, or I'll come find you." With that, he's gone while I'm left trying to figure out what the fuck is going on with me today.

Taking a seat at the nearby empty bench, I sigh in relief when I realize we were lucky no one was out here when he pulled that stunt. Swiping my hair from my face, I look for my phone in my bag. Six missed calls from my dad. Clearly, this must be what Luna has talked about.

Taking a deep breath, I press my dad's name on the screen. The phone barely rings before I hear my father's voice through the phone.

"Pumpkin?"

"Hey, Dad," I murmur nervously, not wanting to be the one to take the lead with this conversation as I run my fingers over the grain of the wood in front of me.

"Pumpkin, how do you know Juliana Gibbs?" His voice isn't harsh. He actually seems relatively calm.

"She's close to my best friend, Luna." I don't want to explain it all in great detail. I just want to hear from his lips what is going on.

"Alright, she spoke very highly of you. Something about your time in New York? You never mentioned you went there." Now he seems upset, but a lot was happening after The Pyramid. I haven't even let myself deal with the fact I was practically being hung, never mind a quick phone call to say I'd left the state.

"Uh, yeah. I went with Luna, and Juliana took me shopping."

He's silent for a moment as if trying to choose his words. "I didn't want to hand over guardianship, Pumpkin. I love you with all my heart, but I saw a path for at least one of us to get away from your mother, and I took it."

There, he said it, and my heart feels like it may burst at the seams. He just released the shackle around my neck, hurting himself in the process, and it's the most selfless thing anyone in our family has ever done for me. A single tear tracks down my face, but I quickly wipe it away, not wanting anyone to see me vulnerable.

"How did you get Mother to agree?" I ask, wanting to be sure.

"Don't worry about her, she doesn't know yet, but I did get her to sign them over. She just didn't know what she was signing. Leave her to me."

"Dad, you know things are never this easy with her. When she finds out, there'll be hell to pay." I respond, fearful for her reaction when it eventually comes.

"Leave it to me, Pumpkin. I will protect you from her." I hear the determination in his voice, and it surprises me.

"Okay, Dad. Thank you." I sniffle, feeling the emotions of such a weight being lifted off my shoulders.

"I love you, Pumpkin."

"I love you too, Dad. Speak soon."

Ending the call, I look up at the sky as I take a deep breath. I feel so free at this moment, like I could fly, but even though the shackles may have gone from around my neck, the prison of Featherstone still remains.

KC KEAN

THIRTEEN

Jess

I did not realize I had enough stuff to fill this freaking room. Back at Diamond, I had kept at least fifty percent of my things in suitcases, rotating what I pulled out. Now all of my little trinkets, photos, and memorabilia have a place on display. Luna and the guys have left, and I finally get a little peace and quiet in my new home without Oscar around. That guy gets on my last fucking nerve, rooting through my underwear drawer like he has any right to order me around. I'm just thankful he didn't open the lingerie box, along with my selection of battery-operated boyfriends.

I spent way too long explaining to Luna that she wasn't

allowed to set up any of her surveillance cameras in my room or outside in the hallway. I need my privacy, and she finally agreed when I explained how important it was to me. I think our conversation at lunch earlier, about my mother, may have impacted her agreement, but there is still a lot to discuss there. Especially now that Juliana is technically in the picture.

As crazy as it is, this seems a lot more like home than my last room. I can tell it's Juliana's taste that has made it so homey. I know Rafe would have avoided all of this like the plague. My bedroom is painted lilac, with a floral feature wall opposite the California king four-poster bed. The walk-in closet is smaller than Luna's but still impressive compared to anything else I've ever had. The lounge has a rustic feel to it, brown leather sofas, cream units, and subtle grey walls. Whereas the bathroom is stunning in all white, and the kitchen is deep grey cabinets, oak wood worktops, and white walls, with a dining table to match the rest of the room.

I am in love and totally not taking any of this for granted. Ever. Juliana already sent me a message. She's a little busy right now but promised she would call in the next few days to make sure I'm settled in and answer any questions I may have. Overall, she's been nothing but warm and welcoming to me, just like back in New York.

Glancing at the time, it's a little after seven. I'm all caught up on my work, so it's time to shower and put a boxset on the TV while I read more of the SC University series. It's my date for the evening, and I'm so ready for it.

Stepping into the bathroom, I turn on the shower and wipe off my make-up for the day. When I step out of my clothes, a little white piece of paper falls from my bra, startling me. Reaching down to pick it up, Aiden's number in bold black ink looks back at me. I'd completely forgotten it was there. Today has been a whirlwind. From my Combat class, which went from fighting off Reece to my confusing moment with Maverick to my brief, passionate kiss with Aiden and moving blocks. I haven't had a moment to think.

I never expected Aiden to approach me ever again, let alone kiss me too, but damn I'm glad he did. It just doesn't make any sense, yet he wanted me to message him by the end of the day. Looking between my phone and his number, I weigh the pros and cons of doing so. The only con may be that he breaks my heart, but if I keep my heart out of the situation, it magically isn't an issue anymore. Besides, I want all the men, and to have all the men, I need to offer no commitment and expect no commitment from them either. Remembering the brush of Maverick's thumb across my nipple earlier has a zap of electricity running through my body again, only solidifying my wants and desires.

Me: Hey. I met your deadline. Do I get a reward?

Before I can chicken out, I hit the send button and jump in the shower. The water falls down my back as I tilt my head under the spray, running my fingers through my hair. I take my time, letting the stresses of today float away with the water. Once I feel fresh and relaxed, I shut off the shower and wrap a fluffy grey towel around my body. Shit, these towels are like heaven. As I head for my bedroom to moisturize and get dressed, a knock sounds from the door, and I freeze. Another knock sounds again before I move, and I hear them call out from the other side.

"Hey, it's West."

West? Why would he be here? I don't consider the fact that I've just stepped out of the shower with only a towel wrapped around my body until I swing the door open, and I watch him look me over. Damn, he always looks so good. In his distressed denim jeans and fitted grey t-shirt, with his brown hairstyle to the side, I could lick him. But I remember the fact this fucker ghosted me.

Clearing my throat, his eyes finally make their way up to mine, and I watch as his Adam's apple moves when he gulps. "West. What are you doing here?"

Rubbing the back of his neck, he doesn't take his eyes off me. "I met Luna and Roman today to give them the keys for this place, and when I heard they were for you I wanted to see how you were." He knows he fucked up when he never responded.

"Honestly? Today has been a rollercoaster of a day, and you showing up here is like the final drop, and I don't freaking like fast rides. You have my number. You could have messaged." I fold my hands over my chest, gripping the towel tightly in position as I wait for him to respond.

"I know, it was shitty of me not to respond after I said I would be there for you, and I wanted to apologize in person." The sincerity in his eyes is what makes my mouth move on its own accord.

"You can come in if you like. I just need to get dressed."

"I want to, I really want to, but I would like to get to know you better, properly."

"What does that mean?" I ask in confusion as he braces his arms on the door frame. Holy fuck, that's hot.

"It means I want to bring food over, maybe watch a movie…"

"Like a date?"

"Yes, like a date. If I haven't lost my chance all together." The hope in his eyes is hotter than any of his sexy features right now, even his deep voice that always hits me high on the swoon factor scale. He's looking at me like I'm a goddess while I stand here with no make-up on and my hair dripping wet.

"I would like that," I whisper. "But I need you to know that I seem to have a connection with someone else, well maybe more but…"

He smiles down at me as I struggle to find the words. The back of his hand strokes down my cheek in a gentle caress, and I'm a goner.

"Did you know I was meant to marry Luna, along with Roman? That was our family's agreement years ago."

"What?" How the hell did I not know this?

"No, not now, everything has changed now, and I've never seen Luna in that way. I'm very protective of her, and I'll go to the ends of the earth for her, but that's because she's my family, my moon, just like you seem to be my sunshine. As blindingly beautiful as you are, I can't seem to stop myself from coming back to you every time." All I can do is gape at him, my heart pounding rapidly in my ears as I remember him calling me sunshine on the phone when I was in New York. "All I'm saying is, I'm familiar with the prospect of sharing, and the fact that you are open and honest with me, makes me want to do whatever it takes to make you happy. If that means you're dating other guys too, I can figure it out as we go along."

"Wow." He looks at me with a frown as my mouth continues to operate without a filter. I never, *ever* thought I'd say that to someone and get such an open and positive response. As much as West let me down, he's here now, and he has a way about him that makes me feel comfortable being myself and expressing my truth. Staring up into his bright blue eyes, I don't know what to say.

As if in slow motion, we gravitate toward each other, my eyes closing as I feel the gentle kiss of his lips against mine. There's no rush, no groping, just his hands on my waist and one of mine on his chest while the other holds my towel in place as we explore each other. The desire that hums through my veins at the slow drag of his lips against mine makes me moan softly.

Leaning back, he places a gentle kiss on my forehead, just like I've seen Kai do to Luna, and I understand that look of pure bliss on her face when he does. All in one movement, I feel special and cherished. Blinking my eyes open, West smiles down at me.

"So, dinner and a movie?"

"Can we have the little Italian bistro delivered?" I ask, and he nods. "Then you can choose whatever movie you like as long as it's not a horror because I don't need that shit in my life."

He chuckles as he steps back, "You're cute when you swear." He winks, making me blush. "Thursday?"

"Thursday," I answer, not even checking to see if I have plans already.

"Lock the door now. I'll text you a time." I raise my eyebrows at him since his texting skills seem less than adequate so far, and he gives me the scout's honor sign. He's never been a scout for sure, but I trust his word, and if he lets me down again, I know where I stand.

"Okay, bye."

"Bye, sunshine."

Closing the door, I instantly turn, slumping against it.

Holy fuck. Holy fuckity fuck. Pumping my fists in the air, I can't stop the need to happy dance. Pushing off the door, I kick my legs out as I jump up and down, barely containing a squeal. Completely lost in the moment of happiness, I don't even realize my towel has slipped from my body, and I'm literally happy dancing around my lounge naked. Totally fucking worth it though.

Quickly throwing on a pair of checkered cotton pajamas, I grab my Kindle and get comfortable on the sofa, until I remember I left my phone in the bathroom. Grabbing it, I fall back into the cushions on the sofa, and check the messages on my screen.

Aiden: Beautiful, I'm your reward! But tomorrow, I'm going to give you a prize.

West: Look at me, just casually confirming I do indeed have the texting function on my phone.

Wow. Two hot guys, both are texting me out of choice. Who the fuck would have thought?

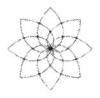

West

Taking the stairs down to the ground floor of Ace, I can't believe how today has gone. When Jess said she'd had a rollercoaster of a day, I felt like I'd been sitting on the same damn ride. When Luna agreed to meet this afternoon, I was excited to finally have a chance to talk, and as much as Roman is a douche, it actually helped that he was there. Hopefully, he'll eventually catch up on the fact I'm not into Luna or planning on marrying her.

I'm just glad she's finally finding some happiness. When I saw her and Rafe a few years back, I wanted to grab her by the shoulders and shake her till the darkness left her eyes. Luna wasn't living her best life out near Philadelphia, and one day she'll look back and recognize that. Even though Featherstone Academy comes with a lot of challenges, her life seems to be hopefully changing for the better.

After Luna's memory of Roman, her, and I, out at the lake house, when she was too scared to go in the water, it felt like she saw me in a different light. When I wrapped my arms around her tight, for the first time in so long, and I whispered in her ear, something shifted inside of me.

"You're stuck with me no matter what, Moon. If this brat or any of the others get out of hand, you just let me know."

After I called her moon, all I could think about was how much I missed the presence of my sunshine. I'd barely spent any time with her, but I couldn't help being drawn to her. My dumb idea to put some distance between us after what Maverick said, felt stupid. I needed to be around her and see where this might be able to go, other guys around or not. Although my brain hasn't really caught up with that whole situation yet, but I'm not going to focus on it right now.

The thought of her lips against mine is all I need. Fuck, the softness of her lips, and her skin under my touch, has me on fire. Damn, I wanted to push her into her room, slamming the door behind me as I walked in and ripped the towel from her body that was teasing me so badly. Biting my knuckles, I take a deep breath, but I know I'm going to need a cold shower when I get in. She makes me feel like a teenage boy, ready to explode at a blow of a kiss from her.

Stepping into the garage, I climb into my charcoal grey Audi R8 and get ready to hit the gas pedal when my phone rings. It instantly links up to the in-car entertainment system, so the shrill sound of my ringtone fills the car as Rafe's name flashes across the screen.

"Hey," I answer, pressing the fob to open the garage door.

"Hey, I need you in on Friday, by dinnertime. It'll be a two-man job, so we'll go together." No messing around, always straight down to business first. Fuck. This is why I scheduled Thursday with Jess. They'll never pull me away on a day I'm teaching, which means Tuesdays and Thursdays are always locked in, but the weekends are never guaranteed to be mine. Not when my other Featherstone job role is involved.

"Okay, where to?"

It's quiet around campus tonight, but I chose my R8 because of the tinted windows, and it helps that I have the key for the Morgan's bloodline apartment in Ace. So, if anyone asks what I'm doing here, I can link it back to that.

"L.A., we'll likely be there until Sunday."

"Fine. It's not like I had plans yet anyway," I grumble, which makes him chuckle.

"How did your chat go with Luna today?" He asks, getting personal now he has the business over with. Neither of us wants to do this shit, but it's usually a more satisfying job when Rafe tags along.

"Better than I expected, even if she did bring the big brat with her."

"Rivera?"

"Yeah," I answer as the security guards open the gates, and I tear out of there. The condo building all the teachers live in is only minutes away, so I keep my speed low while I'm talking.

"Did you tell them the new agreement between the families? That you're no longer expected to get married?" Rafe asks, and it's my turn to laugh.

"No. He was being a mouthy little shit, and it's obviously still a concern of his, and I didn't feel like easing his mind." Rafe laughs along with me until the line goes quiet.

"And Jess?"

"Goodnight, fucker," I respond, ending the call before he tries to pressure me into girl talk. He already grilled me with questions when I officially announced amongst the Steeles, Morgans, Riveras, and Gibbs that I did not want to commit to the long-standing agreement to combine our families. I eventually relented, on a one-to-one level with him, and explained what I felt in a single moment with Jess is worlds apart from the brotherly love I have for Luna. Now there is a new, more fitting agreement, and it couldn't be better.

I'll never forget his soft smile as he patted my shoulder and told me Bryce, Luna's father, would be proud of me for recognizing my own feelings yet caring for Luna deeply. It felt like a weight had been lifted. Pulling up outside of the condo building, I parked in one of my three allocated bays, right in between my SUV and Holly, my Honda Blackbird motorcycle.

Friday, and the stress it always brings can wait. I now have Thursday to look forward to, and a movie to choose.

RED

KC KEAN

FOURTEEN

Maverick

"Boy, do I have a special treat for y'all tonight. Next up in the cage, I give you Freddy 'Fury' Mellor and the one and only Ricky 'Rage' Mills!" The announcer's voice booms through the speakers strategically placed throughout the dingy warehouse basement we all stand in.

I always cringe when I have to react to the name Ricky Mills, but I couldn't exactly give my true name, and I didn't want to stray too far from the truth. I still haven't fully healed from my last trip out handling business for Featherstone, but I need this fight right now. I barely slept last night, after everything that happened yesterday with

Jessica, and that little fucker Reece, I need to channel all this pent-up energy somewhere.

All I could think about was the fact she had come to me before the sparring started, asking to switch partners because she felt uncomfortable. She fucking knew, and I brushed her off and pushed her into that situation. When I saw his hands pinning her down to the mat, I felt something wasn't right in my gut. So when I moved around them and saw his other hand gripping her breast through her sports bra, I saw red. I barely contained my rage until we got in my office, and that motherfucker is lucky I only punched him because I really want to wrap my hands around his neck and not stop until his face was blue.

Then, to top off all of my mistakes, I blamed it all on her. I didn't mean it, not really, but she fucking stood before me, her wild red hair framing her pretty face and I wanted to drop to my knees and give her everything. Which is the most ridiculous shit I've ever heard. I'll never drop to my knees, not for anyone, and especially not for some tantalizing eighteen-year-old who ignites something inside me I've never felt before.

Of course, that didn't stop my fingers from moving on their own, brushing against her pebbled nipple beneath her sports bra, bringing my dick to attention instantly. But my words upset her so much she slapped me, and I fucking deserved it. Yet the pain and despair in her eyes are what I feel more. Jessica clearly isn't a violent person, but I pushed her so far her body took over and defended herself from me. It took more strength to push back and not comfort her in that moment than it did to not kill Reece. Moving around the desk, I had to conceal my reaction to her, my cock so hard it was completely noticeable through my loose shorts. The combination of touching her, and the pain from her slap having me close to combusting.

I haven't been able to get the situation off my mind ever since, so when Rafe called and asked me to make an appearance as Ricky Mills, I agreed instantly.

The music picks up, as I stand at the exit of the locker room, forcing me to get my head in gear and shake off this shit playing on my mind. Here, I'm not Maverick Miller, Academy Combat tutor and official Featherstone brawler. Here, I'm Ricky Mills who just loves to fight and get dirty, hoping to get noticed by the owners so I can work my way into their business. Their system of drugs, prostitution, and guns. All of which is not operated or sanctioned by Featherstone, so we're going to tear these guys down.

Nobody gets to run any kind of criminal activity without Featherstone's authorization, and these guys think they can make up their own rules. I don't really care who runs the criminal world, but any excuse to get rid of sick motherfuckers and I'm in.

"You got this, Ricky boy," Brian says as he approaches, patting my shoulder as he passes. "The owners are in the house tonight."

"Good looking out, man," I answer, playing my role perfectly as I straighten my shoulders, making it seem like I'm wanting to impress them. Brian is the guy getting me in, but it's important to stay focused the whole time I'm here.

The music dims and the chants of the crowd increase, which I take as my cue to head for the cage. Bodies fill the space as I make my way through the cleared path, the sound of clapping and stomping meets my ears as I eye my opponent already in the cage. I'm known here for being a ruthless son of a bitch, and the crowd always knows when I'm here by the fact that I enter the ring to no music, not a single beat.

Bare-chested, with my loose grey shorts drawn tight at the waist and my feet wrapped, along with my hands,

I'm ready to get dirty. Stepping into the cage, a calmness settles over me. In here nothing else matters, none of the usual bullshit I'm dealing with, just what my body can do, and what I can control. The guy waiting for me smirks as I circle around him, testing the tape around my hands. He's shorter than me, but a wider build and the glint in his eyes tells me he hasn't heard about my reputation, and what I'm capable of.

The rules of the cage out in Petersburg are simple. No ref, no weapons, winner takes blood and leaves an unconscious body. Taking a moment to see past the ring, there must be easily three hundred people in here, all standing except for the VIP zone over to my right, opposite the DJ booth. That's where the wannabe gangsters sit with their pussy of the hour, picking and choosing who to pull into their ranks.

The bell sounds, and my opponent moves straight away, not missing a moment to try and charge me, but I'm too quick on my feet, stepping to my left and spinning to face him. I watch as this guy's face tinges red with embarrassment, his teeth clenching as he raises his fists high, finally taking this a little more serious now.

Matching his stance, I grin, letting my playful side

come out, goading him to make the first move again. It works every time, like a charm. Moving in closer, almost toe-to-toe, he looks me over just before pulling his right arm back, and that's his biggest mistake. Pulling back like a rookie, lets me know his move. Before he can make contact, I take the opening he just gave me, extending my arm straight out and connecting with his face. His head whips back with the impact, and blood instantly drips from his nose.

"Fuck," he grumbles, swiping his forearm across his face in an attempt to clear the blood away.

Not giving up easily, we circle each other a few times as the crowd chants 'blood' around us, noting the first sign towards victory. Rage burns in his eyes as he charges me again, this time swinging his arms in succession. I manage to catch the first with my arm, but his second hook is stronger than I expect, hitting me square in the jaw. Turning straight to the crowd, he encourages their cheers, either underestimating what I can handle or overestimating his actual strength. Either way, this fucker is an idiot.

Kicking the back of his leg his weight sags beneath him, and I throw my elbow into the side of his head, knocking him to the floor. Following him to the mat, I punch him in the face two more times, and he rolls to his side as I swipe my hair from my face, sweat coating my skin. He must think I'm willing to give him a second to breathe, but that's not how this works. Crouching beside him, I hook my arm under his shoulder, I wrap the other right around his neck, pulling my arms in tight, straight into a crab choke, leaving him utterly defenseless.

Rising to my feet, I bring him with me, letting him dangle before me as I take his weight while he swings his legs around trying to kick me. With his arms above us in the air, he has no way to fight off my hold, and within seconds I have the unconscious body I need to win. Not caring for his now sleeping body, I carelessly drop him to the floor as the music booms through the speakers at my victory. I look past the cheering crowd, the beer sloshing everywhere as the parties jump around, searching straight for the VIP area.

The guy who runs this joint raises his glass of whiskey in my direction, a grin on his face, and it's the first time in three months he's acknowledged one of my wins. I'll take that as my real success of the evening. Not waiting around, I step out of the ring, heading straight for the locker room so I can shower and change. I fucking love the feel of the adrenaline pumping through my veins, shaking my shoulders out as my body tries to relax.

Yet my mind wanders to my pretty redhead, the sting of her hand connecting with my skin, and the sway of her ass as she leaves, making me growl. I'm nowhere near as fucking calm as I should be after fighting.

What is she fucking doing to me?

RED

FIFTEEN

Jess

The second I step into Science the next day, my eyes instantly search out Aiden who is sitting with Trudy and their friends at the back of the lab. His gaze flicks to mine, but the moment it looks as if he would acknowledge me, Oscar throws his arm around my shoulder, creating a barrier between myself and everyone else in class, making me stiffen in response.

"What are you doing, Oscar?" I growl under my breath. His constant protectiveness gets on my nerves, he thinks I'm a child.

"Making sure no limp-dick thinks he can get close to

you," is the only response I get as he guides me to my seat, and takes the one beside me.

"Whoa, no way, Oscar. Go and sit in your usual spot. I'm not dealing with you right now," I mumble, pushing at his arm but he refuses to budge. Dustin, who usually sits beside me quiet and focused, approaches us, but one glance from Oscar and he's backing away.

"Jess, you are like my sister. Your sense of innocence gives me this crazy need to protect you, just like I would my sister Niamh. I know what guys think about, remember, I am one. Now, focus." Turning back to the front, waiting for the tutor to begin, I stare at him in shock. When he puts it like that, he almost sounds like a nice guy, but he's still cock-blocking me.

Great. Fucking great. I definitely won't be sneaking glances at Aiden today with Oscar beside me, and I can already feel his eyes burning the back of my head. I feel somebody else watching me, and when I look past Oscar I spot Reece frowning at my new Science partner. My heart rate instantly picks up and my palms begin to sweat. After yesterday, I don't want to have to deal with him at all.

Quickly turning to look straight ahead, I feel a little better with Oscar's presence. Although, I may not have had Reece's attention if Oscar wasn't sitting there, but my heartbeat slows knowing Reece won't get near me with him around. I can't deal with the guys in here right now, whether I like them or not, I need to focus on anything but the stress I'm feeling. That means focusing on my work, not the emotions they're drawing from me.

Mr. Perez spends the entire lesson explaining the compounds of different explosives, and I try to listen, taking plenty of notes, but the feel of my phone vibrating in my bag at my feet has been distracting me the whole time. When the bell finally rings, I've never been more grateful. Although, I am surprised with Oscar. He has written down everything Mr. Perez said, taking this way more seriously than I expected. Maybe having him as my Science partner won't be a bad idea after all.

"That's it for today, everyone. Next lesson we will meet out by the Weaponry building where I will be showing the uses of the various explosives we have learned about today." He doesn't say anymore as he focuses his attention on the tablet on his desk, effectively dismissing us all. Packing my laptop away, I slip my phone out of the inside pocket, noticing eight text messages waiting for me. Seven from Aiden, all while he's been sitting behind me, and the other from West.

I darken the screen as Oscar tries to glance at my phone, frowning as I avoid making eye contact with him, acting as though I was simply checking the time. I'm thankful I decided to change their names in my phone last night, for occasions like this. I don't want Oscar or any of the others knowing anything before I'm ready to share. This is my private life. So, Aiden is now saved in my phone as *Grey Fire*, for the color of his eyes and the way his touch makes me feel. While West is saved as *Deep Blues*, because of his deep voice and ocean blue eyes.

Following Oscar out of the room, I force myself to not look back at Aiden. I am not that girl, and this is all just some light-hearted fun, but damn, I want to know what my prize is. Just before Oscar starts down the stairs, I grab his arm.

"I'm going to go to the restroom, I'll meet you down there." He stares me down for a moment, but he eventually nods in agreement, and I take off to the right. Stepping into the restroom, there doesn't seem to be anyone else here. So I take a moment to look through my messages as I stand by the sinks, dropping my bag on the side.

Grey Fire: You look fucking beautiful!

Grey Fire: How do I get you to be my Science partner?

Grey Fire: It's turning me on that you're not responding to me right now, but I can hear your phone vibrating from here.

Grey Fire: Are you ready for your prize?

Grey Fire: I can still feel your lips against mine.

Deep Blues: Hey Sunshine, I hope today is good! I can't wait until Thursday, you don't need a Weaponry class before then, do you?

Grey Fire: Do you know you bite your lip when you're concentrating? So hot.

Grey Fire: Fuck I hate your bodyguard right now.

Who even is this guy? His simple texts make me blush,

turning me on without a single touch, just from his words alone. And West, he's definitely making his intentions clear and I could scream with excitement, but I need to play it cool. Sending a quick response to West, I consider what to even say to Aiden.

Me: Hey West. Today is okay so far, although I wish Weaponry was on my schedule! Have you chosen a movie yet?

Clicking on Aiden's name I re-read his texts, trying to think of something sexy and sassy back to him, but I jump in surprise when the girl's restroom door swings open. Dropping my phone to the counter, my brain takes a moment to catch up as I watch Aiden lock the door and stalk towards me.

"Hey," I whisper, staring into his grey eyes as he smirks down at me. This guy is hot as fuck, even in his Featherstone uniform, with his blonde hair swept to the side and his sexy grin on full display. After admitting to him I've only ever had sex of the boring variety, I know he could show me what I've been missing. Because even though he's standing before me, pursuing me, I know once he's fucked me he'll be gone again. That's his usual M.O. and I'm prepared for it.

He doesn't stop until we're chest to chest, invading my personal space, his woodsy scent with a hint of cinnamon surrounding me. His eyes zone in on my lips, and his hand finds my neck tilting my chin up, and the whole movement has my skin heating with need. Biting down on my lip to contain my moan, I watch as his pupils dilate.

"Fuck, beautiful. You are so tempting. All pristine and pure, but underneath, I see your devilish side." I can't stop my grin at his words. His description of me, combined with his touch, makes me feel sexy as hell, giving me the confidence boost I want.

My hands find the lapels of his blazer, pulling him the smallest inch closer, and his mouth descends on mine. My hips press into the counter behind me as Aiden crowds me, taking from my lips as I take from him too. Fuck, I want more. I don't know what I want more of exactly, just him in general. But right here isn't the best of ideas because someone will be up here in a minute if I don't get to Business soon.

Using all my strength, I pull back slightly. "Someone is going to come looking for me in a minute."

"So, I can handle Oscar," he responds, kissing me deeper, but it isn't just about that.

"Aiden, I'm a private person, and I would rather not look like one of your has-beens when you've got what you wanted from me. So, whether you can handle Oscar or not, I don't want anyone to know." Resting his forehead against mine he takes a few deep breaths before he finally looks me in the eye.

"Okay," he breathes, standing tall and tucking a piece of my hair behind my ear. "Are you free after Business, or tonight?"

"I can be," I answer, too turned on to say no to him. Brushing his lips against mine once more Aiden takes a step back to rearrange himself and I trace every movement.

"That glint in your eyes tells me you like having this effect on me."

"Then you can read me very well," I say with a smirk, keeping my eyes fixed in between his legs.

"There is more to me than my man meat, you know?" He gripes, and I reluctantly pull my gaze to his.

"I'm sure there is, but if I find those things, I'll end up with my feelings hurt when you leave." He frowns at my words, but I just shrug my shoulders. I'm just saying the truth and he knows it. Maybe he's used to girls tripping over themselves to find out more about him, but I haven't given myself a pep talk all morning to fall at the first hurdle with him.

Finding my backbone, I grab my phone from the counter and throw it in my bag before stepping around him. Reaching the door, I flick the lock and turn to look at him over my shoulder. "Let me know when, and you can come …"

"As soon as possible. After Business, text me your room in Diamond and I'll be there."

Fuck, hearing a guy so eager turns me on more than it probably should. "I've been moved to Ace. I'm in Gibbs on the first floor." I don't say anymore, turning and leaving before I give in and let him take me on the restroom floor. Heading straight for the open staircase, the floor is clear of students, but it is just my luck that when I reach the stairs to go down, West and Maverick are coming down from the floor above. They are murmuring between themselves, both looking as delicious as always, when West spots me.

"Hey, Sunshine," he smiles, like seeing me made his day and the butterflies in my tummy I'd just calmed down, flutter just as strong again. Maverick frowns at me, as a door slams behind me and I know it's my fucking luck that Aiden just walked out. I watch as West and Maverick, glancing between Aiden and me, with my blush brightening my cheeks, and I have not got the balls to act casual right now. I take off down the stairs, offering the smallest smile as I leave.

Fuck. There is no reason for me to feel embarrassed, but I know the three faces that will be in my orgy dream tonight.

West

What a complete waste of our time. Gina Williams, the History tutor here at Featherstone, called Maverick while we were in the gym, frantically needing help, so we rushed over. It was another one of her ridiculous attempts to get one of us alone, so her face lit up when we'd both walked in. The woman is quiet and shy, but the second she has us alone, she becomes some psycho vixen.

Expecting it to be just Maverick, she'd dressed in only see-through black lingerie which would have been hot as shit on someone I'd actually wanted to see wearing it. It isn't the first time she's done something like this. The first week back, she'd called me for help at her apartment, and when I'd shown up, her shirt was undone and she was braless. I fixed her damn lightbulb and hightailed it out of there.

This is all because we may have got too drunk at the end of year party back in June, and one thing lead to another, which was Gina between Maverick and I. I have never been so wasted and out of it before, Maverick either, but now we're definitely regretting letting our guards down because this woman does not stop. She's had a thing for Maverick since they went to Featherstone High together, and apparently I just completed the damn fantasy.

"Man, we need to find a way to cut her loose. She's driving me crazy," Maverick grunts as we step out of her classroom. Gina said some students were vandalizing her classroom and threatening her, tears and all, but when we showed up, that's when we realized we'd been played. Again.

"We need to stop answering when she calls, that's half of our issue. Although, her little lingerie set was good, I'd just prefer to see it on Sunshine." The second part of that sentence was not supposed to be said out loud. My big fucking mouth.

"Sunshine?" Maverick asks, confused, like I knew he would. Rubbing the back of my neck I don't stop, instead heading for the stairs.

"Yeah, I have a date on Thursday, and she would look stunning in something like that."

"A date? With who? Where's the usual fight and fuck guy I'm used to? West Morgan doesn't usually date," he grunts, in a foul mood since Gina inconvenienced us.

"With someone who deserves more than a fight fuck, obviously," I answer, shaking my head at him. I'm used to fighting, fucking, then leaving, and Jess deserves more than that.

"Just because someone deserves more than a quick fuck to wear off your adrenaline, doesn't mean it has to be us that gives it to them."

I agree with his words, but Jess is different. There is just something about her that makes me want to give her more. Even if there are other guys in the picture, I just need to have a deeper conversation with her at some point.

"I know what you're saying, Rick, but she's something else."

"Whatever you say man, but we do not need to be

dealing with anymore crazy bitches when your dating goes south."

As we reach the next floor, movement catches my eyes, and I don't respond to him as the beauty herself stands before me.

"Hey, Sunshine," I call out before I can stop myself, and the intake of breath beside me lets me know I just gave it away. What is it with my big fucking mouth when it comes to her? I can't watch what I'm saying or stop myself from bringing her up. I'm an idiot.

Jess's steps falter as she sees us and I can tell she doesn't really know what to say or do with Maverick here. The girls restroom door slams shut from behind her and Aiden Byrnes steps out. I don't teach the guy but his reputation precedes him. I watch as Jess's cheeks redden and she refuses to look behind her, as if she already knows who is there.

Wait? Is he the guy she was talking about? I can see the panic in her eyes, and she offers the tiniest of smiles before bolting down the stairs in her heels. Aiden frowns at us standing, gaping between him and the girl who just fled, and follows after her.

What the fuck just happened here?

"Jessica? Jessica Watson is your date?" Maverick growls beside me, and I sigh at where this is going. I know I'm a tutor and she's a student, but it wouldn't have been any different if Luna had attended here under different circumstances. Everyone had known the family arrangement, and that wouldn't have changed because of our roles. There is no rule against this kind of relationship specifically because of situations like that, and I refuse to defend myself.

"Rick, I know she's a student, but that's irrelevant…"

"You want to date someone who clearly just ran off because you caught her with that little dickhead?"

Clenching my teeth, I try not to overreact. "She told me last night someone else was already in the picture when I went to see her. She has a lot going on right now, and from what Rafe mentioned, when Juliana called her parents to try and arrange the guardianship to move her into Ace, her father agreed to anything to get Jess free of her mother. I don't know why, or what for, but I've learned with Luna, that I need to let Jess be who she wants to be, and I'd be lucky if she brings me along for the ride."

Not wanting to continue standing here discussing my damn feelings, I continue down the stairs and Rick follows me. "Whatever you say, man. It's your death wish."

His words are likely supposed to put me off the whole situation, but instead he makes me grin. "Rick, the touch of her lips last night signed my death warrant, and I couldn't give a shit."

And that's the damn truth. Stepping outside, I could have sworn he murmured something about him seeing her first, but he was gone before I could question what he meant.

KC KEAN

SIXTEEN

Jess

Holy shit, I still haven't been able to relax my heartbeat since it felt like my life imploded outside of Science. I'm glad I got to Business when I did because Luna was literally at the door coming for me. I already felt like I'd been caught doing something wrong, even though I knew I hadn't. She didn't say anything as I took my seat, but my heated cheeks likely had her confused.

So, after lunch, I was glad when Luna and the guys headed over to their Weaponry class and I got to head back to Ace. Luna made sure it was Ian taking me back since I was alone. I don't know what made her so sure he would protect me, but I went along with it.

As Ian started the engine, I pulled out my phone and decided to try Juliana. We keep missing each other. I have no idea what she does in the daytime, but her 'Icy Ring Queen' demeanor has no room for my phone calls, which she apologizes for profusely. But when she tries to return my call, it's gone past midnight, and I'm sleeping. Neither of us gives up trying, but we always end up texting. I just like that she feels like a constant, even though I haven't heard her voice since New York. I'm not surprised when there is no answer, so I pull up the messaging app.

Me: Hey, Ju-Ju. I hope you are having a kick-ass day. We need to have this phone call soon, nobody else is giving me details, and I know you will. No stress though, I know you're so busy! But you have to stop buying me things! Speak soon.

I can see that she opens my message straight away, which means she's going to text back under the table like she'll get in trouble for responding, and the thought makes me chuckle.

Ju-Ju: Stop with the Ju-Ju! I promise we will talk soon, when I'm not dealing with fucking idiots, I swear. Don't be doing anything I wouldn't do!

She has officially been christened Ju-Ju, so she needs to get used to it. It's crazy that she's technically my guardian, but she's more like a sister. We need to talk about the fact she sent a parcel yesterday with a brand-new laptop, credit card, and gift cards for stores available on-site at campus. I don't want her money, but she keeps throwing things at me. There was also a warning that if I hadn't spent the gift cards in the next week, she would be sending actual clothes instead. But she had put far too much money on there. We need to have a rational discussion.

The Rolls Royce pulls up outside of Ace, and Ian beats me to the door, as always. "Thank you. Have a great day, Ian." He offers me a smile and a nod before climbing back in and waiting outside of Weaponry for Luna.

There are a few groups of students in the square, around the water fountain, and I can feel some of their eyes on me. I haven't heard any whispers yet about me being moved into Ace, but I know they're coming, and I need to be prepared.

As much as my feet are aching in my heels, I take the stairs since the lift isn't already waiting on the ground floor. Scrolling through the academy's internal social media, nothing catches my eye or piques my interest. It'd definitely be more fun if Luna actually used it after I downloaded it for her, but instead I'm left with the boring shit like what people have had for their dinner. I'm not opposed to a little gossip sometimes, like who's sleeping with who, but I don't actually post anything myself.

Pulling my keys from my bag, I don't spot the piece of paper stuck to my door until the key is in the lock. My nose scrunches as I pull it from the door, looking around to see if anyone else is here, but I'm alone. A simple white sheet of paper with thick black inked scrawled across the center.

STAY THE FUCK AWAY FROM HIM!

What the hell? Where did this come from? Feeling a little panicked, I turn the key in the lock and step inside my room, slamming the door shut quickly behind me. Leaning back against the door, I take a moment to calm my breathing before I make sure to put the chain on.

"Hey, beautiful." I hear from behind me, and I scream. Like the scream is so high pitched even my own eardrums feel like they're going to explode but I can't stop it. Spinning around, I find a shirtless Aiden sitting back on my sofa watching the television.

"Aiden!" I yell, leaning forward, with my hand on my chest, as I will myself not to cry. "How the fuck did you get in here?" I feel him approach me, but I can't focus on him right now as I blink back my tears and pick my heart back up off the floor.

"Well, I'm good with locks, but I didn't think I'd scare you this much." Feeling his hand rub gently on my back, I'm surprised by how much it actually makes me feel better.

"Did you do this?" I ask, holding the piece of paper up to him to read. Taking it from my hands, he shakes his head as I turn to face him.

"No," he murmurs, turning to check if there is anything on the back. "Where did you find it?"

"On my door," I answer, stupidly pointing behind me.

"It wasn't there five minutes ago."

"Don't worry about it. We need to discuss you letting yourself in here while I was out," I answer, wanting to deal with one thing at a time, and right now he can give me answers, the piece of paper can't.

"No, we need to figure out what they mean by this. And from the way you ran off before, the 'him' could be one of a few options."

I stare him down, meeting his gaze and refusing to back away. "Is that a problem?"

My question surprises him, I can tell by the way his eyes widen in surprise, and his bottom lip drops open ever so slightly. He didn't expect me to give him an honest answer, but this has been mostly about attraction since Friday night, so I can understand the lack of conversation around it.

When he doesn't respond, I continue with how I feel. "I like the idea of more than one guy. I see Luna do it, and I read about it on the daily. So, I won't shy away from it when it's about the only thing I know I want in my future. I understand if that makes you uncomfortable, but, well, I care enough about myself to let you leave."

He looks me over for what feels like hours as I stand my ground. Then suddenly, my bag is dropping to the floor as he lifts me off the ground and presses his lips to mine. Propping me up against the door, my heels dangling from my feet with my legs wrapped around his waist, and my skirt rising up my thighs. I feel hot all over with the need to be touched.

"Do you know how fucking hot it is that you know what you want and refuse to mold yourself to meet other people's standards?" He breathes out against my lips, and his words set me on fire. Threading my fingers through the blonde hair at the back of his head, I pull him back in, loving the taste of his lips against mine. "Do you want your prize now, beautiful?" He asks, and I nod eagerly.

His wicked grin is all I get in response as he carries me towards my bedroom, not asking for a single direction. What the hell has he gotten up to in the five minutes he's been here?

"We need to discuss you being in my room, Aid," I whisper, and his response is to drop me on my bed, making me bounce a few times. Grabbing my ankles, he pulls me down to the edge of the bed, hovering over me in only his uniform pants and bare chiseled chest, and the move feels so alpha I could orgasm without him even touching me right now.

Bending down, his lips graze my neck, causing goosebumps to flair up across my skin. "Say it again."

What the hell is he on about? "Aid, I'm serious."

His lips vibrate against my skin as he hums in appreciation. "We can discuss boundaries now, or after I've tasted you. Which would you prefer?"

I try to act as though it took a lot more consideration on my part, but really I'd be lying if I was ever going to say anything other than, "Later."

As he leans back, I prop myself up on my elbow, slipping my blazer off and throwing it to the side. Feeling the heat of his palm against my thigh, I'm confused with why he's not moved. Glancing down at him, it takes a moment, but I realize what has his attention. His hands cover the lace at the top of my suspenders, which are usually hidden beneath my skirt.

"Who the fuck are you, Jessica Watson?" He asks, and I giggle at the appreciation in his voice. Inching my skirt up higher, he doesn't bother to try and unzip the back, happy to leave it scrunched up around my waist. I feel his eyes rake over the apex of my thighs, taking in the sexy white lingerie I'm wearing. "Fuck me, beautiful. How can something as angelic as white make you look like a sinful devil, hmm?"

I feel almost frozen in place as I scramble for anything

to say in response, but my thought process is cut off when his hands grip both sides of my blouse, ripping it open and making the buttons scatter around us. Holy. Fucking. Shit. Kill me now and send me to sex heaven. I thought this kind of thing only happened in my RH books.

"Tell me you want this, Jess?" He whispers in desperation, and I nod in response.

"Yes," I breathe out, and in an instant he's biting my taut nipple through the lace exposing them, and my back arches off the bed. A moan slips from my lips as my fingers grip his hair tight, holding him close. "Fuck." The feel of his fingers tracing their way to my core has my heart pounding in my ears in anticipation.

"Holy shit. Jess, are these fucking crotchless?" He almost shouts, as his fingers gain instant access to my opening. The heat of his fingers as they slowly glide up to my clit and back down makes me hiss.

"For all this talk, I seem to have you a lot more speechless than the other way around right now," I brazenly answer, and the grin he gives me tells me I'm going to get exactly what I'm hinting at. Dropping to his knees at the foot of the bed, I lift myself to sit before him, my legs on either side of his hips as I pull his lips to mine. The need between us feels raw. The bite of his fingers digging into my ass cheeks as he holds me close has me biting into his bottom lip, our moans mingling together.

His hand presses me back slightly. "Now, I want a real taste of you." He barely finished his sentence as his tongue peeks out, trailing a path from my clit to my pussy, and my toes instantly curl.

I can't stop my hands from clenching the cover beneath me as his lips wrap around my clit and sucks hard. Shit. My head falls backward, a flush creeping up my neck and across my cheeks. The feel of his mouth and fingers, all while the lace of my lingerie remains in place, has me ready to explode with how hot I feel and how primal his touch is.

Two fingers slowly press deep inside of me, a high-pitched moan shoots from my mouth uncontrollably as my hips begin to move on their own, meeting the slow thrust of his fingers.

"More. Please, Aid. More." I beg like my life depends on it, and right now it does because I can feel the edges of my orgasm tingling in my toes and fingertips. Without pause, his tongue swipes against my clit as his fingers swirl inside of me, finding my g-spot like they're magnets.

My fingers ache as they fist in the sheets, and just when I think I can't take anymore, his teeth graze against my clit. In slow motion, the explosion inside of me ricochets throughout my body.

His movements slow, dragging out every inch of pleasure as wave after wave of my orgasm races through my body. All I can see is the back of my eyelids, and my ears are filled with the sound of my blood pumping. When I finally begin to enter the world again, it's to see Aiden's thick fingers wrapped tightly around his length, his eyes settled on my body as he cums in his hand. The intenseness I feel as he meets my gaze makes my skin heat.

Watching him come apart like that sends another ripple of bliss through my body, but I pout. "I wanted to taste you too," I murmur, and his eyes widen.

"Is that so?" He asks, offering his hand out to me as a challenge, but I refuse to back down. Leaning forward, I wrap my lips around his finger, tasting his cum as I slowly make a show of cleaning it off with my tongue. As I release his finger, his mouth finds mine, surprising me as he devours my mouth and the taste of us both lingers between us.

Flopping back on the bed, my eyes close as I try to

catch my breath. I can't explain or dissect how I feel right now. I need to harden my skin, prepare for him to leave as if my world wasn't just flipped upside down. But when I open my eyes, he's barely moved, standing over me with his eyebrows pinched together.

"Are you okay?" I ask tentatively, confused with what has him so stressed.

"Yeah," he murmurs. "I just, uh." Rubbing the back of his neck, I can see him trying to figure out what to say.

"You can leave. I won't start crying and begging you to stay if that's what you're worried about." My heart sinks a little at my own words, but I refuse to fully acknowledge it. Standing I discard my blouse and skirt which were crumpled by his touch. Searching for one of my few oversized t-shirts that I relax in sometimes, I step out of my lingerie and slip it over my head.

Glancing over my shoulder he's still staring at me, making me feel like a million dollars, and before I ask what's going on he finally responds, "I'm not leaving."

"What?" I ask, my confusion likely matching his as I turn to face him.

"I said, I'm not leaving. Well, unless you want me to. But right now, I would really like to get your duvet and snuggle up on the sofa to watch Peaky Blinders." He points at my t-shirt, Tommy Shelby looking back at him, with a cigarette hanging out of his mouth like the badass motherfucker he is.

I look for any sign of uncertainty, but his eyes are as bright as ever and the smile on his face is mesmerizing as he slowly steps towards me. I don't know what the fuck this is between us, and I know I might regret it later, but I don't want him to leave.

"Okay," I answer as he wraps his hands around my waist, looking deep into my eyes as if he's exactly where he wants to be. "But if you don't get fat eating ice cream with me while we watch it, then you can forget it." He kisses the corner of my lips, and I remember what this little shit did. "And we need to discuss the fact that you broke into my room, Aiden."

The puppy dog eyes he gives me means he won't take whatever I say seriously, but I'm speaking to Luna and Rafe about upgrading the actual locks on the damn door. I'll worry about all that later though, for now, I'm going to enjoy my post-orgasmic bliss.

KC KEAN

SEVENTEEN

Aiden

Sinking beneath the water, I try to clear my brain, but it's no use. Red hair and a sassy mouth consume my mind. What the fuck is wrong with me? I never give anyone my number, no matter how good of a time we may have had. Yet I practically threw it at Jess, along with a warning to make sure she used it.

I told myself it was because I only got to kiss her at the party on Friday, but when I pulled her in close again at lunch yesterday, I knew there was more to it than that. I know I shouldn't have picked her lock, but I didn't want to give her a chance to dismiss me. I won't do it again. She's just addictive. I could see it in her eyes, she thought once I fucked her, I would go, which is why she's holding me at a distance, and it won't do.

After I got a taste of her heaven, I could have fucked her into next week, but I know she would have cut me off completely after that, and I'm just not ready. So, I finished myself off, giving me an excuse to continue chasing her. The way she knows what she wants and doesn't hide behind words she thinks I want to hear, makes me want to drop to my knees and bring her to climax over and over again. Especially with the cries that pass her lips and the way she begs so good. Now, I need to figure out which tutor she's connected to because I know there is something there, and she didn't deny it. I want to know who else holds her attention.

Pushing my feet off the bottom of the pool, I gasp for breath when I reach the surface. The swimming pool here at Featherstone Academy is better than the one back at high school. It's the only reason we come out to the Combat building, and it surprises me that nobody else cares to come here, but it suits me better. There's only Trudy and me here, like usual, which means I can swim until my lungs burn and forget about whatever is bothering me.

Swiping my hair back, my mind goes back to last night when I convinced her to watch TV with me. I'd have watched anything just to spend more time with her, but her t-shirt gave me the inspiration I needed to convince her. Sitting on the sofa together, eating ice cream and engrossed in the show, I could have stayed all night. So, I was surprised when she finally kicked me out, but I made sure to leave her breathless before I did.

"Aiden, are you okay?" Trudy asks from behind me, and I shake my head out of the memories replaying in my mind.

"I'm fine, Tru," I murmur. I don't know what I am, confused for sure, but I don't need to be discussing that with Trudy.

"Are you sure? You know I can feel your confusion from here?" Swimming closer to me, I sigh. She reads me like a book every time I have something going on in my mind, and I'm sure it's that twin shit. I just don't seem to get it like she does, and I know she won't let this drop until I talk to her.

"I am confused, Tru, but I don't really know why. Don't worry about it." Her hand lands on my shoulder, and my best friend in the whole world, my sister, gives me that damn look that tells me I'm going nowhere until she gets more details.

"My spidey senses are telling me this has something to do with Jessica Watson."

"How do you fucking do that?" I question, gaping at her and her big mouth with a calculating mind. She just smirks at me for a moment, before giving me her serious look.

"Let's be honest, Aidy, you're going to be moving on to the next conquest by the end of the week. Don't get mixed up with someone so close to the Aces because when you break her heart, that's who she'll turn to, and I'd rather not lose my brother over a girl."

"I haven't thought about dick since Friday," I blurt out, even making myself cringe, but it's the truth. Usually, once I've felt the touch of a female, my cock is itching to brush up against another, but I've had nothing. "I mean, I still love the D, but I haven't craved it like I usually would." Trudy remains frozen in place at my words as I rake my hands through my hair. "What? You wanted to talk about it."

"But that's more details than I needed," she grouches, but I just shrug my shoulders.

"So, what is it you think is going on between you two?" She asks, and isn't that just the million dollar question.

"She thinks I'm a player."

"You are a player," she responds with a frown, and I flip her off.

"Well, she told me I could leave yesterday."

"Okaay?"

"And I didn't want to."

"You ... didn't want to?" I nod in response, waiting for her advice, but she just continues to stare at me blankly, as if I'm talking a foreign language.

"Help me out, Tru. Everything is about sex, everything. Which is why I'm stuck with you as my best friend because, ya know, that'd be gross." She fake gags and I shudder along with her. "But everyone else is just sex. Yesterday, I practically begged her to watch TV with me, so I didn't have to leave. I even sat eating cookie dough ice cream. Let me tell you that should be no one's favorite, especially when there is chocolate fudge brownie out there," I say exasperated, and Trudy just fucking laughs.

Clearly seeing the distress I'm in, she stops, tilting her head as she looks me over. "I don't know what you want me to say, Aidy. You seem confused because there is someone you actually want to spend time with in a non-sexual manner, which is new for you, but you just need to be careful. I know your reputation, and you *always* lose interest, bear that in mind."

My shoulders sag with my annoyance at her words. I don't want to hear that, as much as it's the truth. Offering a single nod, I turn and head for the steps. The water no longer offers me the calmness I'm looking for. Grabbing my towel, I rub my hair and throw it around my neck. Glancing at her peach towel on the table next to me, I look over my shoulder at her and grin.

"Don't you even think about it!" She yells, but it's too late. The towel is already sailing through the air and splashing into the water. "Aidy! You're such a dick!" I simply wink and stroll for the locker room. Just as I'm about to step through the door, she calls my name, halting my step. Looking over my shoulder, she smiles softly. "I'm sorry, okay. Maybe I'm wrong, and if I am, at least half-baked ice cream is a thing, right?"

Frowning at her words, I shake my head and step into the locker room, surprised when I find Maverick Miller, the Combat tutor, stepping out of the showers. I know his workspace is in this building, along with his office, but

I'd assumed he would have had his own shower room or something.

His usually messy brown hair is swept back off his face, and my eyes catch on a droplet of water as it trails a path down his abs. I can quite happily guess what this man is packing behind the towel around his waist, but as I finally bring my eyes to meet his, he's already glaring at me. Clearly, he doesn't like a guy checking him out, noted.

Turning my back to him, I walk in the opposite direction of the showers, to where my locker is. Deciding it'd be better to shower back in my room, I slide my swim shorts off, drying myself quickly with the towel and stepping into my grey basketball shorts and white t-shirt. Slipping into my running shoes, you could hear a pin drop in here. It's that quiet, but I refuse to turn around to address him. That's when I remember he was one of the tutors from yesterday when Jess ran off. They were both looking at her with hunger in their eyes, but I don't know which one made her run when I stepped out of the restroom. Wrapping my wet swim shorts in my towel I throw them in my backpack, when he finally speaks.

"What were you doing with Watson yesterday?" He growls, breaking the silence, and I turn to look at him.

"That's not really any of your business now, is it?" I answer, clenching my fists at my sides. Who the fuck is this guy? He hasn't put any clothes on, still glaring at me with the towel wrapped around his waist as he steps closer, his finger pointed in my direction.

"Listen here, motherfucker. You keep your hands to your damn self, or…"

"Or what? You're gonna spank me? Newsflash, I'd like it. Now, are you done?" I interrupt, as he comes to stop right in front of me, chest heaving as he tries to calm himself. He's so close I can feel his breath against my face as we almost stand nose to nose. He's slightly taller than me, only a few inches, but he makes it feel much more the way he crowds me.

"Hurt her, and I'll snap you in half," he growls, and I grin. I can't tell what's getting under his skin more, the fact I'm close to Jess, or me in general. But I love to fuck with people, and this dick is just asking for it.

Maintaining my position, I angle my head back ever so slightly. "Roger that, boo," I answer before brushing my lips against his. Grabbing my bag, I don't wait around for him to explode at me. Rushing for the door, I slip out without a backward glance.

Fuck, I know I said I hadn't craved any dick since kissing Jess, but I could definitely spend some time wondering what he's carrying around with him. Assholes always have the best dick, including me. I grin, adjusting myself as I start the long jog back, leaving the Club car for Trudy to take.

KC KEAN

EIGHTEEN

Jess

Parker wraps his arm around my neck, holding me firmly in place. "Get out of my hold, Jess," he says calmly, and I take a moment to register his stance behind me and remember how Luna said to get out of this position. Standing in the far corner of our Combat class, I was relieved when Maverick paired me with Parker and placed Reece at the opposite end of the open space to me. He doesn't know half the shit I've been dealing with from Reece, but he's making sure to keep him as far away as possible from me, and I appreciate it.

"Luna told me to grab on to my attackers nuts, and pull

them fuckers until you hear a pop," I say sweetly. Parker's hold around my neck instantly slacks, allowing me to bring my elbow back and hit him in the stomach, winding him, so I can spin out of his hold and turn to face him.

"Damn, Jess," he groans, and I can't help but smile. Just as I'm about to respond, I hear Maverick from behind me.

"We're supposed to be sparring, not fucking training self-defense. Go and give Luna a break and spar with Roman, Parker," Maverick orders, but he doesn't move until I nod that I'm okay. Well, I hope I am. Once Parker is completely out of earshot, I turn to glare at Maverick, folding my arms over my chest as I do. I refuse to check him out while he can see me do it, he does not need to know I think he's hot as hell even when he's a dick to me.

"Can I help …"

"No attacker is going to give you that much time to consider your actions."

"I didn't say …"

"Let's go again. This time you need to react instantly if we're going to have any chance of building your strength and fighting ability, other than a slap across the face of course."

All I can do is gape at him. How fucking rude is this

guy? "Fuck you, jackass," I seethe. "How dare you belittle me! Every time there is a conversation between us, it consists of me attempting to talk and you cutting me off with some bullshit, like I'm not a human being. You don't know me, anything about me at all. You don't get to touch me, because I have enough respect for myself to know when someone means you harm." I know my words are likely harsher than needed, but he brings out the pent-up anger in me. "You prove just how weak you are, being harsh to others, it's gentleness that requires strength," I add, and I don't think he likes that.

Crowding my space, he glares down at me, keeping an inch between our bodies, and my heartbeat pounds in my ears. My nipples pebble as I smell his signature sandalwood and leather scent, but my brain is screaming at me to push him away.

"Ahh, but if I was to slip my fingers in your panties, just like West or Aiden, you'd let me wouldn't you?" Fire blazes in his eyes and I don't know what this guy's fucking issue is.

My face burns bright red, but I refuse to back down. "I want them to touch me. I want them to bring me to the edge over and over again. I want to taste them," I purr, surprised by the confidence in my words, watching my words wash over his face, his pupils dilating before me as his breathing becomes heavier. "But I wouldn't even offer you mouth to mouth if you needed it because you make me feel like nothing, and I've had enough of that in my life already. I know my worth, even if you don't. So, fuck you."

Before he can consider responding, the bell sounds and my shoulders sag in relief as I instantly step back and head for the locker room, not looking over my shoulder to search for Luna, just wanting to put as much space between Maverick and me as possible.

Not wanting to change again and end up here any longer than is necessary, I throw my uniform in my bag, except for my blazer, which I put on over my sports bra. Luna steps up beside me, doing the exact same, and we're ready to go.

West hasn't messaged me yet about tonight, but I don't want to check my phone in front of anyone here, so I follow Luna's lead as she heads for the guys who are already waiting outside.

"You're riding with me, Jessikins. Let's go," Oscar says with his arms out wide as we join them, and I groan internally because he annoys the shit out of me on purpose.

"Even I can tell you're pissing her off with your presence alone right now," Kai says, making me smile slightly at his observation. "I'll ride with you, save you from the stupid idiot." Walking towards the front Rolls Royce, I climb in the other side, giving Oscar the finger before I do and slamming the door shut, hoping he doesn't chase after me.

It's not often I ride with Kai, but I love it when I do because he doesn't pester me or try to make small talk. He does his thing, and I do mine. So I know I can pull my phone out and check my messages in the car. When my screen brightens, I'm surprised to find messages from West, Aiden, and an unknown number. The sight of the unknown number reminds me of the note stuck to my door yesterday. A tremor of fear rushes through my body, leaving me anxious and paranoid, trying to discreetly look around to check if someone is watching.

I still have no idea who could have even put it there. I don't want to worry anybody with this, everyone has enough going on already. Luna doesn't need to deal with my anxiety over someone playing pranks. I wish Aiden didn't know, but he doesn't seem to have mentioned it to anyone, so I'm okay for now. Focusing on the messages in front of me, I try to take my mind off it, answering as I go along.

Grey Fire: Hey, beautiful. What are you doing tonight?

Me: I have plans tonight, Aid, and you better not be in my room when I get there!

Deep Blue: Sunshine, I should be there around seven. I'm set with the movie. I just need to know what you'd like to eat from the Italian place?

Me: Hey, seven is great. I would kill for their lasagna right now, please. See you soon.

Unknown: I'm sorry.

Focusing on the unknown number, I try to figure out who is trying to apologize to me.

Me: Who is this?

It feels like I'm waiting forever for a response, as the

three little dots appear and disappear repeatedly until a text finally comes through.

Unknown: Maverick

Holy shit. Maverick fucking Miller has my number and is apologizing. Is he for real? Quickly adding him to my contacts as Deep Storm, I text him back.

Me: How the hell did you get my number? And an apology via text DOES NOT COUNT!

Ha! Take that, asshole. I sigh in frustration as I throw my phone in my bag. Kai glances over at me, but I pretend to not notice as we slowly come to a stop outside of Ace. I feel a boost of confidence in myself for not accepting his apology so quickly. In fact, if he even messages me back, I'm not going to respond. I'm going to enjoy my evening, like I deserve.

Climbing from the car, Luna is there instantly, wrapping her arm around mine as we head for the lobby. "Do you want to come up to my room with the guys, do some work and eat some pizza?" She asks, and it kills me on the inside to turn her down, knowing I'm going to lie about why too.

"I'm actually going to have a bath, relax, and read, if that's alright? Today feels like the longest day ever," I answer, and she smiles softly in response as we step into the elevator.

"Of course. I just don't want you to feel like you're not important because these douches are here, okay?"

"Hey, I heard that," Oscar chimes in, and Roman slaps him around the back of his head making me grin wide, sucker deserves it.

"Like I would let that happen," I answer, and as the doors open on the second floor, I step out. Coming to a stop in front of my door, I turn back to see Roman's arm stopping the elevator door from closing so they can watch me enter my room. Shaking my head, I step in. Rafe said the updated locks would be done tomorrow, so I check through every room to make sure that no one, especially Aiden, is in here.

Happy I'm alone, I put the chain on the door, kick my heels off and grab my kindle. If West isn't getting here for a few hours, then that means I can carry on reading about my current favorite hot biker boys who are a part of the Ruthless Brothers.

West

Holy shit, I don't think I've ever actually been this nervous, and I've done some life-threatening things in my life, but this has my heart pounding. With the bag of hot food in one hand, and a bag full of treats and a bouquet of flowers in the other, I can't figure out how to knock, so I lightly kick the door.

The door swings open after a few moments, and I'm left speechless as her smile stretches out across her face when she sees me. Standing before me in a loose black dress with little white flowers scattered around it that sits midthigh and shows a little cleavage, she looks stunning. Her red hair is wavy over her shoulders, her lips shiny with lip gloss, and I'm already desperate to find out what flavor it is.

"Hey," she says softly, opening the door wider as she steps back, letting me in.

"Hey, sunshine. You look stunning," I finally say, picking my jaw up off the ground. The blush in her cheeks at my compliment makes my heart beat rapidly, and I can't get enough of this feeling. Being in her presence makes me feel more alive than anything I've had to do for Featherstone. "These are for you."

Handing her the bouquet of flowers, she holds them to her nose, smelling the floral scent like it's her favorite task to do. "Thank you so much, West. Where did you even manage to get hold of coral roses?"

"I know people in places," I answer with a wink as she leads us to the kitchen. "How did you know they are coral and not just light pink?" I ask curiously, placing the bags on the dining table.

"My mom is obsessed with the smallest of details, and this is possibly the only subject I was happy to learn. The fact that flowers have their own meanings and language blows my mind." I love how open she is, and how natural this feels, being here with her. "But the real question is, do you know what coral roses mean?"

Opening a few cupboards, she finally finds a vase. Thank god, I forget this isn't her original room, and it seems she's still finding things. Stepping up beside her at the sink, I take the vase from her hands and turn the faucet on letting her focus on the flowers.

"When I mentioned all of this to my Grandmother she

broke it all down for me. It was eye-opening for sure," I say, turning to face her with a wide grin on my face, loving how her blush deepens. God, it's addicting.

"Desire, huh?" The twinkle in her eyes surprises me, the brazen confidence coming from her lips doesn't match the tinge of her cheeks, and it makes me love it even more. Leaning forward slowly, placing a gentle kiss on her cheek, I whisper in her ear.

"Like you wouldn't believe, sunshine."

Feeling her shiver against me has my cock jerking to attention, but that isn't what tonight is about right now. Putting a little distance between us, I open the bag of food. "So, would you like to sit in here and eat, or would you prefer to watch the movie at the same time?"

"Do I get to know the movie before I make a decision?" Pulling it from the bag, I turn to face her holding it up for her to see, nervously waiting for her reaction. "Oh my gosh, don't tease me with DC comics right now. Wonder Woman is my girl, and I haven't seen this movie yet! I freaking love it!" Moving it closer she takes it from my hands. "Definitely dinner and the movie at the same time. I'm too excited to wait."

"I'm just glad you're not kicking me out for being a

little classic with the DVD," I say with a grin.

"I love the DVD, if anything you get brownie points for it," she murmurs, her eyes lighting up as she glances at me.

"I'll take all the brownie points I can get, sunshine," I respond honestly. The way I feel from making her happy is intoxicating. I want to make her smile like this all the time. Her hand strokes up my chest slowly, as her gaze finds mine. Curling her fingers around my neck, she lifts up on her tiptoes and brings her lips to mine. The softness of her plump lips seems to stop time as she invades my senses. The raw need I feel for this girl is something else. Finding her waist, my hands grip her tight and pull her in closer, making the most of this moment between us.

Slowly pulling back, my lips follow hers, wanting just a little more, and she giggles softly against my lips. Her thumb suddenly brushing where we were just joined, and I miss the contact already.

"Why don't you put the movie on while I plate the food?" Only able to offer a nod in response, I take the DVD from her hands and slowly back away, trying to shake the fog of desire from my brain. Thankfully, the entertainment system is like the one in my apartment, so I easily set everything up, and we're good to go when she walks in with our plates.

Smiling as I pass her, I quickly run back into the kitchen to grab the sweet tea I brought with me and grab two glasses from the cupboard. Joining her on the sofa, she's dimmed the lights and lit a few candles on the coffee table, and everything feels perfect.

Jess hits play on the movie, and we both sit with our eyes glued to the television as we devour our food, barely any space between us. I had to get a lasagna like Jess did, it's the best I've ever tasted, and you never pass on the opportunity to eat yourself into a food coma. The silence that surrounds us is surprisingly comfortable, but the occasional moan that passes her lips has me going crazy.

Relaxing back on the sofa, our empty plates on the coffee table as we watch Wonder Woman. Clearly going with girl power worked in my favor. My arm around the back of her neck as her palm warms my thigh. As much as I love the movie, I want to get to know her more too, and as if she can read my mind, Jess turns to face me better.

"It's just dawned on me that you're a tutor here. I guess because you're not directly my tutor it didn't enter my mind, but is this actually an issue?"

Stroking a loose strand of hair behind her ear, I answer her. "No, not really. Some may frown upon it, but there aren't any rules or regulations against tutors and students dating or even being bound by marriage. Featherstone operates slightly different from other educational institutes if you hadn't noticed."

Smiling up at me, she rolls her eyes. "Well, I would never have noticed if you hadn't mentioned it." Glancing down at her hand, I can feel her wanting to say more, but I don't push, waiting for her to do so when she's ready. "I don't know what this is, West, but I don't want Luna or the guys to find out."

Her words make me frown. "I know you mentioned other guys, Jess, but I want more with you. However that looks." Finally meeting my gaze again, she smiles softly.

"I want to see where this leads too, and if it goes in the right direction, I'll tell them, but right now, I want this to be ours." I can understand her logic, and I can respect her enough to agree, but I don't want it to be forever.

"I can do that." Her shoulders relax in relief, and I'm glad I'm able to set her mind at ease. "Can I ask about the others?" I don't say what specifically, but she nods in understanding.

"Uh, well, you saw Aiden the other day. I think I'm his latest chase, so he might be around for a hot minute and then gone again," she murmurs, but any guy would be fucking crazy to step back from this girl. "The other guy is a complete dick, to be honest, so that's irrelevant, but this is important to me."

"What is, sunshine?" Squeezing her hand against my thigh in comfort as she rests her head against my arm.

"Guys, plural." Taking a deeper breath, her eyes close as she tries to find the right words. "I have lived the past eighteen years pretty lonely. Valerie was my friend when I was younger, and I have Luna now, who comes with some of the most annoying guys that ever existed. But I see them, and I read about similar dynamics in my books and I crave it." Her eyes frantically search mine, making sure I'm not getting mad before she continues. "I have so much love to give, West, I know I do, and I need every kind of love language possible. Which is too much for one guy to handle, I know that. I'm trying to find who I am and I'm probably rambling, I just …"

Tilting her chin up, I crush my lips to hers, cutting off her little speech when I feel like she's about to doubt herself. When I feel her soften under my touch, I rest my forehead against hers. "Sunshine, I just want you to be happy, and to be a part of that for you. As long as nobody is a nobhead, I'm good. I have a demanding job which means I can't always be here. So, knowing there would be someone else to protect what's important to me, really makes me feel better."

I mean what I say, and the hope in her eyes makes me want to go and knock some sense into this Aiden guy and the one she's dismissing as an asshole. Neither of us asks any other questions. Instead, our eyes fall back on the movie. At some point we lay on the sofa, and Jess pulls the blanket from the arm to cover us, and just like that, we make complete rookie errors as we fall asleep peacefully together. Not exploring more between us for the night. How can you do something for the first time, and have it feel like the most natural thing you've ever done?

RED

KC KEAN

NINETEEN

Jess

Placing my Kindle in my bag, I stretch out my body. I've been curled up on a bench behind the Ace block reading, since we got back from Kai's birthday lunch. I could see the sadness in his eyes, and I noticed nobody wished him a happy birthday, so I didn't either. Luna has taken him out to her secret garden to spend the afternoon together. So, I get some peace and quiet with a healthy dose of fresh air.

Time to read, and contemplate what has happened this past week with West and Aiden. Aiden has been blowing up my phone wanting to see me since he found out I was busy on a date with West the other night. While West has been pretty quiet. He mentioned he was having to go away to do some work for Featherstone, and I didn't want to ask what or why. I know we all have our role to play here, but I have to remind myself that West has already graduated and has a role within Featherstone, as well as being one of the next in line to become a member of The Ring when his Grandmother steps down. I haven't asked him how all that works, or if his parents are going to move up the rankings first, but if this leads somewhere, I'll eventually know.

I loved getting to know him better, and his attention to detail with the flowers gave me butterflies. Desire. I feel it too, rooted deep in my veins. West has a way of making me feel special, like he smiles when he sees me happy, and I've never felt that before. So, when I fell asleep in his arms on Thursday, I was so mad at myself, yet I still felt like I was floating on cloud nine. I really wanted to see how deep our connection would feel, skin touching skin as our breaths mingled together between us, but I would have to wait a little longer for that.

The message on my phone that has held my attention the most has been from Maverick. Pulling up the messaging app, I cast my eyes over it again, still not finding a good enough response to send back.

Deep Storm: It doesn't matter how I got your number. Tell me what would count as an apology.

I couldn't seem to bring myself to tell him to fuck off. As much as I didn't know what an acceptable apology would look like, I knew I wanted one. A small part of me was drawn to him, despite his cruel approach at times. The way his stormy brown eyes swirled with a mixture of pain and need, made me want to look closer. Like a cliché moth to the flame, I couldn't look away.

My phone vibrates in my hand, making me jump as a text message comes through. This time from Aiden.

Grey Fire: Get ready to open the door. I'm coming up!

What the hell? This is obviously what I get when I deny him for so long. I haven't seen him, except in passing, since he left the other night, and I'm excited to see him too. Straightening my pale blue oversized chunky-knit sweater, and brushing off my black skinny jeans, I run around for the staff door of Ace. Lifting my bag over my shoulder, I slip my phone into my pocket quickly, and head down the hall to the lobby, my eyes set on the stairs. Climbing them two at a time in excitement, I step onto my corridor, and he isn't here yet.

Fluffing my hair, I drop my bag at my feet so I can open the door. As soon as it's unlocked, I glance down to pick my bag back up, hooking my arm through the strap, but frown when I see a piece of paper hanging out of the pocket. Slowly crouching to see what it is, I don't recall why it would be there. I can't stop the tremble in my fingers as I slowly pull the folded paper open. Thick black capital letters fill the page with my warning.

I'VE WARNED YOU ONCE,
I WON'T DO IT AGAIN.
KEEP THE FUCK AWAY FROM THEM.

Is this linked to Aiden, or West? It must mean one of them because no other guys have been here.

Without warning, hands grip my waist lifting me off the ground, and I scream in a blind panic as I'm lifted off the ground. On instinct, I swing my elbow in the direction of my attacker, making contact at their throat.

"Woah! Woah, Beautiful," they splutter. "It's me, Aid," he grunts, with his head buried in my shoulder. "I'm sorry, I didn't mean to scare you."

Wait, what? Forcing my eyes open, Aiden steps into my room and kicks the door shut behind us. Holding me against the door, our bodies pinned together, my heart rate begins to slow.

"Oh my gosh, I'm so sorry!" I cry, dropping my bag, and holding him tight against my body as I try to catch my breath.

"Jess, is everything okay?" He asks, leaning back and stroking his thumb across my cheek in concern.

When I'm sure he's okay, I answer him. "I, uh, I just found another note in my bag," I murmur, still trying to catch my breath as I hold it up to his face. I watch as his eyes quickly scan over the words, before his frowny face looks back at me.

"Did you tell anybody else about the first one?" I shake my head in answer, and he holds me against the door with one arm as he pulls the paper from my hands and throws it over his shoulder. "We can worry about all that in a minute. Let's get you calmed down, alright?"

I don't utter a word in response as I let him carry me into the kitchen, placing me down on the countertop beside the fridge. Releasing me he searches in the fridge and emerges with a can of soda moments later.

"I think you're in a little bit of shock, beautiful. I didn't help with that, I'm sorry, but some sugar should help." Opening the can, he hands it to me, encouraging me to bring it to my lips like I'm a child, but I'm grateful for his help right now.

"I'm useless, Aid," I whisper when I finally feel a little less shaken, refusing to look anywhere but at my hands.

"Hey, you're not useless, Jess. This is some weird shit. Anybody would react this way if they were getting threatening letters." His palms come down on the countertop on each side of me as he crouches down, forcing me to meet his eyes.

Finally seeing him, I get lost in his grey eyes for a moment before I take in his hot look for the day. I forget how stylish he can be when I see him in his uniform so much. Tight black jeans with a fitted black tee, and a red and black checkered shirt over the top, make him totally lickable.

"Are you checking me out, Jessica Watson?" He asks

with a grin, and I can't deny it because I definitely am, so I simply hum in response.

"You are way too stylish for your own good sometimes," I finally say, smiling as I run my fingers up the open buttons of his shirt.

"Trudy says it's the first sign she thought I was at least bi-sexual, because I had way better dress sense than she did, and she was super into sterotyping back then," he says with a grin, but I shake my head.

"Your sexuality does not define your dress sense." His hands stroke up my thighs, gripping my ass and pulling me closer to him.

"I know that, and you know that." Placing a kiss to the corner of my lips, I shiver at his touch. "And the fact that my sexuality doesn't seem to be an issue for you only makes me crave you more."

His admission surprises me. "I mean, I get it. Dick is life." I shrug as he grins at me. "I grew up with set expectations on what a woman should say or do, and I'm trying to break that mold. I want to be myself, whoever that is, so I would never judge anyone else for their choices. Besides, if you saw my porn search…"

I purposely don't finish my sentence, letting him

come to his own conclusion as he gapes at me in surprise. He stands tall, his eyes full of questions, but he frowns suddenly, when he looks to the right. Following his gaze, I freeze. My beautiful flowers are destroyed. Ripped apart and thrown all over the sink. Gone. Stepping around him, I reach out to pick up a fallen petal, my heart sinking.

"Jess, did you do this?" Aiden asks quietly, and I shake my head in response.

"No. I, no one else has a key to get in, not even you since I added the extra locking system," I respond bleakly. "Aid, what if someone is still here?" I ask, the tremble clear in my voice.

"Don't move," he murmurs, taking off to check the rest of the apartment as I stand frozen in place. Who would do this? Break in, and ruin such a beautiful gift? "It's clear, Jess. But, you might want to see this."

Following the sound of his voice, I step into my bedroom, and I have to brace myself on the door to stop myself from falling over. My chest of drawers, specifically for my underwear and lingerie, is open, and all the items are thrown across the room.

Moving to my bed, Aiden nods at the wall behind me, and a sob uncontrollably passes my lips.

JUST IN CASE THE WARNING IN YOUR BAG WASN'T ENOUGH.

"Jess, we need to tell someone this is happening," Aiden murmurs, and I'm shaking my head before he's even finished his sentence.

"The only other people I can tell have enough going on already. They don't need my mess, *you* don't need my mess. I'm sorry. If you have to go, I understand." Aiden is on his feet, and wrapping his arms around me lightning fast, and I soak in his calming touch.

"I'm here for whatever you need, beautiful. I would prefer it if we spoke to someone, but I can respect your wishes, and do this your way."

My response is cut off by the ringing of my phone. Confused with who would be calling me, I pull it from my pocket, surprised to see Roman's name flashing across the screen.

"Hello?" I answer, puzzled by his call as I hook my finger subconsciously through one of the belt loops on Aiden's jeans, keeping him close.

"Jess? I need you to get up here right now. Kai just

called, something's going on. Luna and him are on their way back right now. He wouldn't tell me what was going on, but he said they needed to talk to all of us," he rushes out, and it's the slight panic in his voice that has my attention.

"Okay, Roman. I'll be there in a minute."

"Do you need me to come get you? I can …"

"No!" I say louder than is needed, glancing up to meet Aiden's confused gaze. "No, stay there in case they're close. I'll be there in a minute." I end the call, at a loss for words. What the hell is going on?

"Is everything okay?" Aiden asks as he searches my face for an answer.

"I honestly don't know. Something about needing me upstairs as soon as possible. Luna and Kai are on their way back, and it mustn't be good if it has Roman a little rattled." Sighing, I feel bad for having to leave when he's only just really got here.

"It's okay, beautiful. I get it. If Trudy called right now I would have to leave too." Holding me tighter to him. "How about, I walk you up there, and I'll come back down here and get all this taken care of? Then by the time you're back it'll be like it never happened. But we need to take another look at your security systems, okay?"

"That's sweet, Aid, but…"

"No buts, especially when your sweet voice calls me Aid. I'm a sucker for you apparently," he says with a gentleness in his eyes, and I can't bring myself to argue.

Quickly slipping into my boots, Aiden wraps his fingers around mine and pulls me towards the door. I stumble over my own feet, too caught up in the feel of my hand in his, and he stops to look down at me. I'm the one left gaping at him as I flicker between his eyes and our joined hands. Realization on what has my brain short-circuiting dawns on Aiden's face, and he frowns at our hands too. He must have done it instinctively, without actually realizing what he was doing, but the longer he stares, the tighter his grip.

Bringing our joined hands to his lips, he kisses my knuckles, and I swoon, melting into a damn puddle at his feet. His touch helps to calm the fear building inside of me. Of course he has my heart pounding in my chest, and my need to feel him zapping through my veins, even when this is all happening around me.

I swear there better be a damn good reason for me going up there when I could be down here having the time of my life. Even if it was on top of the mess my intruder made.

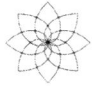

Ah, shit. I'm a bitch. The biggest, most selfish bitch, and worst best friend that ever did fucking exist.

I'm trying to focus on the television, my favorite vampire of all time on the screen, but all I can think about is Luna. Her dirtbag egg donor broke into her apartment, leaving disaster in her wake before getting the fuck out off campus. Not without dropping a bombshell or two, which should probably be expected by now, but Rafe and Luna's dad were together. Like *together* together, and with all her trauma, Luna had forgotten.

It hadn't taken long for Rafe to show up, and it will forever be ingrained in my mind the look on Luna's face as she stepped out of the bathroom and saw him. The pain in her eyes ripped me to shreds, and the way her voice broke when she cried papa still rings around in my head. But I am the biggest bitch because I sat in Roman's room, waiting for Luna and Kai to return, mad that I was missing out on some Aiden time. I feel so stupid for focusing on myself when so much shit is going on around us.

Aiden had been surprisingly sweet. Gripping my hand

tight as he walked me up to the top floor, and kissing me delicately in the stairwell before I had to go. I felt his eyes on me right up until the moment Roman shut his door behind me, and I've missed his presence ever since. He sent me a text a while ago, including pictures of my room looking exactly as it should. I made sure he kept the spare key, but I encouraged him to go home, knowing Luna needed me tonight.

I feel a little awkward sitting with Luna's guys. We're all waiting for Luna and Rafe to come down, but they needed to have a private chat beforehand. Kai is getting everything set up for us to watch whatever footage he can pull from Luna's room, so we can understand who assisted Veronica and set up the surveillance cameras throughout Luna's room.

Kai's living room is all navy and greys, not surprisingly minimal of any excessive furnishings that don't serve a purpose, and it actually feels cozy. It would feel even better if Oscar wasn't constantly moaning all the time, but that's never going to change, but knowing he's doing buzzfeed quizzes on falling in love fills me with joy. This sucker loves the shit out of my girl. He'll figure that out and tell her eventually. They all will.

A knock at the door, and soft murmurs of Luna and Rafe on the other side, has Kai rushing from the kitchen. Oscar begs for us to all keep our mouths shut about his feelings that he's trying to process as Luna moves into the room, Kai instantly wrapping his arm around her shoulder.

"What did I miss then?" Luna asks, and when I go to respond Oscar glares at me, making me giggle as I try to steer the conversation into light chit chat, even if it's only for a moment.

"Oscar's Team Damon." Pointing at the TV I smile at my number one bad boy while the guys all look at me in confusion.

"Err, what?" Luna asks, and I roll my eyes at her lack of knowledge and understanding.

"You haven't watched The Vampire Diaries have you?" I ask, but it's a statement because anybody who has knows how freaking awesome Damon Salvatore is. Unless you're team Stefan, which, meh. Somebody has to, like my friend Valerie did. I almost feel sad for my girl when she shakes her head at me. "Girl, where have you been? Damon is the bad boy player, who eventually … Actually, no. I'm going to make you watch," I decide, pointing at her sternly.

She doesn't give me a response, knowing she'll give

into me anyways. Just as quickly as the lightness had spread across the room, it diminishes while Kai sets up the footage. Making us all take a seat, I pull Luna down to sit between Roman and me. Watching in silence as Veronica, Wren, and a guy I recognize by face but not name, fill Luna's room with cameras and leave her mother waiting. We all heard through Luna's ear piece what came after that. We don't need to see it in action, everything is raw enough for her right now.

I sit back and listen as they start to form a plan, promising vengeance, and I know people will die because of this. As long as it isn't anybody in this room, I can deal with that. When Parker's father, Rico, fills the screen, I watch as Parker slowly starts to sink into himself, but I watch as everyone moves to give Roman and Luna space to soothe him, and it's a beautiful thing to witness.

Sadly, that makes Oscar come and sit beside me, and I instantly feel his eyes on me, thinking of a way to rile me up to take his mind off what's happening around us.

"Phone check," he calls out, holding his hand out between us expectantly, and my nose wrinkles in confusion.

"What?"

"Phone check. Let me see your phone to make sure

there's no flirty or dick pics going on under my nose." He raises his eyebrows at me expectantly, and I want to throat punch this motherfucker like Luna taught me, but I refrain myself, keeping my phone in my pocket.

"Oscar, I'm only going to say this once and in the nicest way possible, but, fuck off." I smile politely at him, but I watch as his eyes assess my face and the pocket where my phone is. I feel him move before he even does, and I'm quick to react, swinging my arm around his neck and pulling it in tight, effectively catching him in a headlock.

"Fuck. Jessikins, let go. You're strangling me," he whines, trying to pull his head back and I can't help but giggle. I hear a chuckle from across the coffee table, and I see Parker smiling lightly over at us. Remembering the seriousness of the moment right now, I release my hold and move further away from him on the sofa.

"Okay, so I think we need some form of trap for Wren. She clearly knows more than we do, but we can't just grab her in the middle of the afternoon. We need some form of disguise, like a party or something." Luna rubs the back of her neck as she thinks of the best plan of action. "Does Trudy usually host a Halloween party?"

"She does, they're usually pretty epic too. So, everyone

goes," Oscar says, thankfully standing up and walking over to her. The thought of the last party we went to runs through my mind, and I have to bite my lip to stop myself from smiling when I remember the first taste of Aiden's lips. Yes, I could definitely be down for another party like that. I just need to figure out how to get me some alone time.

"So, Maverick is going to help work on the tracking of Veronica, and I also advised him that Jess needs some extra training. Luna, I know you're putting the poor girl through her paces, but you need to tighten up your lessons to prepare for The Games. Maverick has agreed to come up with a training plan."

"What?" I yell, jumping up from the sofa. "That's not necessary. One of these guys can help me, right?" I ask in a panic, do not make me spend one-on-one time with that asshole. Fuck.

"Everyone else in this room is also entering into The Games, Jess. It's best for everyone to up their training. Besides, Maverick is the Combat tutor because he's the damn best," Rafe offers. I gape at him for a moment, and I know any argument I come up with will be blocked. Unless I told them how he'd acted towards me, but I couldn't go that far, especially not when I had a text on my phone wanting to know how to be forgiven.

Crossing my arms over my chest, I bite my lip, thinking of a way to bow out. "I'm getting tired. Can I go back to my room and lay down now?" I look to Luna, and she thankfully nods in response, linking her arm through mine and walking me from the room.

"Are you okay?" She asks as I unlock my door and turn the newly installed alarm off. "I know this is a lot, Jess, I'm sorry."

"No, don't you apologize. It's just been a hectic day, that's all, so the Maverick thing just caught me by surprise." Kicking my boots off, I force a smile to my lips. She has enough going on to be worrying about me as well.

"Tell me about it. I need a huge distraction from today." I can see the heaviness in her eyes, and I want to make it all go away.

"We could have ice cream and watch Pitch Perfect? Sing all our troubles away in a riff-off?" I ask, loving the sound of the idea, but not wanting to put any pressure on her.

"You know what? That would be amazing right now. Give me two minutes, and I'll be back."

"That's a different movie," I say with a chuckle, and she tilts her head to the side in confusion. Sighing, I ruin the joke by having to explain. "I'll be back is Arnold Schwarz... You know, it doesn't matter. Go do what you need to do, and I'll get everything ready."

Shaking her head at me, she closes the door to, and I get the entertainment system set up. Feeling my phone vibrate in my pocket, I glance to see a new text has just come through.

Deep Storm: You won't be able to avoid me now, petal. I know you have a free period tomorrow after Combat, so plan to stay longer. I can't wait.

Shit.

"So, Pitch Perfect?" Luna asks, catching me by surprise, and I lock my phone quickly and toss it on the sofa.

"Yes, sit. I'll grab snacks," I murmur, running to get some chips and popcorn from the kitchen. When I step back into the living room, Luna's already kicked her shoes off, and curled up on the sofa with the blanket off the back.

"Hurry up, Red," she calls out, not taking her gaze off the television as she sets everything up. Falling into the seat beside her, I push my shoes off too as Luna holds the blanket up for me to slip in.

Wordlessly, Luna hits play and I open the bags of goodies. "So, do you want to tell me more about your mom?" She asks, keeping her gaze forward, and my heart stutters at her gentle approach. Shit. I was hoping to pretend all the shit around us wasn't going on, but that's completely out of the window now. I owe it to her, to be open about my life, just like she has been open with me.

"Not really, she's vile." I sigh, wishing I'd brought a strong drink in with me too. "She is the ultimate stepford housewife of Featherstone. Everything must look a certain way, be done just right, and the end goal always leads me to a life that isn't meant for me."

"All of that kind of blows my mind. I guess that's because I grew up away from this world." I finally meet her eyes, and there is nothing but support there, which makes me feel a little better. I don't need sympathy, I need to get my life in order.

"Well, I know from the adults that surround you that they would never treat you like that," I respond, squeezing her arm as I look back at the TV "She has an extra special way of making me feel like nothing. Always analyzing everything I do, and trying to force me into the most ridiculous mold that matches her expectations."

"She definitely sounds like a class A bitch," Luna mutters, and I smile slightly at her words.

"I feel very lost, Luna. Having you as a friend has changed my life, but being here is not where I actually wanted to be. Yet, I feel relieved to be anywhere but near my mother." Linking my arm through hers, I lean my head on her shoulder. I feel like a weight is lifted from me as I voice my form of hell.

"Red, you are anything but nothing. You are everything, and I see you grow into yourself more and more every day. I am here for you, no matter who you want to be, okay? But I want to make myself very clear, if I ever see your mom I won't be held responsible for the actions I take."

I squeeze her arm extra tight, as I soak in her words. "Thanks, Captain," I whisper, and just like that, my love for this girl grows ten-fold. I just hope she never has the unfortunate pleasure of meeting Lucienda Watson.

KC KEAN

TWENTY

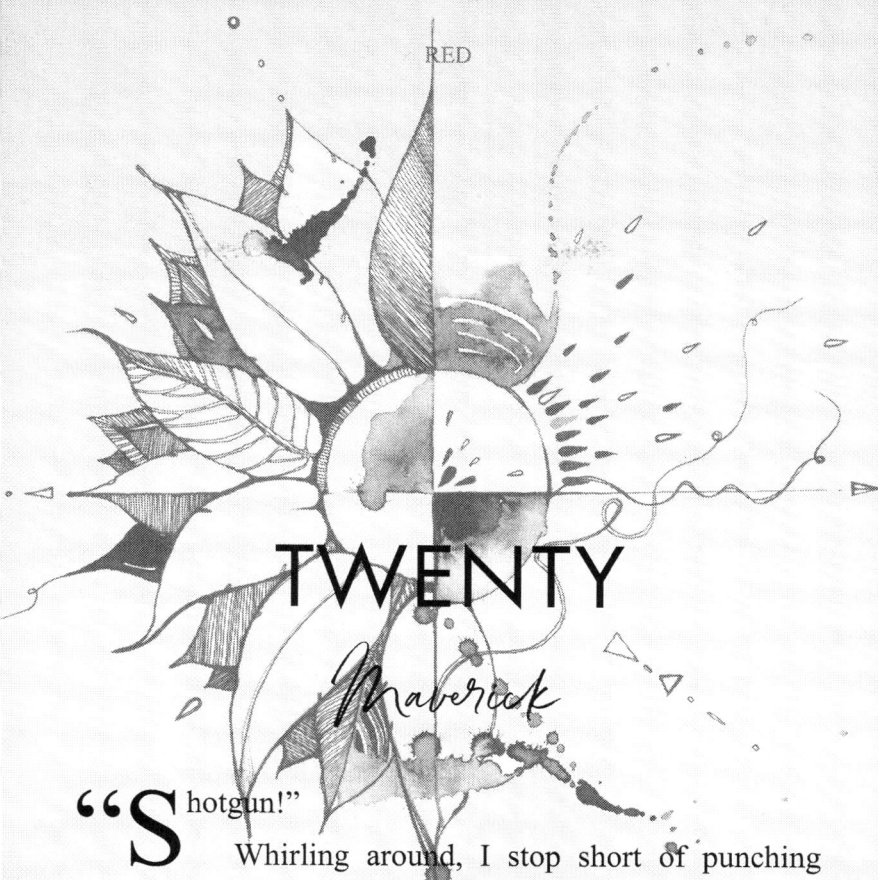

Maverick

"Shotgun!"

Whirling around, I stop short of punching whoever called out from behind me when I see it's West.

"What the hell, man. Don't fucking do that," I grunt. "And why the fuck are you yelling shotgun?"

Stepping up beside me, he nudges my shoulder with his. "So I can sit up front with you, duh."

"West, it's a fucking two-seater," I answer, swiping my finger down the side of my car door, to open the door of my matte-black carbon-fiber Tesla Roadster. Any chance this shithead gets, he'll ride with me, like he doesn't have his own fast car or motorcycle.

"You're spoiling my fun, Rick," he moans, climbing in on the other side. Taking my seat behind the wheel, I wince slightly, and I groan internally when I know West caught it. "You okay?"

"I'm fine. Just a little bruising on my ribs." Putting the car in drive, I focus on the road, hoping he'll leave it at that, but I know he'll push for more. "I was down in Petersburg again on Saturday night. They thought it would be good to test my strength against two opponents."

"Well, you obviously showed them the reason you're sent to do all the fighting," he responds with a grin, and I shake my head at him. "Make sure you take it easy today, you don't want that bruise turning into a cracked rib."

"I've got a one-on-one training session after classes today, but no one will make them any worse, West. Student or not, I'd give them fucking nightmares if they tried." Turning into the campus grounds, I drop my speed, taking us straight over to Combat and Weaponry. If we can avoid mingling with the other tutors, we do, and Mondays are perfect for that when there isn't a meeting being called.

"One-on-one? With who? Usually, you tell everyone to fuck off." I snicker at his words because they're true.

"Well Rafe set it up, and I couldn't say no."

"Why would Rafe ... Wait. Are you going to be training Jess?" He asks, turning to face me as I keep my eyes on the road, my knuckles tightening around the steering wheel. I know he didn't come home until Friday morning after going to see her on Thursday, and I want to know where exactly he touched her, then beat the shit out of him because she's mine.

After my run-in with Aiden the other day I want to strangle somebody. I've shared on occasion, even with West, but my primal instincts with Jessica make me want to pick her up and keep her to myself. Although when Aiden was trying to push my buttons and brushed his lips against mine, my dick was hard instantly. The thought of them together pissed me off until that point, then I wanted to see it and join them.

Fuck. Clearing my throat, I focus on the road and the question West is waiting for an answer to. "Yes," I murmur, refusing to meet his stare.

"Take it easy on her, Rick. She's not built for this shitty life, but she's trying to find herself amongst it all."

"She needs to be able to defend herself. Rafe asked me to get her combat skill set up as quickly as possible. So, I'll do what I have to do," I grind out, slamming my foot on the break a little too harshly as we come to a stop outside the Combat building.

"Woah. I'm just saying don't be an asshole to her. I know you, and you'll take your past out on Jess when she's just trying to find her way." His words slice through my chest, as I clench my teeth, trying to not let the past consume me, or the fact I've already been a complete dick towards her for no reason at all.

"Shit, you haven't spoken to her already, have you?" He asks, and I sigh, wiping a hand down my face in frustration.

"Of course I have. She's in my Combat class, dickhead."

"What did you say to her?" He demands, and I swing the car door open. Straightening my leather jacket as I step out of the car, he follows suit.

Glaring at him over the top of the car, I ball my fists at my side. "It's complicated." Slamming the door shut I leave, not wanting to continue this conversation, and he must know it because he doesn't attempt to follow me.

Stepping into the staff entrance, I bypass the medical center and swimming pool, heading straight for my office outside of the Combat hall. I need to calm down before class starts. Since I only have one lesson on a Monday, I show up right before, so the students will be here any minute, and I need to act like West didn't just flare up emotions inside of me. I'll act however I want to act, like I always do. I'm not going to soften myself because of some bratty girl getting under my skin. I've seen others do that before, and watched where it led them. No thanks.

Just before I make it to my office, I spot the Aces walking in, Luna and Jessica right in the middle of them. The blue in her eyes seems brighter today, and the way her hair floats around her face makes me pause. She's beautiful, and West was right, my past does make me taint her.

Her eyes meet mine, and the smallest hint of hope flickers back at me. I need to find a way to apologize, then not treat her like shit, in that order.

"Maverick, when are you starting your training sessions with Red?" Luna asks, and the name confuses me for a moment until I realize she's talking about Jessica. All of the guys stop too, waiting for my response. It seems she has got quite a support network here. Good.

"Today. After we've finished with this class, it'll be best for you to take a break, eat something small and then we can go again," I answer, looking directly at Jessica, who nods softly in agreement.

"So, you expect her to travel back here on her own, then find her way back to Ace afterwards?" Oscar grunts, clearly not impressed with my plan or treating Jessica like a grown-up apparently.

"It's fine, Oscar," Jess mutters, elbowing him in the stomach as she passes. Making eye contact with me she repeats her words. "It's fine, I'll be back here after lunch." With that, she turns and walks away, Luna follows after her, and I have to force myself to not watch Jessica's ass sway as she leaves.

"When she's in your care, she is your number one priority. Anything happens to her, and I'll be coming straight for you," Kai mumbles, and I'm surprised to see the rest of the guys nod in agreement. Rolling my eyes, I head for the Combat hall.

"You fuckers have two minutes to be ready, or I'll have you running drills for the next ninety minutes," I call out over my shoulder, not looking to see their response. What have I gotten myself into?

RED

Jess

My palms sweat as I change into a fresh pair of black sports shorts and a pink sports bra. According to Featherstone's rules, I had to change back into my uniform to go for lunch, and I didn't want to change back into dirty clothes, so I rushed back to my room for a fresh set. Keeping my feet bare, like I do when Luna or the guys train me, I scoop my hair up into a ponytail before making my way back to the Combat hall.

When I was in here earlier, Maverick kept his distance, and didn't pick apart everything I did for a change. Probably because he's going to do it now instead. I feel nervous, my stomach in knots with anxiety, but I refuse to let his attitude stop me from learning. I need this, I know I do, especially with the weird threats I keep getting.

Pushing the door open, I step into the hall and spot him in the center of the room. His head whirls around to see me when he hears the door shut behind me. Straightening my back, I square my shoulders and make my way towards him. Fake it till you make it, just like Luna taught me.

"Hey," he murmurs as I come to stand on the red mat with him, and the softness in his voice is a huge contrast to the Maverick I'm used to, making my walls melt slightly.

"Hi."

"I was thinking we'd start with you showing me what you've learned so far, then I can put a plan of action together. Is that okay?" He asks, coming to stand right in front of me, and my heart rate picks up as I tilt my head back to meet his gaze. I feel all of my five foot three inches in this moment compared to him as he towers over me.

"Sure," I respond, looking down at my feet, already feeling awkward, and I don't fully understand why.

"I'm sorry," he says and my gaze snaps to him in surprise. "You can still think of an appropriate apology. I just wanted to say it in person too." Stuffing his hands into the pockets of his shorts, he looks at me nervously. "I'm an asshole, we know that, but you didn't deserve what I said." Wow. I have never heard any guy sound so sincere in my life, and all I can offer in response is a nod of my head.

Happy with that, he shakes his shoulders out and spreads his arms out wide. Wait. "You want me to come at you?" I ask, my eyebrows pinching in confusion.

"Yeah, hit me with what you've got." He pounds on his chest, with the tiniest of grins on his face, and I look around us like someone's going to jump out and catch it all on camera.

"You're joking, right? They've been teaching me self-defense. I need you to come at me," I respond, not moving from where I stand, which just makes him roll his eyes at me.

"And I told you, my Combat classes aren't for self-defense. You may find yourself in a situation that may be easier for you to escape by attacking first. So, let's go." He's fucking serious, okay then. Taking a deep breath, I shake my hands and think about how I can adapt the moves Luna showed me in a way I can attack first.

As I step towards him, he shifts his feet to make us start circling each other. Peckerhead. "I thought you wanted to see what I could do?" I ask, frustrated, but he just grins.

"I do, but I didn't say I would take it easy on you."

Holy shit. A smart-ass cocky Maverick is a rare sight. His green eyes are sparkling with a hint of mischief, and the slight curl to his brown hair as it flops above his eyes makes me want to stroke it off his face. I'm getting too distracted, dammit.

Stepping closer, I bring my arm back, letting him see the movement like Roman taught me. I see when his arm goes to block me, which is when I push my left hand out, punching him straight in the throat as his defensive arm blocks my fake move.

Hearing him cough and splutter instantly makes me giggle as he leans over, bracing his hands on his knees, trying to catch his breath. When he finally calms his spluttering, he looks up at me, and I can't stop the wide smile from spreading over my face.

"What the fuck, petal?" He gasps, and I give him the finger, feeling fucking awesome.

"You said to come at you, you didn't say I had to take it easy on you," I answer, playing on the words he gave me only moments ago, and his eyes narrow at me. All while I try to act nonchalant with the fact he used the nickname he called me in his text and trying to dampen the butterflies in my tummy.

"Who taught you that?" He questions, standing to his full height again.

"Roman." I shrug, maintaining eye contact with him. The way he's looking at me right now makes my skin prickle.

"Good. What other moves do you have?" Bending his knees slightly, he beckons me to go at him again, but I need to get something off my chest.

RED

"Can I be honest with you, Maverick?" I ask quietly, and he drops his stance, nodding in an instance.

"I know the moves, and in a setting where you give me time to think I can execute them." Crossing my arms over my chest, I rub my arms nervously. "But I feel like the second I'm put on the spot, or in real danger, my brain shuts down and I'm left scrambling, too late to protect myself."

He moves to come and stand eye to eye with me, crouching slightly to do so. His hand settles on my shoulder in comfort, imprinting his palm into my skin. "The Pyramid?" He murmurs softly, and I sigh.

"Among other things, but that day they sent numerous people to grab me, and they only needed one. My brain froze, and when I finally came around, I was slowly being hung in front of the whole campus. I can't keep feeling helpless. I think that hurts more than the physical pain." I'm shocked by my own admission, so willing to get the words off my chest, and to Maverick of all people.

I feel like he stares at me for hours, searching my eyes, trying to rip me apart to get inside my brain. "Okay. By the time I'm done training you, these moves will be ingrained so deep into your mind you'll do them without even thinking. Understood?"

The determination in his eyes and the steel in his voice has me nodding in agreement, and before I can take a breath he moves. His arm pulls on my shoulder, turning me before pulling me against his chest, his arm lifting to wrap around my neck. I squeal in surprise, and no sooner has my back hit his chest, he's kicking my legs out from under me, my knees hitting the mat. The second they do, Maverick releases me and steps back, as my hands fall in front of me, breaking my fall.

Glaring up at him, he stands with his legs parted and his hands on his hips. "You're a dick." I pant but this motherfucker just grins.

"You basically just told me we need to work on surprise attacks, stop bitching. Let's go again."

"Give me a minute," I grunt, rising to my feet, but the second I'm standing at my full height, he's charging at me. An arm around my waist as he knocks me off my feet, I feel all the air rush out of me as my body tenses, bracing for the impact of hitting the mat. At the last second, I feel his other hand cup the back of my head, his forearms taking the force of the fall as he cradles me against his body.

It takes a moment for me to register his weight above

me, his hand still holding my waist and the other tangled in my hair. Trying to catch my breath with his swirling green eyes looking down at me is difficult. The brush of his hair against my forehead makes me acknowledge how close we are right now, staring at each other, our breath mingling between us.

I don't know who moves first but the crush of his lips against mine has my whole body reacting. My hands cup his face, holding him closer to me as his stubble grazes my skin. His mouth is brutal against mine, both of us needing more of the other. The touch of his tongue against my lips has me opening myself to him, letting him take everything from me.

I hear him hiss as my nails bite into his skin at the back of his neck, but I can't stop, my body needing to mark him as mine as he claims me with his mouth. Wanting more of his skin against mine, I claw at his t-shirt, and he lets me slip it over his head, our lips joining again the instant it's tossed aside.

"Fuck," he murmurs against my lips, and I know I have to have more of this man.

"Please, Maverick," I beg, his fingers trailing up my thigh, as his other hand holds my hip tightly. His hooded eyes peak at mine, and the desire burns brightly, matching what I feel. "Please."

The feel of his fingers stroking a path under my shorts, has my breathing falter, my eyes glued to his as he hovers above me. His fingers brush against the lace between my legs, and I know the moment his brain catches up.

"Holy fuck. Are these crotchless?" He whispers in disbelief as I bite my lip, stifling a moan as he ghosts his fingers over my clit. His eyes brighten, my choice in underwear surprising him and fueling his lust.

My hands trail over his chest and abs, ingraining every dip and hard edge to memory as he teases me. Just when I'm on the brink of begging, he slowly penetrates me with one of his fingers, and his jaw tenses when he feels how wet I am for him. Thrusting two fingers into my core, I revel at the delicious stretch as he brings his thumb to my clit.

My body feels like it's on fire from head to toe. His thick fingers working me over, and bringing me close to the edge before retreating or changing pace. Both slick with sweat, and pure primal need pulsing between us, I want it all. Just as I feel the edge of my climax approaching, I know he's going to drag this out even more, and my body can't cope with it one more time. Slipping my hand into the front of his shorts, I find the head of his cock standing tall, begging for attention, precum leaking from his pulsing length.

Squeezing my hand around him, he moans against my throat, his fingers moving erratically against my core. Grinding my hips up off the mat against his hand adds the extra friction I need as I feel my pussy clamp down around his fingers. I scream in pleasure as my body tingles with ecstasy, my orgasm crashing into me from every direction, all while staring into Maverick's eyes. My hand squeezes uncontrollably around his dick, and he gapes down at me while he makes sure to ring every ounce of pleasure from my body.

Frozen in place, we stare at each other, my hand around him, and his fingers still inside of me. My brain stumbles to find away to convince him to fuck me right now, when my thoughts are interrupted.

"Fuck sake, man. Put your dick away," I hear West grumble, and my heart seizes, but when I look in his direction, it's not Maverick he's talking to.

Standing just inside the door I entered earlier is West and Aiden. It's Aid's dick that's offending him as he stands beside him jerking off, clearly at the sight of Maverick and I. Holy shit, how long have they been standing there? Realizing he has our attention, West looks between Maverick and I, smiling softly with a slightly awkward wave of his hand. Shit. Aiden pulls his swim shorts back over his dick, but I can see his hand still tightly wrapped around it.

"Fuck," Maverick grunts from above me, and in a flash he's climbing off me, leaving my body begging for more of him, but he doesn't notice. I can see it in his eyes. The Maverick I was just with has left the building, and it's Maverick-the-jackass who stands before me right now.

"Maverick, wait," I murmur, jumping to my feet, but he's already shaking his head. I try to grab his arm, but he shakes me off. Heading straight for West and Aiden, I see West reach out too, but nothing stops him. "Maverick, please. Don't run. That's your apology." I rush out, and he stops just before the door, frozen in place. Hope builds inside of me, but as I take a step towards him, he pushes through the door and the sound of it slamming behind him ricochets around me, breaking me a little as it does.

"Is he the 'complicated' you talked about?" West asks, walking up beside me, and when I meet his gaze, I'm relieved to not see any anger or tension. It's one thing saying you are happy to share, but it's another to see it with your own eyes. I nod in response, and he wraps his arm around my shoulder. "Sunshine, he's complicated, period. It's not just you, you're gonna need to be patient with him." Tears prick my eyes. When I first heard West's voice, I thought there was about to be a fight, but instead, he gives me comfort and supportive words.

"Well, I just want to say that was hot as fuck, beautiful," Aiden says as he comes to stand on the other side of me. All of us staring at the door Maverick left through. "West, do you want to carry on the show with our girl here so I can finish fucking my hand to the visual?"

His words make me chuckle, but it's West's response that leaves me speechless. "Raincheck."

Holy shit, yes please.

KC KEAN

TWENTY ONE

Jess

I feel my phone vibrate in my pocket, but I kick my feet up on Luna's sofa, getting comfortable. I know it'll be West or Aiden messaging, and I'm still not ready to speak to either of them after they saw what happened between Maverick and me on Monday. I've done a great job avoiding them since it's now Saturday, but I've taken to hiding out at Luna's as much as possible. Not that she seems to mind. She's supposed to meet some special agent with the Aces, but I'm staying put, ready for some downtime so that I can dive into my new book.

I've made great progress on my TBR list without the

guys distracting me, even if I have been a little lonely and desperate for their touch. Especially after reading the second book in the Allstars series. I still can't seem to get past how I practically begged Maverick not to run, but it made no difference. He left anyway. I feel so embarrassed for showing my vulnerability to them and letting West and Aiden see him reject me. Like I hadn't just laid myself bare for him, letting him pull me apart and bring me to climax. Fuck, I'm letting the old me, and not the new and improved *Red* handle this situation right now.

I need to rein my feelings back in, I'm letting them all get under my skin, and I'm leaving myself exposed. They seem to have the power to destroy me, and I still haven't finished piecing myself together since getting out of my mother's clutch, so I don't want to give anyone that level of power again.

"Red, are you sure you want to stay here on your own? You can come with," Luna asks for the tenth time, but I just shake my head.

"What and spend my time sitting in the truck with this group? No thanks, I have better things to do with my time. Like eat all your snacks, pretend to do this work, and watch TV." I look at her, putting on my best smile as I point to my assignments laid out on the coffee table. There is no way I am actually going to do any of it, but these guys don't need to know that.

"Bye, Jessikins," Oscar shouts, but I don't answer him. Instead, giving him the middle finger and making everyone laugh. The door shuts behind them, and I sigh in relief. Pulling my backpack close, I rifle through my bag for my Kindle when I feel my phone vibrate again. My heart stops when I see Aiden's message.

Grey Fire: Beautiful, I'm done with you avoiding me. Now I know everyone just left and you weren't with them. So, you're either ignoring my knocks on your door, or you're in someone else's room. Do I need to come and find out?

Shit. He can not come up here. Luna's security system won't recognize his face, and I'll have them all back here in minutes, with Rafe frantic on the phone too, if Luna isn't here to override the system with whatever techy stuff she does.

Me: Fine. Just wait there. I'll be there in a few

minutes.

The message barely sends before he's responding, and I want to poke his eyeballs out.

Grey Fire: I'm counting.

Asshole. Throwing my phone in my bag, I pack up all of my assignments and store my Kindle away. Annoyed I'm not going to be able to read like I had hoped. Heaving my bag over my shoulder, I make sure to lock Luna's room up properly before taking the stairs down to mine. When I step out of the stairwell and see Aiden, he's leaning back against my door, foot propped up behind him and a baseball cap on his head, I'm at a loss for words. He should not be allowed to look this good.

"You took your time," he mutters with a raise of his eyebrow, and I just glare, refusing to offer him an explanation. I know he hasn't done anything, but he's demanding, and I don't need that right now.

Pulling my key from my pocket to open the door, he doesn't move from his position, and the heat radiating off him has my pulse pounding in my neck. The hum that passes his lips tells me he knows the effect he has on me, and when I glance over my shoulder at him, his grey eyes capture mine. The pad of his thumb strokes softly over my cheek as he holds my head in position.

"I missed you, beautiful. But you don't get to avoid me for days like that again, okay?" Aiden whispers against my lips, and I can't breathe. His lips brush gently against mine, and a shiver runs through my body. Pulling back, I remain frozen in place as Aiden quickly opens the door, encouraging me inside before he shuts it behind us. Seeing him now makes me feel guilty for punishing him. I just needed some space after Maverick hurt me, but I don't know how to explain that.

"It's okay, Jess," he says, coming to stand in front of me. I love how he always crouches so he's eye-level with me. He makes me feel like an equal, like he's willing to meet me on my level, instead of always expecting me to rise to his. "You don't have to explain. I get it. I think we all needed a little time to wrap our heads around the reality of all this." His words catch me by surprise and make me feel even more guilty because I hadn't considered anybody else's feelings except my own. "Stop frowning." He smiles, smoothing his thumb over the frown marking my forehead, and I relax under his touch.

"I'm sorry," I murmur, placing my hand against his chest, feeling his heart beat rapidly.

"Don't be sorry, just kiss me." Without hesitation, I lean in to bring my lips to his. It's only a quick touch of our lips, but the passion that flares between us is electric. "Now, smile for the camera so I can show West I found you." Holding his phone out, he stands behind me, propping his chin on my shoulder as he smiles at the camera. Rolling my eyes, I do the same, giving a little peace sign as well.

"Since when have you and West been texting each other?" I ask, curious about this new change to the dynamics.

"Since the woman we're both interested in started avoiding us." His eyebrows raise at me again as he hits send on his phone.

"I wasn't avoiding you," I grumble, but he doesn't even respond, knowing that's a load of shit.

"You can spend some time with me now, make it up to me," he says with a wink, and I smile at the usual mischief in his eyes.

Dropping my bag at my feet, I kick my shoes off and link my fingers through his, pulling him towards the sofa.

"And what is it you want to do?"

"I don't care, beautiful, I apparently just need to be in your presence, and I feel better." His words make me melt. As he drops to the sofa, he pulls me onto his lap. I can feel his hard length through his denim jeans, and as I grind against him, a moan slips through my lips. "I missed the sounds you make," he murmurs against my lips, and I have to agree. Aiden squeezes my ass cheeks, and my back arches as I wrap my arms around his neck.

"I didn't actually think you would be this bothered about not seeing me," I respond honestly, and I'm stunned by the glare he gives me as he tightens his grip on my ass. I know his fingertips are going to leave bruise marks.

"That's because you seem to underestimate me and what's going on here."

Licking my lips, I stumble over what to say in response. I can sense a slight hint of hurt in his words, and that's not what I want. "I'm scared of you hurting me, Aid," I whisper, trying to offer him the same level of honesty he gives me, and that leaves him gaping up at me, clearly at a loss for words too.

Before either of us can say anymore, 'Savage', by Megan Thee Stallion, starts playing out around us, and

Aiden sighs. "Shit. Sorry, that's Trudy calling." He says it so casually, I can't help but laugh at the lyrics and the fact he assigned them to his sister.

His eyes stay on me as he lifts the phone to his ear. "Hey, Tru. I'm busy, right…" She must interrupt him because he stops short of his sentence, and his body tenses. "Trudy, calm down. I'll be there as quickly as I can."

Aiden sighs as he drops the phone to his lap and looks to the ceiling. Clearly, something is wrong, and I don't want to stand in the way of anything, so I slowly extract myself from his lap.

"Do you need me to do anything, Aid?" I offer, but he's already shaking his head.

"Thank you, beautiful, but it's all good." Standing in front of me, he tucks a small piece of hair behind my ear. "She seemed a little upset, and I don't want her to…"

"No, of course. Go, I hope Trudy's okay," I say, rising on my tiptoes to kiss his cheek, but he grips my chin and takes my mouth. Stepping back, he leaves me gasping for air, and I watch him head for the door, giving me a wink before he leaves. Flopping down on the sofa, I try to catch my breath.

What the actual fuck just happened here? Usually, I'm

the one being called a tornado, and now I think I know what it feels like to be on the other end. He rushed in here, completely obliterated my brain then had to leave unexpectedly. I need a nap. The whole thing has me exhausted. Doing an extra check around my room, making sure I'm truly alone, I do exactly that.

West

Aiden: Look who I managed to find!

I look at the photo that fills my screen of him with Jess, and my stress eases a little at the smile on her face and her cute peace sign. I can tell she's entertaining him with the photo, but the happiness in her eyes is real.

I've been worried since Monday. After Rick stormed out of the hall, and the rest of us went our separate ways, I felt the distance between us stretch. The way her pain was so evident on her face when he just walked out, broke me. She left herself raw and exposed when she practically begged for him to stay, but it didn't stop his feet from carrying him straight out of the door. There was a lot more to Rick than the harsh exterior he gave off, but I'd seen the way he looked at her too, as he brought her to climax.

I'd headed over to make sure everything was okay between them after the conversation in the car this morning, but when I'd got there, Aiden had been blocking the doorway. Dripping wet from the pool in just his swim shorts, but when I got a peek of what had his attention, I was captivated too. Nudging him into the hall silently, we watched as they got lost in each other. I thought I might have felt a hint of jealousy seeing her with someone else, but to my surprise, I was hard as steel, watching the pleasure ripple through her body. But when I caught Aid stroking himself as he watched the scene before us, I couldn't keep my mouth shut. Little voyeur.

Since then, Jess had avoided my calls and messages, and as much as I wanted to give her the space she clearly needed, one of us had to check in with her. Rafe had called me up on Thursday night, so I didn't get a chance to check in on her myself. It unnerved me a little, having to put Featherstone first, but yesterday evening I'd accessed the academy's systems and found Aiden's number. If I couldn't be there, I needed him to be, and he didn't disappoint. We seem to be on the same page, and he jumped at the chance to check in on her today.

As I pull the R8 into my car parking bay outside the tutors' apartment building, I know I need to corner the other person who had avoided me too. Maverick.

Climbing out of the car, I walk through the deserted lobby, heading straight for the elevator, not wanting to climb the four flights of stairs since I'd barely had any sleep since I'd left. Rafe had me set up with our snipers watching the Russian mob bosses who had shown up two weeks ago unexpectedly, and Featherstone expected to have eyes on them at all times. Watching them board a private jet this morning, handing the job over to the tech experts to trace their next steps, I was glad to head back to her. But as much as I wanted to crash, I needed to check in on my friend first.

Pressing the button for the fifth floor, I slump back against the glass wall at the back of the elevator, and just as the doors are about to fully close, a hand swings out, forcing them back open again. The second I see her face, I internally groan. I do not need to deal with Gina right now, or ever for that matter.

"West!" she exclaims, instantly stepping into my personal space, brushing her hand down my arm. Now, I'm trapped between the wall behind me and the crazy lady as she blocks me in. "I've missed you. How have you been? I haven't seen you in so long!"

"Uh, I've been good, thanks, Gina," I answer, short and sweet but not politely returning the question, which doesn't seem to bother her as she moves in closer, her hip pressing against mine, and her breath fanning across my neck as she strokes her hands up my chest.

Thankfully, the lift chimes, signaling we've arrived at Rick's floor, and I extract myself from her claws as quickly as I can, which still somehow manages to make her gasp like I just licked her clit. I refrain from rolling my eyes at her eagerness, not even looking back at her as I head straight down the corridor to Rick's room. Banging like I'm about to put the door through if he doesn't answer, the door quickly swings open, a glaring Rick waiting for me on the other side. But I don't want to risk our chances that Gina has followed me, so I barge in and slam the door shut behind me. I can feel him about ready to go off on me, but I hold my palm up between us, resting back against the door with my eyes closed, just like I'd wanted to do in the lift.

"Sorry, Rick," I murmur, a yawn taking over my face for a moment before I continue. "I've barely slept, then I stepped in the elevator and was cornered by Gina. I just need a second." He doesn't respond, clearly seeing the bags under my eyes and understanding the energy Gina just drained, even though I was only in her presence for less than sixty seconds.

When I finally pry my eyelids apart, he's leaning against the kitchen island to my right, looking every inch of the asshole he usually does, except his head is down as he avoids my gaze. "You gonna offer me a beer, Rick?" I ask, but he barely grunts as he stands in the exact same position.

I've been here enough to know where everything is, so I walk past him to the fridge and help myself to a cold bottle from the top shelf. Our apartments are practically identical. Mine is just a little bigger and on the top floor because of my bloodline. My body wants to lie down or sit at least, but I can feel the stress in the air around us, and I know it's because of Jess.

Placing my bottle on the island, I fold my arms as I lean against it on the opposite side of him. "Have you finished sulking?"

"I'm not fucking sulking, West," he grunts, whirling around to glare at me, and I just raise my eyebrows at him.

Fucker's sulking right now.

"Well, at least you're talking." Patting the table, I force myself to stand properly. "Have you spoken to Jess?"

"And why the fuck would I do that?" Grabbing my beer, he turns his back on me and stalks towards the sofas, unpausing the game playing on the television as he slumps back.

Clenching my hands, I try to stay calm with his short and shitty answers, but it's difficult when my protective instincts of Jess take over. "Do you even realize how broken she looked when you walked out the other day?" I grind out, and I'm glad to see a hint of guilt in his eyes. He should know how his actions impacted her. Knowing an argument won't get us anywhere, I need to say what I want him to hear, then sleep. "Listen, I just came by to say it's okay if there is something between you and Jess. That isn't an issue for me, but you need to tread very carefully in the future because I won't let you continue to treat her like that."

I watch as his knuckles turn white as he grips the bottle in his hand tightly. "Whatever, it won't happen again anyway. It was a moment of weakness, nothing more."

His words sound strained, and I know he can sense it

with the crinkle of his eyes. He's not going to listen to anything right now, too set in his ways to see what is right in front of him.

Sighing, I speak the truth. "Under the surface of your skin, you feel itchy, Rick, and it somehow disappears when she's near. I feel it, Aiden feels it, and I know you feel it too. We all do. So what are you going to do about it?"

With that, I leave, let this fucker have some food for thought.

TWENTY TWO

Jess

Stepping into the elevator on Tuesday with Luna and the guys, I can't stop gaping at them all. It's been two days, but my best friend is freaking married. MARRIED. Yet, I can't even get a guy to hang around for more than five seconds after giving me an orgasm. Well, that's a lie. If it had been West or Aiden, it wouldn't have ended there, that's for sure.

It feels crazy, looking at how far Luna and her *Aceholes* have come. I've known of these douches for years, and I never thought they'd be brought to their knees so easily, but my girl is a badass bitch. Looking at the guys, it blows my mind how I can notice slight differences in them all of a sudden.

Roman isn't constantly growling, and the gentleness in his eyes when he thinks no one's watching as he stares at Luna hits me in the gut every time. Parker seems to stand taller, if that is even possible, a new level of confidence pouring from him. Kai now openly gravitates towards Luna more than ever, wanting to show his emotions to her and touch her whenever possible, which is a huge contrast to the quiet and isolated guy he used to be. Oscar doesn't lead with his mouth as much as he used to. He looks as though he's becoming more observant, as if she's his queen, and he's willing to defend her to the ends of the earth.

I want that. Damn, do I want that.

"You're riding with me this morning, Jessikins," Oscar says, wrapping his arm around my shoulder, and I have to force myself to smile at Luna as she glances over, but I know she sees right through me when she rolls her eyes at us.

"Whatever you say, Ozzie," I murmur as the elevator doors open, and we all step out. As much as this sucker annoys me, deep down, I appreciate the way he wants to protect me too. He just has to take it to the extreme, as always.

The rain is hammering against the glass, and bouncing up off the floor, so my feet and legs in this uniform will end up soaked, but I appreciate Thomas as he stands by the door with an umbrella ready. Murmuring my thanks, Oscar takes the umbrella, holding it above us as he keeps his arm around me, trying to keep us as dry as possible. I walk as quickly as I can in these heels to the Rolls Royce and quickly climb in before Oscar, and the driver shuts the door behind us.

There's a small grey towel on the armrest, and I've never been more grateful for the attention to detail the drivers have in these Rolls. Using it to try and dry my legs, I struggle with the stockings I'm wearing since the watermarks look more noticeable, but there's no point stressing over it.

"So, how does it feel being a married man, Oscar?" I ask, hoping to avoid his annoying ways with a deeper conversation. I can't deal with him irritating the shit out of me this morning.

"Jess, I feel like a new fucking man," he murmurs with the widest grin on his face. "Do you want to see my new bloodline tattoo?" He asks enthusiastically, but when I shake my head, he gives me a pout.

"Oscar, you've shown it to me at least six times in two days. I do not need to see it again." I grin at him, not wanting to argue. It is kind of cute how attached to the tattoo he is. "I love how happy you all are, though. Which is why I need you to keep our girl safe in The Games, okay?" I murmur, letting my fear take over for a moment, as his face morphs into the lethal Ace I've not seen in some time.

"Nobody will touch her, Jess. I'll fucking gut them all, blow their dicks off, and burn those motherfuckers alive if I have to." I nod at the fierceness of his words, which surprisingly offer me comfort.

"Thanks, Oscar," I respond honestly, needing to hear the depths he will go to, to protect Luna in Featherstone's own brand of torture. Kill or be killed; it's why I want to be a nobody in this world. At least I can keep a clear conscience that way. Don't get me wrong, I want to get all stabby on Luna's mother, Veronica, for some of the shit she's pulled, but I know I wasn't made that way.

"One day, you're going to feel like this, Jessikins, and you're going to be flashing me some tattoo, and I won't even complain about it." His smile is back on his face as he looks at me. "When I allow it, of course."

What the ... this fucking guy. "Oscar Steele-O'Shay, you make me want to boil your teeth while they're still attached to your jaw," I growl, furious at his audacity. "When you allow it? Fuck off, peckerhead." I fume as the car comes to a stop outside of the academic buildings. Too mad at him to stick around, I climb out of the car without the umbrella when I notice a huge white gazebo between the two buildings.

I spot Luna at the edge of the space, taking in the scene around her, and I rush to join her, linking my arm through hers as I sneak under her umbrella. This must be the set up for the announcement of The Games that Luna mentioned this morning. Tables line the edges of the gazebo, filled with Featherstone Academy swag and pamphlets. At the opposite end, there is a small podium where Barbette Dietrichson stands, ready to address us all. Her eyes are glued to Luna though, making the other students whisper and gossip as they watch her blatantly glare.

"Good morning, my Featherstone students," Barbette calls loudly. "I'm ever so disappointed with the dull weather, especially on such a day for celebrations." This woman is bat shit crazy, for sure. Glancing around the space, my eyes fall to Aiden, who is already staring back at me. His grey eyes caress my body from afar, making my cheeks pink with nerves as I glance back to the podium.

"One day, she'll be knocked clean off her high horse," Parker whispers beside me, and I couldn't agree more. She reminds me of my mother. Always putting on some kind of performance, believing everyone is lucky to be in her presence.

"I wanted to be the one to announce to you all that The Featherstone Games have been rescheduled for next week. Monday, November second, to be precise, and I'm so excited for those of you who will participate." Raising her arms at her side, she draws everyone's attention to the tutors operating the tables under the shelter. That's when I catch sight of Maverick. There's another tutor talking to him, I think it might be Gina, the quiet History tutor, but I can't see properly from here with all the people between us. Whatever she says makes his frown deepen, and I have an overwhelming urge to make sure he's okay. Even after he disappeared on me, I can't seem to shift the pull that I have towards him.

"As you are all well aware, any member of The Ring's bloodlines will automatically be entered into The

Games. Anyone else who wishes to participate may do so at their own risk. Surviving The Games will increase your reputation, and bloodline, within the Featherstone foundation if you are not an Ace."

My heart stops at the thought. If my mother were here now, she would be pushing for me to participate if she thought it would increase her stature. The thought does give me pause though, because I haven't heard from her since leaving back in August, and I can't decide whether that's a good or bad thing. Especially now that Juliana is my guardian, she can't be happy about it, but I'm sure I'll find out eventually.

A few students edge forward, eager to participate, and I just can't comprehend their mindset. I understand Luna and the Aces have no choice, but to take that path by choice leaves my stomach queasy.

"Hearing her talk is like someone is using a cheese grater on my actual ear," I whisper, making Luna smile as chatter rises around us, and it almost feels like excitement in the air.

"You have until the end of the day to complete the forms to be entered into The Games. Any submissions after midnight tonight will not be counted. First lessons have been canceled this morning to allow you enough time to complete the necessary forms." A quick clap of her hands, and I know she's finally ready to finish her damn speech. "I will be away on business for the rest of the week, so I wanted to wish you the best of luck. Try not to die," she murmurs, glaring straight at Luna before leaving.

"Ace block, if you could come to my table, please. Anyone else wanting to participate, go see one of the other tutors!" Maverick shouts, and the sound of his voice hits me square in the chest. I need to figure out a way to get into class while Luna and the guys sign up. I don't want to be around him right now.

But I don't have a chance to flee as Luna tightens her hold on my arm and starts pulling me in his direction. "What are you doing, Luna?" I ask, but she doesn't respond. Instead, she continues to part the crowd, leading us closer to Maverick.

Luna moves around the side of the table, closer to Maverick, and I can't lift my gaze from my feet.

"Hey, have you got a minute? I have a favor to ask," Luna says, which has me confused. Why would she need a favor from Maverick? I can feel his eyes on me, but I don't move, and he must agree for her to continue.

RED

"I was wondering if Red could come and stay with you while I'm in The Games?"

"What?" I balk, my eyes crashing into Maverick's as he asks the same question, and Luna sighs.

"I need you to be somewhere safe, Jess. We both know the shit they like to pull. Maverick helped after The Pyramid. I trust him to keep you safe." My brain kicks into overdrive as I try to process what she's saying. Her hand wraps around mine as she tries to comfort me. She would never be asking me to do this if she knew any of the shit going on with me, but I decided to keep this to myself and look where that has got me now.

How the fuck do I make him say no?

Maverick

Holy mother of shit. How can the sky be falling around us, drenching everything in sight, yet she still manages to look so damn radiant? I felt her the second she climbed out of the car, and I wanted to march over there and find out what that fucker Oscar must have said to make her storm out of the Rolls Royce like she did.

Then I had to remember it wasn't my place and remind myself that I wasn't supposed to care about shit like that. Now, she stands before me, with Luna by her side, asking me to take care of her when they leave for The Games. It's obvious Jessica hasn't uttered a word about what happened between us to Luna. Otherwise, she'd be over here punching me in the face instead. The panic in Jessica's eyes as she bites at her lip tells me she wants me to say no. I should say no. I *need* to say no.

"I'm sorry, Luna. I don't think that's a good idea," I finally say, but the words burn my tongue, and the look of panic that was just in Jessica's eyes is now replaced by disappointment, and I hate that I put it there. Again.

"Oh. Okay, no worries then. I'll speak to West instead," Luna responds, her eyes widening in surprise by the fact that I said no. I watch as Luna turns to leave, ready to pull Jessica along with her, and it takes me a moment to process what she just said. Instinctively, my hand reaches out, grabbing her arm to stop her from leaving.

Turning to face me, Luna looks at me with her eyebrows pinched in confusion as Jessica slowly turns around as well, her neck and face flushed with embarrassment.

Lost in her gaze for a moment, I remember Luna is

waiting for me to speak. "West? Why, West?" I ask, trying to stop myself from frowning at the thought of her going to him next. He won't say no. West would say yes before she even finished asking the question.

"Why not? I need someone I can trust enough to keep her safe. My first choice was you, but you said no," Luna responds, and her words leave me speechless as I look between her and Jessica.

"I'm standing right here, Luna," Jessica grinds out, but neither of us responds.

"So, what you're saying is, you trust me with Jess the most?" I ask, making sure to use her nickname like everyone else. I can't stop the grin from spreading over my face as I let her words sink in. She came to me first. Me. To protect Jessica in her absence, and my gaze sweeps back to the woman of the hour. Her blush darkens before she drops her gaze to her feet. She isn't arguing against this whole situation because that would cause suspicion, and the actual thought of her in my apartment for a week straight has my dick perking up.

"Will you help or not?" Luna grunts, clearly getting fed up with waiting for an answer.

"Yes. Yes, I will." Holy shit, what the fuck did I just

say? Forcing myself to stand taller, I nod in agreement while internally questioning why I just made my life so much harder. I'm never going to be able to survive in her presence, in my personal space. Shit.

"Good. I'd rather she came to stay on Sunday after the Halloween party. I don't know when they're going to do the whole snatch and grab for The Games, so I'd like to be prepared. Red, how about you give Maverick your number? That way, it'll be easier to work things out more specifically, and we can sort out getting some of your things over."

Jessica does nothing but glare at Luna. Clearly she wasn't aware this conversation was going to happen, and was caught off guard as much as me. But seeing her snark makes me chuckle.

"Don't worry, I have her number… On file. On file, of course. We have all students' cell numbers in your profiles. I'll get it off there. Right?" I ask, backpedaling a little because I already have her number saved in my phone as Petal, now I'm the flustered one.

"Right. Thank you, Maverick. Now, show me what I need to do with all this shit here," Luna groans, and I wordlessly grab the clipboard for her. Releasing her hold on Jessica, she looks it over, and I watch as Jessica murmurs something in her ear and turns to leave. No goodbye, no see you later, nothing. Not even a last glance over her shoulder, and I watch her until she is completely out of sight.

If this hurts me, I dread to think what I did to her, but I refuse to dwell on it. Placing the clipboard on the table in front of me, Luna gains my attention. "You guard her with your life, do you understand? Nobody gets close enough to hurt her."

I nod in agreement, but what if I'm the one causing the pain?

KC KEAN

TWENTY THREE

Aiden

I love a party, a good time. Getting lost in the music and the sex. But setting all this shit up gets on my nerves. Especially since Trudy showed up to bring Luna to the back room, she would be using, then left again. Something is going on with my sister, and I don't know what. When she'd called me, while I was with Jess, she was sobbing uncontrollably down the phone, panic in her voice. I ran to her and when I showed up, Trudy was sitting on the sofa, her face void of any emotion. Since then, she doesn't seem as put together as usual. Her shoulders seem hunched over, and the perky step she always has is non-existent, nevermind the baggier clothes.

Her blonde hair was scraped back in a bun on the top of her head, and I'd never seen it like that before. Her eyes were red and swollen from crying, but she wouldn't speak a word to me. Not a single one, and I didn't know how to get through to her. So, I'm trying to give her the space she needs while taking a more hands-on approach with the Halloween party.

Usually, I just set up the sex tent and make sure the liquor is on point, but taking the weight off Trudy means I need to make sure the narcotics pass the chemical quality testing and all the other gazebos are set up just how Trudy does it. I'm currently learning how much shit I leave for her to do, and now I feel bad. I'm glad we don't have to test the narcotics ourselves, otherwise I'd get nothing done.

Happy with the bar's alcohol selection, I head over to the DJ booth, making sure everything is good to go there too when I hear Luna call out to me.

"Hey, Aiden."

"Luna," I respond with a nod, glancing around to see who is with her, and my eyebrows waggle when I catch sight of Kai up in the tree opposite the gazebo where we're standing. "And you brought some eye candy too, huh?"

RED

She laughs as she rolls her eyes at me, and I brace my elbow against the booth.

"I did, didn't I?" She smiles all dreamily as she glances at him, and I can picture this is how I look at Jess. Wait, where the fuck did that thought come from? And why am I not freaking out? Cracking my neck, I focus on responding to Luna.

"You did, but where's the brawler? I want to keep my face pretty tonight," I say with a wink, and she throws her head back with laughter, and I'm hoping that means no one is going to come at me throwing fists.

"You're good, for now. Are you okay with me putting this camera in here?" She points to the lighting system we have set up in front of the booth, and I nod in agreement.

"Whatever you guys need. Do you need help with anything else?" I ask as I stretch my shoulders out, but she shakes her head in response, focused on the task at hand.

"No, we should be all set after this. Then I have to go and meet Red so she can force me into my Halloween costume." The mention of her nickname for my favorite girl has my ears pricking to attention, and it takes a lot of effort to remain calm.

"Oh yeah? And what are you going as?" Damn, I don't

care what it is, I'm just excited Jess will be here tonight, and I need to try and get her alone.

"I have no clue. Jess won't tell me because she knows I'll say no. So, I'll have no choice but to go along with whatever she says when I get there," she answers with a shrug, and it makes me smile.

"You're soft on her." I nearly say too, like me, but I bite my lip at the last second.

"If you ever try to use that against me, I will gut you, do you understand?" Her words catch me by surprise, and I nod subconsciously.

"Like I would risk the wrath of you and your four fucking horsemen, I'm going to start calling you Apocalypse." She laughs whole-heartedly at my response just as Kai comes to stand with us, and the conversation is cut short as we take him in. God, this guy was always hot, he still is hot, but my dick is not pulsing against the seam of my jeans to get to him like it usually is. No. It only wants to do that for Jess.

"Sakura," he murmurs at Luna, and the mischief in her eye makes him frown. "What am I missing?" Kai asks and can't help but chuckle along with her.

Trying to calm her laughter, she holds her hands up

parallel to each other, moving them closer to each other before pulling them further apart.

"Nothing, handsome. It's just that Aiden wanted to know how hung you are, and I was trying to measure it out for him." Spluttering on my oxygen, I burst out laughing at where she just went with that, and I can't believe she just made Kai Fuse blush. Fucking blush, and I still have no movement in my pants. Jess has officially broken me.

In. The. Best. Way. Possible.

"So gorgeous, Kai Fuse. It's a shame someone has caught my attention. Otherwise, I would have been trying to convince you to let me rock your world," I add, still chuckling as Luna shoves me backward a little.

"That's not funny," she grunts, and it makes me laugh harder. I can see why Jess likes being around Luna. When you get past her 'RBF' attitude, she's fun to be around. Glaring at me once more, she pulls her phone from her pocket, and a moment later, her hand is wrapping in Kai's, and they're leaving. They're so wrapped up in each other they don't even say goodbye, and I can't say I blame them.

Feeling my phone vibrate in my pocket, I pull it out, and it vibrates again and again. What the hell is going on? Unlocking my phone, I find I've been added to some group chat, and when I click to open the messages pending, my heart starts to pound in my chest.

Maverick added you to the group chat.

Maverick added West to the group chat.

Maverick renamed group chat to The Jonas Brothers

What the fuck? I think I know why there is a group chat for the three of us, and my dick does twitch at the thought of the reason why. But why the fuck did he name the group The Jonas Brothers?

As if reading my mind, a text comes through from West.

West: I'm all for a group chat, but why The Jonas Brothers? We look nothing like Kevin, Nick, and Joe.

I smirk at his message, but I can't argue with his reasoning when Maverick's response comes through.

Maverick: Cos, you know we're all 'Suckers' for her.

Me: Agreed.

West: I can't argue with that, but I'm curious to know what made you change your mind?

It feels like it takes forever for him to respond, and just when I'm about to put my phone away, the screen lights up.

Maverick: I haven't. But I'm a smug motherfucker, and I wanted you both to know I have a house guest next week! Guess who Luna trusted to take care of Jessica while she's at The Games?

He isn't wrong. He is one smug motherfucker.

West: Fuck. We live in the same building, nobhead, I'm staying over!

Me: What the fuck? Don't be assholes. I'm packing a bag, one of you can take me in too!

There is no way in hell they are keeping her away

from me for a week, especially not since I've had huge withdrawal symptoms this week when I was giving her space.

Maverick: Fuck you, suckers.

Oh, that asshole doesn't play fair, and I know just the way to fuck with him.

Jess

Oh my gosh, I'm so excited about tonight. I love dressing up, and Halloween is one of my favorite holidays. Christmas is my number one, but Halloween is a close second. I can't get over the nerves in the pit of my stomach though, and they have nothing to do with tonight. My worry and stress are over next week when Luna and the Aces are due to begin The Games. I've heard the horror stories, and I'm scared I'm going to lose my best friend.

Shaking it off, I try to relax. Tonight is about having fun and no stress. I know Luna and her guys have a plan in place regarding Wren, and as much as I know the details,

I have no involvement, so I'm hopeful I might be able to see Aiden.

Straightening the wig on my head, I look myself over in the floor-length mirror. White closed-toe wedges on my feet cover the fact I have my stockings on. The lace at the top sits just inside the leg of my denim shorts, so no one knows they're there except me. Tucked into my shorts is my long-sleeved silver sparkly latex shirt, with a zip going all the way down the front. I leave the zipper open from right in between my breasts, taking full advantage of the lingerie I have on underneath that enhances my chest.

Over the top pink eyeshadow frames my eyes, and I've drawn thick freckles over the bridge of my nose and cheeks, with a silver lipstick coating my lips. I feel hot, but to top it all off, I have my hair pinned back and a shoulder-length dusty pink wig in place, with a pair of silver antennas on the top of my head.

Happy with my look, I call out to Luna. "Luna Moon Steele, will you get a move on?" When she finally steps in, I see the surprise on her face at my outfit. Sensing her protests, I put her mind at ease. "Don't worry, Captain. No wig for you. I want to put your hair in two buns on the top of your head. Now, get a move on." Giving me a classic

Luna eye roll, she starts to move as I point her towards the stool at her dresser.

"Red, we're aliens?" she asks for clarification, and I nod in response. Seemingly happy with that, she starts to get changed. "I was expecting something super over the top like a skintight suit or a skimpy nurse's outfit covered in blood."

"Wait till you see the guys," I scoff, turning to give her some privacy while she gets the rest of the outfit on. "I thought you would be able to wear your combat boots with this outfit. Even I can accept that heels are not appropriate for tonight," I offer, turning to face her when I sense she's done.

"Well, I appreciate your thought process," she says with a smile, as I encourage her to take a seat so I can do her hair. I've already done her make-up. Her lips are blue, like neon glow in the dark blue, with green eyeshadow framing her eyes and giant freckles across the bridge of her nose, just like mine.

"Is everything okay with you, Red? I know I kind of forced you to go and stay with Maverick while I'm away, but I hope you know it's to keep you safe," Luna murmurs as I comb the brush through her hair. My heart burns for me to answer her honestly, tell her about what happened at my one on one session with him, but I can't bring the words to pass my lips. So, I steer the conversation towards the other thing playing on my mind.

"It's not that Luna, honestly I don't mind. It's just ..." How the hell do I word this without putting more pressure on her shoulders. "I'm petrified. I know you're strong, Luna, the strongest person I know, but I'm so scared you aren't going to come home from these Games. You guys are my family now, and I don't want anything to happen." My eyes well with tears, and I force them back down.

"Red, I'll be damned if I let these fuckers get the best of me," Luna says, standing to face me with her hands on my shoulders. "Can I promise nothing will happen? No, but I will do everything in my power to get back in one piece. Besides, we still haven't taken a trip together yet, and that's high on my to-do list, okay? Now, stop crying before you ruin your make-up and blame me."

Her words bring me comfort, I know her strength and determination, and I have to believe that everything will be okay. Wrapping my arms around her neck, I squeeze her tight.

"Hey, you ladies okay?" Parker calls from the lounge,

and I smile, excited to see Luna's reaction when she steps out there.

"Yeah, we'll be out in a minute," Luna shouts as I fan her face. Taking a deep breath, I relax my shoulders.

"Fake it till I make it, right?" I say, and I instantly feel stronger.

Stepping into the lounge, Luna stops dead in her tracks as she sees all her men dressed as cowboys. I fucking love it, and I don't even know how I convinced them to do it.

Now, I'm excited to see what Aiden does, and I'm hoping the rumors are true that the tutors attend the Halloween party too so that I can feast my eyes on West as well. Even Maverick too, because he might be an asshole, but his body is to die for.

RED

KC KEAN

TWENTY FOUR

Jess

Pulling up to the Halloween party, I can feel the excitement zinging through my veins as I take in all the decorations. Sugar skulls are everywhere, hanging as streamers, actual skulls lining the tables and scattered across the ground, along with brightly colored petals. It's so beautiful, and I feel like I'm on the set of a dark and twisted Disney movie as I stare around at all the vibrant colors.

Over near the food and drinks tent, there are a variety of Halloween party games. I can see a few people bobbing for apples while a group of guys I recognize from Diamond are preparing a scavenger hunt, and if I'm right, there will be some girls from Hearts ready to play spin the plastic pitchfork. They're boring Halloween twists on the classic spin-the-bottle. I'd rather not make out with someone under those circumstances, or by playing three minutes in the closet either. Which I know will be a thing later, when the students are either high or drunk. I can't stop my shudder at the thought.

As I make my way through the crowd with Luna and her guys, my eyes are discreetly searching for West, Aiden, or Maverick. *My guys*. It's funny how a few weeks ago, I would have scanned every guy here, but now my focus is on them alone, even if the feeling isn't reciprocated. Well, West does at least. Maybe he could give the other two a little shake for me, or a lesson in communication.

I pout slightly as I don't see any of them, while Parker leads us to the exact same spot we sat at the last party. I don't miss the heat in Kai's eyes as he looks at Luna, clearly remembering the body shots they took from her before we danced, which lead me straight to Aiden. Luna received a phone call as we were leaving Ace, from the special agent she had met last week, and whatever he said had hit a nerve. So, we need her to be able to relax a little before she makes her play against Wren.

"I'll grab the drinks. What does everyone want?" Roman asks the table, and they all mumble for a glass of water. Wanting to see if I can catch a glimpse of my guys, I follow after him. "I can get your drink, Jess," he murmurs as we head for the bar.

"I know that, I just don't mind helping," I respond, continuing to glance around the party, cringing when I see Reece and his friends dressed as zombie football players, and his eyes take me in.

"Is everything okay?" Roman asks, catching the look on my face, and I quickly act natural. "You're important to Luna, so you are important to us too. I'm glad to see you coming out of your shell more at the minute, even if you are almost as sassy as Luna, but if you ever have something going on, we are all here, you know."

When we stop at the bar, I stare up at him, completely surprised by his declaration. They may seem like nothing, but I've never heard nicer words from Roman, especially since they aren't aimed at Luna or one of the guys.

"Thanks, Rome," I say sincerely, and he ruffles the wig on my head, making me glare. "Don't fucking ruin it," I grouch, but it's nice seeing this playful side of him that

Luna brings out.

When the bartender sees Roman, he rushes over, quickly taking his order of six waters. I offer my thanks before we carry them back to the table, and I make sure to avoid looking back over in the same direction as Reece again.

"Let's run through the plan one more time. I don't want anything to go wrong," Parker murmurs as we take a seat.

"Me and Parker will head into the red tent first, about fifteen minutes before everyone else. Kai and Red are going to hang back here with the monitors running on their phones to make sure we're not being followed. Roman and Oscar will approach Wren and hint at some alone time. *Hint* being the keyword," Luna says, glaring at the two of them, but there is no way in hell they would even want more. She just doesn't truly see the way they look at her. It seems she is still adjusting to being married because these guys have committed themselves to her, and she's still worried they're not sticking around.

"Then we'll take her to the room you guys have set up. Kai will direct us through the earpiece we'll each be wearing and the micro camera on my cowboy hat," Roman adds, continuing the plan. "Then Luna and Parker will join us in the room. Where Luna and I will stay with Wren, and Parker and Oscar will head into the main area until we give the word."

As everyone around the table nods in agreement, I can't help but frown. "I still don't understand why we don't have time to dance a little." I take a drink of my boring water, wishing it was a shot of Sambuca like Aiden gave me.

"Fine, come on. One dance, but honestly, after that, we need to get the ball rolling, okay?" Luna says, and I can't contain my smile. Looping my arm through Luna's, we head for the dance floor when 'Confident' by Demi Lovato plays through the speakers. Squeezing through the crowd already dancing, I let the beat take over as I sway to the music. Predictably girls in slutty outfits covered in blood surround us, but I block them all out, focusing on dancing instead.

As I let the music flow through my body, I can feel eyes on me, and that's when I see them. West and Maverick standing side by side around a table near the apple bobbing stand and my heart stutters in my chest. I can't take my eyes off them. West is wearing a classic grey suit, waistcoat, and all, with a flat cap on his head, and if that isn't his attempt at Thomas Selby, aka the king of the Peaky Blinders, then

I don't know who he is. But I could dream up a few ways of stripping him out of the outfit for sure. It's either a lucky coincidence or Aiden has told him about my obsession with the TV show.

Searing his outfit to memory, I cast my eyes over Maverick. His overgrown wavy hair falls around his face, with the collar of his leather jacket flipped up. He's wearing his classic black leather jacket, straight-cut denim jeans, and combat boots, but when I read his t-shirt, I chuckle. 'I'm Sam Winchester. Now, fuck off' is printed in white across his navy v-neck t-shirt. The fact that his Halloween costume is so simple doesn't surprise me at all, and a part of me envies how much he always stays true to himself, even if he is a walking billboard for what bad boys look like. It draws me in, *him*, everything he is, under all his leather and anger.

Around the table are a few other tutors, including Gina, the history tutor, and Penny from my Business classes, and they're dressed more outrageously than the girls grinding around us. Just as I'm about to point it out to Luna, hands wrap around me from behind, stroking against the thin material of my shirt. I panic at first, worrying Reece is finally making an appearance as the press of a hard cock touches my back, but the murmur in my ears has me relaxing instantly.

"Hey, beautiful." Glancing over my shoulder, I see Aiden, but I have to do a double-take when I look at his face. His face has been professionally painted to make it look as though his skin is being unzipped, and the blood seems crazy realistic. His blond hair is slicked back away from his face with red devil horns on the top of his head. He's wearing black pants and shiny black shoes, with no top, and he reminds me of Lucifer Morningstar. Hot as fuck.

"Hey," I finally respond, meeting his grey eyes. He holds my hips, pulling me in tight, swaying along with me to the music. This feels like heaven.

"You look fucking stunning. Even if you covered your pretty red hair with this wig." I smile at his words as I look to the roof of the tent above us, lost in him and the music. "They're watching us, beautiful. Why don't we give them a little show?" Feeling him dance behind me and their eyes on us, I can't stop myself from grinding against him. I don't know when I closed my eyes, but I force them open slightly to peer in their direction.

West is watching us without shame, his hands in his

pockets as his eyes rake over us. While Maverick has his hands fisted on the table in front of him, practically growling at us, as Gina hangs off his arm, but it's as if he doesn't even notice she's there.

Turning my gaze to Luna, I'm surprised to find Parker dancing up behind her, and for a moment, just a moment, we are two eighteen-year-old girls dancing carefree at a Halloween party. As if hearing my thoughts, Luna nods at whatever Parker is whispering in her ear, and her eyes find mine. I know the moment is over, and we're back to being Featherstone Academy students.

Knowing they will want to take me back to Kai, I slowly start to pull away from Aiden, but he holds his arm out, talking to Luna. "Let us dance for a few minutes, bossy pants. We're having a little fun." Resting his chin on my shoulder, Luna looks to me, and I smile and nod in response. Seemingly happy with that, she squeezes my hand and leaves with Parker.

"Hmm, so your friend trusts me with you too, huh?" Aiden murmurs in my ear, and I spin around to see his face, wrapping my arms around his neck.

"I guess, but what does that mean?" I ask, confused with why he said that.

"It means, Maverick made sure to let us know where you'd be staying next week." My eyes instantly look over his shoulder to where West and Maverick are still standing. I'm surprised and intrigued by the fact he shared that little nugget of detail with the others. Is this supposed to mean something?

"It's only a week, Aid," I whisper in his ear. As I pull back, my eyes lock on his lips. Fuck. I'm desperate to taste him, to ruin the perfect face paint around his lips. Damn it. Fuck the consequences and who's looking. It'll be worth it.

My hands grip his neck, locking him in place as he holds my waist. His lips are almost to mine when someone grabs my arm, pulling my attention from Aiden in front of me.

"Jess, we need to move now!" Kai growls, pulling me from Aiden's grip.

"Hey, man. What the fuck is going on?" Aiden shouts, placing his palm in the center of Kai's chest, stopping his movement, and the glare he gets back sends chills down my spine.

"They were set up, Jess. Someone just knocked out Luna and Parker, and I'm pretty sure it was Rico and Veronica if the voices were right coming through the earpiece. We need to get the guys and figure out what the fuck Wren did."

The more Kai said, the lower Aiden dropped his arm, and I don't wait to say anything, needing to help Kai and save Luna now. Following Kai's lead, I run in my wedges, straight towards where Oscar and Roman are standing with Wren between them.

My blood boils. Who the fuck is this bitch? And why does she always have some involvement in injuring Luna? I'm done with her shit, and she's going to give me some answer right now. As I near them, I don't slow my pace, and Roman must realize there is no way to stop me as he steps aside. Charging into her with all my force, I pin her to the table, her head smashing off the wood with a resounding thud, with my hands wrapped around her throat.

Caging her in, I bring my face to hers, "What have you fucking done? Where are they?"

Wren starts to laugh, even though her face is pinned to the table, and blood is pouring from her nose. This bitch just loves to get on my nerves. Clearly, she thinks I'm joking, and I need to prove her wrong. Letting my body take over, I try not to overthink my actions as I wrap my fingers in her hair, pulling her up off the table before slamming her back down again. Holy shit, where is everyone? I try to look over my shoulder to where I left Aiden, but I can't see him anywhere. My back is completely to West and Maverick, and I don't want to loosen my grip on Wren.

"Kai, what's going on?" Roman growls frantically from somewhere behind me, and it feels like forever before Kai responds.

"Someone has them," he finally murmurs, my heart pounding uncontrollably in my chest. "I'm trying to find them on the cameras we set up, but I think you two need to head in there now. Leave Wren with us," Kai says, his voice dark and void of any emotion.

Wren doesn't have the answers to what I want, so I throw her to the ground beside the table as her so-called friends continue to sit at the table with their mouths wide open. Someone needs to get better friends that will stand by her side and protect her, not these assholes. I don't bother to check if she's going to come back at me, I need to help, and we need to find Luna.

Turning to the guys to figure out what the fuck has happened, but Oscar and Roman are running towards the tent, leaving Kai and me here with his surveillance system. Paying no attention to anyone around us, I move in close, getting a closer look at what he's seeing, and he holds out an earpiece to me. I don't take my eyes off the screen as I place it in my ear, listening to Kai guide a frantic Oscar. Hearing the fear in his voice sets me on edge. I've never heard anything but anger, laughter, or love pass his lips.

"Kai, I'm…" I start to talk, but I'm suddenly pushed from the side Kai was standing on. If it's that bitch Wren, I'm going to smash her face against that table again, hopefully, knock some fucking sense into her. Spinning around, I'm frozen in place as I watch as one of them lifts Kai's limp body over their shoulder, another doing the same with Wren. They're already moving across the grounds, bypassing the dance floor, when I finally find my voice.

"No. No, get off him. Get off him!" I scream, chasing after them, but there are too many bodies around for me to move quickly, and I stumble over on my ankle in these stupid damn wedges. Falling to the ground at the edge of the dance floor, I remember my earpiece. "Roman! Oscar? Ozzie, they've got him! Please, they're taking Kai!"

"Jess, I need you to focus, okay? This is really important," Roman grunts back, and I try to catch a calming breath. Pulling my wedges from my feet, I stand, limping towards the DJ booth. I might be able to see a little more from up there. Where is Aiden? He would be able to get me up there for sure.

"Okay, I'm focusing," I sob, I slowly make my way through the crowd.

"What were they wearing? The people who took Kai?" Roman asks, and I take another deep breath.

"Black tracksuits with the Featherstone emblem embroidered on the front. They had sunglasses on too." My brain processes what I'm saying, and it slowly begins to dawn on me that it might be for The Games, but they're early. Why today?

"Good girl, Jessikins. You did brilliant. Where are you now?" Oscar asks, and I focus on his words, the music pounding around me, and the flashing lights making me disoriented.

"I'm over by the DJ booth. They pushed me aside and took Wren too, and I didn't want to be alone with her crew," I mutter, which is a total lie. I let them down. I let them take Kai. That's when I freeze, no longer scanning the area around me as all my attention is focused on him. It's as if the crowd has parted perfectly for Reece to have direct access to me. He's dressed as a quarterback, covered in blood, with a helmet in his hand and black lines on his cheeks. I watch as a grin slowly takes over his face as he steps towards me.

A movement to my right catches my attention, breaking the tension building with Reece, and I see Maverick suddenly at my side. "Maverick, what are you doing here?" I ask, but he doesn't respond. Instead, he grabs my waist, throwing me over his shoulder in a fireman's hold. "No, no, they've taken Luna and Parker. I need to help them, Maverick!" Not listening to a word I say, he spins us around and starts walking towards a moving SUV. "PUT. ME. DOWN!" I scream at the top of my lungs, but he does nothing.

"Jess, go with him. It's the only way we can keep you safe if they're looking for us too." Roman sighs, making me feel completely defeated. The noise coming through the earpiece goes radio silent as they turn theirs off, leaving me with this neanderthal.

The strain on my neck hurts as I twist myself to watch where we are going, and I see the SUV come to a stop, and West jump out of the driver's seat, opening the rear door for Maverick to toss me in the back. Quickly dropping me into a seat, I try to get my bearings as Maverick slams the door and sits beside me.

West jumps back into the driver's seat, and just as he's about to hit the gas, the passenger door swings open, and Aiden climbs in frantically, taking me in as he shuts the door behind him.

"What the fuck are you all doing? They need us!" I yell, my eyes welling with emotion with the anger and stress I feel, but when I turn to glare at Maverick, he simply shrugs.

"Luna asked me to protect you. This is me protecting you."

"Funny how you can listen to her and do as she asks, but when I ask you to fucking stay and not run, you don't even know what language I'm speaking!" My voice rings in my ears, and any other time I would cringe at my outburst, but he deserves it. Clearly, I like to hold a grudge. I hear him sigh heavily, likely annoyed with my outburst, but he doesn't argue back, and I think that makes me angrier, but I do see him flinch slightly at my words. Neither of the others say anything, but West doesn't stop the car. So, it seems I'm being pulled away from the scene whether I like it or not.

Slumping back into my seat, I close my eyes, too

worked up to look at any of them right now. I jump at the brush of Maverick's hand on my hip as he fastens my seatbelt, and I glare at the side of his head when he doesn't turn to look at me. Pulling my wig from my head, I rest my face in my hands, trying to steady my breathing as I do. I can hear the guys murmuring to each other around me, but I don't focus on them. Too angry to even listen to whatever bullshit comes out of their mouths.

Fuck you, douchebags. Fuck you with a twelve-inch ribbed dildo and *no* lube.

RED

KC KEAN

TWENTY FIVE

Jess

We don't seem to be in the SUV for long, especially not with the way West is driving, but I don't lift my head from my hands until the door to my right swings open, and someone unclips my seatbelt. Sighing, I find West standing at the open door, looking down at me with a softness in his eyes I don't care for right now. He's holding his hand out, patiently waiting for me to step out of the vehicle.

I can't seem to calm myself down, and I know it's because I believe I deserve to be mad right now. I don't know where Luna is or if she is safe, and I don't know what to do with myself when I feel utterly helpless. I hear the door to my other side slam shut as Maverick storms off, entering the building we are at. Aiden stands in between the two, his eyes scanning me from head to toe on repeat.

Leaving the wig and my wedges in the SUV, I step out, pushing West back a little so I can move, as my feet touch the rough gravelly floor. I barely take two steps before West is lifting me into his arms, bridal style, and the moment I turn to glare at him, he speaks.

"You can continue to be mad, sunshine, but I refuse to let you walk on the ground barefoot when you could hurt yourself." I gape at him in surprise, the sternness in his deep voice catching me off guard. Does he not know what just happened back there, though? A little graze or cut to my feet is nothing compared to what I know just happened, but I don't fight him. That hasn't worked for me so far.

As West walks by Aiden, he falls into step beside him, his fingers stroking my calf, and I feel his eyes shoot to mine when he feels the material of my stockings. I don't meet his gaze as I hold myself stiffly in West's arms, arms folded tightly across my chest, refusing to allow myself to bask in his comfort. The second we step inside, I keep my eyes straight ahead.

"Put me down now, please," I state, trying to keep my voice neutral as I do.

"Jess, it's…"

"I said, put me down now, please," I repeat, finally bringing myself to look at him, and he sighs reluctantly as he does as I ask. Slowly lowering me to the floor, dragging my body down the length of his body. Damn, my nipples react instantly to the sensation, but I won't let him see his effect on me. Not when I can feel my emotions swirling inside.

My body screams in protest as I pull away from him, and Aiden stands beside him silently, begging me to turn back to them, but I walk to the elevator where Maverick is waiting, holding the doors open. He fills the space, his arms propped above his head on the frame of the elevator doors, his t-shirt rising slightly with his stance, offering me a sneaky view of his abs and happy trail. Licking my lips, I step through the gap at his side, my small five-foot three-inches frame slipping by untouched.

Standing in the far corner of the mirrored walls, I keep my head cast down at my feet and hands fisted at my sides. Closing my eyes, I try to regulate my breathing, control myself, but it's no use. The elevator pings before I've even realized we're moving. Following Maverick's lead, I stand behind him as he unlocks the door to what I assume is his apartment. I hear the door click shut behind me as the others step in too, the silence that otherwise surrounds us is deafening, and I need to be on my own right now.

Not taking in the large open space around me, I look straight to Maverick. "Where are my things? And where will I be sleeping?" My voice barely above a whisper, all my energy drained.

"Jess, I think we should all stay together right now," Aiden murmurs, coming to stand at my side, stroking his hand down my arm comfortingly.

"I need to be alone right now," I respond, as West comes to stand by my other side.

"Sunshine, a lot of shit just went down. Let me explain what the next process is for them. I've been there." His hand cups my chin, bringing my eyes to his, and I try to see him through all the red fog filling up my brain.

"No, West. If she wants to run off crying, leave her to it. Your room is to the right of the bathroom. Your belongings are in there. Come back out when you're ready to listen," Maverick's voice booms around the room, but West doesn't release his grip on my chin. His body is tense, and I can't decide if it's because I won't listen or the way Maverick is growling at me, and right now, I just don't care.

A part of me is grateful for Maverick appearing out of thin air. The dark look in Reece's eyes as he was walking towards me had scared me, and Maverick showing up had stopped him. But he still pulled me away from the bigger issue at play here.

"Back off, man. She needs a minute to process," Aiden growls defensively, his hand tightening around my arm in support, and feeling the both of them at the same time starts to help ground me.

Keeping my eyes trained on West, "This douche doesn't get to tell me about running off, does he?" I ask, making sure I'm hearing him right.

West's lips lift slightly, but before he can respond, Maverick chimes in. "Petal, I heard your outburst in the car, and these are two completely different scenarios. Your friends were taken for The Games, and they knew this was coming, they…"

"No, Maverick Miller!" I yell, stepping out of West and Aiden's hold, turning to glare at him. "Luna and Parker were taken by someone else. Kai's surveillance and the earpieces we've been wearing points towards Rico Manetti and Barbette Dietrichson, maybe even a third person, but they were not taken the same way as Kai," I cry, pulling the earpiece from my ear, throwing it down on the floor at my feet in defeat.

I watch as his face morphs with confusion, his eyebrows pinching as he looks to West. "I'm getting Rafe on the phone," West says as Aiden wraps his arm around my shoulder, Maverick pulling his phone out too.

"So now you want to listen? It's a little too fucking late now!" I yell, unable to contain my anger.

"Let's leave them to make the phone calls, beautiful, while I get you a sugary drink. You've had a lot of adrenaline running through this little hot body of yours, and I don't want you to crash," Aiden murmurs in my ear, and I let him lead me towards the open plan kitchen. When we near the fridge, he lifts me and places me on the countertop, just like last time I had a mini-breakdown in front of him. Oh god, this is apparently becoming a habit, how embarrassing.

As he takes a look in the fridge beside me, I focus around the room. I love how the living room and kitchen are all one space. The high gloss kitchen cabinets balance perfectly with the dark wood furniture in the living room.

Grey paint covers the walls, and the black leather corner sofa separates the two spaces. I'm actually impressed with how clean it is in here too, although it's so Maverick I shouldn't be surprised. Glancing to the owner, I see Maverick setting up a laptop on the coffee table, with his phone wedged between his ear and shoulder. Growls coming from the other side of the room, near the front door, pull my gaze to West as he paces back and forth while on the phone to Rafe.

"Here we go," Aiden says with a smile, pulling a can of soda from the fridge and bringing it to my lips. Taking it from his hands, I drink half the can in one go. "May I say, beautiful, you looked hot as fuck when you smashed Wren's face into the table like the badass chick you are." I choke a little on the soda, forgetting for a moment that'd actually done that. I'm actually proud of myself too, for standing up to that bitch.

"That was an awful thing for me to do, but that bitch deserved it," I mutter, then a thought occurs. "Where did you go?" I ask, looking up to him. I can't take him seriously with all this face paint on, which reminds me of the state of myself too. "When I ran from the dance floor, you saw me hit Wren, but when Kai was taken, I was panicked, frightened, and on my own. Where were you?" I'm not mad, I just need to understand the bigger picture from that moment, not just what I felt because I barely saw anything after they carried Kai away.

"I'm so sorry, beautiful." Cupping my face, he strokes his thumb against my cheek delicately. "As you were smashing Wren's face off the table, I was making my way through the crowd towards you when Trudy called. She was hysterical, and she needed me. I was stupid to think you would be safe because you were with the Aces. I didn't realize they were going to be taken, leaving you all alone." Resting his forehead against mine, he looks deep into my eyes, and I see the pain it causes him to know he left me alone, but it wasn't his fault. "The second I knew things were going south with the Aces, I ran straight back to you, which is when I caught you guys in the SUV before you pulled away."

My heart pounds in my chest as I feel his emotions mix with my own, and I squeeze his wrist, keeping his hand in place on my face. "It wasn't your fault, Aid. I just didn't want to leave when everything was so up in the air." I sigh. "Is your sister okay though?"

He smiles softly at me as he leans back a little. "How

is it you were just caught up in the middle of all the drama tonight, yet you want to make sure my sister is okay too?" I smile back, not knowing how to respond, and he places a gentle kiss on my head. The touch of his lips against my skin washes over me, a sense of calmness taking over. "I'm not sure, to be honest. She wasn't in a good state, but Ethan, the on-site doctor, was at the party thankfully, and she seemed safe with him. So, she sent me back to you."

"If you need to go and be with…"

"I'm not going anywhere, Jess. I'm right where I need to be."

Aiden's words leave me gasping for breath as I gape up at him, and he must know the effect he just had on me because, in the next moment, his lips are crushing mine. My hands land on his chest as I drag my fingers up to his shoulders, trying to pull him closer, and the feel of his bare skin beneath my touch has heat radiating through my body.

Hot damn, this is the distraction I need. Wrapping my legs around his waist, he has one hand around my throat as the other grips my ass tightly. I moan against his lips, and a growl from the other side of the room meets my ears, but I'm too lost in Aiden right now to care.

"Sorry to interrupt, but Rafe wants to talk to you, Jess,"

West says, as I feel him come to stand at my side. Aiden slowly releases my lips, and as I blink up at him, I'm rather pleased to see his face paint has smudged around his mouth, just like I'd wanted it to. He doesn't step back as I turn my gaze to West, whose gaze is filled with heat as he looks me over.

Before I can take the phone from his hand, he tilts my head back and claims my mouth too. Only for a moment, nowhere near as long as I'd like. The desire pulsing through my veins has me wanting to pull him in closer, but when he silently holds the phone to my ear, I remember what's going on.

"Rafe?"

"Hey, Jess. Are you okay?" His rough voice softens when he speaks to me like he thinks I'm too delicate for his harsh tone, and the caring factor behind it makes me smile.

"I'm alright, Rafe. I'm just worried, they took Kai from right in front of me, and I did nothing, Rafe, nothing. They were trying to figure out what had happened to Luna and Parker, and I…" He cuts me off as tears begin to fall down my face.

"Jess, darling, I need you to calm down, okay? What happened to them is not your fault, and we will figure it all out. I'm at The Games already, and I have some of my men looking into where Luna and Parker may be if they don't show up here in the next twenty minutes or so. But I need you to be strong, and the second I know more, I will call. I trust Maverick and West to take care of you. They did the best thing getting you out of there when they did."

Of course he agrees that pulling me away from the situation was the best option, but it still frustrates me that I froze. He doesn't need to deal with my insecurities and strains right now though. I need him to be ready to go to war if Luna doesn't show up there.

"Okay, Rafe. Please keep me up to date," I murmur, realizing both West and Aiden have their hands on my thighs, trying to offer me comfort, but my eyes find Maverick, who is standing by the sofas, his gaze frantically searching mine. It's as if he could hear me cry and reacted to the noise but didn't actually know how to handle it.

"I promise, Jess. Speak soon." The phone line cuts off, and West pulls the phone away from my ear. Swiping a hand down my face, I get my emotions under control.

"Hey, it's going to be okay, sunshine," he says with a gentle smile on his lips. "We just need to distract you." He winks before looking around the others. "How about you take a shower, I'll grab a few things from my room, including some clothes for Lucifer here, and we can try and relax?"

I nod in agreement as Aiden murmurs his thanks for some fresh clothes when Maverick steps in. "Yeah, of course, why don't you all make yourselves at home in my apartment. I love it." His sarcasm drips from every word, and the glare on his face has me questioning how mad he is.

"If it's an inconvenience for you, I can take Jess and Aiden up to my room, so you have nothing to worry about?" West grunts in response. Maybe that might be for the best if Maverick isn't happy...

"No!" He shouts, rubbing the back of his neck as he sighs. "Stay. All of you stay. It's fine." Meeting my gaze, he tries to drop the frown from his face, but it looks as though it's proving difficult. "Let me show you to your room so you can get comfortable."

Aiden lifts me from the counter, kissing the corner of my lips before he places me on my feet. Maverick starts walking towards the door to the right of the kitchen, and I follow his lead. Opening the door, he swings his arm out wide for me to step in first, and just as I'm about to step through the door, I turn to look at West.

"You were right, West. I definitely need a distraction. So, don't change yet. I have a thing for a Thomas fucking Shelby," I say seductively, and I don't know where that confidence came from, but I'm rolling with it. Especially when West nods rapidly in agreement, and Maverick and Aiden groan.

Shutting the door behind me, I sag against it. How on earth am I going to cope, surrounded by the three hottest guys in my life, for the next week?

KC KEAN

TWENTY SIX

West

The door slams behind Jess as my heart pounds in my chest. Did she say what I think she just said? I need to grab what I need from my room and get back down here to my sunshine. Holy fuck.

Glancing at the other two who are still gaping at her door, I spin on my feet and run from the room, not even shutting the door behind me. I'm on the sixth floor, the elevator looks like it's on the second floor and I haven't got time to wait for that. Taking the stairs, two at a time, I fumble for my keys in my pocket. When I finally get the door unlocked, I scan my thumbprint, deactivating the alarm, before rushing for my bedroom.

Stepping into my walk-in closet, I pull a duffel bag from the top shelf and drop it to the floor. Grabbing a few outfits for Aiden to wear and something I can change into tomorrow, I stuff them into the bag and zip it up as quickly as possible.

"West?" I hear from the living room, and my back stiffens. Heels click on the hardwood flooring as I throw the duffel bag over my shoulder and rush to the open plan living space, not wanting the intruder to be in my personal space any longer than necessary.

Slamming my bedroom door shut behind me, I come face to face with Gina, dressed in a black and white maid outfit with fake blood smeared across her arms and legs. If she turns around, I'll probably see her ass cheeks with the little 'fuck me' outfit she's in. I try not to sigh or let my distaste show on my face, but this woman is starting to get on my fucking nerves.

"Gina, what are you doing in my apartment?" I ask, but I know it's coming across as a growl. As she steps up against my body, I groan internally. The semi I'd been sporting in excitement to get back to Jess instantly deflates at her touch. I really don't have time for this or being nice for that matter.

"I saw you leave the party, speeding off campus, and I needed to make sure you were okay," she purrs with pouty lips and a flutter of her lashes, and my politeness is gone.

"I'm actually still dealing with all of that, so if you don't mind, you need to leave."

"I can help you, baby. Just tell me what to do." Her fingers stroke against the lapel of my blazer, and I grab Gina's wrists with one hand, stopping her attempt at seduction.

"I just did. You need to leave, and so do I." Not wasting any time, I drop her wrists and head for the door. When I open it wide, I look back at Gina for her to move. With her head lowered in disappointment, she brushes past me, and I quickly reset the alarm and lock the door behind us.

"Are you walking me back to my room?" She asks, hope in her words, and I don't even feel bad for popping her balloon when I shake my head.

"No," I answer sharply, fuck I feel as grumpy as Rick right now. Heading for the stairs, I feel her hand wrap around my arm, trying to stop me from leaving.

"West, please. We had such a good time together. Why do you keep avoiding me? I want you and Maverick too.

Why can't you give me that?" She hisses in annoyance, making me sigh. I need to be brutally honest with her. Otherwise, this is never going to end. The cold shoulder just isn't working.

"Gina, there is someone else, okay? There is never going to be a 'me and you', or a 'you and Maverick,' so definitely no 'me, you, and Maverick.' You need to get over it. You're only embarrassing yourself."

Her hand slips from my arm, and I take that as my cue to leave. I don't need to be dealing with her emotions right now, especially when Jess needs me and I need her. I hear her scream as the door to the stairwell shuts behind me, but I keep on going. I'm glad Gina's apartment isn't on Maverick's floor because I don't need her to see where I'm heading to.

Stopping at Maverick's door, I knock hard since one of them clearly shut the door after I left, and it takes a moment for Aiden to open the door.

"Will you tell this asshole," he grunts, pointing over his shoulder at Maverick as he walks backward in his direction. "He seems to think that because Jess is staying in his apartment, he gets to decide *everything*, and I'm not above giving him a turnip if he carries on." Shutting the door behind me, I frown at the two of them. Maverick has taken his leather jacket off and is running his hand through his hair with a sigh. While Aiden stands in front of him, hands on his hips and the devil horns still on his head.

"What the hell is a turnip?" Rick grumbles, and the cheshire cat grin on Aiden's face tells me I'm about to find out.

"I thought you'd never ask," he mutters before reaching out, pinching Rick's nipple through his t-shirt and twisting his hand to the left.

"Ahh, what the fuck man?" Rick shouts, jumping back and rubbing his chest, and I can't stop the laughter from taking over me as I watch the two of them. "Don't fucking laugh, West. You're encouraging him."

Swinging his arms out wide, Aiden looks between us with his mouth open wide, but I can't take him serious with that face paint smeared around his mouth and the top half of his face looking like it's being unzipped. "You asked me what a turnip was, so I gave you a demonstration." Stretching his right arm in front of himself, he makes a turning motion as he breaks it down for us. "Tuuurrrrnnnn," he drags out slowly, like were children. "Nip." He finishes tweaking his fucking nipples, and I'm done, especially when he winks and blows Rick a kiss.

"You are too fucking much, Aiden," I say with a chuckle as I drop the duffel bag on the sofa. As fun as this is, we need to have a serious conversation. I've read Aiden's file. His bloodline operates narcotics and sex clubs, so I don't know how he'll feel with the parts of Featherstone we run, but if he wants to be here for Jess, he'll have to get used to it. "Rick, did you find anything on Luna and Parker?" I ask, and Aiden instantly drops the humor.

"The surveillance shows two SUV's leaving the campus, just as the other SUV with the F.A. guys showed up. The first two SUV's were completely blacked out, so no one can get a visual yet, but if Luna and Parker were in there, it wasn't to take them to The Games." My heart sinks at his words, as he drops to the sofa. Aiden says nothing, but my gut is telling me they were in there. I know it. Pulling my phone from my pocket, I press Rafe's number on the screen. It's not been long, but it feels like hours. I need to know what is happening with Luna Moon, and I need to put Jess's mind at ease.

After three rings, the line picks up, but I don't hear Rafe speak for a moment, just the sound of a door clicking shut. "Rafe?" I say into the phone.

"I'm here, and she is too. Fuck, West, give me a second." Holy shit, holy fucking shit.

Looking at the others, I point to Jess's door. "Someone go get Jess, she's there. Luna's at The Games." Thank god. A sigh comes through the phone, and I feel the weight of the world resting on Rafe's shoulders from here. Aiden dashes to Jess's room and is back within moments with my sunshine, while Aiden looks as though he's texting. It may have something to do with the fact his sister was crying as we left the party, but it's not my place to ask.

"West?"

"Yeah, I'm here." Putting the phone on speaker, I place it on the oak coffee table and sit on the sofa beside it. Maverick stays where he is around the other side, Aiden takes a seat in the corner of the sofa, while Jess climbs into my lap.

Wrapping her arms around my neck, she rests her chin on my shoulder as I hold her close. She's changed out of her Halloween costume, her face is clean of any make-up, and her red hair is in a messy bun on the top of her head. She has never looked as beautiful as she does right now, in my lap, where she belongs. In just her short pajamas, my hand instinctively strokes her thigh, loving the feel of goosebumps rising at my touch as she sits sideways on my lap.

"Rico, Barbette, and Veronica took Luna and Parker," he growls at the phone, and I feel Jess still at the fierceness in his voice. "They were drugged, West. Drugged. But it clearly wasn't the one they wanted because Luna and Parker woke up much quicker than they expected."

"Are they okay?" I ask, feeling Jess lean towards the phone, waiting for him to answer.

"Yes, although the same can't be said about Veronica," he murmurs, and my eyebrows pinch in confusion.

"What do you mean?" Maverick asks, clearly the only one not stuck on Rafe's words.

"I mean, I just watched my daughter shoot her mother in the head, in front of everyone." He sniffs down the phone, but he isn't mad at her actions. "Eighteen years, we have had to deal with that bitch, thinking it was always the right thing to do to have her mother be a part of her life. Yet when she pulled the trigger, I watched her shoulders sag in relief, knowing Veronica wouldn't be getting anywhere near her again."

Jess squeezes me tighter as I let his words sink in. My moon had to kill her own mother to protect herself, she shouldn't have to live with that burden. "Is she okay?" I ask.

"She's fucking brilliant. How crazy is that? I'm proud of her." He snickers as his emotions get on top of him. "What fucking father says they are proud of their daughter for shooting her mother? For taking a stand and showing Featherstone, and Rico, who she is? For showing all these motherfuckers they've been underestimating my girl." He could be crying, I'm not sure, but he's venting, and I'm glad we are here to help him get it off his chest.

Slipping from my lap, Jess kneels on the floor by the phone, taking it off the speaker and bringing it to her ear. "Rafe, you are the best dad I have ever met. *Ever*. We don't live in the normal world. We have to say and do things to survive, and our Luna is the most badass bitch there is. You're taking pride in this because you know you raised her to be strong, unbreakable, and resilient."

My heart beats rapidly at the sincerity in her voice, and I fall a little harder for her as I watch her comfort Rafe through the phone. I don't hear his response, but she continues to prove her point.

"Well, you should also take pride in the fact that Luna has lived through all of this bullshit, yet she still knows how to love and care. Her loyalty knows no bounds, and that is because of you. Family is everything to her, and that is also because of you. Everything she values and protects is what you instilled in her." I watch as a single tear drops down her cheek at whatever he says back, and she whispers into the phone the sweetest words. "I love you too, Rafe. Get some sleep, okay? She's going to need you."

She places the phone down on the coffee table, and no one says a word. Not a single one as the three of us stare at her in awe. Sitting here, in her presence, I know this is something special. Something we can't take for granted because she is the lightness to brighten all our darkness in some shape or form, and I don't want to lose that. Not when she's choosing to be surrounded by us.

Glancing at Rick, I see him rub his hands together roughly, as if he wants to reach out to comfort her but is stopping himself. Nobhead. Aiden crouches down beside her, whispering in her ear as he wraps his arm around her shoulder. I don't hear a word they say as they sit on the floor in front of me, but a moment later, Aiden is standing to his feet and helping Jess to hers.

Turning to face me, Aiden kisses her gently on the lips and grabs the duffel bag from beside me. "I'm going to go and shower. Shout if you need me, okay?" She smiles at him appreciatively before gazing back down at me.

"Are you okay, sunshine?" I ask, slowly rising to stand with her, and her hands instantly stroke up my waistcoat. Playing with the buttons as she goes.

"My brain is a mess, I don't usually have so much going on in my life like this, and I don't think it's going to shut down so I can go to sleep."

"Is there anything I can do to help?" I murmur, stroking her cheek as we stand chest to chest.

"You can make me forget," she whispers. Make her ... wait. My eyes must widen in question, and she nods slightly as her teeth sink into her bottom lip. "I need you, West."

Lightning fast, my palms are gripping the back of her thighs and lifting her in the air, holding her against my body as I start walking her in the direction of Maverick's spare room. I think I hear him call out, but all I can hear are her giggles in my ear. It seems my sunshine needs her little corner of darkness brightened, and I'll do whatever it takes, especially if it brings us closer.

Kicking the door shut behind us with my foot, her hands clasp my face, drawing my lips to hers as I walk us blindly to the bed. When I feel my knees hit the mattress, I slowly lean her back, refusing to pull my lips from hers as I guide us down to the bed. Her legs wrap tighter around my waist, refusing to let me go, as we explore each other.

"Tell me what you want, sunshine," I say against her lips, and she smiles at me, her eyes remaining closed.

"I want you to make me feel anything other than anger, fear, and helplessness," she mutters back, and I stroke the hair from her face.

"Are you sure? I don't want you to think that's all I ..."

Her eyes shoot open, and she frowns up at me. "West, why would I think that's all you want when it's me practically begging you to take me?" Well, she does have a point.

"I guess it's because in my head you consume me, and if you knew how many times I pictured you naked tonight at the Halloween party, you would probably understand." She grins up at me, the smile taking over her face, and meeting her eyes.

Pulling the flat cap from my head, she drops it to the floor. "I thought you wanted the full effect?" I ask with her smirking as she pulls my blazer down my arms.

"I want the full effect of West Morgan right now."

Shrugging my blazer off, I lean back, letting her undo my waistcoat buttons before I pull my shirt over my head. Releasing her hold on my waist, Jess props herself up on her elbows as she watches me undress all the way down to my boxers, and with each scrap of material I remove, the more heated her gaze becomes. My dick is pulsing at the attention she's giving every inch of my body.

"You are so fucking beautiful, sunshine."

"Show me," she breathes out, rising enough to pull her pajama top over her head, and the sight of her pretty pink nipples has me wetting my lips. Kneeling on the bed in between her legs, she lies back as I hook my fingers in the waist of her shorts, slowly slipping them over her hips, and discard them like the rest of my clothes.

Laying bare beneath me, she doesn't shy away, the lamp on her bedside table offering the perfect glow over her pale skin. Her fingers stroke against my abdomen, following the scar that marks me from my rib cage to my pelvis.

"What is this from?" She whispers, continuing to drag her finger along the puckered skin.

"A stab wound, from a Featherstone assignment. It's a lot more superficial than it looks." I don't say that the assignment was my time in The Games, she doesn't need that level of stress right now, and she thankfully doesn't push for more information.

Tracing a line from her collarbone, down between her breasts, to her hip, my eyes fall on the little beauty spot right where her thigh meets her core. Holy shit. My finger moves to circle around it, and she moans softly at the gentle caress. Leaning over her, I place a gentle kiss on her neck before following the path my finger took. As I stop to brush my tongue against her nipple, her hands lift to my shoulders, her fingertips biting into my skin, and I can't stop my cock from grinding against her core. We both moan at the contact, and I bite down on her nipple, making her roll her hips up to join me.

"Fuck," she whispers, and I blow gently against the pebbled peak before continuing the trail down to her core. Kissing her belly button, I lift from her slightly, nodding my head for her to move further up the bed. The second her head is nestled amongst the pillows, I kiss her beauty spot, following it with a trail of kisses to her clit. The second I stroke my tongue against her sensitive nub, her back arches, and her moans fill my ears. Holy fuck, I could cum from just listening to her.

"Please, don't tease, West," she begs, and it's like music to my ears.

"Sunshine, I'm going to taste you until you cum on my tongue, and then I'm going to sink my dick deep inside of you, bringing us both to ecstasy." I don't wait for her response as I suck her clit into my mouth and thrust two fingers inside of her. Her walls clench tightly around them as she moans louder in surprise. "That's it, let them hear you," I murmur against her core as her thighs wrap around my head.

Thrusting my fingers a few more times, I smile against her clit before I graze my teeth over the swollen nub, loving hearing her chant my name. When I feel her tighten around my fingers, I circle them over and over again, maintaining the same pace as her thighs tighten, her hips rocking up against my face.

"West, fuck, West!" she cries, coming apart against my tongue as waves of pleasure wash over her. I grind my cock into the mattress, squeezing my hand around the tip to stop myself from spilling too soon, but holy fuck does she looks gorgeous as she writhes beneath me.

Making sure she feels every ounce of her orgasm, I finally pull away to grab a condom when she covers her face, trying to catch her breath. Dropping my boxers to my feet, I hear her intake of breath. I look up to meet her gaze, but her sole focus is my cock.

"Holy shit. Your cock lives up to your ability to dirty talk me, West. Full of surprises." Biting down on her bottom lip, my dick flexes towards her, making a grin creep over her lips.

"Surprises, huh?" I don't question what she means because the look in her eyes tells me it's more than positive. "Come here."

Crawling towards me, she kneels at my side, so I lift her by the hips, bringing her down on top of me, with her legs on either side of mine. She slides her pussy against my cock, testing her weight against mine, and she throws her head back with a soft sigh. As she strokes back up, the entrance to her core meets the tip of my dick, so I lift off the bed slightly, watching her face as she slowly takes every inch of my cock. Her lips form the perfect O as she takes a moment. I try to catch my breath. The tight feel of her core wrapped around my cock has my pulse throbbing in my ear as my dick swells inside of her.

"I've never… I've never done it this way before," she pants, her fingers combing through the hair at the back of my head, and if I thought this was ecstasy a moment ago, she just knocked it to the next level with that little statement.

"Fuck, sunshine," I murmur, straining to keep my dick from rutting into her like a goddamn animal. "Let me feel you ride me." Squeezing one hand on her ass, I bring the other to cup her breast, trapping her nipple between two fingers.

At first, she slowly rises on her knees and sinks back down on top of me, taking every inch of my cock like her pussy was made just for me. I don't move, keeping my grip on her body but letting her explore what makes her feel good. Slowly rising again, leaving only the tip of my cock inside her, she slams back down, making us both grunt in pleasure.

"Oh god," she whimpers, and before I can respond, she does it again and again, and my body feels like it's on fire. Changing tactic, she slides backward and grinds against me, her clit rubbing against my shaft as she does.

Bringing both hands to her ass, I encourage her to do it again, wanting to see the look of pure bliss on her face one more time before I find my release. I watch as she bites her lips and her body flushes, from her chest to her cheeks, as my hips rock into hers, and I see it, the moment her orgasm rips through her body. The way her hips grind against me and her nipples brush against my chest only add to the feel of her pussy clenching around my cock. The tingles of my orgasm start at my feet, every hair on my body standing on end as I find my release. My eyes roll to the back of my head as she drains every ounce of cum from me.

When I finally open my eyes, her arms are curled around my neck as her head rests on my shoulder. Our bodies glisten with sweat as we try to catch our breaths. "Holy fuck, sunshine."

"Holy fuck indeed," she murmurs against my neck, and it takes me a minute to turn us over, so she is laying on the bed. My dick twitches still as I slowly pull out, making quick work of the condom as I look down at her.

"Give me a second, and I'll grab you a wet cloth unless you'd rather take a shower?" I offer, and she smiles up at me through half-mast eyes, her body exhausted from our little workout. "Wet cloth it is, sunshine."

Quickly stepping into my boxers, I run a hand through my hair, my heart still pounding in my chest. "Okay," she whispers in response, and I slip from the room.

The moment I step into the living room, I'm met with

two sets of eyes glaring the fuck out of me, and I simply grin. These motherfuckers heard every moan she made, and every single one was for me. Raising a two-finger salute at them, I head for the bathroom, take that, nobheads.

KC KEAN

TWENTY SEVEN

Jess

Damn, it's hot in here. Swiping my messy hair back off my face, I stretch, and the second I do, I feel the hard lines of a body beside me. West. My face scrunches as I peek through one eye at him lying beside me. Sunlight filters into the room through the window brightly, since the blinds were never closed last night, casting the perfect light over his god-like chiseled jaw.

Last night was amazing. Perfection. After the shit storm from earlier in the evening and consoling Rafe over the phone, I needed someone to consume me, my mind, body, and soul, and West didn't disappoint. I can still feel how our bodies moved together, I have never felt as sexy as I did last night. I wanted to feel the level of intimacy I had felt with Aiden, with West too, and it was like magic. My body knows it belongs to them the second their hands touch my skin.

I try not to move as I rake my eyes over him. His arm is under my head, while his other hand grips my waist, and my leg is thrown over his hip. Still naked from the night before and comfortable in his presence, I could wake up like this more often.

"I can feel your eyes on me, sunshine," he murmurs, a soft smile on his lips with his eyes still closed, and I move closer, resting my head on his shoulder as his arm tightens around me.

"Good morning."

"Good morning to you too," he responds, kissing my forehead lightly, and it feels like heaven. "Do you know what time it is?"

"Nope, but I'm hungry, so it should be breakfast time, right?" He chuckles lightly in response, squeezing me tighter for a moment before leaning back.

"Breakfast can be arranged. I love this little diner not far from here, I could go and grab us some food."

"Oh my god, yes, please," I agree, kissing his cheek quickly before he climbs out of bed, and I can't take my eyes off his hot, naked body. Stretching out, I finally take a look at the room I'm going to spend the next week in. Pastel mint green walls surround the room, making it feel light and airy with the white wooden furniture around the room. Apart from the bed, there are bedside tables, a vanity, a chest of drawers, and a walk-in closet.

I spot my suitcases sitting by the closet, and I know I need to arrange my things today. It's embarrassing to have to bring two suitcases for just a week, but a lot of it is the damn uniform. Propping myself up on my elbow, I watch as West pulls a plain black t-shirt over his head. His dark denim jeans finish off his casual look, and I could stare at him all day.

"What would you like for breakfast, sunshine?" He asks with a smile, likely enjoying my attention.

"You," I mumble, and he grins at me like the Cheshire cat but doesn't respond. Instead, he raises his eyebrow, waiting for a real answer. "Fine, pancakes, with all the chocolate and peanut butter they have, pretty please," I grumble with a pout.

"It'll cost you a kiss, pretty lady," he says, crawling up

the bed, trapping me under the cover, and I feel like I'm living a dream. I just need them all, even the one that hates me. As if knowing where my thoughts were leading, the door swings open, but it takes a moment to see who it is with West smiling down at me.

"Okay, I'm done fucking waiting. Let me see my redheaded beauty, right now." I giggle at his attempt at a stern voice, and when his megawatt smile comes into view over West's shoulder, I sigh with happiness. "Get off her now, man," Aiden grunts, shoulder barging West off me so he can place a kiss on my lips.

"Good morning, beautiful. Sleep well?" Shaking his head, he grins. "Who am I kidding? Of course you did, all that energy you were burning last night." He winks down at me, but it doesn't stop the blush from creeping up my neck.

"Leave her alone, nobhead. You're embarrassing her," West mumbles, climbing from the bed and blowing me a kiss. "I'm going for breakfast, Aiden, want anything?"

Scrunching his nose, he glances over his shoulder, "Do I want anything? Do bears shit in the woods? Of course I want something. The only thing in that fucking fridge is fruit. Fruit. I need carbs." He pouts down at me and I laugh at his mood. "I need pancakes, bacon, syrup, but enough for three people, okay?"

"What the fuck is this?" Maverick roars, but he sounds distant, a door slamming shut follows his shout as I hear his boots thump along the wooden floor. Pulling the cover over my chest as I sit up, West and Aiden move towards the door to see what's going on.

"What's going on... Ahh shit," Aiden murmurs, looking to West, who is frowning in confusion. "West, I'll come and get breakfast with you. Jess..." Sighing, he turns to me with his lips turned down. "I think the little issue we thought you were dealing with, just got a whole lot bigger." With that, he hightails it out of the room, pushing West out with him, which just leaves Maverick, with his eyes burning into the piece of paper in his hands, as he fills my doorway.

"You better get dressed, petal. Cos I want to know what the fuck this is about, and what the hell Aiden just meant." He turns the piece of paper my way, and my heart drops. I wordlessly nod as my hand clutches the sheet tighter. Maverick continues to stand in the door, looking at me expectantly, and I finally find my voice.

"I need you to leave so I can get dressed."

His eyes crinkle in confusion. "You were okay a minute ago with the others and West last night." Is this guy for real?

"And that's probably because they respect me, and I feel comfortable and safe in their presence," I grind out, and the hurt is evident in his eyes. I know I'm over exaggerating, but this jerk needs to realize he can't be a dick and expect me to be fine with it.

"You have two minutes," he bites out, slamming the door shut behind him.

Fuck.

Flopping back on the bed, I give myself a moment to try and cling to the happiness I felt only moments ago before I have to get up and face my issues that just won't leave me alone.

"Ninety seconds," Maverick shouts, and I growl in frustration.

Quickly making the bed, I pull the orange suitcase up onto the top. Putting on my tight navy joggers and matching cropped hoodie, I bypass any underwear since I'm going to shower once I've dealt with this asshole. Pulling the loose hair tie from my hair, I comb my fingers through the mess before piling it back on top of my head.

Swinging the door open, I expect to see him waiting on the sofa, but he is right in front of me, hands braced at the top of the door frame as he looks down at me. Crossing my hands over my chest, I glare up at him.

"Can I see it?" I ask quietly, lifting my gaze to his and I get lost in the storm brewing in his green eyes. Finally holding the piece of paper out to me, I look over the words.

I FUCKING WARNED YOU.
YOU DIDN'T LISTEN.
NOW YOU HAVE TO FACE THE CONSEQUENCES.
I CAN REACH YOU ANYWHERE,
AND I'M COMING.

Holy shit. My hand lifts to my mouth as I read the words over and over again, my hands trembling as I let them sink in. Who the fuck is this?

"Do you have any idea who this could be from?" He asks, anger in his voice and a tick to his jaw, and I shake my head. "Are there more of them?"

"Yes," I whisper, finally returning my gaze to him.

"Did you bring them here, petal?" His thumb brushes

across my bottom lip, dropping it from the clutches of my teeth, and knocking my hand away. I hadn't even realized I'd been biting it. Nodding in response again, I step back to grab my handbag from the suitcase. My shaking hand clutches the other two tightly as I walk them over to him.

I hand them over without a word, and he reads them over a few times before stuffing them in his pocket while I stand and watch helplessly. His hands fist at his sides as he takes a deep breath or two, followed by the heaviest sigh I've ever heard. I don't know what I'm supposed to do. As I raise my hands to cover my face, his fingers stroke under my chin, holding my head high, as he crouches down to my height, and my heart stops.

"We will figure this out, Jessica," he murmurs, but I can't respond. Dropping his hand, he suddenly lifts my thighs, pulling me to his chest and placing my legs around his waist, just like I did with West yesterday. Gripping his shoulders, I look down at him as he moves us to the living room, dropping down onto the sofa and holding me in place.

Neither of us say anything as we stare into each other's eyes, and I feel myself getting lost in him, just like I did back in Combat. I can't let him hurt me like that again.

Pushing against his chest I try to move, but his grip tightens, and he pulls me in closer, our lips millimeters apart.

"I'm sorry," he breathes, and my eyes shoot to him, surprised by his words. "I'm an asshole, I know that, but I will protect you, and get to the bottom of whatever this shit is. Okay?" His words may be softly spoken, but the determination within them hits me hard in the chest.

"Okay."

"Okay?" He repeats, and I nod, his lips capturing mine gently in response. My heartbeat rings in my ears at the soft touch of his mouth on mine, slowly taking everything from me. My fingers cup his face, the feel of his stubble under my touch has my nipples perking beneath the cropped hoodie. His callous hands move up my waist, and the skin on skin contact sets me on fire.

His hands continue to travel up my ribs, and I hear him hiss when he realizes I have no bra on. My hips grind down on him automatically, and I feel his hard length through his sweatpants. His lips travel to my neck as my fingers curl around the hair at the back of his, just as the door swings open.

"Fuck," Maverick mutters, as the chatter of Aiden and West fills the room. Resting my forehead on Maverick's shoulder, I notice they go quiet as they clearly see what they've walked in on.

"Holy mother of fuck, you two together gets me so fucking hard. West, you have to agree with me, right?"

"Yeah," I hear West murmur, and I lift up, shaking my head in embarrassment. "You guys, are too much."

"Well, duh," Aiden responds. "Now come eat, beautiful."

They both empty the bags of food on to the table, and it looks like we're going to be feeding a football team with the amount of stuff here, but since Maverick showed me the note, I've lost my appetite.

"I'm not hungry." Climbing off Maverick's lap, I sit beside him, watching as he readjusts himself. I have to put my hands under my thighs as I bite my lip. All this shit has me needing a nap, but I don't know how I'd even get myself to sleep. Someone is watching me, and they don't like what I'm doing.

"You need to eat, sunshine. How about we eat and talk at the same time, yeah?"

Before I can argue back, Maverick is turning my head to face him. "Don't even bother arguing. You need to eat, and we need to figure this shit out."

Sighing, I take the box from Aiden, and the second I open the lid and smell the fluffy pancakes coated in chocolate sauce, my tummy grumbles. Refusing to meet their knowing gazes, I take the plastic knife and fork and dig in. Holy shit, this place really is good. Thankfully, the guys follow suit, and we all eat in silence.

When my pancakes are all gone, and I've devoured every inch of peanut butter and chocolate sauce, I place the empty box on the table, and Aiden holds a bottle of orange juice out to me. I smile at him in appreciation as I take it from him, but he stops me in my tracks as he swipes his thumb at the corner of my lip.

"You had a little something." I watch, open-mouthed, as he sucks his thumb clean.

Oh. My. Days. Yes. Please.

Aiden grins, knowing his effect on me as Maverick clears his throat. "We need to talk about this threat. Someone is clearly watching you and warning you against one of us, unless there's someone else?"

"As much as you like to think it, I'm not a whore." I spin my head around, glaring at him, but he actually raises his hands in surrender, surprise mixed in the grey of his eyes at my outburst.

"I didn't mean it like that."

Deciding honesty is the best way to handle this, I look down at my hands. "Well, since I've been at Featherstone Academy, there have only been three guys, and you are all in this room."

"And what about Reece Wicker?" I cringe at the name on Maverick's lips as I look to the others who are staring at me expectantly. "He was trying to grope Jessica in a Combat class," he adds, fueling the fire in West and Aiden's eyes.

Sighing again, I rub my sweaty hands down my thighs, as I push myself to openly answer his question. "I slept with Reece at the beginning of summer, at a party, and I didn't see him again until he was standing in my mother's dining room, planning for a wedding."

"The fuck?" Aiden mutters, as West clears his throat.

"My father got me out of there after I insulted Reece and his dick, infuriating my mother, and since I've been here, he's hinted a few times that he wants more. But nothing has happened with him since you punched him in the face," I say, looking to Maverick.

"Fucking scum," West growls, and it catches me off guard hearing anger in his voice.

Leaning forward, bracing his arms on his knees, Maverick holds my gaze. "You can't be alone, at any time, especially outside of this apartment. One of us will be with you at all times, even if that means you are sitting in on Combat or Weaponry lessons."

"What? Don't be crazy, that's completely…"

"The right thing to do," Aiden interrupts, and I stare around at all of them.

"You can't be serious!"

"Deadly," Maverick grunts. "Your safety is our number one priority. Get used to it."

West and Aiden nod in agreement and I roll my eyes. Apparently, what I want or think, means nothing. I need to clear my head, and I can't do that here with them dictating where I will and won't be going.

Patting my legs, I stand. "Well, if that's all you need from me, I'm going to shower." Without a backward glance, I storm for the bathroom. I hear West call out my name, but I'm done talking. Slamming the door shut behind me, I lean against it.

I need to get my shit together, and I need to do it quickly.

KC KEAN

TWENTY EIGHT

Jess

Fresh out of the shower, I glance at all the outfits I brought here, trying to organize them so I can hang them in the closet. The sooner I get this done, the quicker I can dive into a book on my Kindle and escape in the best possible way. Wearing a pair of high-waisted black leggings with a cropped white tee and a checkered shirt, I put the last item away as a knock sounds at the door.

"Come in."

"Hey, sunshine," West murmurs with a soft smile as he sneaks his head around the open door. "Luna's calling your phone." I rush at him in an instant. I hadn't even realized

I'd been without a phone.

"Thank you, West," I whisper, placing a kiss on his lips as I take the phone. "Luna? Luna, I swear to god, this better be you calling! I have been going out of my damn mind over here!" I yell, my heart pounding as I wait for a response.

"Hey, Jess. You okay?"

Oh, thank god. My hand clutches the neckline of my t-shirt as I sigh in relief, until I process what she actually said, and I frown in confusion. "You only call me Jess when things are serious. What's going on, Luna?"

"It's a little hectic, but we're okay. How are things at Maverick's? All good?" She asks, and I can tell she's trying to change the subject. I want to hear everything and anything about what is going on over there with her and the Aces, but I understand not wanting to discuss it.

Looking to West, he must sense I need some privacy. Giving me a wink, he steps back, and I shut the door. "It's fine, everything's fine. Don't worry about me, just stay safe, okay?" Taking a seat on the bed, I jump a little as the door swings back open, and Aiden steps inside, clearly not respecting my space. I shake my head at him as I shush him so that I can focus on my conversation with Luna.

"Alright. One other thing before I go, I need you to stay away from Trudy. She was somehow involved with them drugging us and taking us."

"What?" I murmur, shocked, and devastated by her words. My eyes instantly fall to Aiden, who is looking at me with concern from where he stands near the door, but my heart pounds in my chest. Did he know? Did. He. Fucking. Know?

"Yeah, something Veronica said, you know, before I killed her," Luna continues, not knowing that she may have just shattered my heart. Pushing through the pain pulsing through my veins, I hear what else she just said. Deciding not to mention Rafe already told us, I react as calmly as possible.

"Thank god. That bitch had it coming, and when I see Trudy, I'm going to give her a piece ..."

"Keep away from her, remember? Let her sweat it out. I'll deal with her eventually," Luna mumbles, and I sigh, pinching the bridge of my nose as I get lost inside my own head.

"Red, I'm gonna have to go. I'll check in as often as I can, okay?"

"Yeah, of course. Love ya, Captain. Make smart

choices!" I shout, trying to stay positive, but not feeling it in my bones like I usually do.

"I love you too, sassy pants. Behave." The call ends, silence the only thing that greets me through the phone before lowering it to the bed beside me.

"What's wrong, Jess?" Aiden asks as he takes a seat beside me on the bed. I need to decide whether to keep my mouth shut, so Luna has the element of surprise with Trudy, or ask him point blank right now if he knew and broke my trust.

Looking into his eyes, I feel my emotions bubble inside, and my eyes tingle with fear. "Did you know?" I whimper, and I hate myself for sounding weak.

"Did I know what, beautiful?" Placing his hand on top of mine, I clench my hand into a fist, denying him the ability to lace our fingers together like he was trying to.

"Did you know Trudy had something to do with Luna and Parker being drugged?" I scrutinize his face, watching for his reaction, and it scares me how relieved I am to see the shock and disbelief on his face.

"She didn't, she wouldn't, Jess."

"Well, something's been said, and Luna knows."

Cupping my cheek, he brushes his thumb against my

skin, and I can't stop myself from leaning into his touch. "I swear, Jess, I have no idea what it is you're talking about, and I'll do whatever you need to prove that to you."

I don't know what to believe or say, but my gut tells me he's telling the truth. The bedroom door swings open again, this time Maverick steps into the room, glancing between us as we pull apart. "You done on the phone?" I barely nod in response before he continues. "Good, get your shit. We're going down to the Weaponry Hall to teach you how to use a gun."

Well, okay then.

West

Unlocking the door to the Weaponry Hall, I step back to let the others through. Maverick knows his way around here, so he leads the way, flicking the lights on as we move towards the safe. I can't say I'm not excited to show my girl her way around a gun, especially if she is in any danger. If I can help protect Jess in any way, I will, even if that means encouraging her to defend herself by any means necessary. The use of a firearm within Featherstone is vital, and I want Jess to have the best advantage possible to survive in this world.

I can tell something has shaken her since she was on the phone with Luna, but she hasn't mentioned anything. Frown lines come and go from her forehead as she massages her temples, while Aiden hasn't stopped tapping away on his phone, and swiping a hand down his face. I'm sure we'll find out eventually, but I don't want to push her. Not when I can tell she is already out of her depth emotionally.

I watch as Jess takes in the room, looking over every inch of the space with curiosity, as Aiden and I check her out from behind, and Maverick continues to look over his shoulder at her. She has us all hooked, and I can't say it makes me mad. Everything may seem a little strained right now, with having to stay at Maverick's and Luna away at The Games, but I'm falling for her, and I don't want it to stop.

She looks stunning, in her leggings, cropped white t-shirt, and loose red and black checked shirt. Her sexy lace-up black ankle boots and gold hooped earrings give her an edgier look than usual.

"Stop staring at her ass, and open the safe, West," Maverick grumbles from the far corner of the room, making Jess look over her shoulder at me. I just shrug and offer her a wink, not denying his accusation, and I watch her blush slightly before stopping in front of the safe too.

Pressing my palm to the electronic screen, I let it scan my print, before I enter the six-digit code and the sounds of the locks turning fill the room. This safe is massive, bigger than any of the vaults on campus, and it's literally filled with guns in all shapes and sizes.

Maverick steps in first, the rest of us following his lead. "Have you used a gun before, Aiden?" He asks, and Aiden nods in response.

"Yeah. You learn to pull a trigger as soon as you learn to start mixing chemicals in my family."

Glancing at Jess, I watch as she looks around at all of the guns, this must be daunting for her. I try to look at the four walls filled with guns, from rifles and shotguns to sniper rifles and automatics, from her perspective, and I know it must be difficult.

"Maverick, grab a few of everything with Aiden. I'm going to take Jess and a Glock 17 to the far corner. Come meet us in a minute," I say, grabbing the pistol and a box of ammunition from the shelf by the door. Looking to Jess, I nod my head towards the door for her to follow me.

Walking us to the opposite corner of the room, where the easier targets are set up for beginners, I place the gun on the table. "Are you ready to learn your way around a gun?" I ask, and she raises her eyebrows at me.

"Sure." She shrugs her shoulders and moves to stand in front of the black and red target.

Offering her a pair of ear defenders, Aiden and Maverick come to stand with us. Maverick drags another table closer to place the other guns and bullets on. They clearly don't want to miss our girl's first time with a gun, and I can't say I blame them.

Our girl. *Our girl.* We need to talk about this and make it official, because she is mine, ours, and I need to make sure she knows that.

Grabbing the Glock from the table, I click the safety off and move to stand beside Jess, holding the gun out for her to feel the weight. Watching her hand squeeze around the grip has my dick stirring in my pants. Holy fuck. A firearm should not look so good in her delicate hands.

"So, what you want to do, sunshine, is hold the gun with your dominant hand and place it high on the grip." I watch as she does as I say, and I can't stop myself from stepping up behind her, bringing my chest to her back.

Wrapping my hands around hers, I continue. "Wrap your last three fingers around the base of the grip, below the trigger guard. Don't use a death grip. We want to simply hold it firmly."

She listens to what I say, and I can feel the guys edging closer to where we stand, drawn to her. "Place the heel of your non-dominant hand underneath like this." Guiding her hand into position, I murmur in her ear, turned on by the whole situation. "Feet shoulder width apart, square your shoulders, lock down your sight, and take a deep breath." Giving her a moment to get comfortable, I give my last instruction. "When you're ready, sunshine, shoot."

Bringing my hands to her waist, I wait patiently for her to find her zone before she pulls the trigger. That motherfucker hits the red eyed center. I can't believe it. Glancing to Maverick beside me, I see the look of surprise in his eyes too.

Before anyone says anything else, she pulls the trigger, again and again, hitting the mark every time. What the fuck?

"So, would someone like to finally ask me how much experience I have with a gun, or should I continue to play dumb for a little longer?" Jess asks, knocking the safety off, and releasing the magazine from its chamber. Stepping out of my grip at her hips, she moves to the table, reloading the gun like a pro, all while maintaining eye contact with me.

"Yes, girl, you fucking sass us. I love it," Aiden says, bursting into laughter, and I shake my head as I grin too.

"Okay, maybe I should have asked."

"Damn right, you should have asked," she says with a fake glare. "Now, take me to the long-range zone." Dropping the gun to the table, she takes off for the other end of the space as we all watch her ass sway as she leaves.

"Holy fuck," Maverick mutters, adjusting himself, just as turned on as us. Holy fuck indeed.

Aiden is the first to move, running to her side and wrapping his arm around her shoulder. "Beautiful, that was so fucking hot, I am not worthy of your presence."

Screw off, fucking ass wipe. "He's such an ass licker," Maverick grouches, and I grin.

"Yeah, but he's not fucking wrong." Grabbing the guns from the table, we follow after them, and she smiles with pride at me when I kiss her cheek in passing. "So, where did you learn to do that?" I ask, intrigued.

Rubbing her hands down her leggings, she looks

around the room nervously. "Did you know my mother was the original parent with a link to Featherstone? Her Academy assignment was to bring my father into the fold by any means necessary, so she chose marriage." Wow. "When that happened, they allowed my mother and her bloodline to take a backseat, wanting to push my father's abilities within the Science field, which is what I'm here for." Sighing, she looks to the ceiling. "That didn't stop my grandfather from making sure I knew how to use a gun or a weapon in general. It's just my actual body strength I seem to have an issue with, and not feeling panicked under pressure."

Processing her words, I'm surprised as Maverick steps in front of her, bending his knees to bring his eyes level with hers. "We're working on that, petal, remember?"

"Are we?" She asks, refusing to look away from him. "Because we haven't trained since I let myself be vulnerable with you. You got scared and ran."

Biting his lip, I watch as his hand's fist at his sides. "It won't happen again," he finally grinds out, and she slowly nods in response. His hands relax at her acceptance as she kisses him quickly on the lips and steps back.

"It better not. Now, pass me a motherfucking gun. It's

surprisingly calming."

Yes, ma'am.

RED

KC KEAN

TWENTY NINE

Jess

Holy fucking shit. When Maverick said I wouldn't be left alone outside of his apartment, he wasn't fucking kidding. They are everywhere, yet I can't seem to bring myself to complain about it. Yesterday, Maverick dropped Aiden and me off at the academic buildings, where Aiden sat beside me in LFG, which was completely strange. I usually sat alone in here, and he would sit with Trudy, but no one seems to bat an eyelid. I sensed him looking towards his sister throughout the whole lesson, while his hand remained on my thigh, and I could feel the tension building between them the entire time. I believe Aiden when he says he didn't know, but he needs to have a talk with Trudy. I just don't want to get involved, so I hope he figures it out.

I spent the rest of the day having Combat class with Maverick and a one-on-one session afterward. He worked me to the bone, but I already feel much more confident in myself. So, when he said we should have another training session in my free period this afternoon, I agreed. Any excuse to watch him in just a pair of shorts, flexing his muscles, and I will be there willingly.

Walking into the Combat Hall in my sports bra and fitness shorts, I'm surprised to find West and Aiden with Maverick. Phone in hand, I walk towards them, just as Parker's voice filters through the phone.

"Hey, Jess," he answers, and I can hear the exhaustion in his voice.

"Hey, Parker. Sorry, I know she said she would call me when she could. I, uh, I just got worried." I rub the worry marks from my forehead as I walk towards the guys.

"No, it's okay. Luna's just in the bath, I can get her."

"Well, she's only alive if I actually speak to her," I say with a smile, and he chuckles lightly down the phone. "How are you all doing? Okay?" I ask, wanting to make sure they are all intact.

"We're good, Red." He pauses for a moment, cursing down the phone. "Shit, sorry, even I'm calling you Red now. Luna has a cut on her cheek, and Oscar has a couple of bruises, but we're all in one piece. One second, she's here." I hear him murmuring with Luna, but I'm still caught on the fact he called me Red too. Since Luna started calling me that, I feel like my life has started changing, and I love the reminder it gives me.

Hearing a door click shut down the other end of the phone, I call out. "Luna?"

"Hey, Red."

"Luna, Parker said you were cut on your cheek. Are you okay?"

"I'm fine, it didn't even need stitches. Becky's aim could have used some work," she responds, and her complete casualness catches me off guard. West stares at me intently as I react to her words.

"Becky? Becky did it? I hope you buried her," I growl through the phone, Aiden's hand squeezes mine in comfort.

"The last time I saw her, she was bleeding out on the floor. I didn't look back to check if she was still breathing or not."

"Why do you always attract the crazy bitches, Captain?"

Luna laughs at me, as Maverick raises his eyebrow at me. "Same way I attracted you apparently," she chuckles down the phone, and I scrunch my nose at her shitty jokes.

"Not funny. Now, tell me everything."

"There isn't much else to say, except Brett is dead. Otherwise, it was the usual fucked up Featherstone event."

"Brett's dead? How?" I squeak down the phone, my hand gripping Aiden's tighter, as my frantic eyes search for West.

"Oscar and Parker." She sighs.

Knowing she is okay, my mind can stop worrying for a minute. Talking for a little while, even West speaks to her, and it surprises me how much I love hearing West talk to her, not a single ounce of jealousy. The fact that they could have been married once upon a time doesn't even register in my brain because they never grew to be those people. I can see the love he has for her, but it's the family kind, and I'm glad she has him.

"Sorry, I had to check in," I murmur, dropping my phone to the mat.

"No stress, I'll just make you work harder, for making me wait," Maverick says with a grin, and I think he's trying to be funny, but who is ever sure with him?

"Oh, really?"

"Hey, sunshine," West says with a resigned look on his face, and I step straight into his arms which he holds out wide.

"Everything okay?"

"It is now that I have you." He kisses the top of my head, and I can't stop the shiver from running through my body.

"Oh, you have me, huh?" I ask with a grin, trying to lighten whatever is playing on his mind.

"Yeah I do. So does Aiden, and Maverick, when he pulls his finger out of his ass," he winks down at me, holding me tight, and I relish in it.

"Do I get a say in any of this? Because this is a pretty shit way of claiming me," I state, and it doesn't pass by me that Maverick and Aiden don't argue with what he's saying. I fake being inconvenienced, but inside, my heart is about to leap out of my chest with happiness.

"I'll make it up to you when I get back, but you are most definitely mine, sunshine." Lifting me off my feet, he twirls me around, making me giddy from his attention.

"When you get back? Where are you going?" I ask

with a pout, and he sighs.

"I've been called away, more Featherstone related work, but I should be back by Thursday." I look at him in confusion, wanting to know what he's talking about, but Maverick interrupts.

"I'll explain later on, petal. West needs to leave if he's to catch his flight."

I feel a little out of my depth with what they are and aren't saying right now, but I have to trust in them and shelf this information for later, like they're asking.

"Okay," I answer, and West nods appreciatively, claiming my lips with his for a moment before he backs away, and I watch him leave, still staring at the door when it shuts behind him.

"I hope you stare longingly at the door like this since I have to leave now too," Aiden says, wrapping his arm around my shoulders.

"Where are you going?" I ask, looking up at him, and he kisses the tip of my nose.

"Trudy has finally agreed to meet me." I offer him a soft smile, seeing the strain in his eyes. Wrapping my arms tightly around his waist, I squeeze him tight until Maverick groans.

"Okay, shithead. Go, do what you need to do so I can put our girl through her paces."

"Our girl, huh?" Aiden asks, with a waggle of his eyebrows, and I feel my blush take over my cheeks. "Don't blush, beautiful, he likes me when I'm playful, don't you, boo." Blowing a kiss in Maverick's direction, he turns and leaves.

"I can't fucking deal with you all," Maverick sighs, and I chuckle, seeing the heat in his eyes.

"Wait, does Mr. Broody get a little stiff over Mr. Sassy?" I ask, completely bypassing any filter on my mouth, and the surprise in Maverick's eyes says it hasn't gone unnoticed, but then they darken and he's coming back at me just as quick.

"I could think of much more useful things for him to do with that mouth of his, for one, if that's what you're asking," he responds, baiting me to stammer at his response, but he has no idea what I'm fucking into.

"Do not tease," I purr, stepping into his space, looking up at him with my eyes wide. "I've been looking for some new porn material, the ones that usually do the job have been lacking lately." He gapes down at me, and I offer him a playful wink. "Now train me, hot stuff, I need to defend myself."

Maverick

Jessica Watson will be the fucking death of me from blue balls. The way she always seems to surprise me brings me to my knees time and time again. She killed it again today in our one-on-one session. Her reaction times were much quicker as I made sure not to give her any advance notice for what was about to come.

Now, she's smiling at me like I hung the moon because I agreed we could have pepperoni pizza while it was just the two of us. Sitting on the sofa, The Vampire Diaries plays on my television, she looks perfectly in place, yet I can feel myself wanting to push her away. My brain wanting to put a safety net up between us.

Taking a seat beside her as I place the pizzas on the coffee table, I make sure to keep some distance between us. Freshly showered, with her hair falling around her face in waves and no make-up, I could stare at her for hours. I can see the questions in her eyes though, wanting to discuss what West mentioned earlier, and I know I need to word this right, or I'm going to fuck it all up.

Pulling a bottle of water off the table, I gulp half of it down in one go. Sighing, I look in her direction. "What do you want to ask first?"

"How about you start wherever you think is best," she answers with a sigh of her own, but I don't miss the way her back straightens, as if she's preparing herself for whatever I'm about to say. I take a moment, trying to decide where would actually be best to start, without me giving her a huge history lesson.

"So, I need you to tell me if I'm not explaining things right, or if I'm making you want to run for the hills, okay?" Brushing my hair off my face, I watch her, waiting for her to acknowledge what I'm asking, and she offers a small nod. "West and I have more than one job within Featherstone."

"And what do those other jobs entail?" The question is casual, but the way she takes a huge bite of pizza straight after shows me her nerves.

Clearing my throat, I make sure to meet her gaze. "It means we take care of business; however they need us to, depending on our skillset." I watch as she processes my words, figuring out what they expect from us based on our bloodlines.

"So, that means when West is called away, it links to him using a gun?" She looks to me for confirmation, but there isn't any fear in her eyes yet.

"Yes." Before she can ask her next question, I answer it for her. "I'm one of the brutes of the Featherstone. I get sent to do the beat downs or infiltrate other crime organizations to help bring them down."

"Are you pulled away for that a lot?" I frown, never really considering the answer to her question before. "I mean, I guess, sometimes, but nowhere near as much as I used to."

Her eyes search mine, assessing me. "I can feel a story there." I don't answer her because she's not wrong, but I'm not going there. Clearly taking the hint, she presses in a different direction. "Should I be worried about your safety?" I still at her words, frozen by the sincerity in her voice, and it does something to my soul.

Forcing myself to take a deep breath, I try to be as honest as possible. "There is always a risk with what we do, petal, but that comes with everything in life and in Featherstone." Looking down at her hands, I give her a moment to consider what else she wants to ask, when my phone vibrates in my pocket.

Shit. "Yeah?" I grunt, answering the call, refusing to look in Jessica's direction.

"Ricky boy, they're calling you up. You're on in two hours, see you then." As simple as that the line goes dead. Fuck.

"Is everything okay?" Jessica asks, her hand reaching over and squeezing my thigh.

"Duty calls, apparently. I need you to try and get a hold of Aiden for me because I need to leave, and I refuse to leave you alone." She looks taken back when I turn my gaze to hers, but she nods rapidly, grabbing her phone from the cushion beside her. Standing, I pace the floor as I watch her meet a dead end. Trying him a further two times, she looks at me helplessly.

"It's okay, do what you need to do, Maverick. I'll be safe here."

Trying to call Aiden myself, I'm met with the same sound of the call ringing out and sending me to voicemail. Shit. "Not a chance in hell, petal. It looks like you're about to get a live view of what being called up looks like." Holding my hand out for her to take, I sigh, knowing I'm risking more than just my life right now. "Let's go."

KC KEAN

THIRTY

Jess

My heart is pounding in my chest, and I don't know whether it's with excitement or fear. Looking up at the warehouse from Maverick's car, it looks as if the place is shut, but he assured me it will be buzzing inside. Running my fingers against the edge of the leather seat beneath me, I look across to Maverick, still feeling the rumble of his damn race car before he shuts off the engine.

Luna would love this car, fuck, even I love this car, and all I know is it has four wheels and a stick, but the throttle had me squirming in my seat. The grin on Maverick's face the whole way here tells me he fucking knew it too.

"When we get in there, you keep your eyes down and your mouth shut. The people on the inside of those walls are not safe, and I barely trust one guy to watch you while I do what I need to do, as quickly as possible." He has one hand braced on the steering wheel, and the other is clenched in his lap. I can tell he doesn't want me here, but he preferred that to leaving me alone.

"God, if I didn't think you were saying those things to protect me, I'd punch you in the dick for being a bossy jackass," I say, glaring at him, but he pays me no attention. "Are you finally going to tell me what you are expected to do here?" This is the part that has me nervous.

He sighs, looking out of the window instead of meeting my gaze. "I'm here because the people who run this joint are messing around in guns, prostitution, and drugs. They don't seem to have gotten the memo that Featherstone runs the criminal underworld, that or they just don't care. So, I'm here to infiltrate their system, then we can shut these fuckers down and teach them a lesson." I gulp at his words, it's one thing knowing what Featherstone does as a whole, but it's completely different knowing someone's specific role. Although I don't feel sick at his words or what he has to do, if anything, I feel like I understand. It's even crazier that I know this role suits him.

"Okay, and how are you infiltrating them tonight?" I ask, watching his face for any sign of a lie, but the truth is all I see.

"I'm a fighter on their books. I've been coming here to fight in organized matches for the past four months to work my way in." Well, his combat training definitely comes in useful then.

"So, I'm going to be watching you fight?" I ask, excited by the thought, and he grunts in response.

"Let's go."

Shaking my head, I step out of the car, glancing down at myself. He said I had to fit in but not draw attention to myself, but he's been calling me a distraction the whole ride over. I had to make do with what I had available at his apartment, to make myself look edgy and a little grungy. Wearing my cropped hoodie, with a pair of leather-looking leggings and wedges I shiver a little at my midriff being exposed to the breeze. I have my big gold hoop earrings in, and my hair French braided down my back, with heavy make-up and deep navy lips.

Meeting him at the front of the car, he places his hand on my lower back, guiding me towards the entrance.

The heat from his touch combats the cold around us as I try to keep up my pace with his. He raps his knuckles on the metal door, and the second it opens my senses are overloaded. Music hums heavily in the distance as we step inside, and the door slams shut behind us. Maverick's hand doesn't waver as he guides me down the narrow corridor and opens the door to the right at the very end. I step in, but not before seeing all the bodies in the open space we just turned away from.

Looking around me, we're in a locker room. The yellow walls are lined with benches and coat hangers, and the tiled floor feels sticky beneath my wedges. So gross. No one is in here, but the showers are off to the left, and I can hear one running.

Releasing his hold on me, Maverick drops his duffel bag on the bench and instantly starts undressing. Watching his tanned chest come into view as he lifts his t-shirt over his head fills me with tingles, making my stomach clench. I probably should turn my gaze away, but I can't get my eyes to move.

"My eyes are up here, you know," I hear him murmur, and I can hear a hint of humor in his voice, but I don't lift my gaze.

"Uh huh, I'm aware." His hands clutch his t-shirt at his waist, and I can see his veins bulge as his forearms flex. Holy fuck. I don't realize he's getting closer to me until his thumb brushes against my bottom lip, releasing it from my teeth. My eyes shoot up to meet his, and he grins down at me. I hadn't even realized I'd been doing that.

"When I'm done out there, I'll make you feel good, petal, as long as you do as I say, okay?" I nod in agreement, clamping my lips shut when I realize I'm gaping up at him in awe. "You have to say it, Jessica. Consent doesn't come from a nod, it comes from words, and what I want to do to you requires consent."

Holy mother of... "Yes. Whatever you say." I practically shout, wanting to feel his hands on me again, and he smiles down at me, heat in his eyes as he steps away to finish getting changed. "How old are you?" I blurt out. Not that it's an issue, he already has me in knots, but I actually don't know.

"Old enough to know better."

"To know what better?" I ask in confusion, and he rolls his eyes at me.

"When I'm letting someone consume me, knowing someone is going to get hurt." I go to step towards him, but he raises his palm, and I stop myself. "I went through my darkest hours alone, petal. I didn't let you in, you just crawled under my skin without my permission, and I can't seem to bring myself to push you away."

"Then don't," I answer quietly. This moment right here feels a little raw, like he's offering me a small peek inside his soul, but he closes the window quickly. The door behind me swings open, and an older guy with grey hair and his arms covered in tattoos steps in. He seems nice enough, in his shorts and t-shirt, he looks like he's ready to fight too.

"Ricky boy, you ready to go?" He asks before his eyes find me. "Who is this little piece?"

"She's under your protection, Brian. If anything happens to her while I'm in that ring, I will gut you and strangle you with your fucking intestines. Understood?" Maverick growls and I stare at him with wide-eyes, but this guy just chuckles.

"Whatever you say. Come on, pretty thing, it's about to start."

Maverick glares at him for a moment before he nods at me to follow the guy. "Remember what I said, petal." Folding my arms over my chest, I smile softly in acknowledgment but before I leave he calls my name, making me turn back. "Twenty-four." I mouth my thank you, and he nods at me. It's just a number, but anything personal about him feels like a new milestone.

Following Brian, who heads straight for the crowd, I'm surrounded by people, and the further into the open space I get, the more people I see. It's beyond rowdy in here, the smell of stale beer fills the air, and every guy I catch a glimpse of looks deadly, making the hairs on my arms stand on end. There must be hundreds of bodies, and they're all hovering around the cage in the center of the room waiting for the next fight, Maverick's fight. It's that realization that has my heart beating wildly in my chest.

"Come on, sweetheart. You don't want to be swallowed up by the crowd," Brian says, steering me towards a small platform on the opposite side of the room to the locker room. Standing behind the metal railing, I hear the music change, and an announcer begins speaking.

"Ladies and gentlemen! I give you, Gregg Weller and our rising star, Ricky Mills." The crowd goes wild when I hear what I can only assume is Maverick's name here, but it's the other guy who appears in the ring first. I don't recognize the song booming through the speakers, but he's lapping up the attention. His arms raised above his head, he throws a few fake punches out, grinning wide and winking at all the ladies. The whole thing makes me cringe.

Then the music stops altogether, and I look to Brian in confusion, but he just grins and nods towards the locker room. Maverick steps towards the cage, and the crowd has to be separated to let him through. It's like everybody is trying to get closer to him. He's clearly a favorite around here. They're hyped, and he didn't even have any music to add to his vibe. That's when I notice his hands aren't wrapped, and a quick glance at the other guy shows me the same. Holy shit, this is bare-knuckle fighting. My heart starts to pound in my ears for fear of his safety.

"Are you ready to watch him beat the fuck out of this guy?" Brian asks, and I offer a weak smile. Checking out the space from our slightly elevated position, I glance around the room, my eyes locking on a man sitting in what looks like a VIP area. Dressed in a fitted black suit, with a white shirt with the top few buttons open, he looks every inch of a mafia boss. Bodyguards stand to either side of him as a woman trails her lips down his neck, and her hand gropes his dick through his pants. He wets his lips as he looks me over, and my skin crawls under his scrutiny.

Dark brown hair, and even darker eyes, I feel him trying to undress me in his mind.

Quickly turning to face the ring again, I answer Brian. "I'm not sure, to be honest," I murmur truthfully, but Brian is looking up at the guy whose eyes haven't left my body.

"You might want to be careful there, sweetheart. That's Frankie Winters, this is his place, and he sees women as toys. He'll chew you up and spit you out broken, whether you wanted to be a part of his little bubble or not. Some don't make it out alive." I don't respond to his words as I focus on the cage, distracting myself from his gaze. Those are some heavy words, and I do not need to dig any deeper into them.

The sound of a bell rings, and Maverick's opponent leaps into action. He charges straight at Maverick, but my guy is quick on his feet, moving out of his reach at the last moment, and following through with a punch to the face.

I wince as I hear the contact of skin on skin from here, but the crowd loves it. They go around in circles a few times, this Gregg guy is continuing to try and catch Maverick off guard, but Maverick always has the upper hand, outsmarting his moves, and defending every attempt of an attack. I can see the frustration in Gregg's eyes. He's about to react with real rage, his eyes and body language calculating some kind of dirty move, but Maverick must see it too as he pounces on him for the first time. His moves are swift, accurate, and practiced. The way his muscles bulge and the determination shines in his eyes has me filled with need.

Squeezing the railing in my hands, I try to calm myself down, but watching him do his thing is intoxicating. His fists are raised, and I watch as he rains down punch after punch on his opponent, clearly having had enough of playing around. I watch as Gregg's body falls to the floor, blood pumping from his nose and a cut above his eye, and he lies motionless. Sweat drips from Maverick's forehead, as he looks in my direction. A bell sounds, I think the crowd goes wild at the win, but I don't hear anything, and the only thing I see is Maverick climbing from the cage and beckoning me over.

My feet move on their own, wanting to get to him as quickly as possible. People jostle me as I try to make my way to him, but he meets me halfway, holding his hand out for me to take. His hand clamps around mine, and the feel of blood on his knuckles has my heart stuttering. Glancing to my right, I pause, is that … is that Gina? My History tutor? A guy cuts across the direction I'm looking, and when I glance again, she's gone. Shaking my head I must be losing it. Squeezing his hand tighter, I focus on moving with Maverick. I should be scared of him, frightened by what he can actually do, but I need him now more than ever.

I let him pull me along, knocking people out of our way as they try to get his attention, heading straight for the locker room. The second the door shuts behind us, he looks around the room for anybody else, but it's empty and he locks the door.

The hunger in his eyes matches my own as he crowds my space, pushing me back against the door. His bloodied hand cups my cheek as he stares deeply into my eyes.

"Please," I murmur, not knowing what I'm asking for, but his mouth descends on mine with force, and I gasp against his lips. Wrapping my arms around his neck, I hold him closer, and he lifts me off the ground, pinning me to the door. His cock nestles between my legs as I wrap my legs around him, and my head falls back against the door with a thud as pleasure courses through my body. "I need you, Maverick."

"I don't want you to hate me for fucking you in a

dirty locker room," he mutters against my throat, and his consideration only makes me hotter.

"Please, Maverick. I need you now. Hard and fast. Don't make me wait," I beg, raking my fingers through his hair. "If you put me in that car right now, I'm going to cum all over the seat, and I'd rather explode on your dick."

His green eyes darken as he searches my eyes, looking for any uncertainty, but he won't find any. I mean every word. His hold on the back of my thighs loosens as he drops my feet back to the floor, an overwhelming sense of disappointment taking over. Before I can protest, he spins me around to face the door, pulling me back against his chest. I try to catch my breath before he places a hand in the center of my back, encouraging me to bend towards the door. Bracing my hands on the wooden door, his hands slowly stroke up my stomach, slipping under my cropped hoodie to find my breast bare for him.

"Fuck, Jessica," he hisses, rolling my nipples between his fingers and I moan with pleasure.

Feeling his hand slowly trail down my stomach to the waistband of my leggings, my back arches at the sensitive touch, but as he slowly pulls them down I gasp as the cool air meets my exposed skin. Leaving my leggings midthigh, his hands stroke over the globes of my ass, my tiny thong the only thing covering my pussy. Looking over my shoulder at him, his eyes are focused on my ass as he lifts a hand and spanks me.

"Ah, shit," I whisper. He fucking spanked me, and I liked it. Maverick's eyes find mine as he strokes the reddening skin, and my mouth falls open, a moan desperate to escape.

"You look divine when your body is screaming for me to leave my mark, your body is begging for me to cover your ass in this pink glow."

"Then do it."

His eyes flare at my words, and in the next second, he's ripping my lace underwear from my body, dropping the torn material to the floor as his hand comes down on my backside again. I moan in pleasure, and as his hand strokes between my legs, he finds the evidence of just how much I'm enjoying this.

"Fuck," he grunts, tilting my hips up and spreading my legs as far as they will go with the restriction of the leggings. Stroking a finger around my pussy, he slaps my ass with his other hand, and I cry out in ecstasy.

Wrapping his hand around my waist, I groan as his

fingers pull away from my pussy, but a moment later, when his cock is thrusting inside of me, stretching me in the most delicious way, I whimper in bliss.

"You feel like heaven, petal," he strains to say. His grip on my hips tightening as he holds himself deep inside of me. "Are you sure you want hard and fast?" He asks, and I can't remember how to talk.

"Please," I slur, high on the ecstasy pumping in my veins, and he doesn't disappoint. I feel every ridge of his hard cock as he slowly pulls out before he slams into me hard and fast, just like I asked. Over and over again, he repeats the same pace, taking his sweet ass time pulling out of my pussy before thrusting deep inside of me like his life depends on it. My body feels electric, drowning in the pleasure of every move.

Stroking the pad of his finger on my swollen clit, I cry out, feeling my orgasm rising. My hands slip slightly on the door, unable to hold me up properly. As he hits my g-spot, his whole hand comes down in between my legs, and slaps my clit, jolting me, and I scream. My pussy clamps down, tightening around his cock as he suddenly pinches my clit too. My head falls against the door, trying to hold me up as his other arm catches my waist, and he grinds into me, and I feel his cock pulsing deep inside of me as he cums with me.

Frozen in place, I let the world surround me again, but all I hear is our heavy breathing as our bodies come down from the high.

"Are you okay?" He asks, and I hum in response. Slowly trying to hold my own weight again, Maverick pulls out of my body. "Shit," he grunts, and I look at him over my shoulder, my eyes only half-open.

"What's wrong?"

His stormy green eyes swirl with uncertainty as he meets my gaze. "Condom. We didn't use a condom. I'm so sorry, I've never… Fuck. I was just so caught up in you, it left my mind. It never leaves my mind."

"It's okay. I'm on the pill. I've never, uh, without a condom either, and my mother always made me go for physicals every three months. Since my last one, it has only been you and West, and we, uh, used one." I can feel his cum slowly beginning to coat my thighs, but I don't want to move until I know he's okay. It's not ideal, but we are still protected.

I can see the strain around his eyes, but he nods, and I'm just grateful he isn't pushing me out of the way to run from the room.

"Why don't you go and clean up?" he asks, pointing towards the shower. "I'll have us ready to go in a minute."

I can feel the distance growing between us, after some of the hottest sex of my life, and I don't want him to push me away again.

"Please don't push me away again, Maverick. You told me you wouldn't do that, don't break my trust, not again," I whisper, and I can see the pain in his eyes.

"This is fucking with my brain, Jessica. I feel reckless, and I don't do reckless." He sighs. "I really prefer to distance myself when I'm lost in my own head. I turn into the most heartless person you'll ever meet, and you're going to hate me even more for that."

This isn't about me, I can feel it. Otherwise, he wouldn't offer me anything at all, he would just give me the silent treatment. But this has stirred something inside him, and I have a feeling it falls back to what West has said previously, about Maverick and his past, and his darkest time he mentioned earlier.

Swallowing the questions I want to bombard him with, I step towards him like he's a wild animal, ready to attack at any moment. Cupping his cheek, I can feel a tremor running through his body. Keeping my eyes locked on his I whisper my truth, just like he just whispered his. "I'm scared of losing you before I even get a chance to have you. So, I'm going to go and clean myself up and give you the space you need. But one day, I will know everything about you, just like you will know everything about me, because you are mine, and I am yours."

KC KEAN

THIRTY ONE
Jess

He hasn't left. He hasn't run, and he hasn't been a total dick, which is why I'm being put through my paces in Combat class. Maverick didn't say anything on the ride home, or before I climbed into my bed last night. He even managed to give me comfortable silence this morning at breakfast, and during every move between us in class. As I knock him to the floor, a triumphant grin on my face, the bell sounds throughout the room, calling time on the class.

"Alright everyone, get the fuck out of here," Maverick grunts, but I don't miss him adjusting himself in his pants. Someone likes it when I knock him down.

Sticking to my 'don't push Maverick' mantra, I head for the locker room. Quickly showering, I get changed in the corner, avoiding the other girls as they stick to their cliques. I'm surprised nobody has come at me yet, with Luna gone, but it's almost as if everyone has forgotten who I am again when she isn't near.

Well except West, Aiden, and Maverick. My very own WAM sandwich. I chuckle at my internal joke as I step out of the locker room, and find Maverick waiting for me, his phone to his ear.

"She's here now," he grouches, handing me the phone and nodding his head towards his office.

"Hello?"

"Hey, sunshine, are you okay?" I hear West through the phone, and it makes me smile. Dropping my bag to the chair at Maverick's desk, I lean against it.

"Hey, West. Is everything okay?"

"Yeah, I'm okay over here. What's wrong with that grumpy nobhead?" He asks, and I chuckle at his choice of words. Looking at Maverick, he's glaring right back at me, likely hearing West's question, and I'm gonna give him the god's honest truth.

"Maverick is having a little breakdown because he

fucked me without a condom last night down in Petersburg, and the way his hormones are acting up today, I think he might be pregnant already."

"What the fuck?" He splutters with laughter at my choice of words, as Maverick growls from the door. "Wait... Petersburg? What the fuck was Maverick doing taking you to that fucking warehouse?" He yells down the phone, and my heart stops.

Frozen in place I gape at Maverick, who rips the phone from my hand, and wraps an arm around my shoulder in comfort at the same time. "Raise your voice on the phone like that to her again and I'll rip you a new asshole." His words are like razor blades as he spits them out, but I don't miss the anger in West's voice as he yells at Maverick. He clearly isn't happy that I went with Maverick to Petersburg, but there is nothing he can do about it now, and it was *totally* worth it.

As the two of them argue with each other, a knock sounds from the door of Maverick's office, and Aiden's face appears through the gap. He frowns at the tension in the room, as Maverick continues to growl on the phone. Deciding I'd be better leaving them to hash it out between themselves, I slip out of the door with Aiden.

Walking as fast as I can, with Aiden at my side, I find Ian waiting outside by the only Rolls Royce here. West arranged it so Aiden could ride with me, a complete fuck you to the protocols around what block we fall in.

"Did Luna get the bag, Ian?" I ask, since Maverick brought me to campus this morning, I haven't seen him to ask, and he nods with a smile.

"She did, Miss Watson. Are we going over to Business now?"

"We are, thank you, Ian."

He shuts the door beside me as Aiden climbs in on the other side, and I stare at him patiently with my eyebrows raised. The second he settles in and looks my way, he sighs, dipping his head. "Is everything okay with you and Trudy?"

His chin rests on his chest, the smile dropping from his face. "Luna was right, Jess. Trudy provided Rico with two syringes because he backed her into a corner. She still won't tell me what they held over her head, but I know she risked it all when she gave them two syringes filled with vitamin D since she knew they were going to hit them in the head."

What the fuck? Is he serious? What on earth had Rico

done to force her to do that? Even if she didn't actually provide them with what they wanted, she was still scared enough to allow them to take both Luna and Parker.

I'm getting involved too much with thinking about this. "I need to ask you a question, Aid, and I need you to really think about it before you give me your answer, okay?"

"Of course, Jess," he murmurs, lifting his gaze to mine.

"I need to know how serious this is to you? Me, you, and the others." I squeeze my hands together as sweat coats my palms. I didn't want to be the girl to ask this kind of thing, but this is all getting a lot deeper than I expected.

"I'm very serious about you, Jess. I've been serious since we first started our game of twenty questions, and your lips touched mine. I just didn't say anything because you kept saying how temporary this all was, expecting me to ghost you."

My heart beats rapidly in my chest at his admission, and I could do a happy dance right now if I had space. But first, I need to address what happened yesterday, and the whole Trudy situation. "This is more than I expected it to be, Aiden, but it's everything I've ever wanted all at the same time." He smiles, lacing his fingers with mine as he brings our joined hands to his lips, brushing them against my knuckles.

"I want to be everything you want, beautiful. I even want West and Maverick there because I can see how we all bring out a different side of you." Well, fuck me. I've melted into a puddle and started the cycle of condensation because his words have me steaming up.

"Then whatever is happening between Trudy and Luna has nothing to do with me, okay? I can't get involved with that, otherwise, it could come between us, and that's the last thing I want."

"Agreed," he blurts out, keeping his eyes on mine, and I smile.

"But I need you to be a little more reliable than you were yesterday." I can see he wants to interrupt me, but I don't give him a chance. "I called you so many times because Maverick was called out for a Featherstone job, and I had to go with him because you weren't answering. Now, I know you're not my keeper. That's not what I expect, but when you didn't answer, and the only message you sent was at midnight letting me know you were safe, I was scared."

Aiden gapes at me, as I watch him panic with his response. "Jess, I…"

Placing my finger against his lips, I stop him from continuing. "Whatever it was, or whatever you had to do doesn't matter, but going forward I expect you to respect me enough to understand if this is real, I will worry about you when you go off the grid, and that just might be a hard limit for me."

"You are something else, you know that, beautiful?" He asks with a smile, and I shrug as the car comes to a stop outside of the academic buildings.

"Damn right I am, now, we need to talk about the fact that Maverick mentioned he had better uses for your mouth than all the shit you talk, and I definitely think we should explore that."

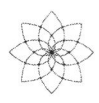

History is the only class I have without Aiden or Maverick present, and since the door gets locked, Aiden demands he waits outside. Business class was difficult. With Aiden sitting beside me, I could feel Trudy's gaze, and I know she's going to try and talk to me. Use me as her way to try and smooth things over with Luna, but I promised Luna I would stay away from her, so that's what I need to do.

Gina, our history teacher, plays another recording to

the class, explaining the fucked up way things are run around here, and how Totem made it worse. I'm used to sitting with Luna and Parker in here, and it feels lonely without them.

My mind wanders for most of the lesson, daydreaming about reading, and my current situation with the guys. I can sense feelings developing and it gives me butterflies, but I still feel scared, like I'm waiting for the other shoe to drop, and everything will be gone. The three people consuming my mind, body, and soul will vanish. I guess I'm not used to people appreciating me for who I am, and not who they expect me to.

"Okay, that's it for today," Gina murmurs quietly, as she unlocks the door. "Miss Watson, could you hold back for a moment please?" She asks, and I nod slowly as I lift my bag over my shoulder. I have no idea why she would need to speak to me, she never asks students to stay behind. Gina is probably the most softly spoken tutor we have, all delicate and out of place, just like me, Luna says.

I watch as everyone filters out of the door, and I hold a finger up to Aiden, letting him know I will be a minute and he smiles. The second the last student leaves the room, she clicks the door shut softly, but when she turns to face me, it's like I'm looking at a completely different person.

Her eyes are filled with rage, her nostrils flaring as she comes to stand on the other side of my desk, slamming her fists down on the table in front of me. "Do you want to fucking explain to me why I have seen you in the tutor's apartment building numerous times this week?"

What the fuck? Is the woman crazy?

"That's not really any of your business, is it?" I respond, stunned at her burst of anger.

"I think you will find it is, Miss Watson. Why have you been in Maverick Miller's apartment?" Deciding that walking away from this situation right now is the best option, I push my chair with my legs to stand, but her hand wraps tightly around my arm, her fingernails digging into my skin.

"Get your fucking hand off me!" I shout, and the door swings open, Aiden's eyes frantically looking between the two of us. It catches Gina off guard, and she releases her hold on me. "It's fine, Aiden, we're done here," I say calmly, walking towards him. "If she knows what's good for her, she won't ever lay a finger on me again," I add, looking over my shoulder at her with a glare of my own, but she doesn't hear my threat as she picks a chair up and throws it across the room towards her desk.

Pulling Aiden from the room, his hand squeezes mine. "What the hell was that?" He asks, but all I can do is shrug in response.

"I honestly have no clue, Aid. She was asking questions about me being at Maverick's place," I murmur, glancing to make sure she isn't following us. Damn, I need a minute to calm down. I'm glad lessons are done for the day, I don't need any more drama.

Stepping into the elevator with Aiden, he captures my lips with his as soon as the doors shut and we're alone. Gripping the lapel of his blazer I pull him towards me. I love our secret touches and moments around campus, but I would love to be able to touch him whenever I wanted. As he pulls away, I know I need to build up the courage to tell Luna and the Aces about my relationships. I don't want to hide in the shadows or have them be my dirty little secrets anymore.

Letting Aiden pull me towards the Rolls, I hear him murmur to Ian that he needs to grab a few things from his dorm before we head to Maverick's, as my phone vibrates in my bag. I start to panic when I see Juliana's name flash across the screen. I know she's at The Games with Luna, and it's Wednesday, so there has been a trial today.

My heart pounds in my chest as I bring my phone to my ear, the world seems to still as my hands shake, fearing the worst. "H-Hello?"

"Jess?" Juliana sounds frantic, and I think I'm going to be sick.

"Please, Juliana, don't... don't say it," I whisper, tears filling my eyes. I can feel Aiden's hand on my thigh but I can't see anything.

"Jess, she's okay, but things got bad. I need you to calm down for me, okay?" My breath rushes out of me, relief flooding my system.

"I'm sorry, Juliana, I thought... Never mind, tell me what happened, please?" My hand finds Aiden's on my leg, and I squeeze with all my strength, petrified of what Juliana is calling for.

"The Games have been called off, Jess. Totem showed up, setting explosions off, and Luna made it out with the guys, but Kai was shot."

No. No no no no. "Kai? Oh god," I cry, my eyes finally finding Aiden. "Is he okay?"

"He will be from what Rafe said. But it turned into complete chaos, and everyone separated. A lot is going on, but they are safe. I need you safe as well, Jess. I've called West, he's on his way back and Maverick is at his apartment. He said something about you being with someone he trusted to get you to his apartment safely?"

"Yeah, yeah I am," I murmur, as Aiden cups my cheek, a soft smile on his lips, keeping me grounded even when it feels like everything is going wrong. "Keep me posted, Juliana."

"I will, Jess. Love you," she mutters before the line goes dead and my heart stops. She just said love you, to me. My mother has never uttered those words to me. The only female to ever say them to me is Luna, and now Juliana. The emotional rollercoaster consumes me as tears trickle down my face, a complete mixture of happiness and heartache.

The Rolls comes to stop outside of the Club block, but Aiden doesn't move. "I can get my stuff later. Let's get you back to Maverick's, yeah?" He says, kissing the top of my head, but I wipe at my tears.

"No, we're here now, grab what you need then we can head over." He looks at me for a moment, making sure and I nod in encouragement. Placing a gentle kiss to the corner of my mouth, he climbs from the car, talking to Ian before he runs inside.

Closing my eyes, I try to calm myself. What the fuck is today? First, Maverick and West arguing about last night, then Gina, and now Luna and everyone else at The Games. My life used to be drama-free, bar my toxic mother, but now it seems like I'm drawn to everyone who is in some form of danger.

Fake it till you make it. I repeat Luna's words, encouraging myself to be stronger, braver. Doing a double inhale, followed by a slow exhale, like I saw someone do on an app, I try to calm my mind. When the door opens, I finally open my eyes, ready to get back to Maverick's with Aiden, but when I see Trudy climb in, I freeze. She looks completely disheveled. Her usually pristine blond hair is up in a ponytail, unbrushed, and no make-up on.

Ian's eyes meet mine for confirmation in the rear-view mirror, but I shake my head, we don't need a scene here.

"Trudy, this is nothing to do with me. I can't..."

"Please, Jess. I know how much you mean to Luna, and I know how much you mean to Aidy, alright? But I just need you to hear me out, I need... I'm so scared. Not of Luna, I deserve whatever she throws at me, but please, I need to tell someone in case anything happens."

Her hands are shaking, her eyes red raw from crying, and I notice the bruises around her collar that she's trying to hide with her shirt. I don't know what use she thinks I'm going to be, but I can't leave her in this state. There is clearly something she needs to get off her chest, and I can't deny her.

"Okay, Trudy, talk to me."

She whimpers at my approval. "I need you to keep Aiden safe, alright? Wherever you guys are staying, I need you to keep him there. I screwed over the wrong person, and I don't want them to come after Aidy as payback."

"Rico?" I ask, and she nods, tears pouring from her eyes. "Do you need to come with us, Trudy?" She frantically shakes her head.

"No, no. I'm as safe as I can be here. I'm not staying in my dorm, but I need you to swear you won't tell Aiden."

"I don't know if I can do that, Trudy. He's worried about you. You need to talk to him."

"Jess, how do I tell my brother that Rico burnt my flesh, and branded me?" It's barely a whisper, but I hear it, and I hear her voice lose all emotion as she says it, feeling the pain and weight of the word. "It was me or him, Jess, and he's my number one, always. This will break him, and

I won't allow it, just like I couldn't allow them to leave a single mark on his skin."

"Why would he do that?" I ask, my eyes wide in shock at her words, but she simply shrugs her shoulders in response. "Oh Trudy, we need to get you some help," I say, squeezing her hand tight. I can't imagine what they did to her, but the way she holds her stomach gently, I can guess where they did it. I just can't imagine the pain, or what the mark is, and I know it isn't my place to ask.

"I already have it, I swear. I'm being taken care of in a way I feel safe, but I'll sleep better knowing Aiden is safe too."

"Okay, but I think you need to tell him eventually, you can't go through this alone."

She nods, a watery smile on her face, as Aiden opens the door. "Ah, shit. Sorry, Jess…"

"It's alright, Aid. We are okay. Text Trudy my number." Looking at Trudy, my determination to protect her increases. "Trudy, if you need me, no matter the time, you call me. When Luna gets back, I'll be there when you talk to her, okay?"

She squeezes me tightly, and my heart breaks for her. Stepping from the car, I hear her whispering with Aiden, and she makes him promise to not push me for what we talked about.

Today can go to hell, and not fucking come back with all the shit that's going on. I'm done.

RED

THIRTY TWO

Jess

Four days. It's been four days since Juliana called, and ever since I got back to Maverick's with Aiden, I haven't been allowed to leave. Apparently, we're on high alert, and it isn't just me cooped up, but I've already had enough of being indoors. I can't imagine doing this for much longer, having it become the new normal around here. It's Maverick I'm worried for most. I don't think he can deal with my sass, and constant pestering for much longer.

I was glad when West came home, I feel whole when we are all together. Even if we're not actually doing anything together, I just feel an overwhelming sense of calm when I'm around them. Relaxing on the sofa, with my feet in Maverick's lap as he types away on his laptop, and my head in Aiden's lap, I scroll through buzzfeed, pausing when I get to the perfect quiz.

"West, come sit down. I've got a good one," I call out, and I hear Maverick groan.

"What's this one for?" He walks over from the fridge with a bottle of iced tea for me and I smile in appreciation. As he takes a seat on the other side of Aiden, I pull up the quiz on my phone.

"This one is called, what's your love language?" I hear Aiden chuckle, and when I look at West, he grins too.

"Well, I think that one is definitely for Rick to do." Hearing his name, Maverick groans, but before he can respond, West continues. "And I would like to remind you, Maverick, that you are still in the phase of making it up to Jessica since you put her in danger down in Petersburg."

"I'm confused because I know if I offered Jessica a repeat of Petersburg, she would jump on the chance, right, petal?" Maverick asks with a cocky grin, and I nod in agreement, making him squeeze my ankle in his lap. "So, who am I actually apologizing to? Cos it sure as shit isn't her."

"Just entertain our girl, Rick. Be a good sport." Maverick rolls his eyes but looks at me expectantly.

"Okay, only honest answers though," I flick my gaze to his and he nods in agreement for me to continue. "What's your ideal date? Going to a live show, making dinner together, going for a drink and a round of pool, staying in and watching a movie, or a candlelit dinner?"

Maverick looks at me like I'm crazy, but when he sees I'm not going to stop until he gives me an answer, he sighs. "Fine, staying in and watching a movie." Progress.

"What is a big turn-off for you on a date? They don't like where you chose to go, were rude to the waiter, they show up late, isn't cuddly, or is constantly on their phone?"

"Phone," he mutters, his fingers drawing a circle around my ankle. "That's one thing I like about you, petal. Whenever we are doing something, we always have your full attention." I smile at his words, liking the fact he recognizes I give them my attention. "It's a shame we give you the time to find random quizzes online."

Aiden laughs, stroking a hand through my hair, as I continue. "What's the best present your partner could give you? Jewelry, tickets to an event, a back massage, breakfast in bed, or a little love note?"

He surprises me when he takes a moment to think over his answer, and when he does finally speak he takes my breath away. "The note."

I can sense West is about to wind him up, so without taking my eyes off Maverick's, I throw my left arm out and punch West in the thigh. I hear him hiss, but he doesn't utter a word, clearly getting the message, while I lock that information away for a later date.

"What do you think your biggest flaw is? Too type A, getting pissed off easily, forgetful, not the best at communicating? Actually, I can answer that one for you."

"Wait a damn minute, what did you press?" He asks, and it makes me chuckle.

"Clearly the wrong one, Mr. pissed off," I murmur with a grin. "I pressed communication, and do not tell me I'm wrong." He stares at me with his eyebrows raised but eventually nods in agreement. "Good, next question. What is most important to you in a partner? Kindness, loyalty…"

"Loyalty," he blurts out, cutting off the rest of the answer, and I hear the importance of that word in every syllable he speaks. Deciding to answer the last question on my own, I get to his result.

"Your love language is quality time," I whisper, and he

nods, turning his gaze back to the laptop, showing me his lack of communication again. Silence falls around me as the guys go back to doing their own thing, and I bring up my latest book. Relaxing between Aiden and Maverick, I get lost in the story.

I don't know how much time passes, as I dive further into the amazing world created, but Aiden stirs beneath my head, and I assume it's because he has a dead leg or something, until I hear him groan.

"Holy fuck you guys, she's reading porn right now, and my dick is aching because her chest is a little flushed." The others stop what they're doing as I drop my phone to my chest, but I refuse to be embarrassed, I love my books.

"What are you reading that has you all hot and flustered, sunshine?" West asks, with a sexy grin on his face.

"Just a new release from my favorite author," I answer, not getting too specific, since he wouldn't have a clue.

"No, you little smut slut, let him hear it," Aiden groans, grabbing my phone from my chest. "It says, 'she writhed above Aaron, grinding against him as she swallowed Warren whole. Leaving Marcus to fuck Aaron's mouth. All. At. The. Same. Time.'" He stares wide-eyed at the other two as he dramatically reads the words on the screen.

"Holy fuck," Maverick whispers, rearranging his hard length at my feet. "That's some hot shit."

"I know, right? The author really knows what she's doing with her words," I respond with a wink as Aiden's hand strokes down my collarbone and in between my breasts.

"We know what we're doing too, beautiful. We could bring those pages to life."

"All I'm hearing are words, Aid. Still no action," I say with a pout, and in an instant, Maverick is gripping my waist and lifting me onto his lap as my pulse throbs in anticipation.

"Petal, we're gonna make you scream."

Aiden

I couldn't read another word over her shoulder without easing the strain of my cock against the waistband of my jeans. The words on that damn page had me on fire. Nevermind our girl, and the heat in both West's and Maverick's eyes after I read the short passage, tells me I'm not the only one. She looks so hot, even when she's casually relaxing with us in the apartment. Today, her hair is in loose curls, and she's wearing a tight ribbed grey dress that hits midthigh, with short sleeves and a high neckline. Effortlessly beautiful.

Watching as Maverick lifts Jess so easily into his lap, I stare in awe. After Jess mentioned what Maverick said about my mouth, I've been eager to see where that might lead, especially knowing Jess is hot for it. Maverick may have also mentioned that she'd dropped a little hint about her man-on-man porn addiction.

"What did Aiden say?" Maverick asks, glancing at West and I before focusing on Jess in his lap. "You want us to bring the pages to life, Jessica?" Her teeth sink into her bottom lip as she stifles a moan, nodding eagerly. "Words," Maverick adds, the grip on her hip tightening, and I have to stop myself from moaning too.

"Yes," she responds, desperation burning in her eyes.

Slowly stroking his hand up her side, dragging his fingers over her breasts, Maverick cups her chin, ever so slowly bringing his lips to hers, and the moment they touch, electricity zaps throughout the entire room. I can't even pull my eyes away from them to see how West feels because I know he'll be as lost in them as I am. Jess's hands claw at Maverick's loose-fit t-shirt, and when she tries to drag it up his chest and over his head, he lets her, although his lips find hers again quickly.

"Aiden, why don't you undress our girl?" Maverick murmurs against her lips and I don't waste a second. Jumping to my feet, I crouch down behind her as West moves to sit beside Maverick. Holy shit.

Gliding my fingers up her thighs, I reach the hem of her dress and slowly push it up, making sure my pinkies drag along the thin material of Maverick's shorts as I do. Damn, the feel of his thighs tensing beneath Jess, mixed with the softness of her skin has me breathing rapidly. Leaving her lace panties in place, followed by her matching bra, she raises her hands above her head letting me discard the dress.

"Fuck," West grunts reaching towards her chest, and I stand so I can see what has his attention. I swear she is so fucking sexy, and her lingerie has me on my knees. Her little white lace bra has no padding and little slits for her nipples to peek through, teasing us. That's when I remember.

"Check her panties, Mav. The last time I got a taste of our girl, she had crotchless panties on," I breathe out, capturing Jess's lips as she looks up at me. Our faces are upside down to one and other, but that just makes it hotter. As Jess squirms against my lips, I know I was right about the panties, and one of the others just found what I meant.

"Holy fuck," one of them grunts, and I smirk against her lips. She's always full of surprises, and every single one of them is hot as hell.

Trailing my hands over her ribs, I slowly drag my fingertips over the lace encasing her breasts, heading straight for her pretty pink nipples. Pinching them lightly, she grinds down against Maverick, as West teases at her exposed clit.

Nudging Jess high up Maverick's lap, I slide on right behind her, whipping my t-shirt over my head so I can feel her bare skin against my own. My cock is ridged against the zip of my jeans, but no readjusting is going to help me right now. With one hand playing with her breasts, I bring my other hand to stroke the inside of her thigh as Maverick crushes his lips to hers. My dick pulses in my pants, begging for me to grind into her at the sound of her whimpers and moans.

Continuing the path up her leg, the heat of her core luring me in, I tease the entrance to her pussy as West continues to draw circles around her clit. We're all desperate to give her the attention she desires, and she's thriving under our touch. Slowly sinking my fingers inside of her she moans, long and deep against Maverick's lips, and he pulls back slightly to see what we are doing. Watching as she rocks against my fingers, Maverick's gaze flashes to mine.

In slow motion, his hand wraps around my wrist, pulling my fingers from Jess's heat, and slowly brings them to his lips. Making sure he has Jess's attention, he licks her from my digits, humming against my skin as he gets a taste of her.

"Fuck, I need more of that, petal," Maverick mutters, and she nods eagerly. "Bedroom, or right here?"

"Here," she breathes, and I jump up from behind her, swiping my arm across the surface, sending all the papers and devices to the floor as quickly as possible as West places a cushion down for her. Taking West's hand, she stands from Maverick's lap, letting him pull her against his body, his teeth nipping at her shoulder lightly.

"How about you lay down on the coffee table, sunshine? Spread your legs wide for us so we can make you feel good," West murmurs, and his hot words have me gasping for breath right along with her.

Nudging her backward to lie on the table, the desire in her eyes is bright, and her eyes widen when Maverick drops to his knees before her. "Don't touch the lingerie," West says. "She wore this pretty outfit with the perfect access to her hot spots, it stays in place." Neither of us argue as Maverick leans forward and trails his tongue from her entrance to her clit, making her back arch up off the table.

Kneeling by her head, West captures her nipple with his teeth, and I watch as her eyes roll back. Dropping down beside Maverick, I run my fingers across her clit, slowly adding pressure that matches Maverick's tempo as he fucks her with his tongue.

Listening to her gasp and moan beneath us all is like music to my ears, I want to hear her scream like I know she can.

"Please, I don't want to cum yet," she begs, but West just tuts, shaking his head at her in disbelief.

"Sunshine, we're gonna make you cum like this, then we are going to give you the scene from your book and bring you to orgasm all over again. Understood?"

She stutters in agreement, as I pinch her clit, and Maverick trails his tongue up to my hand, thrusting two fingers deep inside of her, making her cry out. Continuing to tease her clit with my fingers, I move further up her body, bringing her nipple to my lips as West takes her mouth. Working together in perfect sync, it doesn't take long for her to scream against West's lips, her body tightening like a bow, then releasing, as wave after wave flows through her body, bringing her to ecstasy.

Looking down at my beautiful girl, the pure bliss etched into every inch of her dazed smile, I'm lost in her pleasure. "Aiden, sit on the sofa, at the end," Maverick murmurs, his voice thick with desire as I place a kiss on Jess's belly button and rise to my feet. Quickly dropping my jeans to the floor, I pull a condom from my pocket as I watch Jess's eyes widen in surprise. Someone likes the fact I have nothing on underneath. My cock, sighs in relief without the strain of the zipper cutting into the tip, but Jess's gaze has it twitching for attention.

Taking a seat as Maverick instructed, I gasp as his thick hand wraps tightly around my cock, and Jess whimpers from the table. "Look how ready he is for you, sunshine. So eager to please you, we all are," West whispers in her ear, her pupils dilating with pleasure.

"Come on now, boo, you can't touch my dick without

grazing my lips, that's not how this works." I look up to Maverick, a grin on my lips as I push him, but I should have known he wouldn't back down. His lips touch mine with brute force, and I relish in it.

"Holy fuck," Jess breathes out, clearly liking our little show as I bite down on Maverick's bottom lip, making him moan, and that feels like an achievement. I love the differences between a man and a woman. Jess's lips are soft, delicate, heaven. Whereas Maverick's are rough, demanding, and brutal. I love that I'm in a scenario where I can have both, but as long as Jess is here, she's all I need.

Feeling the sofa dip on either side of my thighs, Maverick sucks my tongue into his mouth, leaving me gasping for breath as he takes the condom from me, and rolls it down my cock. Holy shit. Feeling the smooth skin of Jess's thighs, I feel her lift up onto her knees, and slowly, really fucking slowly, sink down on my dick.

This is paradise, what dreams are made of, and I never want to leave. Holy fucking hell. Maverick pulls his lips from mine so I can see my girl. Her hair is wild around her face, falling over her shoulders with her eyes wide and lips pouty. The way her body moves as she grinds against me leaves me breathless.

She looks at me with a knowing eye as she watches Maverick and West lose their pants and stand beside us, just like her hot book. Dicks in hand, Jess stops her movement, holding me deep inside of her, as West holds his dick out for Jess, and Maverick grins down at me with the tip of his cock in reach of my tongue.

"Let me show you what I meant about the other ways to use your mouth," he chuckles, but I sneak my tongue out, swiping it against the slit of his bulging tip, leaking with pre-cum. Jess grins at me before turning her head to take West too.

Maverick wraps his fingers in my hair as he thrusts deeper into my mouth, and I relax my throat. This motherfucker is about to find out I have no gag reflex, and the glint in his eyes tells me he's desperate to have my eyes watering. I can't stop myself from humming against Maverick's cock in my mouth as Jess starts to grind against me. My left hand grips her waist as I soak in the pleasure of her touch. I'm desperate to see her, watch her take me, but I love the extra layer of need I feel like this, sandwiched between Jess and Maverick.

The sound of skin on skin fills the room as Maverick thrusts to the back of my throat, and I watch his gaze lock with Jess's, a reminder this is all for her. His eyes flare with realization, and he pulls out and thrusts straight back into my mouth over and over again. My head throws back in ecstasy as I hiss with pleasure at Jess's pussy wrapped tightly around my cock. There is so much going on, my body can't handle all the sensations, I'm close, and I refuse to go out alone.

"Play with yourself, sunshine. Let me see you stroke your little trigger button," West grunts, his breath coming in short succession. Fuck, I want to see her do that too. Hollowing my cheeks I suck hard around Maverick's length, making his fingers tighten in my hair as he continues to take from my mouth. I can feel my orgasm ready to rip me apart so I use my right hand to squeeze gently on his balls, making his moves stutter as I swallow him to the back of my throat and he bursts in my mouth, just as I explode inside of Jess. Her pussy clamping down tight on my dick, squeezing every ounce of cum from me as she finds her climax too.

Flicking my eyes towards West, I hear him moan deeply as the cords in his neck strain and he cums down Jess's throat. "Holy fuck," Maverick growls, an intense burn in his eyes as I hold myself still, letting him ride out every inch of his orgasm. Finally turning to see Jess, I'm in awe of her. Her eyes are watery, her skin flushed pink, and her body coated with sweat.

Her mouth meets mine in a slow sweet kiss, and I can taste the remnants of West on her tongue, just as she'll taste Maverick on mine.

"Are you okay, beautiful?" I ask, my body exhausted as I cup her cheek, and she smiles dreamily at me.

"Never better, Aid," she whispers, her eyelids closing as she rests her head on my shoulder.

"Good, cos I'm gonna marry you one day," I whisper in her ear, but she's already asleep.

RED

KC KEAN

THIRTY THREE

West

Slipping my arms into the sleeves of my jacket, I brush my damp hair back off my face, shutting my apartment door behind me. Maverick will be back from the Academy any minute now with Jess, and I need to update them on the call I've just had with Rafe. Luna and the guys are all on their way here, and we need to be ready for the war brewing.

Taking the stairs two at a time, I pull Maverick's spare key from my pocket, letting myself in, and finding them both already here. Maverick has placed Jess up on the kitchen island as he gets her a drink from the fridge. She has us all falling over ourselves wanting to please her, and she doesn't actually ask for a single thing, except our time, and I love it. I didn't expect us to fall into such a comfortable dynamic so quickly, but we all play our part, and I care for every single one of them. It's starting to feel like the family I've been desperate for.

Especially after yesterday. The only thing that could beat the sexual experience we shared yesterday, is if I was the one inside Jess. I'm keen to know what other scenes happen in the books she reads because I could definitely get behind that again. Maybe, I should sneak a look at her Kindle library the next time it's lying around, or maybe see if there is some kind of social media group I can get recommendations from.

"Hey, West," Jess says with a smile, swinging her legs as she looks over at me. Her soft voice, settling my soul.

"Hey, sunshine. Good day?"

"She spent time with me, of course it was a good day," Maverick answers, bracing his arms on the counter facing Jess, who shakes her head at him.

"Well, I just got off the phone with Rafe, and they're on their way here. A few hours tops, and you'll be able to see Luna." Jess's eyes widen, and her hands clasp together under her chin as I watch the emotions wash over her face. It's clear how much they mean to each other, and I'm glad she won't have to stress over Luna's whereabouts when she's back here. It's just the risk that comes with it that's the issue.

"That's fantastic," she murmurs, her eyes closing as she tilts her head back to the ceiling.

"Well, they're also going to be putting Ace on lockdown, and Maverick, Aiden, and I will be coming with you. At least until the threat of Totem has gone."

"Really?" Maverick asks, his eyes crinkling in confusion.

"Really. Every room will either be filled with members of The Ring, Luna and her guys, us and trusted guards, ready for Totem when he attacks."

"When?" Jess asks quietly, and I watch Maverick squeeze her thigh in support as I move in closer to her too.

"He won't back down now, so it isn't a case of *if* he will strike, but when. Then we can get on with our lives, sunshine," I murmur, stroking her hair behind her ear. "We are going to be there to protect you and keep you safe, Jess."

"I don't want you guys to feel obligated…"

"Of course we feel obligated, Jessica, but that's because we want to be there, so it's an expectation of our own," Maverick whispers. "It's exactly where we're meant to be." Placing a gentle kiss to her temple, her eyes close at the contact as I continue to stare at him in surprise. It's as if he opens up to her more and more every day.

"So, we better get packing then, huh?" She whispers, her voice not as joyful as I expected. "You know I'm going to make you all squeeze into my king-size bed like we did last night though, right?" She adds with a grin, and we both nod in agreement. After she passed out on Aiden's lap, I carried her to her bedroom, and none of us wanted to leave, so we all slid in beside her. It was perfection.

She sighs a little, as if remembering how happy she was when she woke up this morning. Surrounded by the three of us and allowed to go to classes again. She was walking on cloud nine. "I'm not going to lie though, I'm a little sad our bubble is being popped."

I can't help but agree with her words, and the grip Maverick has on her thigh tells me he feels the same. It'll be an adjustment for all of us, but we'll figure it out. I know it in my bones that this is meant to be, so we will do whatever is needed to get us there.

"When all of this shit with Totem is over with, I don't want us to be a secret anymore. I'm not sure how we do that, and if that's not something you want individually, I understand, but I'm done hiding."

Her words have my heart pounding in my chest as I see the truth in her words, and the power she feels sparkling in her eyes. "This is all for you to take the lead, sunshine. However you want this to go is what I'll do." Maverick doesn't say anything, he just nods in agreement, and I hope that isn't him isolating himself in his mind again.

I feel like I'm finally starting to live, and it's all because of my sunshine.

Aiden

What is it with these Aces monopolizing my girl's time? I understand Luna is there too, but I want to be by her side, and until they know, that's not going to happen. West mentioned in our group chat that she doesn't want us to be a secret anymore, but everything with Totem needs to be over and done with first. I should appreciate the lengths they go to, to protect her, but I can't stand seeing their arms wrapped around her shoulder. I feel like a pouty child who isn't getting their own way.

We've barely been at Ace for twenty-four hours, and I haven't got to see Jess as much as I would like. It's nice being back in her room though, being surrounded by all of her things, and all having to share her bed. I love the smile on her face when she wakes up sandwiched between all three of us.

Now I need to put on a bored facial expression, as we walk through Ace block to their personal gym, where Luna asked Trudy to meet her. Trudy still won't tell me what happened, but I will protect her with everything I am. I just pray it doesn't actually come between Jess and me, because that's one ultimatum I can't handle.

Conor opens a door on the opposite end of the hall, and I watch as Trudy straightens her spine before entering, and my body goes on high alert. Stepping through the door, my eyes instantly find Jess, sitting beside Oscar on a bench. Parker and Luna stand in front of them, but it's Roman fucking Rivera that has me glaring like a bitch. I don't know what was happening before we entered, but he's squeezing Jess's shoulder supportively, and I want to rip his hand from her body. I wish they would stop touching what's mine, well ours, but definitely not fucking theirs.

Luna stands to her feet, slowly moving towards Trudy and none of the Aces move with her. Just as she gets close to my sister, I step in front of Trudy protectively, and the second I do, I sense all three of the Ace boys ready to pounce.

"You don't get to fucking kill her," I grind out, making it clear they don't get to fucking play god around here, especially not with Trudy's life. She might have fucked up in their eyes but there is a good reason I know it, she's not the same Trudy from two weeks ago. Luna laughs in response, giving me a raised eyebrow, but I don't back down.

Trudy steps around me, never wanting to be the damsel in distress, and as she goes to talk, Luna swings her arms back and punches her straight in the face, watching her drop to the floor. Fuck. My fists clench at my sides as I grind my jaw. My heart is beating like thunder in my chest, and I glance at Jess, who is looking down at her lap. Clearly not wanting to see Trudy be hurt, but not stopping it from happening, and I have to remember that I agreed the issues going on between them do not affect us.

"Who said anything about killing anyone?" Luna

huffs out, crouching down in front of Trudy and gaining everyone's attention. I watch as Trudy prepares herself for another hit, but I catch Luna looking over her shoulder at Jess, who nods slightly, making Luna murmur, "Get up."

What? What did Jess just agree with? She said she wouldn't get involved. It pisses me off more that Roman's hand still rests on her shoulder. "I said, get up," Luna repeats, and Trudy does as she says, brushing her uniform skirt back into place as she does. "Conor, go and get her an ice pack before her face swells too much," Luna murmurs before glancing at me. "Aiden, I don't know what you're glaring at, but your frown is giving me a fucking headache."

Sighing, I try to gain control of my emotions, but I need to be close to Jess right now, since it seems Luna isn't going to hit her again, at least not yet anyway. Shaking my head, I make my way over to Jess, taking the seat beside her where Oscar had previously been sitting. "Hi Jessica, long time no see. Why don't you extract yourself from Roman and sit with me?" I can't stop the growl from lacing through my words, and Jess looks at me with wide eyes. Forcing a smile on my lips, I turn my gaze back to Trudy before I make this worse with Jess. I can already tell my outburst is driving her crazy.

"Aiden, either sit down and shut up, or leave, you aren't helping," Trudy mutters, and I smile wider at her, attempting to play my happy-go-lucky persona.

"I was fucking sitting there," Oscar grouches, coming to stand in front of me, but I just shrug my shoulders.

"Move your feet, lose your seat," I answer, not even meeting his gaze. Take that fucker. I remember his little speech at the beginning of the semester in Science, warning everyone away from Jess, he's probably part of the reason why she doesn't want them to know.

Conor steps back in with a frozen bag of peas wrapped in a towel and hands it to Trudy, who smiles slightly in appreciation.

"I want the fucking truth, and if I ask you a question, you answer. Understood?" Luna grunts and Trudy nods in agreement, wincing as the cloth touches her already bruising cheek. "Tell me what the hell happened?"

Trudy's gaze holds mine, almost like a silent apology, and I know it's because she's going to tell Luna things now that she hadn't yet told me. "So, after you and Kai came to the tents to set up the cameras, Barbette Dietrichson showed up. Apparently, she had video footage of Aiden and I coming over to your room, the day we discussed setting up a spot at the party for you to get Brett. She also watched Kai set the camera up in the tree and wanted to know why."

I know this bit, but I want to hear the rest, and when she glances back at me, I lean forward, bracing myself on my knees as I nod for her to continue. "Tell them, Tru. You promised," I murmur, not wanting them to know I don't know much else, but she did promise to try and fix this.

"I told her I didn't know what she was talking about. That you and I were friends, but she wouldn't believe it. Then Rico, the member of The Ring, showed up." I watch as she gulps, her hand coming to her chest. "I'm still waiting for him to come back and finish what he started. Now he knows I didn't do everything they asked me to do," she whimpers, tears forming in her eyes, and I growl. What the fuck made my sister so fucking scared? I'll kill him, I don't give a fuck who he is. Rico is going to die.

"He's dead, Trudy. He won't be returning," Luna says openly, and Trudy's eyes play like a film, the emotions filtering through her as she processes her words. The sheer relief in knowing he won't be coming after her makes her breakdown into tears, and I'm grateful Conor is here to comfort her as I sit frozen in place.

When she finally catches her breath, she continues. "He, erm, he was quite forceful in his mission to get me to help, and I was too weak," she whispers, swiping her hands at her cheeks. "But, uh, he wanted me to help catch you off guard, and he knew my bloodline is in Science. So, he wanted some paralysis stim shots, because the one's they'd been banking on, hadn't come through."

Oscar growls beside me, which makes me think that the ones they were banking on would be coming from him. I catch Parker whispering in his ear, and I'm taken back by the familiarity there. Is he? Are they? Wow. Intriguing.

"We weren't paralyzed, Trudy," Luna murmurs, pulling my attention back to them. "We weren't far from the Academy before we were awake again."

"I know," she sniffs, her face blotchy and red. "I gave them vitamin shots instead. I knew I wasn't strong enough to go against them, but you are."

Luna stares her down for a moment before finally responding. "Okay, you guys can leave. I don't trust you, but I believe you."

I feel Jess's fingers trace over my hand, clenching the edge of the bench beside me, and I look to her with my own relief. I don't know what she did, but deep down I know Luna's calmer approach had something to do with her, and I'll be forever grateful for that.

"Trudy, can I ask what Rico did?" Parker asks, and Trudy stops dead in her tracks as I stand to follow after them.

"You seem like a sweet guy, Parker Steele. Rico has tainted enough of us already. I won't add to your pain, this is my burden to carry." With that, she turns and leaves, and I pick up my pace. The second we are outside of the Ace block she breaks down, and I wrap my arms around her in comfort.

"I know you don't want to tell me what happened, Trudy, but I'll need to know one day. I hate seeing you like this," I whisper into her ear as I hold her close. When she whispers ever so slightly in my ear, before slipping from my hold and heading back to the Clubs block, I'm left frozen in place.

That motherfucker deserved a far worse death than he clearly got, he should have been tortured by every single person he destroyed.

RED

KC KEAN

THIRTY FOUR

Jess

I hate being cooped up inside, but on the plus side, I have Maverick, West, and Aiden keeping me company. I just wish they could catch Totem and it could all be over with. My body aches with the training Maverick put me through today, but Aiden has promised me a back rub to help me relax, and I'm not going to say no to this new addition to our dynamic.

It's getting a little late in the evening, and I yawn with exhaustion, checking my phone again to see if my dad has messaged me back. I haven't heard from him in weeks, and it has me a little stressed out. His phone is still switched on, but he's not answering or returning my calls.

Deciding to ask Juliana about it, I send her a quick text. She's here in the building since The Ring are all staying in Ace with us, but she's sharing with West's grandmother and that has me all kinds of nervous, to the point I've been avoiding them. What if she doesn't like me? What if she recognizes me as the nobody I am? I can't deal with that level of rejection right now, especially since I can see how important family is to West. The way he has looked out for Luna all these years, and the fact he was so shaken to find out Luna's father, Bryce, is still alive, proves it.

Jess: Hey Ju-Ju! Sorry to bother you. I haven't heard from my dad for a few weeks now. His phone is switched on, I'm just not getting any response. Is there anything going on I don't know about?

Placing my phone down on the coffee table, West takes a seat next to me on the sofa, pressing play on the remote, and the Fast & Furious movie starts. Aiden lifts my legs up over his from the other side of me as he settles in too. Apparently the way to get them all to sit and watch a movie is by putting fast cars on, so here we are. Although, Maverick is sitting on the other sofa tapping away on his laptop.

I can't deny how natural this feels though. The four of us, all together, how it's supposed to be. My heart has never felt so full, and every time I learn something new about them, I fall just a little more, and if I'm being completely honest with myself, it scares the living hell out of me.

Aiden and West start singing along to the opening track, their heads nodding as they do, both of their lips silently mouth the dialogue too. They weren't impressed when I said I'd never watched any of the movies, so now we have a nine series saga to watch.

"Damn, can you hear the throttle on that 1995 Mitsubishi Eclipse," Maverick adds, and I chuckle at how invested they all are.

My phone vibrates on the table with an incoming call, and I answer it without looking, expecting to hear Juliana's voice through the speaker.

"Hey…"

"Well, I am surprised you were brave enough to answer the phone after what you've been putting me through. Are you proud of yourself? Of what you have done to this family?" My mother's voice yells down the phone, and I'm stunned silent.

West pauses the movie, clearly sensing something is wrong as Aiden rubs my thigh, and Maverick holds my gaze. Taking the strength I need from them, I push back my shoulders and take a deep breath.

"Mother, what is it you're calling for?" I ask, hoping it isn't to just rant at me down the phone.

"What am I not calling for, Jessica Watson! Do you know how I feel, having let your father trick me into signing over your bloodline rights? I won't allow it. I know it has something to do with that whore Juliana Gibbs, otherwise your father would never have been able to do it. You are my daughter, and you will do exactly as I say." I try to interrupt, but she continues to power over me, her voice getting higher in pitch the more she goes on. "I will never hand you off to anyone, letting you do whatever you want, don't be ridiculous. What is this I hear about you being moved into the Ace block? Then Reece says you have only just returned there, after being seen leaving campus every evening. I don't know what games you think you are playing, but I have had enough."

Closing my eyes, I sigh. This woman will never change.

Her love for dictating my life, sinking her claws into me, will never dampen, and I was foolish to think it would.

"Mother, I don't know why Reece is reporting anything back to you, but I am my own person, and you do not have the right to push me into the ridiculous mold you think I should fit in."

"How dare you! Blood is everything to Featherstone, and to me. Now, you will do what your bloodline expects of you or face the consequences. You will marry Reece, and join our bloodlines like I have arranged, do you hear me?" Her voice is dark and sinister, and as much as she usually yells and screams, she's never set the fear of god into my life like she is right now.

The phone is suddenly pulled from my grasp, as West brings it to his ear, his face red with anger. I gape at him, and look to the others, who all have the same rage in their eyes.

"West Morgan here. I'm assuming this is Jessica's mother?" He asks, his voice like steel as his hand clamps down on my knee. His touch helps ground me as I try to take a deep breath. I can't hear my mothers response, but the words that leave West's mouth surprise me. "Let me tell you something Mrs. Watson, my grandmother is a member of The Ring, I'm sure you've heard of her. The lady who has also taken guardianship of Jessica is Miss Juliana Gibbs, also a member of The Ring. I'll see to it that you get a phone call from one of them, that way it won't result in me putting a bullet through your damn head for speaking to Jess like that."

He ends the call and throws the phone on the coffee table. I know what West does, what his bloodline links to, but I've never heard harsh, threatening words leave his lips before. I'm used to the sweet guy who wants to be with me, but this alpha protector in front of me has me tied in knots all the same.

His eyes finally find mine, riddled with guilt, and I refuse to let him think he did something wrong. Wrapping my hand around the back of his neck, I pull him towards me, my lips finding his with a hot and heavy need. He matches me stroke for stroke, letting me take from him for a change, and my body tingles with an unfamiliar feeling.

"No one has ever stood up for me like that before," I murmur. "She is my biggest critic, and the main source of all my internal struggles. She won't back down though, unless the upgrade in status benefits her, she will fight this every step of the way."

"And we will protect you along that same path, beautiful," Aiden responds, pulling my hair over my shoulder and kissing the back of my neck.

"Exactly what he said, petal," Maverick adds, coming to crouch down in front of me. Everytime he brings himself down to my level I see the difference in him, compared to the man I first met. "What she says doesn't make a difference here, and you'll marry Reece fucking Wicker over my dead body." Picking my hand up from my lap, he laces our fingers together and brushes his lips across every knuckle.

Holy fuck. I'd love to know what was going on in his head right now, for him to be this gentle with me. I want to say something strong back to them, but all I can do is offer my thanks. Maverick wordlessly lifts me off the sofa, taking my seat, and placing me in his lap. West turns the movie back on as Aiden settles back down too, and the three of us sit in tranquillity, the touch of all three of my men relaxing me like nothing else.

Maverick

My eyes flicker between the television and the laptop in front of me. The Vampire Diaries is still playing on the big screen since Jess was watching it before she went to bed, and I haven't been able to bring myself to turn it off. I keep telling myself it's because it feels like she's still in here with me, but deep down she has me hooked.

It's a little after one in the morning. I wasn't ready to sleep, so the others went to bed, giving me the space I asked for, and leaving me to get lost in my own mind a little. I can feel Jessica pulling me apart, and slowly piecing me back together again. I think she deserves to understand what I've been through, why I struggle with this level of intimacy she's asking for, what hardened my soul. I just need to find the strength to do so.

I've got no scope on the letters that Jessica has been receiving. I've dusted the paper down for prints too and there is nothing there. Now I've set up surveillance outside of my apartment, and Jess's. I don't care if she wants it or not, to protect her, I need to be able to see what's happening.

Since there isn't anything else I can do with that at the minute, I've been focusing my attention on tying everything up in Petersburg, but Frankie Winters is proving difficult.

Brian hasn't called with a new fight since I was there with Jessica, and it concerns me a little. I sent him a message a few hours ago, and I've had nothing in response. He was our inside man, and I'm worried we've lost the connection.

My phone vibrates on the cushion beside me, and I quickly pick it up, hoping to see Brian's name, but it's Rafe that flashes across the screen. Why would he be calling in the middle of the night?

"Hello?" I murmur, trying to not wake the others, but the second I hear Rafe's panicked voice, I know the whole building is going to be awake.

"Mav? Totem's here, he has Mia. Luna has a plan, I need you with Kai and the others, can you do that?"

"Fuck. Yeah, of course. I'll be there in two minutes." Dropping my phone and laptop to the sofa beside me, I start for her bedroom, but when I look to the door, Jessica is already standing there watching me, in nothing but West's t-shirt.

"He's here, isn't he?" she murmurs, and I silently come to stand in front of her, nodding as I do. "You're going to help them." It's not a question, it's a statement because she knows I care, and will do anything to protect those that matter to her and the people around us. "You're going to come back here in one piece though, Maverick, or I'll be your worst nightmare." She doesn't say anything else or ask me to promise the impossible. Instead, she brings her lips to mine, wrapping her arms around my neck, and I lift her off her feet, moving her towards the bed where I slowly place her down.

West and Aiden stir, and as if knowing their roles already, Aiden wraps Jessica in his arms as West places a kiss on her temple and climbs from the bed. "Is he here?" West asks, wide awake and alert already, and I nod.

"I know keeping me here is protecting me, but if I can be of use for anything at all, please ask, okay?" Jess whispers into the darkness, as Aiden holds her tight.

"Of course, sunshine. Aiden, we will call ahead when we are near the room. Otherwise, don't answer the door. There are guns in the bedside tables, linen closet, and under the sink in the bathroom."

Even I look at him in surprise, but I'm glad he's prepared for this. Taking one final look at Jessica, I head for the door. "Rafe wants us to help Kai. Totem has Mia," I grunt, and West pats my shoulder as he quickly dresses and steps into his boots.

Stepping into Luna's room, I'm barely through the

door before Luna's explaining to everyone that Mia is in the library which has just gone up in smoke with an explosion, and Totem is willing to trade Luna for her. The pain in Kai's eyes as he feels his world tearing in two hits me square in the gut. I've seen that look before.

"Kai, I need you to go to the library now," Luna says, looking around the room as everyone processes what she is saying. "Travis, Patrick, Maverick, Bryce, all of you. Go with him, please, we don't have long. Ian already has cars ready to move." Knowing where I'm needed I head for the door as West stops me.

"Take this, just in case, brother." He places his gun in my hand, and I take it without words. I can feel the heaviness of the situation surrounding us. We are so used to taking on jobs that require us to step in, eliminate the target and get out of there. But this is personal.

Taking the stairs two at a time, we are all quickly seated in the SUV, Kai joins us last, his face ashen with fear. The SUV moves before the door is fully closed, heading towards the fire. I've never dealt with Totem before, but he seems to like causing a disaster.

As we pull to a stop outside of the library, I open the door. "I can't tell where the fire started. I'll enter the front with Kai and Patrick. While Travis and Bryce search the perimeter and enter from the second door to the rear," I shout, not stopping my approach towards the burning building.

Testing the door, I slowly push it open. The view that greets us, has us all pause for a moment. Smoke fills the whole space around us, walls engulfed in flames as every book and wooden beam burns before us.

Everyone starts to call out for her, but I don't join them, focusing my energy on what I can see and hear, which is very fucking little. Totem clearly doesn't expect anyone to survive tonight, but he's underestimated our determination.

The smoke is slowly starting to burn my throat, filling our lungs as we step deeper into the space. The structure is falling around us, wood splintering behind us as it hits the floor. We won't be able to go back now, not with the flames blocking our path. Orange and red fills the room, burning brightly against the dark background of the charcoaled building.

I watch as Kai and Patrick slowly start to stumble, with the flames and smoke swamping us, until Travis Fuse calls out, "I've found her! Mia! I'm here. Mia!"

Holy fuck, I sigh internally, trying to figure out the

clearest path to get us the fuck out of here. Covering my mouth with my elbow, I nod for the others to follow suit as I slowly try and take the safest path.

"I can see the exit," I yell above the deafening flames, continuing to lead the way, the exit coming into view. The second I step outside, I drop to my knees, trying to inhale fresh air and clear my lungs, but I end up a spluttering mess.

Lifting my gaze from the ground, I notice a girl off in the distance, but it's the panic on Travis's face that makes me pause. "My son, where's Kai?" Without a second thought, he runs back into the building, and I try to drag myself to my feet to help, but my brain feels foggy, unable to process what I'm doing.

"It's okay, Maverick, stay here," Bryce murmurs, ready to head back in with him, when Travis appears with Kai in his hands. "Where's Patrick?"

"Not far from the door, be quick, it's ready to crumble," Travis yells, dropping Kai to the floor, trying to open his airways. Fuck, this isn't good.

Grabbing my phone from my pocket, I hit Ethan's name and he answers on the second ring. "Maverick?"

"Yeah, library. Multiple people with smoke inhalation,

some worse than others, all the oxygen you can get your hands on, and have at least three beds ready," I call out before dropping the phone. Everyone is safe here now, and Ethan will take care of their medical needs. Now, I need to help Luna and get her to Kai's side.

My heart beats like a rock in my chest, watching everyone tease the edges of death only solidifies how important Jessica is to me, because she's all I can see in my vision right now.

RED

THIRTY FIVE

Jess

How is it, the man raining hell down on Featherstone is finally gunned down, and my life is put on pause? Totem's body was taken care of, along with Barbette Dietrichson in the middle of the night when they were killed. At the exact same time, West was called away to assist his grandmother with everything regarding The Ring. I try to listen to what's going on but, truthfully, it all goes over my head. Maverick also had to join Rafe off-campus in closing up any loose ends with anyone remaining in Totem's camp.

It's been two weeks since I've seen either of them, but

I'm grateful I've had Aiden with me as much as possible. I am now a pro at facetiming them until two in the morning, but if Maverick hints at some phone sex or sexting one more time, I'm likely to give in. It's not been easy with the Aces being back, and protective, but I made sure Maverick didn't give anyone else access to the surveillance he set up outside of my room.

Asshole left his laptop open when he ran to help Luna and Kai, and I saw what he had set up. I couldn't get mad, it's strangely his way of showing he cares. It actually helps now when Aiden is sneaking out in the morning or when he's on his way over because we can see the whole corridor by the way the camera is angled.

I feel like a routine is forming properly again, and I'm up to date on classes, with no further incidents from Gina, or Reece for that matter. Although, she does continue to glare at me like I kicked her puppy or something. I'm so excited for today and what the Aces have planned. I just feel a little disheartened that neither West or Maverick can make it back when I mentioned it. I'm sick and tired of the secrets, and I want to be able to talk to Luna about them. I would prefer to do that with them all on campus, not in a completely different state.

RED

Sending Luna a quick text, I prepare for Project Queen. That's not my stupid code-name idea, but Oscar looked so excited about it that even I couldn't be a bitch to him about it. They're throwing a surprise ceremony and reception to celebrate Luna, Roman, Parker, Kai, and Oscar officially being married, surrounded by family and friends. I've been on hand to take care of the girly things, and the stuff they have no clue about. Like coordinating color schemes and centerpieces.

Taking one last look at myself in the mirror, I brush my hands over the sparkly beads covering my dress. It's a calf-length silver wrap around dress with long-sleeves. Perfect for the early winter weather we're dealing with. Lacing up the straps for my black heels, I'm all set. I've curled my hair, giving myself way too much volume but I love it. The natural toned eyeshadow looks perfect with my deep red lips. Luna will know the instant she sees me something is going on, but I'm being her maid of honor whether she likes it or not.

"Hey, beautiful, are you ready?" Aiden asks from the other side of the door, and I grab my purse.

"I'm coming," I call out as I step into the lounge.

"I fucking wish you were, sunshine." I still, hearing his

voice, my heart beating rapidly in my chest as I turn to see both West and Maverick in my living room. Staring at the pair of them in shock, I flounder for something to say but my brain just keeps short-circuiting. Especially when I see the flowers in West's hand. It definitely doesn't help that all three of these guys are dressed in suits.

Maverick is rocking his dark edgy feel with his black on black, looking every bit a criminal mastermind. While West is wearing a fitted charcoal grey suit with matching tie and white shirt and Aiden has gone for a pale grey suit and white shirt.

Shoving West's shoulder, Maverick steps towards me. "We fucking broke her, asshole. I told you we shouldn't have surprised her." Stepping into my personal space, he bends his knees to meet my height, which is still a noticeable difference, even with the heels. "I'm sorry, petal. We missed you, and West said it would be a good idea to…"

I have to shut his rambling up, as cute as it is, so I bring my lips to his. The palms of his hands wrap around my waist, pulling my against his chest and lifting my off the ground. I squeal as he twirls me around a little, but I don't complain because this playful side of him is a rarity.

"Okay, my turn," West says, wrapping his arms around me from behind, practically sandwiching me between them both, and my cheeks flush at where my mind goes right now. I'm mad they didn't get here before I started getting ready because now I have no time to do the things I want to do.

"Oh, man. Look at the heated gaze she's rocking. I think our girl just took a trip into her mind where she stores all the group sex ideas she has," Aiden chimes in, and Maverick grins down at me.

"Hell yeah I did. I'm needy, and I haven't seen you in forever," I pout. "Poor Aiden has had to deal with my sass and bitching all on his own."

"It was worth every second, beautiful," Aiden responds, stepping in to kiss my cheek. I smile at his words and turn my gaze to West.

"You brought me flowers?" I ask, my heart pounding in my chest, and his smile melts my insides.

"I did." He doesn't ask if I know what they mean, yellow roses with red tips are the most beautiful roses because they mean falling in love. They also mean friendship, but I'm going to hope that's not what he means. As if reading my face, he nods slightly, confirming their meaning. "I'll put them in a vase, sunshine," he murmurs, kissing me gently before taking them back.

"Thank you," I whisper.

"Now, let's get you away from these heathens so you can help Luna, and we can get this party started," Aiden says with a smile. Maverick reluctantly steps back too as I straighten my dress.

"You are so fucking gorgeous, Jessica," Maverick murmurs, and I blush at the way my tummy fills with butterflies. I hope this never gets old, but for now I need to surprise our beautiful bride with her dress and hope she doesn't take any of this the wrong way.

Glancing over my shoulder, taking in the three guys that have appeared in my life, helping me find myself amongst all of the craziness that is Featherstone, I've never felt happier. What could possibly go wrong?

Opting to take the elevator, I take a deep breath as I step out onto the top floor of Ace block. I try to calm the need to race back downstairs to spend more time with my guys. I've missed us all being together so much, but I need to help set my girl up first. I knock quickly on the door, and Luna is just as fast to open it.

Stepping into Luna's room, with my hands filled with

the white boxes that contain her dress and accessories, she quizzes me instantly.

"What the hell, Red. What's all this?"

"This is Project Queen. No, I didn't get to name it, but it'll be worth it. Even if it does have a stupid name," I say, rolling my eyes and making Luna chuckle. "Well, don't just stand there. You guys all overslept, and Roman refused to wake you. So now we have about forty minutes." Nodding to her room, I head straight for the walk-in closet, placing the boxes on the floor before I start looking through her make-up.

"I have to wear make-up?" Luna asks, and it makes me grin.

"Nope, they actually told me to give you the choice, but screw them. I deserve some fun too." Giving in so easily, she relaxes into the chair in front of me.

It feels good being in her presence again. It felt like she was away for years, and I've missed my girl time. "How's Kai doing? You know when I ask him, he just shrugs me off," I ask as I start to apply her make-up. I'm surprised she hasn't commented on my outfit yet, but she seems happy to enjoy the ride.

"He's actually doing really good. He completely

refused to take any medication, but it helped having him use the oxygen machine daily in the beginning. He doesn't have any scarring on his lungs or throat, so we just have to make sure his shoulder heals properly, and we're all good." It fills me with relief, knowing everyone is indeed okay, and in one piece. "What's been going on with you?"

"Not much really. A lot of school work and training really."

"That's it? No sexting or hot make-out sessions? Damn, Red. We are monopolizing all of your time, and keeping you from the good stuff.I swear I will be an amazing wing-woman just say the word, okay?" Her enthusiasm makes me chuckle, and I feel my cheeks tinge pink with embarrassment.

"I'm good, Captain. I'm just so glad everything is hopefully getting back to normal, although it's definitely quiet in my room now," I answer, focusing on her mascara.

"How was all that? Staying with Maverick, then having him and a few of his *trusted* guys taking up your space?" She asks, rolling her eyes, and it makes me smile. Maverick is a little protective, even when he's apparently explaining to everyone how he was guarding me with his life.

Thinking about him, West, and Aiden, makes my heart pound in my chest, and my skin tingles in anticipation for their touch. Especially after they left me so needy earlier.

"It was amazing," I murmur, lost in thought, and when I meet her gaze I can feel my mouth start to move on it's own. "Actually, there is something I need to talk to you about. He, well they, are, uh…"

A knock sounds from the door, making me jump back.

"Done," I mutter.

"Red, what's wrong?"

"Nothing, nothing. Just emotional, that's all. Would you look at that, saved by the door. You grab it, I'll get the boxes ready."

I feel her gaze on me as she pauses her movement. She wants to know what I was talking about, and I want to be able to tell her what's been going on with me, but now isn't the right time. As I hear her footsteps lead away from me, I tilt my head to the ceiling and take a deep breath. Tomorrow. I need to rip the band-aid off, and finally tell my best friend everything I've been dealing with. Love life included.

THIRTY SIX
Jess

Arriving at the reception party before Luna, I make sure everything is perfect. That was the most beautiful ceremony I have ever seen, and I need to get a grip on myself before I start crying again. Everything represented them all beautifully, and I spent the whole time letting my eyes stray to the guys in my life too. Once today is over, I need to have a girly chat with Luna, finally build the courage to tell her about my guys. Especially since I almost blurted it out earlier.

As the other guests start to enter, I try to see the space with fresh eyes. We decided the Weaponry building would be the perfect spot, away from other students during the weekend, so we didn't have to worry about anyone else. The rose gold and white flowers and décor fill the space perfectly. I had a huge picture of the five of them blown up and placed on the far wall. It's from the beach house with Bryce, and even though they were surrounded by a complete shit storm regarding Featherstone, they look so happy and relaxed.

Taking care of everything means I don't get to sit down and enjoy the reception until it's really in full swing. I've spent so much time looking around the room at my guys, I hate that they are separated. West is sitting with his grandmother, and the other members of The Ring, while Aiden is sitting with Trudy and Conor, and Maverick is sitting with the tutors. The tutors that have no real reason to be here, except to shut up their moaning for not being invited. I wish I could sit down with them all surrounding me.

"Jess!" I hear my name being called and glance to my left.

"Juliana, oh my gosh, finally!" I say as she wraps me in a hug. God, why does she feel like home? Like my safety net from the outside world? I haven't seen her since New

York, or even spoken to her properly, but she impacts my life so much.

"I have missed you, girl." Keeping her arm wrapped around my shoulder she guides me towards her table with Rafe, and Bryce. I guess this solves where I'm going to be sitting then. "Come and sit with me, we need to catch up. I have plans for Thanksgiving and Christmas, I wanted to run by you," she continues, as she drops me down in the seat beside Rafe.

"Hey, Jess," Rafe says as Bryce smiles at me. I haven't spent as much time with him as I have with Rafe, but I can already tell how protective and loving he is of my extended family.

"Hey Rafe, Bryce," I murmur as Juliana takes a seat beside me.

"So, Thanksgiving, and Christmas, want to come to New York? It is always so amazing over the holidays, maybe you could stay for New Year and we could watch the ball drop?" She's talking a hundred miles a minute, but her enthusiasm is intoxicating. I nod along eagerly with excitement.

"I would love that, Juliana, thank you," I respond, my eyes drifting to West on the table beside us, who smiles at me as his grandmother whispers in his ear. She's feisty, I can see it in her gaze, and that's what has me so nervous.

"Oh, West will be joining us. I'm glad you two are getting along so well," she murmurs with a knowing smile, but wait... how does she know anything? "Maybe we could bump the date up and do it over one of the holidays, wouldn't that be stunning?" She gushes excitedly, but I have to refrain myself from frowning as I try to understand what it is she's actually saying.

"Uh, bump what up?" I ask, flickering my gaze to West who looks tense.

"The wedding, silly."

"The wedding?" This time unable to keep to confusion from my gaze. "Whose wedding?"

"Yours and West's, of course. He told you about the bloodline agreement we came too now you're a Gibb's and he's a Morgan." The look on my face must clearly tell her I have no fucking clue what she is talking about. "Right?"

"When was this agreement made?" I ask, feeling tears trying to prick my eyes. I feel stupid. Stupid and so fucking blind to not have realized that this is what it has always been about. Never me, or us, always some stupid fucking Featherstone bloodline shit. I need to know when this was made. If it was only just made while he's been away the past two weeks, I can calm down and let him explain. There has been no time for him to tell me yet, and of course he'd want to tell me to my face right?

"When I signed off on your guardianship. It was part of the agreement for the rest of The Ring to allow me to do it." She looks at me with the smallest frown marking her forehead, nothing like the ice queen she usually is. "Jess, West said he would take care of explaining everything to you, please tell me he has?"

All along. He's known ever since he showed up at my door after ghosting me. Would he have ever actually showed up at my door otherwise? I think I'm going to be sick. Oh my god, do the others know? Why would they play along too? What's in it for them? I need to get out of here. Looking around the room, I see the door leading to the bathrooms, and I decide that's where I need to go.

"Sorry Juliana, he didn't. Can you give me a few minutes?" I ask, but I'm already standing from the table as she looks guilt stricken. I don't hear her response, already moving towards my destination when a hand wraps around my arm.

"Sunshine, is everything okay?" West asks, but the

guilt in his eyes too tells me he fucking knows what she just told me.

"How dare you. How fucking dare you," I growl under my breath at him. "I can't believe I fell for it, more fool me, right? God, if you had just been honest with me, I would have known what I was getting myself into." I can't control the slight sob that passes my lips as he stares at me with wide eyes. I'm trying my best to keep my voice down so no one hears me, but my emotions are a little out of hand.

"Jess, please, I can explain everything, it's not like that at all, I swear." His eyes are frantic as he tries to calm me down. His face wrought with despair, but he isn't the damn victim right now.

Pulling my arm from his grip I glare up at him, "Fuck you, West Morgan. You've had plenty of time to explain, and you chose not to. So now I choose to not hear you out." Straightening my spine, I look him dead in the eyes. "Stay the hell away from me." Turning on my heels, I march for the door. The silence as I step through to the quiet hallway allows my brain a moment to process what the fuck actually just happened.

My heels click against the stone flooring as I step away

from the loud bustling hall where the party continues. I can't stop the smile from gracing my face, remembering the pure love and happiness in Luna's eyes today. A complete contrast to the girl I first met, and how it is nothing like what I'm feeling right now.

I want that so much, the love you only read about in books, but my love life is in complete shambles, especially if Aiden and Maverick are also a part of this.

As I push against the cool wood of the bathroom door, the hand at my side is pulled, and I'm whirled around. My back hits the wall softly, my eyes closing, as the knowing scent of leather and sandalwood invades my senses.

"You look beautiful tonight," Maverick murmurs huskily, my legs shaking at the feel of his knuckles grazing my cheek. I'm not sure if he feels my tears, but if he does, he doesn't mention it. I swallow hard, feeling his body heat surrounding me, his thumb stroking my bottom lip before his mouth meets mine.

Slowly, his lips consume me, my palms stroking up his chest, feeling his heart beating just as frantically as mine. The grip on my waist tightens, as the door to the hall opens and the music fills the space around us.

"Somebody better start fucking explaining what's

going on here," Oscar growls, ruining the moment. Jolting back, I stare up at Maverick, my eyes huge with fear. Someone just caught us, and now it might all have been for nothing if he had anything to do with West as well.

"Oscar, please, not right now," I murmur, trying to calm my beating heart.

"No, definitely right now, Jess. What the fuck is this?" He shouts, turning his gaze to Maverick, who still has his arms at my waist. "Get your fucking hands off her, before I do it for you," he growls, but Maverick's hold only tightens.

"I think you need to calm down, Oscar," Maverick responds, but if anything that only makes Oscar's chest rise and fall faster.

The door opens behind Oscar, and West, Aiden, Kai, and Roman step through the door. Fuck this is causing a scene I didn't want, not today, and especially not after what I just learned.

"What's going on?" Roman asks calmly, but he can see how Maverick and I are standing. He won't release me, and I can't seem to pull myself away.

Ignoring Roman, I keep my gaze on Oscar. "Oscar, this is a special day for you guys, let's not do this now, okay?"

I beg, but he just scoffs.

"I won't repeat myself again. You are a grown ass man, and she is an eighteen-year-old girl," he growls, pointing at Maverick, and I can already sense how bad this is going to get.

"I'm not going to do this in front of Jessica. She doesn't deserve that, but if you want to take this outside and discuss it like men, then that is something I can do." Maverick's voice is almost soft, completely out of character as he looks down at me, squeezing my hips one last time before stepping back.

"What the hell is all of this?" Luna shouts from the open door behind everyone, as more people step in. I can't fucking deal with this, any of it. But before I can ask them to stop, Oscar is charging at Mavericks waist, tackling him to the ground directly in front of me.

"Stop it! Oscar, stop!" I yell, trying to pull him back off Maverick, but he swings his arm out and knocks me backwards. Stumbling on my feet, I fall to the floor beside them, and Oscar pauses as he realizes what he just did and stares at me in horror. I can hear Aiden and West, yelling at the Aces to let them pass, but I don't look to see what's going on.

"Oh my god, I'm so sorry, Jessikins." He's cut off by Maverick punching him square in the face.

Pulling myself back to my feet, I watch as they continue to punch and kick each other. I have never been more mortified or embarrassed in my life. All the noise, the yells, the questions, and confusion is hurting my mind. I need air, I can't fucking breathe. This is all too much.

Glancing at the opposite end of the hall, there is a door leading outside. My feet move on their own accord, and I push through it into the chill of the night air, leaving their screams and shouts behind me. I don't realize I'm not alone until Gina steps in front of me. I can't deal with her as well on top of all this right now.

"Are you okay?" She asks, glancing past me to where all the noise is coming from.

"I'm fine."

I feel her eyes assessing me for a moment. "Do you need to get out of here?" She asks, and I meet her gaze. I do, I definitely fucking do. Nodding in response, she points out an SUV sitting idly.

"I was, uh, just about to leave, but you can take it. You need it more than I do," she mutters, and I sigh in relief.

"Thank you."

I never thought I'd be saying those words to this woman, but I also never thought tonight would turn into such a disaster. Swiping the hair back off my face, as my body begins to cool down with the cold temperature out here, I pull open the SUV door, and climb inside.

My eyes close as I take a seat and a deep breath. "Ace block, please," I murmur to the driver, and a moment later the SUV begins to move. What the hell has happened tonight? Sighing I open my eyes to glance through the window, but I stop short when I realize I'm not alone.

What the fuck?

"Hello, Miss Watson, how nice of you to join us." Wait that's ... that's ... "Put her to sleep before she gets any ideas," he murmurs with a smile as a white cloth is pinned to my nose and mouth.

"No! No, please no," I barely manage a scream as I plunge into darkness. Alone. Again.

KC KEAN

EPILOGUE

Maverick

Fuck. He manages to get another hit on my stomach as I punch this little shit in the fucking face. I didn't want to do this in front of Jessica but look at us. Then when he knocked her to the floor I was done, he fucking deserves every hit he gets now.

"Okay, that's enough! Enough!" Rafe yells as he pulls me off Oscar. "What the fuck do you two think you are playing at?" He growls as I stand to my feet, ripping my blazer from my body as I glance around at the fucking crowd that has formed.

"He was all over Jess, all over her," Oscar fumes, but I

just roll my eyes at his shit.

"Well, lord fucking help you when you find out about West too, huh," Rafe grunts, clearly not happy with the whole situation, but he just made it worse.

"What?" Oscar seethes, as Aiden stands forward.

"Well, me too, if we're having a show and tell, but could someone tell me where the hell she's gone?"

Wait, what? Glancing around the hallway she's nowhere to be seen, she can't have gotten far. She would have struggled to get through all the damn bodies in here to go back to the party, so she must have stepped outside.

Charging for the door that leads outside, it's still slightly open, and as I step out into the night, my ears prick at the sound of a sob.

"Oh Maverick, thank god you are here. I saw a poor student being shoved into the back of an SUV, we have to help!"

My heart plummets at her words, my gut telling me something is really wrong here. "Which student, Gina?" I growl frantically, but she doesn't respond. "Which student?" I repeat, shaking her shoulders as she sobs.

"Jessica. Jessica Watson."

Running to the end of the track road, I try to see an

SUV or any taillights, but there is nothing, nothing. My hands are shaking as adrenaline kicks in. Turning back to the building, West, Rafe, and all the others are outside, confusion on their faces as they listen to Gina repeat herself.

Who would get access to campus? And why the fuck would they be over this side taking Jessica, of all people?

Feeling my phone vibrate in my pocket, I pull it out quickly, hoping to see her name flashing across the screen, but it says Brian. Shit. Raising the phone to my ear, I bark at him. "Now's not a good time."

The line is silent for a moment, before I hear those deadly words.

"I have something that belongs to you."

THANK YOU

So, how much space do I have here to tell everyone how much I appreciate them? I feel like I'm winning an Oscar with a thirty second timeframe to spit everyone's names out.

The biggest thank you must go to my handsome! You have encouraged me, believed in me, and taken control of the house to ensure I can give this my all. There would be no book without your presence.

Next, my beautiful children, you have been amazing supporters. Cheering with me at every milestone, and joining in with the happy tears and dances. You are full of grace and mischief. I love you both to the max!

Then to my girls that I have claimed for all of eternity. Val, Emma, Hope, and Katy! Thank you for being such a strong support network. I couldn't have wished for such fabulous people to help me along this journey.

ABOUT KC KEAN

KC Kean is the sassy half of a match made in heaven. Mummy to two beautiful children, Pokemon Master and Apex Legend world saving gamer.

Starting her adventure in the RH romance world after falling in love with it as a reader, who knows where this crazy train is heading. As long as there is plenty of steam she'll be there.

ALSO BY KC KEAN

Featherstone Academy
(Reverse Harem Contemporary Romance)

My Bloodline

Your Bloodline

Our Bloodline

Red

Freedom

All-Star Series
(Reverse Harem Contemporary Romance)

Toxic Creek

Tainted Creek

Twisted Creek

(Standalone MF)

Burn to Ash

Emerson U Series
(Reverse Harem Contemporary Romance)

Watch Me Fall - coming January 7th

Printed in Great Britain
by Amazon